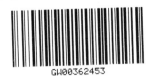

'If the vicar calls, out?' I asked.

'He called earlier,' Robin murmured, looking up from his desk. 'He called while you were having lesbian sex. I told him that you no longer lived here.'

'But how did you know that I—'

'Have you seen my pen anywhere?'

'It's there, on the desk. Robin, how do you know so much about me, about my life?'

'Psychiatrists know everything,' he replied, tapping the side of his nose and grinning.

'*Psychics* might claim to know things they can't have any actual awareness of, but not psychiatrists. Is there anything else you can tell me about my future?'

'The future depends on the past.'

'What do you mean?'

'Whatever happened in the past moulds the future.'

Also by Ray Gordon

Sisters in Lust

Carnal Craving

Depravicus – The Sequel

House of Lust

Lust Quest

RAY GORDON

Sex Crazed

NEW ENGLISH LIBRARY
Hodder & Stoughton

First published in Great Britain in 2002 by Hodder and Stoughton
A division of Hodder Headline

The right of Ray Gordon to be identified as the Author
of the Work has been asserted by him in accordance
with the Copyright, Designs and Patents Act 1988.

A New English Library paperback

1 3 5 7 9 10 8 6 4 2

A CIP catalogue record for this title
is available from the British Library

ISBN 0 340 73336 5

Typeset in Plantin by Hewer Text Ltd, Edinburgh
Printed and bound in Great Britain by
Mackays of Chatham plc, Chatham, Kent

Hodder and Stoughton
A division of Hodder Headline
338 Euston Road
London NW1 3BH

Sex Crazed

I

When I was younger than I should have been to see an
erect penis, let alone hold one in my small hand, a young
lad taught me how to wank him. Rolling his foreskin back
and forth over the globe of his purple knob, I watched his
balls jerking. His sperm jetting from his slit, splattering
the deserted classroom floor as I moved my hand up and
down his solid shaft, he grimaced and moaned as if in
pain. My first cock, my first sight of sperm.

Living in a village community, we all knew each other.
My mother thought nothing of my playing with the boys
in the woods or taking friends up to my bedroom. Had
she not been so naive . . . Sexual experimentation was
inevitable. My early teens were littered with boys who
took it upon themselves to lead me along the path of
sexual discovery. I allowed them to grope inside my
panties, fondle with the fleshy lips of my pussy and
rub the soft folds within my sex valley. But the boys
were inept, fumbling hopelessly between my legs, massaging the wrong places. My quim was never expertly
attended, so I never experienced an orgasm.

One weekend, I stayed at a girlfriend's house overnight. She was the same age as me: too young to learn
about sex, too young to know. We snuggled up in bed
together, our hands instinctively wandering over each
other's barely developed naked bodies. She stroked the

firm lips of my pussy, ran her fingertip up and down my
pink crack. I shuddered, digging my fingernails into the
mattress as she slipped beneath the quilt and licked the
smooth flesh of my most private place.

Again, I'd enjoyed the experience, the intimate stroking and pussy-licking. My clitoris had stiffened, the
small nub becoming painfully solid in my heightening
arousal. My girl-juices had flowed, wetting my young
friend's face as she'd slurped between the smooth lips of
my vulva. But still I didn't come. In my tender years, I
knew nothing of female orgasm. My companion finally
fell asleep, leaving me quivering, desperate for relief. I
felt empty, unfulfilled. I knew instinctively that I should
have experienced something more than those merely
pleasant surface sensations. There was much more to
sex, as I was soon to discover. But it wasn't a young
schoolfriend who would teach me the real joys of oral
stimulation and take me to orgasm.

One Saturday afternoon, my mother sent me to see the
vicar. It was his birthday and she'd made a cake, which I
carried down the lane to his cottage. Dressed in my tutu
because I had a dancing lesson later that day, I wasn't
embarrassed – the villagers had often seen me in my
various dance outfits. I used to dance at the village hall
and had hopes of appearing on television one day. Unfortunately, my dream faded as I grew. But, that fateful
afternoon, a nightmare began. What would I have become had I not visited the vicar? How would I have
turned out had I not been introduced to crude sex at such
an early age? My mother should have protected me.

The vicar invited me in, thanked me for the cake and
then asked whether I'd like a drink. Opting for orange
juice, I sat on the sofa and giggled when he said that I

looked like a princess and was good enough to eat. He was forty-five years old, softly spoken and quite good-looking. I liked him, trusted him. We chatted for a while and then he suggested that I do a little dance for him. He'd always taken an interest in my dancing. On Sundays after church, he'd take me to one side, stroke my long blonde hair and ask me how I was getting on. My father never had the time to take that sort of interest in my activities.

Proud of my ballet, the new routine I'd learned, I did my piece for the vicar and then sat down again. He gave me a funny look, his eyes glazed as he stared at the tight material of my tutu clinging to the mounds of my chest. I had no idea what was in his mind, thinking that he was just admiring my tutu. When he pulled a five-pound note from his pocket and offered to pay me to do another dance, I grabbed the money. My mother had often said that the day would come when I'd be paid to dance and, stupidly, I thought that this was the beginning of my career. In reality, it was the start of a haunting nightmare.

The vicar took his camera from a shelf and began snapping away as I danced. It was fun, but then he asked whether I'd dance for him without my tutu. He offered me another five-pound note and said that he wanted to admire the curves of my young body as I performed. He talked about muscle development and movement of the limbs and then he suggested again that I'd be able to dance properly if I took my tutu off.

I'd never thought much about nakedness. In the cottage where I lived I'd often walked around with nothing on after a bath. The boys at school were interested in my young body, constantly trying to get their hands inside my knickers, but I'd never dreamed that a grown man would have such thoughts. In my mind, groping in the woods behind the school was something that only the young did. The boys rubbing my pussy as I wanked their fresh cocks, their sperm splattering the ground as they gasped . . . Adults would never do such things. And certainly not a vicar.

I finally slipped my tutu and shoes off and stood in front of the priest in my pink panties and white ankle-socks. I danced again and he took several more photographs, which he told me were for his private album. Staring only at the mounds of my small breasts, my ripening milk teats, he seemed to be taking no notice of my dance movements. After I'd performed the routine again, I followed the direction of his gaze and looked down at my chest. My nipples were fairly long, out of proportion to my petite breasts. But what was the attraction? I had no idea why an adult man, a vicar at that, was so interested in something that I myself had never really given a thought to.

I was about to take my tutu from the sofa and put it back on when he asked me to slip my panties off. He must have thought that I felt anxious when I frowned at him. He smiled reassuringly, telling me that he wanted some really special photographs of me. He said that many dancers performed naked, again pointing out that the body could move more freely without the restriction of clothing. Stupidly, I thought that it would be all right since he'd seen me naked a couple of times when he'd come to visit my mother and it had been my bath time. Looking back, I suppose that, in my naivety, I wasn't actually anxious. I'd only frowned because I hadn't understood why he'd wanted me to pull my panties down.

The vicar's explanation seemed plausible, so I tugged my panties down my legs and slipped them and my socks off over my ankles. A strange expression crept over his face, his dark eyes staring hard at the fleshy cushions of my smooth pussy lips. He looked as if he was hungry. I remember thinking that he must have been ravenous as I began to dance for him. Sitting on the edge of his armchair, licking his lips, he couldn't take his eyes off my pussy crack. I was a princess, and he wanted to eat me. Again, I thought that he was taking no interest in my dancing as his stare was transfixed on my pink slit. He was only admiring the curves of my young body, wasn't he?

He was right: the freedom of movement from being naked was incredible, and I danced for quite some time. He took some more photographs and then asked me to sit cross-legged on the floor. I'd enjoyed dancing nude, but I didn't understand why he moved in with his camera and took close-up pictures of my firm pussy lips as I sat with my young thighs splayed wide. He then asked me to lie on the carpet with my legs in the air and my feet wide apart. Although I didn't see the point, I did as he'd asked and he focused on my private parts, taking several more photographs. I was a model, a ballerina. I was naive beyond belief. Finally standing and grabbing my panties and tutu, I was about to dress when he took another five-pound note from his pocket.

'You're a beautiful girl,' he said softly, and smiled. I noticed that his hands were trembling as he passed me the money. 'A *very* beautiful young girl. Why don't you come and sit on my lap?' Again, I did as he asked, dropping my tutu and panties back onto the sofa as I walked to his armchair. I felt something hard beneath my naked bottom as I sat on his lap. He laughed and said that he had a gun in his pocket: I knew that boys had erections – they liked me wanking their cocks. But grown men? I remember thinking that the vicar's hands were very warm as he caressed the teats of my sensitive nipples. What was so fascinating about my small breasts? Not only did I wonder why he was interested in my breasts, but why he was giving me so much money. Had my dancing really been that good?

The priest talked for a while about dancing and then eased my naked thighs apart, remarking on the small mole just above the tight crack of my pussy. 'Would you like me to kiss it better?' he asked, his fingertip running up and down the smooth flesh of my inner thigh. Not knowing what to say as he laid me across his lap and leaned over my naked body, I thought that it would be all right. Again, even with hindsight, I suppose I knew no different. After all, I was with the vicar, in his cottage, and thoughts of right or wrong didn't enter my head. Adults weren't rude, they didn't look at each others' private parts. Mature men didn't want young girls to wank their cocks. Did they?

He kissed my mole, his breathing deep and heavy as he ran his fingers over my barely developed breasts: 'You're beautiful,' he said again softly, the lump in his trousers digging into the groove of my bottom as he pressed his fingertip into the firm cushions of my sex lips. I felt a wetness between the pouting hillocks of my pussy as he kissed my lower stomach. I also felt something stirring deep within the slit of my most private place. My clitoris was stiffening expectantly.

'It's your birthday soon,' the vicar said, his wet tongue delving into my navel as I squirmed and writhed. His tongue running over the smooth plateau of my stomach, tickling me, he moved his head down until he was dangerously close to my tight crack. 'Why don't I give you an early birthday present?' he asked me. Most teenage girls love presents, and I was no exception.

I wasn't too bothered about his interest in my young body until he began to stroke the fleshy pads of my firm pussy lips, sending unfamiliar feelings through my pelvis. I was enjoying his intimate attention, but something told me that things were going too far and I decided to dress. I was about to clamber off his lap when he held me tight. One hand gripping my upper arm and the other holding my thigh, he looked angry. But then he smiled.

'Crystal,' he said softly as I tried to make my escape. 'You're a big girl now. Big enough for me to love you properly.' I remember confusion engulfing me. I didn't know what to do as he released my thighs and ran his finger over the contours of my naked pussy lips. This wasn't right. After all, he was a vicar.

Inexperienced boys had stroked and rubbed my pussy, my girlfriend had licked and sucked me . . . But, as far as I was concerned, the tightly closed crack between my legs was simply another part of my teenage body. The intimate attention from my friends had been pleasant, but nothing more. Had I experienced an orgasm, I might have thought differently and looked upon my pussy as something that could bring me great pleasure. But I was incredibly young for my age, absurdly naive. I'd washed between my legs, of course, but had never experienced pleasurable sensations as a result of touching my quim. It seems ridiculous to me now that I honestly had no idea what had brought about the vicar's interest in my naked young body.

Lying on his lap with my head over the arm of the chair, I allowed him to stroke my pussy lips for a while. Playing about with boys was one thing, but this man seemed so old. An adult should have admonished me for being rude, for allowing boys to play with my pussy. I was confused in my lack of knowledge, my misunderstanding. Finally sitting up, I clambered to my feet and stood in front of the vicar. I'd delivered the cake, done my ballet routine . . . I had to get to my dancing lesson. He frowned, disappointment clearly visible in his expression as I picked up my panties from the sofa.

'Are you all right?' I asked him.

'Yes, yes,' he sighed, lowering his head.

'I really do have to go,' I said, wondering whether I'd upset him: 'I have a dancing lesson.'

'Yes, I know. It's just that . . . I was hoping . . . Never mind.'

'Tell me,' I said, wondering what the trouble was.

'Crystal, I'm afraid that I'll have to speak to your mother about this.' His voice was stern, threatening: 'I'll have to speak to her and—'

'Speak to my mother?' I asked, wondering what I'd done wrong.

'I don't know what she'll say when she hears that you came here and took your clothes off. She won't be at all happy, I do know that.'

I didn't understand what the priest was talking about. He'd asked me to take my tutu off, and my panties. His tone was menacing as he warned me that my mother would be furious. He was making out that *I*'d decided to take my clothes off and dance naked. He'd stroked me, kissed my stomach and licked my navel, and was now making out that I was the one who'd been bad. Confused,

I pulled my panties up my legs and grabbed my tutu from the sofa. When my parents admonished me, they always explained what I'd done wrong. Now this man was implying that I'd been naughty and I just didn't understand what I was suppose to have done.

'I'll phone your mother now,' he said, leaving the armchair.

'Why?' I asked, fear welling from the pit of my stomach.

'To tell her what you've done,' he replied as if I knew very well what I'd done wrong. 'Crystal, you came here and took all your clothes off. You danced around the room naked, you sat on my lap and . . . I'm sorry, but I'll have to tell your mother.'

'You *asked* me to take my tutu off,' I retorted, my mind spinning with confusion. 'And my panties.'

'I was only saying that some people prefer to dance naked. I didn't mean that you should strip off. What will your mother say when she hears that you came here and took all your clothes off? Young girls don't do that sort of thing, Crystal.'

As the vicar went into the hall and rang my mother, I listened at the door but couldn't hear what he was saying. I felt awful, my stomach churning, my hands trembling. I didn't want to get into trouble, and I began to wonder what to say to my mother. If I told her the truth, explained that he'd asked me to take my clothes off, she'd probably believe him and ask me why I was lying. I began to doubt myself, wondering whether I'd misheard him and he hadn't actually asked me to take my tutu off. Perhaps he'd been surprised when I'd slipped out of my clothes. But I definitely recalled him asking me to take my panties off.

When the clergyman came back into the room, he was shaking his head disapprovingly. I dreaded to think what my mother had said, and what she was going to say to me once I got home. Still only wearing my panties, I didn't know what to do or say as he walked across the room and stood with his back to the fireplace. I imagined my mother sending me to my room when I got home and threatening to tell my father of my despicable behaviour. The vicar rubbed his chin, his dark eyes staring hard at me as I stood quaking in the middle of the room, naked except for my panties.

'I didn't tell her,' he finally said. 'You're a lovely girl, Crystal. I don't want to get you into trouble.'

'I'll go home, then,' I said and sighed with relief, about to slip into my tutu.

'I'll have to tell her at some stage,' he said sternly. 'I mean, I can't just pretend that it didn't happen.'

'Why can't you?' I asked fearfully. I was profoundly naive in my tender years. 'Just pretend that—'

'I don't like lying,' he cut in. 'I know it wouldn't be lying, exactly. But withholding the truth is as bad as lying.' Staring at the brown teats of my young breasts, he rubbed his chin again 'I suppose . . .' he began pensively.

'What?' I asked hopefully. 'What do you suppose?'

'Well . . . I suppose there might be a way out of this. If you were to take your knickers off again . . .'

'But I thought—'

'Perhaps you *are* old enough,' he interrupted me.

'Old enough for what?'

'Photographs – just a few more. It's a hobby of mine.' He smiled enthusiastically, clapping his hands. 'I take special photographs for my private collection, like I told you. I'll have to show you them one day. Anyway, slip your knickers off and I'll take some extra snapshots of you.'

'You won't tell my mother if I . . .'

'We'll be helping each other, Crystal. I'll be saving you from a lot of trouble, and you'll be helping me to build up my private collection of photographs.'

I remember feeling a lot easier as I slipped my knickers off again and threw them back onto the sofa. I really did believe that I'd been naughty and was thankful that the vicar was trying to save me from getting into trouble. I did as he asked and lay on the floor as he put a new roll of film into his camera. Funnily enough, his hobby really was photography. He'd already taken several photographs of me, so I didn't think anything more of it. Clutching his camera, he kneeled on the floor and asked me to open my legs as wide as I could. I swung my feet apart, my legs opening like a pair of scissors as he moved in with the camera, the lens about a foot away from the pink crack of my naked pussy.

He took a few shots and then told me to open my pussy lips. I asked him what he meant and he explained that he wanted to take pictures of my body as it should be. Parting the soft lips of my pussy, I thought it odd that he was taking still more close-up shots of my private parts. Looking back, I can see now how he led me along the path and coaxed me to do exactly what he wanted. As the camera clicked, I had this niggling feeling that something was very wrong. First, my tutu, then my panties and dancing naked, then kissing my stomach, threatening to tell my mother . . . And now he was taking pictures of my open pussy again. Step by step, coaxing gently, leading me on with his talk, his so-called help . . .

'I do believe that you're old enough,' he said again and

smiled, placing his camera on the sofa and lying on the floor with his head between my parted thighs. I jumped, releasing my pussy lips as the clergyman kissed my pink crack. I could feel his hot breath between my legs, his tongue licking my slit as I looked up at the ceiling and wondered why he was doing this. My school friend had licked me there, but that had been different. Two young girls in bed exploring each other's naked bodies . . . That *was* different.

The feel of the cleric's wet tongue running up and down my sex crack wasn't unpleasant. In fact, I quite liked what he was doing to me. Concentrating on the solid bulb of my clitoris, he parted my vulval lips with his fingers and licked and sucked my secret spot. My naked body became rigid, my back arching as pleasure built deep within my pelvis. Gasping, I dug my fingernails into the carpet and cried out as my clitoris exploded in a pioneering orgasm. Again and again, he swept his wet tongue over the pulsating tip of my clit, sustaining my new-found pleasure as I cried out in my ecstasy.

I'd never known anything like it as I listened to the slurping sound of the vicar's tongue working within my open sex-slit. My naked body shaking violently, my breathing fast and shallow, I tossed my head from side to side. Waves of pure sexual bliss rolled through my glowing body, on and on, taking me to heights of pleasure I'd never known existed. But, naive and gullible as I was, as pleasurable as his intimate licking was, I felt a great sense of wrongdoing. I suppose it was an instinctive feeling that this wasn't normal.

His tongue running up and down the wet valley of my vaginal crack, the priest grabbed my thighs and forced my legs further apart. I could feel his saliva and my pussy cream running between my buttocks. I thought I'd found heaven as I lay quivering on the carpet. Was this what the boys had wanted to do to me? Did they know about female orgasm? The glorious sensations finally fading, I lay quivering on the floor as the vicar brought out the last of my climax. Was this what my girlfriend had wanted to do to me?

'That's enough,' I said, propping myself up on my elbows.

'Did you like it?' he asked, his wet chin resting on the fleshy lips of my vulva as he looked at me.

'Yes. No . . .' I stammered. 'It's not right to do this.'

'Crystal, if you enjoyed it, what's the problem?'

'I don't know. I . . . I suppose that I . . .'

My words tailed off as he stood up, kicked his shoes off and pulled his trousers down. He tugged his underpants down too and loomed over me with his huge rigid penis pointing to the ceiling. I stared with wide eyes and an open mouth at the awesome thing. His balls were massive, rolling and heaving inside his hairy scrotum. I'd wanked several boys at school, brought out their sperm, but their cocks had been far smaller, young and fresh. Gazing at the vicar's mammoth member, I thought that he was a giant.

Kneeling between my thighs again, the clergyman grabbed his penis by the root and rubbed its purple head against my soft pussy lips, running the smooth globe up and down my creamy-wet crack. His eyes were glazed, his breathing deep and heavy as he massaged the soft folds within my burning sex-slit with his swollen knob. I suppose he could have fucked me then. But he obviously thought better of it, deciding to initiate me gently, lead me carefully along the path to full-blown sexual intercourse.

Leaving my pussy, he moved up my naked body, kneeling beside my head and offering his ballooning knob to my mouth. I stared at the huge purple globe of his knob, his veined shaft and huge balls, thinking that it looked like some kind of ugly monster. The boys' cocks were young and unblemished, nothing like this giant veined python. When the vicar told me to suck his knob, I shuddered at the thought. I'd never dreamed of taking the boys' cocks into my mouth. Why on earth was the priest asking me to do such a terrible thing? Mentioning my mother again, what she'd say if she found out what I'd done, the man of God grinned triumphantly.

He'd cleverly turned the whole thing round. I was the one who'd gone to his cottage, I'd removed my tutu, I'd slipped my panties off and danced naked. Actually, it wasn't so much that he was cunning as that I was gullible and stupid in my inexperience and youth. He knew that my mother was strict, and he was playing on it. She was probably severe because my father was away on business most of the time and she had to deal with everything. The bills, running the cottage, bringing up a daughter . . . The last thing my mother needed was to discover that her young daughter had behaved like a little slut.

I honestly felt that I had no choice as the vicar pushed his purple knob against my unwilling mouth. If I knew then what I know now . . . But I didn't. I protested, mumbling through pursed lips that this was wrong as he pressed the smooth knob of his cock hard against my face. Looking annoyed, he came out with his trump card. The family name, the disgrace, the scandal . . . He told me that my father would probably lose his job if it came

to light that I'd disgraced the family. Noticing my confusion, he tossed another threat into the pot. The villagers. We'd have to move out of the village once the
shocking news broke.

Finally opening my mouth, I felt my cheeks bloat as he
thrust his knob inside. My first sensation was the salty
taste, and then I wondered why he wanted to do such a
thing to me. Rubbing the firm mounds of my young
breasts, he told me to use my tongue and lick his knob. I
felt strange, a mixture of fear and pleasure running
through my naked body as I suckled on his solid glans.
But I also felt that I was in thrall to him. I remember
wondering how I'd got myself into that situation. I'd
taken a cake to the vicar's cottage and had ended up
naked on the floor with his penis in my mouth. Coaxing
me gently, leading me along the path to sexual discovery
. . . Blackmailing me.

Taking my hand in his as I gobbled and licked his
knob, the clergyman made me grip the hard rod of his
engorged penis. He took hold of my wrist, moving my
hand up and down the warm shaft of his cock – wanking
him. He told me about sperm as I sucked on his knob and
wanked his solid shaft. Little did he know that I'd
already wanked those boys at school. He said that white
liquid would come out of his penis and that I was to
swallow it. His eyes were rolling, his face grimacing as he
moved my hand up and down his cock and pushed his
knob further into my mouth. I tried to turn my head,
pulling away to slip his knob out of my mouth as he
gasped and shook. Clutching strands of my long blonde
hair, he held me tight and rocked his hips, the smooth
globe of his cock-head gliding over my wet tongue as I
breathed heavily through my nose.

My mouth filling with salty liquid as he came, I did my best to swallow it. He made grunting noises, thrusting his knob in and out of my mouth as I coughed and spluttered. Drinking the creamy liquid, I wondered whether the schoolboys would like me to suck *their* cocks and drink their sperm. Did other girls suck cocks? I wondered as the vicar murmured words I've never heard spoken before. *Cunt, fuck, shag.* I kept swallowing his sperm as he rocked his hips, mouth-fucking me. His purple knob swelling, the white liquid jetting to the back of my throat, I jumped as I felt his finger slip between the soft lips of my little pussy and drive into my trembling body.

The cleric's finger moved around inside me as I slurped and sucked on his throbbing knob. It felt strange, having my insides massaged. Painful at first, but then most pleasurable. The boys had fingered me, but it had felt nothing like this. They hadn't yet learned the fine art of finger-fucking. Finally taking his wet penis out of my mouth, he pulled his finger from my pussy and smiled at me. I licked my spermed lips, the salty taste of his male cream lingering on my tongue. I don't really know how I felt as I looked at the purple knob of his deflating penis. Was I a woman now that I'd had an orgasm and swallowed sperm?

'You did very well,' he praised me, fiddling with his penis.

'I must go home,' I murmured, clambering to my feet.

'Yes, of course. As you've been a good girl, I won't say anything to your mother. Your father will keep his job, the people in the village will never know about you and . . . Turn round and show me your bottom.'

'My bottom?' I said, looking down at him as he kneeled on the floor.

'Turn round and bend over, Crystal. I just want to take a look at your bottom. It's all right, I won't tell your mother.'

Turning around and bending over, I wondered why he wanted to look at my bottom as he parted the firm cheeks of my buttocks. I'd never seen my bottom-hole, and I couldn't understand why he wanted to look at me there. When I felt his tongue snaking around my private orifice, I jumped. Clutching my buttocks, holding me tight, he pushed the tip of his tongue into my anus. I remember thinking how awful it must have tasted, but he seemed to like it. I could feel his hot breath, his nose pressing between my parted buttocks as he licked inside me.

'I must go to my dancing lesson,' I said, standing up and moving away.

'Of course you must,' he said and grinned, licking his lips. 'You must come and visit me more often, Crystal. I think we're going to become good friends.'

As I dressed, the priest pulled his trousers back on the placed his camera on the mantelpiece. I felt funny inside: my pussy was sore, my bottom-hole wet and cold. I could still taste his cream as I finished dressing and walked to the front door. Salty, tangy. Opening the door for me, he told me to visit him the next day. He said that he'd ring my mother and tell her that I was going to help him in the garden. 'She'll be only too happy,' he said as I stepped out into the warm sunshine. Was I happy? I wondered.

From that day on, the vicar hounded me. He visited our cottage regularly, coming up to my room and slipping his cock into my mouth. My mother suspected nothing. Why should she suspect that the man was mouth-fucking me and spunking down my throat? After all, he was a vicar. Wanking and sucking his cock, I'd drink his sperm as he towered above me, swaying on his trembling legs. In her unawareness, my mother would send me to the church to help the cleric with the flower arrangements. In reality, I helped him by allowing him to fuck the tight sheath of my little pussy.

I grew up and finally decided to leave home, fly the nest, flee the village. My father didn't like my friends, my short skirts, the way I stayed out late at night. He'd never been a teenager himself, it seemed. And I had to be free of the vicar's continual threats to expose me as a slut. If I was going to leave home, I'd need money. I'd need a proper job, preferably a live-in job. I envisaged having my own room, space in which to grow and develop. I'd have friends back for coffee, or stay overnight. No longer would I have to answer to my strict mother and father, or allow the vicar to fuck and spunk my mouth.

The prospect of leaving home excited me, but I'd been to one job interview after another and had failed miserably. I had one more interview lined up. It was a live-in job as housekeeper to a psychiatrist. I must admit to feeling negative as I sat opposite the middle-aged man, but tried not to show it. I fiddled nervously with my long blonde hair as he rested his elbows on the desk and scrutinized me. From his expression, I reckoned that he thought that I was an attractive little beauty. I knew his male thoughts as he gazed at my succulent lips, my sky-blue eyes, my fresh face framed by my long golden hair. The vicar had taught me well. I knew what men thought, what they wanted. Did the psychiatrist want to fuck my mouth and sperm down my throat?

His dark eyes focusing on the deep cleavage dividing

my full breasts, the shrink licked his lips as if he was hungry. I'd seen that expression many times before. He'd have loved my mouth, my wet tongue licking his swollen knob. He wanted to fuck my tight pussy, I was sure. But would he think me suitable for the job? Beauty, full breasts and a tight pussy were one thing, but a live-in housekeeper required other assets – like an ability to cook and clean.

'What is it about housekeeping that attracts you to the career?' he asked me authoritatively. 'Bear in mind that this might be a trick question, so think carefully before answering.'

A trick question? 'Nothing attracts me to the career,' I replied, rather too flippantly. 'Basically, I need somewhere to live.'

'Well, at least you're honest,' he muttered, grimacing. 'And I'll be honest. I'm looking for someone who will be dedicated to the job. Someone who's eager, keen to become involved in hands-on housekeeping. If you simply want somewhere to live . . .'

'Just because I'm not dedicated to hands-on housekeeping, it doesn't mean to say that I won't be able to do the bloody job,' I retorted.

'I'd rather you didn't swear,' he admonished me. 'How old are you?'

'I'm eighteen.'

'At least you're old enough.'

Old enough? I'd heard that before. When I was too young, I'd been told that I was old enough. This wasn't going at all well, I thought, realizing that I should have made out that I'd wanted to forge a whole career from housekeeping. Swearing probably hadn't been a good idea, but I was feeling down, really pissed off. I was desperate to get away from home, the village and the perverted vicar. Despite my despondency, I decided to come across as a pleasant young lady who was interested in the job. Interested in housekeeping as a career? This wasn't going to be easy.

'How long have you been a psychiatrist?' I asked, my pretty face smiling as if I was immensely fascinated by his boring work.

'It all started when my interest in growing runner beans from seed began to rule my life,' he said eagerly.

'What?' I breathed, wondering about his sanity. 'I don't see what runner beans have to do with psychiatry.'

'Ah, well . . . Wait a minute. I'm the interviewer so I'll ask the questions.'

I was wasting my time. Runner beans, hands-on housekeeping . . . He was mad. But his Victorian house was lovely, and I imagined moving in, having my own room and privacy at long last. I imagined being far away from the vicar and his huge cock. Wondering whether to humour the psychiatrist, I mentioned that my father grew runner beans. Pointing at the telephone and threatening to strangle it with its coiling wire if it rang during the interview, he obviously wasn't interested in my father's runner beans.

'OK, here's a scenario,' he said, staring hard at the phone.

'Are you talking to the telephone or to me?' I asked, trying not to laugh at his brown corduroy trousers as he stood up.

'Both of you,' he replied, leaning on the desk. 'I've been working hard all day and—'

'Have you?' I murmured, somewhat perplexed. 'But it's only ten in the morning.'

'This is a scenario,' he sighed, keeping an eye on the phone. 'It's hypothetical.'

'Ah, right,' I said and smiled. 'Another trick question.'

'After a hard day's work, I'm feeling hungry. What is there to eat?'

'I don't know,' I chuckled, wondering what on earth he was talking about as he sat down opposite me again. 'Take a look in the fridge.'

'But you're my housekeeper.'

'I've got the job?' I trilled, my face beaming. Never would I have to face the vicar again.

'What I meant was—'

'Oh, that's brilliant,' I cried, punching the air with my clenched fist in my excitement. 'When do I start?'

'Well, er . . . Can you cook?'

'No.' *Shit.* 'I mean, sort of. Yes, I can cook.'

'You can start straight away. I was never any good at interviews.'

'I was never any good at *any*thing,' I giggled. Apart from cock-sucking. 'My father says that I'm a waste of space. He threw me out of the house.'

'He threw you out?' he gasped. 'In midwinter?'

'Onto the cold and barren streets,' I sighed, going for sympathy.

'Why on earth did he do that?'

'Because I wouldn't suck his cock,' I replied, going for more sympathy. Was I thinking of the vicar? I was confused. I shouldn't have said that. 'This is a lovely house.'

'Victorian,' he said and smiled, adding proudly, 'It's been in the family for generations. I live here alone, apart from poor old Tiddles.'

'Tiddles?'

'The cat. He died ten years ago.'

Did I want to work for a man who was obviously insane? I was trying to move on, get away from the village and the vicar's threats and make something of my life. This was supposed to be a fresh start away from perverted vicars and strict parents. I wanted to grow up properly, become a normal young woman and find a genuine, loving relationship. I doubted that I'd find anything apart from insanity if I worked for the psychiatrist. But, above all, I had to escape the vicar and his huge cock. Working for an insane man had to be a better choice.

'Er . . . should the neighbours ask you anything,' the psychiatrist whispered mysteriously, looking over his shoulder, 'deny all knowledge of it.'

'Deny all knowledge of what? The cat?'

'Anything. Anything and everything. Particularly questions about the toilet. By the way, my name's . . . My friends call me Robin.'

'I'm Crystal.'

'Not that I've got any friends. Crystal. That's a lovely name.'

'I hate it. What's wrong with the toilet?'

'Nothing, nothing at all.'

He was a strange man, I mused as he straightened his bow tie and rubbed his stubbly chin. His left eye twitching, he stared at the deep gully of my cleavage. Even psychiatrists had sexual thoughts, I reflected as he fiddled with something beneath the desk. I've always wondered about men who fiddle with things beneath desks. My schoolteacher used to fiddle with something beneath his desk as he tried to look up my skirt. Schoolteachers and psychiatrists probably had more sexual thoughts than other men. Apart from vicars, of course.

I must admit to having led my schoolteacher on. He'd sit at the front of the class, his eyes scanning beneath the girls' desks, obviously hoping for a glimpse of their bulging panties. I used to pull my skirt up and part my legs, knowing that his eyes would finally spot what he was looking for. He'd begin to stammer as he talked about history or whatever. I enjoyed the game, opening my legs wider and watching him mop his brow with his handkerchief. Perhaps I should have allowed him to take me into the stockroom and play with the crack of my little pussy. Perhaps I should have sucked the sperm out of his throbbing knob. Perhaps *he* should have threatened to tell my mother that I was a slut unless I sucked him off.

Looking around the psychiatrist's office, his consulting room or whatever it was, I was surprised by the amount of books lining the walls. I could well have been back in Victorian times, I thought, gazing at an oil lamp standing on a roll-top bureau. The room smelled musty with time, and the furniture looked as though it hadn't seen a duster in years. But the psychiatrist looked clean enough, I reckoned. His dark hair smarmed down, he was old-fashioned but clean. Still, he needed a housekeeper, that was certain.

'So, Crystal,' he grinned, rubbing his chin again. 'Welcome to your new home. I have one or two things that I must attend to. Your room is upstairs, first on the left. Oh, here's a front-door key.' Rummaging about in the desk drawer, he pulled out a key. 'Don't lose it,' he warned me. 'It cost me an arm and a leg.'

'I'll go and get my things,' I smiled, taking the key.

'I'll have a look at the room and then nip back home. I just hope that my father isn't in.'

'I'd better put that in my diary,' he murmured, rummaging through the drawer again.

'What? That my father—'

'No, no. I'll make an entry in the diary about you. Janice moved in, February the sixteenth.'

'Who's Janice?' I asked, frowning.

'I mean Crystal. I forget things, you see. I might bump into you in the hall and wonder who you are and what you're doing here.'

'Er, right.'

I gazed at the man as he flattened his hair with his palms and closed the desk drawer. He was eccentric, and I wasn't surprised that he lived alone with a dead cat. I doubted that any sane person could live with him for long. Perhaps I'd lost *my* sanity, I mused, wondering whether I'd be safe in a huge house with a strange man. As long as he didn't creep around in the dark of the night . . . I'd have to make sure that there was a decent lock on my door. If I humoured him and did my job properly, I couldn't see that there'd be any problems. Would he threaten to tell my mother that I was a slut if I didn't . . .

'That reminds me,' he said, the telephone leaping into the air as he banged the desk with his fist. 'Christ, I almost forgot.'

'Forgot what?' I asked, wondering whether the phone was in trouble again.

'The house rules.'

'House rules?' I echoed somewhat surprisedly. If he was going to say that I wasn't allowed out at night or . . .

'No eating in the toilet. No food or drink to be taken into the bathroom . . .'

'I don't eat in the toilet, Robin,' I sighed, shaking my head.

'*You* might not, but *I* have a tendency to eat in the toilet. Hence the rule. Oh, and don't throw sanitary towels down the toilet.'

'I don't eat in the toilet and I don't use sanitary towels,' I stated firmly.

'I do. They tend to block the U-bend. You wouldn't believe the number of electricians I've had to call out over the years. I'm now top of the Electricians' Association blacklist, which causes problems when the U-bend is blocked. Would you like to talk about your toilet habits?'

'Er . . . no, I would not,' I replied, wondering whether I'd heard him correctly. *My toilet habits?*

'I feel that you've been sexually abused,' he said, staring accusingly at me. 'Tell me about it.'

'I . . . I've never been sexually abused, Robin,' I said, forcing a laugh. Was my guilt that obvious? My shame? Psychiatrists always came up with a diagnosis of sexual abuse.

'Someone close to you,' he murmured. 'They used to pull your knickers down and play with your little pussy-slit.'

'No one's ever—'

'You're a virgin?'

'No, well . . . I mean . . . I've never been sexually abused.'

'Oh, that's a shame. I specialize in the sexual abuse of young girls.'

'I'm sure you do,' I said, wondering where this was leading to.

'Why wouldn't you suck your father's cock?'

'Because it's illegal.' I shouldn't have said that I was trying to be funny, but . . .

'No other reason?'

'Er . . . none at all. I think I'll go and get my things, if that's OK?'

'Yes, yes, of course. The examination can wait until later.'

'Examination?'

'Don't worry about it now. OK, off you go.'

Examination? Wondering again whether I should take the job as he clouted the ringing phone with his fist, I knew that I had no choice. The prospect of a bus shelter in midwinter wasn't at all inviting. And the likelihood of having to share a park bench with a smelly tramp who probably had crabs and rotten armpit odour sent a shudder up my spine. There was no way I was going to stay in the village. The vicar had threatened and abused me for too long. Besides, my father had said that teenage girls were a nightmare – and I wanted to prove him right. My mind was made up. I'd get my things and move in with the crazy psychiatrist.

2

Bearing Robin's house rules in mind, I went home and collected my things. Fortunately, my parents were out, giving me the opportunity to raid the bathroom. Shampoo, soap, deodorant, toothpaste . . . It seemed strange leaving home. Closing the front door behind me, I walked down the path and looked at the cottage. I'd been born there, had grown up there . . . been sexually abused there. There was no sign of the vicar as I lugged my suitcases down the lane to the bus stop, which was a relief. I'd half expected him to pounce on me and insist that I suck his knob and swallow his sperm. I'd put up with his uncontrollable craving for perverted sex for too many years, and was now moving on. I'd soon be well away from the evil man and his insatiable cock.

Finally reaching my new home, I went up to my room and began to unpack. I felt a lot happier as I slipped a Pulp CD into the hi-fi and sang along while I hung my clothes in the wardrobe. With my ornaments and photographs adorning the walls and shelves, the large room really was homelike. A huge bay window overlooked the back garden so the atmosphere was bright and airy, and I was just thinking how happy I'd be there when Robin popped his head round the door and grinned at me.

'What do you think of the room?' he asked me.

'It's lovely,' I replied. 'A television and hi-fi equipment . . . even a telephone.' I smiled, sitting on the double bed and bouncing up and down. 'It's a lovely room, Robin.'

'It was my great-great-grandfather's bedroom,' he told me proudly. 'He died in here, over there on the floor, with a carving knife through his heart.'

'Oh, I . . . I'd rather you hadn't told me that,' I said, grimacing. 'Who murdered him?'

'His mother. She didn't like him.'

'Obviously not. What's through there?' I asked, walking to a door in the far corner of the room.

'The observation room,' he said, joining me and opening the door. 'This is where I lock up the patients after I've filled their minds with my fears and nightmares.'

'Lock them up? Are they dangerous?'

'Well . . . they're sort of dangerous, I suppose. But only if you provoke them.'

'Presumably this door is kept locked?'

'Of course it is. Good God, do you think I'd leave the door unlocked, with mental patients running wild with guns and knives and—'

'Where's the lock?' I asked, looking at the door. 'I can't see one.'

'There's a bolt on the other side.'

'On *their* side?'

'Yes.'

'But . . . Robin, I want a proper lock on this door. On *my* side of the door.'

'I've already told you that I'm blacklisted by the electricians.'

'We don't need an electrician.'

'What about the toilet?'

'Robin . . . It doesn't matter. I'll get a lock when I next

go into town. Oh, I almost forgot. What pay do I get? We haven't talked about money yet.'

'Er . . . that depends on your compatibility.'

'Compatibility? What do you mean?'

'Well . . . let's say two hundred a week. If you turn out to be . . . If things work out.'

I wasn't going to argue. Two hundred a week for housekeeping? I'd not expected half that. As he left, I sat on the bed, wondering about the observation room. Mentally deranged people running wild with guns and knives? I was living in a madhouse. A crazy psychiatrist who lived with a dead cat . . . I'd buy *two* locks, I decided. Two locks, six bolts, chains, padlocks . . . Despite the lack of security, it *was* a lovely room and an income of two hundred pounds a week was beyond my wildest dreams. I'd have privacy, space, and plenty of money. And I was far away from the perverted vicar and his blackmail threats. Actually, I wasn't too sure about privacy, what with Robin prowling around. Grabbing the phone as it rang, I suppose I wasn't surprised to hear Robin's voice.

'Do you smell?' he asked.

'Smell?' I echoed, wondering what he was going on about.

'I can't abide sweaty armpit odour. God only knows why some people stink to high heaven. The worst thing is standing next to someone on the Tube who insists on forcing their stenching armpit into your face and—'

'Robin, I do *not* smell,' I interrupted him.

'Oh, that's OK, then. Bloody straphangers. I mean, what does a bar of soap cost? A bottle of deodorant is cheap enough so—'

'Was there anything else, Robin?'

'No, no, no. I'll leave you to get on.'

Replacing the receiver, I wondered whether it was a good idea to have a phone in my room. If Robin was going to ring me every five minutes . . . There again, he was right. People with sweaty armpits are a real turn-off. At least we agreed on issues of personal hygiene, so perhaps we *would* get on. I was sure that, once I'd settled into a routine, Robin would go about his business and leave me to it. Hopefully, he'd be kept busy seeing clients during the day while I did the housework and cooking. I'd probably be out in the evenings so we wouldn't be in each other's hair.

'It's me,' Robin said as I answered the phone again. 'I forgot to tell you about the ghost.'

'Ghost?' I echoed. 'What ghost?'

'The one that haunts the house. He's a middle-aged man, a sex fiend, an insane sex pervert.'

'I'll keep an eye out for him,' I said, thinking that Robin fitted the description perfectly.

'I reckon that he'll be keeping an eye out for *you*,' he quipped. 'I'll leave you with that thought.'

'Thank you, Robin. You're too kind.'

'What's for lunch?'

'Lunch? Er . . . I haven't even seen the kitchen, let alone—'

'Lunch at one o'clock, please. Thank you and good-bye.'

Relaxing on the bed, I pondered again on the psychiatrist. He had a problem with the toilet, lived with a dead cat, locked mental patients in the room next to mine, had a thing about sweaty armpits, and now reckoned that the house was haunted by a sexually perverted ghost. There was never going to be a dull moment in the house, I was sure of that. And I was sure that I'd never be plagued by the vicar again.

The kitchen was rather like Robin's mind: a complete and utter mess. I couldn't see the sink for pots and pans and the floor seemed to be home to anything from squashed chips to mouldy tea bags. However, I managed to knock up a sort of vegetable stew. Chucking some curry powder into the mixture gave it a little flavour, and Robin seemed pleased enough with my culinary efforts. After washing up and getting the kitchen into some semblance of order and cleanliness, I went upstairs and lay on my bed.

Recalling the vicar, the way he'd led me gently along the path to seduction and finally blackmailed me into surrendering my young body to his lustful appetites, I wondered why he'd not fucked me the first time I'd visited his cottage. He'd licked and fingered me, he'd come in my mouth, but he'd stopped short of pushing his huge cock deep into my tight little pussy. But it hadn't, in fact, been long before he was driving his hard shaft deep into my vagina. I had to get the vicar out of my head, I knew. I'd moved on, far away from the perverted man and his sexual demands.

I'd started masturbating regularly after that fateful Saturday afternoon. Either lying in my bed or in the bath, I'd part the soft hillocks of my pink pussy and rub the solid nub of my clitoris to orgasm. I couldn't stop masturbating. My first orgasm with the vicar had woken something within me, stirred sleeping desires and brought me to sexual awareness. Thinking about masturbation as I lay on my bed in my new home, I felt my clitoris swell, my juices of arousal seeping between the fleshy pads of my love lips.

In a way, the vicar had left me feeling grown up, almost adult. I told my school friends that I'd *done it*. They were in awe of me, believing me to be some kind of goddess and asking me all sorts of questions about cocks and sex and sperm. I'd felt proud, somehow superior to them as I told them about wanking and fucking. I said that my *boyfriend* was eighteen and that he had a big car and took me out to nice places and spent money on me. I built a fantasy around my experiences with the vicar, pushing the stark reality of blackmail and sexual abuse to the back of my mind. I tried not to think of the things that hurt my psyche.

The trouble was that I grew up too quickly. I gave up ballet lessons and concentrated on clothes and make-up. Drifting away from my mother, I'd go out at the weekends and meet boys in the woods. I'd pull their cocks out, fondle their balls, wank them and bring out their sperm. I loved sperm – creamy, lubricious . . . I often saved some in the palm of my hand after wanking the boys off. Back at home, I'd sit on my bed and savor the white liquid, licking my hand clean. The salty taste would linger on my tongue, driving me to seek out more boys and wank them to orgasm.

Knob-sucking and sperm-swallowing became my speciality, my forte. I must admit to making a bit of a name for myself. I wasn't quite the village bike, but not far off it. Word soon gets round, especially in a small community, and I had boys after me all the time. They wanted to mouth-fuck me, strip me and spunk up my pussy. The attention made me feel good. My eagerness to hold and suck the spunk out of a hard cock, my sexual prowess . . . I was like a princess with boys longing for my intimate attention.

But now I'd left home and was looking forward to . . . actually, I wasn't sure what the future held as I relaxed on my bed. What with the anxiety of the interview and moving into my new home, I was tense and desperately needed to relax. After years of the vicar's threats and crude sex, I needed to put the past behind me and calm my mind. Closing my eyes, I could hear Robin cursing and banging around downstairs. I had no idea what he was up to, and didn't want to know. I was in my room, my new home, enjoying my privacy and . . . Someone came bounding up the stairs and I wasn't surprised as Robin burst into the room and stood by my bed.

'What is it?' I asked, tugging my skirt down to conceal my panties.

'I can't find it,' he complained. 'I've looked bloody every-bloody-where and—'

'Can't find what?' I sighed, swinging my legs off the bed and sitting up. 'You should have knocked, Robin. I might have been naked.'

'Naked? Naked? What's that got to do with my bloody notebook?'

'I might have been naked when you burst in here.'

'That would have been a most delightful surprise,' he said, smiling. 'But it doesn't help me find my bloody notebook. Mrs Doogle will be here soon and I can't find my notes . . .' He frowned at me as if puzzled. 'Why aren't you naked?' he asked. 'I mean, most teenage girls are naked when they're in their rooms.'

'Of course they're not,' I laughed.

'Well, they should be. Were you masturbating?'

'No, certainly not.'

'That's a shame. Were you *thinking* about masturbating?'

'Robin, I was neither masturbating nor thinking about masturbating. Actually, I was hoping to sleep for a while.'

'Sleep? You can't sleep on the bloody job.'

'I thought you didn't like people swearing? Anyway, talking about the job reminds me. What are my hours?'

As he cupped one elbow in his palm and rubbed his chin, I looked at his baggy corduroy trousers. He wasn't so bad, I thought, watching him looking up at the ceiling as if deep in thought. He was wearing an ill-fitting burgundy velvet jacket and a bow tie. Brown corduroys, a burgundy jacket and a yellow shirt . . . His dress sense was as crazy as his mind, but he wasn't too bad. At least he wasn't like the vicar. His dark hair flopping over his lined forehead as he looked at me, he plunged his hands deep into his trouser pockets.

'Well,' he murmured. 'I'd say that your hours are all hours.'

'All hours?' I echoed.

'Are you heavily into sexual slavery, by any chance?'

'No, I am *not*,' I retorted.

'Shame. In that case, we won't bother with the studded collar and chain. Come and go as you please. All I ask is that the meals are on time and the place is kept clean and tidy.'

'I'll need money for—'

'Sex?' He grinned expectantly.

'Shopping. I'll need money for shopping.'

'Oh, right. The money's in the safe in my consulting room. Help yourself to whatever you need.'

'I'd rather you gave me money. If there's a discrepancy . . .'

'I haven't got time to waste on discrepancies. The combination is seven, three, four, eight.'

'I'll leave the receipts on your desk.'

'I don't do receipts, Crystal. In fact, I don't do paper-work.'

'Yes, but—'

'What the hell would I do with a receipt for a loaf of bread, milk, butter, bacon . . .'

'I'll keep the receipts anyway. Just in case.'

'Whatever. As long as you don't throw them down the toilet. Which reminds me, I must find my notebook.'

I couldn't help but laugh out loud as he went down-stairs. He was quite a character. Perfectly harmless, but as mad as a hatter. *What would he have done if I'd been naked?* I wondered, imagining him staring open-mouthed at the violin curves of my young body. His constant and lewd references to sex, masturbation, toi-lets, sexual slavery . . . He was like a comedy act. 'He should have been on the stage,' I murmured to myself, deciding to help him look for his notebook. Leaving my room and walking downstairs, I paused outside his con-sulting room. He was on the phone, and I thought it best to wait before entering.

'She's eighteen,' he said. 'Not bad at all. I hope to get around three hundred pounds.' Spying through the crack in the door, I wondered for a moment whether he was thinking of selling me. I was worth more than three hundred pounds, surely? 'Yes, I'll book you in,' he laughed. Perhaps he *was* thinking of selling me – for sex. 'OK, John. I'll be in touch.'

Creeping along the hall into the kitchen, I filled the kettle to make a cup of tea. I did my best to convince myself that Robin wasn't trying to sell me for sex, but I had my doubts. After all, I knew nothing about him. Were all men like the vicar? Wondering what had happened to Robin's last housekeeper, assuming he'd had one, I took two cups from the shelf as he walked into the kitchen.

'Tea?' I asked, smiling.

'Ah, yes,' he said. 'What a good idea.'

'Did you find your notebook?'

'No, no,' he murmured. 'I can't be doing with bloody notebooks. Bloody waste of time, if you ask me. So, what are your plans?'

'Plans? Well, I thought I might go out for a drink this evening.'

'With a girlfriend?'

'Er . . . I'm not sure. Maybe.'

'Ah, lesbian tendencies,' he chuckled triumphantly. 'I thought as much.'

'Lesbian . . . Robin, I am *not* a lesbian.'

'But you're going out with a girl this evening.'

'Yes, but that doesn't mean that I'm a lesbian.'

'Shame. So what are you? I mean, you don't masturbate in your room, you're not a lesbian . . . What are you, exactly?'

'A girl, Robin. An ordinary girl.'

'There's no such thing. What are your sexual preferences? Vibrators, candles, anal sex . . .'

'Robin, I am not one of your clients.'

'Oral sex is very popular among teenage girls.'

'Robin!'

'And double penetration. You know, one up the vagina and one up the—'

'Robin, will you please stop talking about . . .'

'Is the tea ready?'

'Yes.'

'Good.'

As I poured the tea, I had the strangest thought. I liked Robin, daft and crude as he was. I suppose I sort of fancied him. I say 'sort of' because he wasn't God's gift to women or anything like that. He was . . . I don't know what he was. Funny, crude . . . I fancied him because he was different. A challenge? I realized as he sat at the table that I knew nothing about him. Apart from the fact that he was a complete nutter. Passing him his tea, I sat opposite him and decided to try and discover a little more about him.

'Have you ever been married?' I asked.

'Married?' he echoed scoffingly. 'Good grief, no. Have you?'

'I'm eighteen, Robin. I've hardly had time to—'

'My mother never married. Still, that was her prerogative. Have you ever slept with your brother?'

'Have I ever . . . I don't have a brother. And if I had, I wouldn't sleep with him.'

'Neither would I. So, do you think you'll be happy here?'

'Yes, I do. It's a lovely house. Oh, and I'm really keen on hands-on housekeeping.'

'What are you running away from, Crystal?' he asked, a knowing look in his eyes as he stared at me.

'Running away?' I laughed nervously. 'Nothing. I'm not running away from anything.'

'Aren't you?'

'No, of course not. What makes you think that?'

'We're all running from something, usually ourselves. But in your case—'

'Do you have brothers or sisters?' I asked, trying to change the subject.

'Yes, no . . . sometimes,' he muttered, smiling and sipping his tea.

Sometimes? There was far more to Robin than met the eye. Sexual abuse, running away . . . he seemed to know things about me. There again, psychiatrists moved – and thought – in mysterious ways. They seemed to think that anyone with problems was sexually abused by their father. Psychiatrists, from what I'd heard, put everything down to sex. And Robin was no exception.

'That reminds me,' he said, finishing his tea and standing up. 'I must examine you.'

'Examine me?' I frowned, cocking my head to one side as he moved to the doorway.

'A physical examination. Don't worry, I'm fully qualified.'

'Yes, but—'

'Follow me.'

This didn't seem at all right, I thought, following him into the consulting room. He'd wanted me to talk about my toilet habits, and now he wanted to examine me. There was a hell of a lot more to this psychiatrist than met the eye, and I wasn't sure that I wanted to find out what it was. On the one hand, he was funny, and I liked that. But on the other, he was dark and deeply mysterious. Was I attracted to that? Did I want to suck him off?

'It's the procedure,' he said, closing the door and clapping his hands. 'It won't take a minute. I just need to check you for vaginal worms. Slip your knickers off and—'

'I don't have vaginal worms,' I gasped indignantly. 'What do you think I—'

'The cat,' he smiled. 'I'm worried about the cat getting worms.'

'But the cat's dead.'

'We'll have to have one of those murder evenings,' he said. 'You know, whodunnit and all that.'

Looking around the room as Robin rummaged through the desk drawer, I was once more having second thoughts about the job. A pair of handcuffs hanging from a hook on the wall, a shelf filled with wooden objects resembling large penises . . . I couldn't think why I'd not noticed them before. The place looked nothing like a psychiatrist's consulting room. Not that I actually knew what a psychiatrist's consulting room looked like, when I came to think about it. Watching Robin pull a vaginal speculum from the drawer, my blue eyes widened as he grabbed a jar of Vaseline from a shelf. *Is that what happened to the cat?*

'Shall we get started?' he asked, standing by the leather couch.

Get started? 'You're not putting that thing up me,' I stated firmly. 'You're not putting *any*thing up me. I'm your housekeeper, not—'

'Crystal, I *have* to examine your vaginal canal,' he groaned in exasperation. 'I don't *want* to examine your vaginal canal, but it's the law.'

'The law?' I laughed. Did he remind me of the vicar? Did he want to fuck my mouth? 'What sort of law is it that—'

'Rule seventeen of the 1958 Housekeeper Employment Act,' he cut in. 'All potential housekeepers will undergo a ruthless vaginal examination.'

'A ruthless . . . May I have a copy of the document concerned?' I asked. I knew he was mad, but . . .

'Rule twenty-four, section two. Housekeepers are not permitted to have copies of the Housekeeper Employment Act.'

'I've never heard of such a thing,' I gasped. 'It's ridiculous.'

'I agree. The law is an ass, but a man in my position can't afford to break the law. And the penalty for house-keepers who break the law is pretty severe.'

'I really don't think it's necessary to examine me,' I sighed.

'Rule forty-three. Housekeepers will undergo the vaginal examination with eagerness and zeal. Right, slip your knickers off and lie on the couch.'

'Robin, I am not—'

'There you are, then.'

'Am I?'

'With a certificate of vaginal cleanliness, you'll be able to do your job with a clear conscience.'

Resignedly lugging my panties down my long legs, I lay on the couch with my thighs parted. Was I humouring him? Or did I really want him to play with my pussy? My thoughts were muddled. The vicar looming in my mind, I wondered whether this was the beginning of another nightmare. This all seemed rather odd, I thought as the man pulled my skirt up over my stomach and gazed at my full pussy lips. But I had to accept that Robin was indeed an odd man, and I desperately needed the job. Two hundred pounds a week plus my keep was far more than I'd expected. Besides, this was nothing new to me. Payment for dancing naked, more money for slipping my knickers off, photographs, licking, sucking, swallowing sperm . . . The last time the vicar had threatened me and fucked me had been about two days previously. He'd taken me to a massive orgasm and . . . Was I in need of a man's intimate attention?

I supposed, as Robin smeared a good helping of Vaseline between the fleshy lips of my vagina, that an internal examination wasn't too bad. After all, he'd said that he was qualified. And it was probably a good idea to be checked for vaginal worms, even though I'd never heard of them. God forbid, I was beginning to think like Robin. It had been best to go along with the vicar, I reflected. If I hadn't, he'd have told my mother of my naughtiness. So it was probably best to go along with Robin, too.

The cold steel speculum slipped between the petals of my inner lips and drove deep into my vaginal shaft as I let out a rush of breath. It was a good job I'd had a shower that morning, I found myself thinking, my vaginal canal opening as the man squeezed the levers together. And put on a clean pair of panties. Pondering on Robin as he kneeled on the floor and peered deep into my vaginal cavity, I again thought how strange he was. But he *was* a psychiatrist. And they did say that all psychiatrists were mad. Whatever Robin was, at least I had somewhere to live and a decent income. Even if it was only a temporary arrangement, I'd earn some money and have the chance to look around for something better.

Slipping the speculum out of my vagina, the oddball shrink stood up, moved to a cupboard and began rummaging around. I had thought that the examination was over – until he returned to the couch wielding a huge vibrator. There was no need to use a bloody vibrator on me, I thought angrily as he kneeled again on the floor and parted the soft hillocks of my pussy lips with his fingers. An internal examination was one thing, but . . . .

'No,' I gasped as the tip of the buzzing vibrator pressed against the sensitive tip of my exposed clitoris.

'Crystal, I have to check your clitoral response,' Robin explained, switching the device off.

'Clitoral response?' I breathed, glaring at him. *I just want to take a look at your bottom. It's all right, I won't tell your mother.*

'Rule thirty-six, subsection four. Housekeepers will be checked for—'

'Wait a minute. Rule this, rule that . . . What sort of law is it that says I have to be brought off with a vibrator?'

'Not brought off,' he said, smiling. 'Although, if that does happen, it'll be an added bonus for you.'

'The only bonus I want is in my wage packet. I'm prepared to act as your housekeeper, but nothing more,' I stated firmly.

'Well, I suppose we can forget your clitoral response for the time being,' he sighed. 'Although I *will* have to check it before filling in the Employment Act Report at the end of the week.'

'Report? I've never had to go through this sort of thing before.'

'You've been a housekeeper before?'

'No, not a—'

'There you are, then. This act only applies to house-keepers, Crystal. That's why it's called the Housekeeper Employment Act.'

'Have you finished with my pussy?' I asked, sliding off the couch.

'As I said, we'll leave it for the time being. Would you like to discuss your masturbatory habits?'

'No, I would not.'

'Oh, all right. Would you like to hear about mine?'

'No.'

Clambering off the couch, I pulled my panties up and moved to the door. I'd been stupid to allow him to examine me. Robin was one hell of a weird man. But the more his eccentricity showed through, the more I warmed to him. I'd never met anyone remotely like him before, and I was intrigued. Insane, mad, eccentric, disgustingly lewd . . . For some reason, I liked everything about him. Perhaps I'd wanted to be like him. I supposed that, after years of the vicar's threats and abuse, I wanted a clear mind with no worries or problems. Was that what insanity brought? Happiness, a carefree attitude with no worries or . . . Insanity brought freedom.

As I reached my room, I heard the front doorbell ring. Guessing that it was one of Robin's clients, Mrs Doogle or whatever her name was, I wondered what her problem was. No doubt he'd examined her for vaginal worms. I laughed inwardly. Where *was* the dead cat? As I started to rearrange a few things in my room, a tap sounded on the door. Wondering what Robin wanted this time, I gasped as the vicar walked into my room and grinned at me.

'You should have told me that you were moving,' he said, his dark eyes staring accusingly at me.

'How the hell did you . . .' I began shakily. I felt as if I was staring at a monster. 'How the hell . . .'

'Your mother told me. I called round to see you and she said that you'd moved out.'

'What do you want?' I asked stupidly.

'You, Crystal. I want you. Nothing's changed just because you're living here.'

I couldn't believe that the man who had threatened me, who had used and abused me for years, was standing in my room. I should never have told my mother where I was moving to. She obviously didn't think I'd mind the vicar calling on me. As far as she knew, he was a family friend; he'd probably told her that he'd love to see me and my new home. Not knowing what to do, I wished that Robin had at least called me down to the front door rather than sending the man straight up to my room. There again, he too had probably thought that a priest would be harmless.

'I don't want you coming here,' I said as he lifted his cassock, exposing his erect cock.

'Crystal, you're forgetting that I have photographs of you. Look, we've been through this a hundred times before. You know why I'm here, what I want.'

'Yes, I know, all right,' I hissed.

'Then let's get on with it.'

'No. You're not going to rule my life any more, ruin my life any more.'

'What will your mother say when she sees the photographs? Are you going to risk . . .'

'If I do as you want, you'll be back again and again.'

'Of course I will. We have an arrangement, Crystal. Your body is mine for the taking whenever I wish. That's the way it's been for years, and nothing's changed. In return, I'll not reveal your sordid past. Now, sit on the bed and suck my cock.'

Taking my position, as I'd done hundreds of times over the years, I gazed at his bulbous knob as he stood in front of me and wanked the fleshy shaft of his solid cock. Where the hell was Robin now? I thought, gazing at the vicar's heaving balls. Robin hadn't given me a minute's peace since I'd moved in, and now he'd disappeared. My mind in turmoil, I recalled the lewd photographs the vicar had taken of me. When I'd slipped my tutu off and seen his camera, I should have known that . . . But I'd been too young to know.

'Let's turn this round,' I said, grinning. 'You take pornographic photographs of a young girl, and then—'

'Crystal, you just don't understand,' he broke in, smiling wolfishly and offering his purple knob to my mouth. 'I found the photographs in the church. They were in a bag you'd left behind after helping me with the flower arrangements. Quite a feasible story, don't you agree?'

'Not really. Firstly, I'd hardly leave incriminating photographs like that in the church. Secondly, I—'

'Is anyone going to question *me* when I say that I found them in the church? Is anyone going to accuse *me* of lying? I don't think so. I have dozens of pictures of you naked in your bedroom, pictures of sperm running down your face, oozing from your little pussy crack.'

He was right, I knew. No one would question him. There were shots of his solid cock in my mouth, sperm running down my chin, over the petite mounds of my young breasts . . . Many times he'd delighted in showing me his porn pictures. But I was determined that the evil man wasn't going to be allowed to continue with his threats, his sexual abuse. I'd moved on. A new life ahead of me, freedom, happiness . . . If I gave in now, he'd hound me for the rest of my life.

'I've moved away from home and the village,' I said. 'And I've moved away from *you*.'

'I have boxes full of pictures,' he replied, grinning evilly. 'Apart from your parents, there's your friends, relatives . . .'

'I'll go to the police and tell them that you—'

'Don't be stupid, Crystal. I'm a man of God, a respected vicar. Besides, what evidence have you? Can you *prove* that I took the photographs? No, of course you can't. I'd say that you were simply trying to put the blame onto me in order to . . .'

'All right,' I finally conceded, reaching out and taking his solid cock in my hand.

'Good girl. I knew you'd see sense. I'll call round to see you and—'

'No, not here,' I sighed, interrupting him. 'I'll have to meet you somewhere.'

'As you wish. Now, suck it and drink my spunk like a good little girl.'

Taking the priest's swollen knob into my mouth, I ran my tongue over its silky surface, teasing the sperm-slit. He breathed heavily, as he'd done dozens of times in the past. I really thought that I'd started a new life, moved on and put the past behind me. *It's not always easy to shake off the past*, I thought. Despair engulfing me, I felt that I was back at square one. I was back in the vicar's cottage, sucking the sperm out of his knob at an age when I should have been . . . I had to keep this from Robin. I didn't want him knowing anything about my sordid past, the years I'd spent sucking and fucking the vicar.

'I've taught you well,' the vicar gasped, pushing his taut purple glans to the back of my throat. 'You were very lucky to have me catch you at such an early age. I was able to teach you—'

'*Lucky*?' I hissed, yanking his cock out of my mouth.

'Yes, you were *very* lucky. I taught you things that you might have taken years to learn.'

'I didn't want to know about crude sex when I was . . .'

'You didn't seem to mind wanking the boys in the woods,' he chuckled.

'That . . . that was . . .' I stammered, wondering what he knew about the boys.

'What would your mother say if she saw photographs of you wanking young boys' cocks?'

'I . . . I never did anything of the sort,' I replied fearfully.

'Their spunk shooting from their cocks, running over your hand and . . . How old were you then?'

'Look, I . . .'

'Suck my knob and drink my spunk, Crystal. And don't *ever* threaten me. You'll do as I ask when I come here for sex. Just remember that I could ruin your life. Now, suck my cock.'

Taking his glistening knob into my hot mouth again, I felt my stomach churn. Ruin my life? He'd already ruined my life, and would continue to do so for the rest of my miserable days. His hairy balls tickling my chin as I took his purple cock-bulb deeper into my mouth, the thought struck me that this was the very first prick I'd sucked. Lying on the vicar's lounge floor with his knob in my mouth, his sperm jetting to the back of my throat . . . How much sperm had I swallowed? I wondered, running my tongue around the rim of his glans. Pints? Gallons?

I could hear Robin moving about downstairs as the vicar began to tremble and gasp. What the hell was I doing? I wondered. My new home, my new life . . . Sperm flooding my mouth, I swallowed hard as the vicar rocked his hips. Again and again I swallowed, drinking his gushing spunk as he mouth-fucked me in his crudity. A man of God? He was a man of Satan, the Devil incarnate. Wondering how many other girls he was threatening and abusing, I realized that I'd assumed that I was the only one. He might have used and abused half the girls in the village, each one not daring to tell the others. Sucking out the last of the clergyman's sperm, I looked up at him as he withdrew his cock and shuddered in the aftermath of his mouth-fucking.

'Not as good as usual,' he complained, lowering and adjusting his cassock.

'Tough,' I hissed.

'I don't like your attitude, Crystal. We've been good friends for a long time, enjoying sex and—'

'And it's come to an end. I don't care what you do with the photographs. Show them to anyone and everyone – see if I care.'

'You don't mean that,' he chortled. 'Show them to anyone and everyone? You'd be labelled a slag, a filthy whore. Is that what you want?'

I really didn't know what to do as he moved towards the door and flashed me a salacious grin. The taste of his sperm lingering on my tongue, I recalled my many visits to his church. He liked to have me over the altar, my feet wide apart, my naked buttocks projected ... Many times, he'd forced his huge cock deep into my rectum as I'd pressed my face against the tapestry covering the altar. I'd listen to his lower stomach slapping my buttocks, the squelching sounds of his cock shafting my bottom as his sperm filled me.

After he'd fucked me, he usually licked my vaginal crack, lapping up my creamy girl-juice, pushing his tongue deep into my tight pussy. He'd force the fleshy lips of my pussy wide open, exposing my most intimate inner flesh to his evil eyes. He'd suck hard on my ripening clitoris, sucking and licking until I shuddered in my enforced coming. Sometimes, he'd wipe the sperm out of my pussy with my knickers, telling me that I could suck the stained crotch and think of him fucking me when I masturbated. He was wicked in his perversity.

'I have a surprise for you,' the vicar said, dragging my thoughts away from the altar. 'A friend of mine is very keen to meet you. He's eager to . . . Let's just say that he's eager to get to know you – intimately.'

'No,' I spat. 'If you think I'm going to—'

'I don't *think*, Crystal. I *know*. You'll do as I ask because . . . The choice is yours.'

'I've already said that you can show the pictures to everyone. I really don't give a damn.'

'All right, if that's the way you want it.'

'Yes, it is.'

'Your mother was telling me about your father's promotion.'

'What of it?'

'You know what the newspapers are like. Your father will soon be in the public eye. "Top company man's daughter sucks cock," that's what the tabloids will say. And there'll be photographs of the new director's daughter giving head. I'll leave you with that thought.'

Lying back on my bed as the priest made his way downstairs, I closed my eyes and tried to put my mind at rest. He was right, I knew. My father *had* been promoted recently. Heading an international company, liaising with governments around the world . . . I wasn't sure exactly what he did, but I knew that the newspapers would have a field day with the photographs. There *had* to be a way out of my predicament. I couldn't allow the evil vicar to rule my life, to use my young body for crude sex whenever he wished. And I certainly wasn't going to have another man using me: I shuddered at the thought of two men fucking and spunking me.

'Everything all right?' Robin asked, peering round the door.

'Yes, yes, fine,' I smiled – I lied.

'Do you want to talk about it?'

'About what? The vicar is a family friend. He came to see how I was getting on.'

'Why mention the vicar?'

'I . . . I thought that was what you meant. Talk about the vicar.'

'Perhaps I did mean that.'

'You're confusing me,' I laughed. 'There's nothing to talk about, Robin.'

'Isn't there? When you're ready, should you feel the need to talk, come and find me. I'm going out now. I have to visit a client.'

'Yes, all right. I'll see you later.'

Moving to the window as Robin left the house, I gazed down at the garden. Cold and bare in winter. I'd been looking forward to the summer, hoping to be free to live my life and enjoy the sunshine. But this summer was going to be like the rest. Fucked behind the church by the vicar, my bottom spermed as I lay over the altar, my young body stripped and spanked . . . And now he had a friend who wanted to fuck and spunk my naked body. I should have put a stop to the vicar's abuse long ago, but I didn't know how. I suppose I didn't realize that he'd hound me all though my teens, that he'd continue to make his sexual demands on me even after I'd left home, moved away from the village.

Grabbing my coat from the wardrobe, I left the house and caught the bus into the village. The photographs were all the vicar had on me. No photographs – no more blackmail and crude sex. Simple, I thought. He'd said that he had boxes full of photographs. Once I was in his cottage, it shouldn't be too difficult to find the evidence. He normally hung around the church during the day, which would give me the opportunity to slip into his cottage and . . . Realizing that I'd have to break in, I knew that this was going to be dangerous.

Stealing through the woods behind the cottage, I slipped into the garden and crept up to the back door. To my surprise, the door wasn't locked. But that might just have meant that the man of Satan was lurking somewhere. I knew that I had to take my chances, so I slipped into the kitchen. There were no sounds, no movements, and I went into the lounge and looked around. I hadn't thought that I'd ever stand in the vicar's cottage again, in the very room where he'd used and abused me hundreds of times.

Concentrating on my mission, I decided to take a look upstairs. The photographs wouldn't necessarily be well hidden, I knew as I entered the vicar's bedroom. He lived alone, so why go to great lengths to hide the evidence? Kneeling, I lifted the quilt and looked under the bed. Nothing. Checking the wardrobe, I left the room and stood on the landing. Perhaps they *were* well hidden, I reflected. The kitchen, the attic, or even the garden shed. They could have been anywhere. Wondering what to do, I finally made my way into the spare room.

To my amazement, there was a leather-topped table in the centre of the room and a mass of what looked like bondage equipment. This was evidence enough of the vicar's perverted ways, I mused, eyeing lengths of rope dangling from each corner of the table. Bamboo canes, a leather whip, vibrators, chains, dildos . . . The place looked like a sexual torture chamber. How many young girls had he lured into his den of iniquity? Rummaging through a cupboard, I thought that the torture chamber would be the most likely hiding place for the photographs. Vibrators, candles . . .

'Welcome,' the vicar said softly, leering as he appeared in the doorway.

'Oh, I . . . I was . . .' I stammered, fear welling from the pit of my churning stomach.

'I'm glad you're here, Crystal. I've been wanting to show you this room for a long time. What do you think of it?'

'I . . . I don't know. What do you do in here?' I asked stupidly.

'What do I do in here?' he echoed, laughing. 'It's not that easy to explain. Perhaps I should *show* you what I do.'

'No, no. I have to be going.'

'Going? But you've only just got here. Actually, your timing couldn't have been better, Crystal. I have my friend with me. The one I mentioned earlier.'

'Now look. If you—'

'Ah, Dave,' he said as a young man wandered into the room. 'This is Crystal, the girl I was telling you about. She's so keen to show us her naked body that she's come here looking for us.'

'A nice little piece,' the man said, licking his lips lecherously as he eyed the cleavage of my firm breasts. 'I think I'm going to enjoy her visit.'

'I can assure you that you'll enjoy *your* visit very much. You'll make sure that my friend enjoys his visit, won't you, Crystal?'

'If you dare to . . .'

Backing away as they moved towards me, I knew what

was going to happen. My buttocks pressing against the edge of the table, my pulse racing, I knew that I was going to be fucked and spunked not only by the vicar but by his accomplice too. My mother should never have told the priest where I was living, and I should never have tried to retrieve the photographs. My heart sinking, I realized that I was a slave to the vicar and his perverted ways. And always would be.

3

I decided that it would be best to give in to the men rather than put up a struggle. After all, I had no choice. I'd never had a choice when the vicar had wanted my naked body. My idea to grab the photographs had been futile, I knew as the evil man unbuttoned my blouse. I should have made sure that he was well out of the way before searching his cottage. But it was no good looking back. My blouse open, my bra lifted from the firm mounds of my teenage breasts, I was going to have to endure the men's crude sex acts.

'Let's get you out of these clothes,' the vicar said, tugging my skirt down as the young man slipped my blouse off my shoulders. 'Once you're naked and on the table, Dave can take a proper look at you and decide exactly what he wants to do.' Nakedness was nothing new to me. The vicar knew my body intimately, probably better than I myself did. Every crevice, every mound and dimple . . . Saying nothing as they removed my clothes, I allowed them to lay me on the table and bind my wrists and ankles. My limbs spread, I closed my eyes as they scrutinized my naked body and ran their fingertips over the brown teats of my sensitive nipples.

Someone's hand smeared cold cream over my pubic hair and I knew that they were going to shave me. There was nothing I could do to stop them. Besides, the vicar had often shaved me before. Whenever it had taken his fancy, he'd removed my pubic curls, stripping years off my femininity. I'd quite liked the feel of my panties caressing my naked pussy lips, but I had always worried that a boyfriend would ask too many questions about how come I'd shaved my teenage quim. Not that I'd had many proper boyfriends. My sexual exploits had been brief encounters where I'd wanked or sucked cocks to orgasm. Perhaps I was incapable of enjoying a real relationship?

Turning my thoughts to the photographic evidence of my debauchery, I reckoned that the young man too had copies of the incriminating pictures. Perhaps the vicar sold copies of the photos to other perverts. God only knew how many men had gazed at photographs of my naked body as they'd wanked their cocks and pumped out their spunk, I thought despairingly. Feeling more despondent than ever, I knew that all was lost. I'd never find freedom, unless I moved several hundred miles away from the village.

A razor dragging across my pubic mound, working over the pouting lips of my pussy, I knew that I was again to be transformed into a lookalike prepubescent girl. The vicar obviously had a thing about young girls and hairless pussies, but what was his friend's fetish? As they wiped away the cream and talked about my naked sex lips, I opened my eyes and gazed in horror as the vicar took several photographs of my naked body. Hadn't he got enough photographs of me already? Making sure that my face was in frame, he obviously wanted more evidence of my lewd sexual exploits. How would I explain my shaved pubes to Robin? Christ, what was I thinking?

Standing at the foot of the table, the vicar ordered his

friend to mouth-fuck me. I watched the young man drop his trousers, the purple knob of his erect penis pointing to the ceiling as he stood by my head. He was big, his shaft a good eight inches long. Turning my head and opening my mouth as he pressed his swollen glans against my cheek, I sucked on his cock-head. The vicar clicking the camera as I tasted the salty tang of the man's rounded sex globe, I wondered again whether I should have moved further away from the area. Perhaps I should have gone to another country. Apart from my parents, I didn't have any ties to England.

'Use your tongue, you dirty slut,' the young man ordered me, withdrawing his penis until my lips engulfed just the rim of his engorged knob. Running my tongue over the silky surface of his glans as the vicar's tongue ran up and down my gaping sex valley, I began to believe that I *was* a dirty slut. I'd thought badly of myself when I'd first started sucking the vicar off and drinking his spunk, and I'd felt even worse when he'd forced his huge cock deep into my bottom and fucked me there. I'd slipped my tutu off and danced for the vicar. I'd pulled my panties down and danced naked. I *was* a dirty little slut.

My mouth bloated by the young man's ballooning glans, my lips taut around his broad shaft, I shuddered as the vicar forced at least three fingers deep into the tight sheath of my young pussy. I'd never had two men use different holes of my naked body simultaneously before. I'd been in the woods with two boys on several occasions, held a cock in each hand and wanked them simultaneously. They'd both come at the same time, their spunk running over my hands as they'd stood on their trembling legs, gasping in their illicit pleasure. And

I would have to admit to having taken two lads up to my bedroom after school one day. I pulled their fresh cocks out and sucked their purple knobs into my mouth. They came together, flooding my mouth with their white spunk.

One of the boys later told me that his greatest turn-on was watching his spunk run down my chin and drip onto my young breasts. I already knew that the vicar liked to watch his cream splatter my face and dribble down my chin. I'd enjoyed the boys' double mouth-fucking, but I'd never before had two adult men attend different orifices of my naked body at the same time. Sucking on the young man's swollen globe, I wondered again what his kink was. Did he want to watch his spunk spurt into my long blonde hair? Or perhaps he'd like me to blow bubbles with his spunk. When I'd been virtually the village bike, I'd been known as the queen of cock-sucking. I knew how to use my mouth, my tongue. But I wasn't going to pleasure the vicar's friend with the full expertise of my hard-learned tonguing and gobbling.

My mouth flooding with sperm, I swallowed the man's orgasmic cream as he gasped and trembled above me. Again, I wondered how much sperm I'd swallowed since I'd first taken the vicar's solid knob-head into my mouth and sucked him to orgasm. The queen of cock-sucking? Licking around the rim, tonguing the sperm slit . . . I knew exactly how to use my mouth to bring immense pleasure to men. I felt resigned to the 'job'. Although I'd vowed umpteen times to break free of the perverted priest's hold on me, I supposed that this was my life. My sole purpose in life was to pleasure the vicar, and now his friend.

'Suck it all out,' the young man ordered me, ramming

his deflating knob to the back of my throat. I sucked hard, swallowing the remnants of his spunk as it oozed from his slit. I'd moved away from the village, found myself a live-in job with decent money . . . And yet I was as beholden to the vicar and his perverted ways as I'd ever been. As the flaccid cock slipped out of my spermed mouth, I realized that I was never going to be free. Cock-sucking, sperm-swallowing, licking the vicar's balls as I wanked his cock and he showered my face with his spunk . . . This was my life.

'She's not as good as you made out,' the young man complained.

'She is,' the vicar murmured, dragging his sperm-wet fingers out of my vaginal sheath. 'She's deliberately playing us up.' Moving to the top of the table, he grabbed a fistful of my long blonde hair. 'I think it's time you were taught a lesson,' he growled, staring hard into my blue eyes. 'It's bad enough you moving away from the village, but to play around like this . . .'

'Has she ever been whipped?' the vicar's accomplice asked, taking the leather belt from his trousers.

'Spanked, but not whipped,' the man of Satan grinned. 'I think you're right. A damned good whipping might just mend her wicked ways.'

My naked body was briefly released and rolled over. I lay on my stomach as my wrists and ankles were bound again with rope. The vicar ran his fingers over the firm globes of my naked buttocks, mumbling about correcting young girls, thrashing discipline into naughty girls. He'd spanked my young bottom many times. He loved putting me across his knees and spanking the naked cheeks of my bum as I squirmed and writhed on his lap. He'd fanta-size, saying that I was a naughty little schoolgirl and, as headmaster of the girls' school, it was his job to punish me. Many times I'd got home from the church and gazed in the dressing-table mirror at the glowing pink flesh of my bottom. I'd become used to his hand, but a leather belt?

The first lash sent a jolt through my tethered body, my buttocks tensing as the pain permeated my anal globes. Again, the belt swished through the air and landed squarely across the hillocks of my bottom. I could hear the vicar chuckling as the belt repeatedly whistled down and swiped the burning cheeks of my young bum. I tried to count the lashes, but my mind became muddled as I did my best to endure the gruelling thrashing. Thoughts of trying to escape my life as the evil man's sex slave faded as I realized again that this *was* my life. There was no escape.

My stinging buttocks finally becoming numb, I lay with my face pressed against the padded leather-topped table and wondered how often I'd be summoned to the torture chamber. Once a week? Every day? Strangely, I found myself thinking that I'd have to make excuses to Robin, lie to him when I went out for a couple of hours every day. I could hardly tell him the truth, I reflected. The young man whipped me harder: he obviously realized that my whimpers had stopped. I cried out as the loudest crack yet resounded around the den of debauchery. Once more, he brought the belt down with such force that I yelped, my naked body convulsing wildly.

'That'll do for now,' the priest's young friend finally said, pulling my head up by the hair and grinning at me. 'You might have been gently spanked in the past, but that's not how *I* deal with young girls,' he hissed. 'You'll find no leniency in me, young lady. Your tears and protests will only drive me on, remember that. Mercy, leniency, quarter . . . They are words that have no meaning to me. I've thrashed the Devil out of many a young girl, believe me.'

'You *are* the Devil,' I ventured stupidly.

'Looks like the thrashing worked extremely well,' the vicar chuckled mockingly.

'That was phase one,' the young man breathed angrily. 'This is phase two.'

The belt began lashing my stinging buttocks again – and again. My naked body becoming rigid, I did my best not to cry out. The leather strap swishing through the air and repeatedly biting into my fiery flesh, I knew that I had to hold on and endure the merciless thrashing. Swearing to get my own back, to put an end to the years of sexual abuse, I bit my lip and held my breath. No matter what happened, no matter how long it took, I'd have my revenge on the evil vicar and his accomplice in debauchery.

The thrashing finally over, I felt someone clamber onto the table between my splayed legs. It was the young man, I knew as hands parted the burning orbs of my bottom and a rounded knob pressed hard against my anal opening. Crude, cold sex. A mouth-fucking, a gruelling thrashing, an arse-fucking . . . That's what my young body was for. I'd been indoctrinated and now believed that my purpose in life was to satisfy the perverted craving of men. I was nothing more than a lump of female meat to be whipped, fucked, spunked and abused on a regular basis. Would I ever find love? I wondered as the ballooning glans pressed harder against my anal inlet, trying to gain entry to my rectum. Did I know what love was?

The solid penile shaft entering me, forcing its way deep into my anal sheath, my pelvic cavity bloating, I wondered how many times I'd had my rectum fucked. The vicar must have fucked and spermed my bowels hundreds of times, but he'd never before forced me to take another man's cock up my bottom. My tethered body rocking as the solid penis repeatedly withdrew and thrust into me again, I could feel the brown tissue of my anus dragging along the huge shaft. In, out, in, out . . . His balls slapped the hairless lips of my vagina as he fucked me, his lower stomach meeting the burning globes of my bottom.

My head lifted by its hair, I gazed at the vicar's erect penis standing to attention in front of my face. He pushed his knob against my lips, forcing his rock-hard glans into my wet mouth. Gobbling and sucking the vicar's cock head as another penis fucked my aching bottom, this was a new experience. Both ends of my naked body used, fucked by two solid cocks, I realized that the priest was embarking on a new regime of sexual abuse. Where would it end? I wondered, the two cocks sliding in and out of my young body. Two men, three men . . . My clitoris swelling, pulsating, the sticky juices of my vagina oozing between my smooth sex lips . . . Surely, the enforced double fucking wasn't turning me on?

I'd felt in control when I'd sucked the boys' cocks, taken their purple knobs into my mouth and swallowed their gushing spunk. But now? Perhaps I *was* in control now, I mused, slurping on the vicar's silky-smooth glans. The man was blackmailing me, but he had to track me down and corner me to use and abuse me. Thinking that I could somehow ease myself out of my predicament, I decided to get Robin to say that I was out the next time the vicar called. If I could cut the crude anal sex down to once a week, and then to a couple of times each month . . .

'Here it comes,' the man fucking my arse breathed, quickening his anal pistoning as his cock-shaft swelled within my tight rectal duct. I could feel his sperm gushing into me, flooding my burning rectum, lubricating his throbbing knob. The vicar gasping as he flooded my mouth with sperm, he grabbed my head and repeatedly rammed his orgasming knob to the back of my throat. If I did find love one day, I doubted that I'd be able to enjoy a proper sexual relationship. My young body was for fucking, not for loving.

Drinking the vicar's orgasmic cream as my anal canal swallowed up the young man's spunk, my clitoris painfully hard, I was desperate for the relief of orgasm. I'd masturbate later, I decided. Perhaps I should allow Robin to check my clitoral response with his vibrator? No. My relationship with Robin wasn't sexual, and I wanted to keep it that way. Once we'd embarked on a sexual relationship, everything would change. He was my boss, I was his live-in housekeeper. If we started climbing into bed together . . .

'I needed that,' the vicar gasped, grinning as he slipped his salivated penis out of my mouth. I watched a long strand of sperm hanging from his knob-slit as I licked my lips. The young man yanked his spent organ out of my anal canal and I lay trembling on the table, wondering what they'd do to me once they'd recovered from their illicit fucking and spunking. Another thrashing? I reflected, the tensed orbs of my buttocks burning like hell. They talked about me as sperm oozed from my anal opening, the taste of male cream lingering on my tongue.

They talked about my naked body, my arse, my tight little cunt.

Cunt. I pondered on the word. I didn't like it. It was harsh, with blunt edges. There'd been one boy at school who was bent on using the word. Whenever I'd taken his knob into my mouth and sucked hard, he'd talked about my cunt. My tight little cunt, my wet cunt, my hot cunt . . . It had probably turned him on, but it had done nothing for me. I reckoned that he'd been trying to provoke a response, possibly trying to shock me. Nothing shocked me. I must have had the cock of just about every boy in the school in my mouth. I don't think there was one boy in my class who hadn't had the pleasure of slipping his purple knob into my thirsty mouth and pumping his sperm down my throat.

I remember complaining to my mother of a stomach ache one evening. She'd asked what I'd eaten during the day. I could have told her that I'd swallowed the sperm from about ten boys' cocks. My stomach ache didn't deter me from cock-gobbling. The very next day I sucked off half a dozen boys, taking their stiff penises into my mouth, running my tongue over their fresh knobs and drinking their salty spunk. I was a slut, but that wasn't my fault. I'd grown up with crude sex, the vicar initiating me into just about every sexual act imaginable, teaching me to cock-suck, to lick and suck and fuck.

'I'll expect you here tomorrow,' the vicar said, releasing my naked body.

'No, I can't,' I murmured, hauling my exhausted body up and clambering off the table. 'I have to go to—'

'You'll be here tomorrow, Crystal. You'll be here at the same time tomorrow, do you understand?'

'Either that, or we'll come and find you,' the young man chortled.

Once I'd dressed, I left the cottage and walked to the bus stop. My buttocks burning a fire-red, sperm oozing from my sore bottom-hole, I vowed never to return to the vicar's cottage. When I didn't turn up, he'd no doubt come looking for me. If I got Robin to tell him that I'd gone to London for the day . . . But I couldn't keep making excuses. The best thing was to get Robin to tell the vicar that I'd moved away for good. That had to be the answer. I'd been staying at his house on a temporary basis until I'd found a job in London. The vicar would hang around, spying on the house . . .

'Hi, Crystal,' a male voice called.

'Oh, Brian.' I smiled as one of my old classmates approached. One of my old regulars. 'I haven't seen you for ages. How are you?'

'I've been away, staying with my aunt in Yorkshire. Are you waiting for the bus?'

'Yes, I . . . I've moved out of the village.'

'Oh, that's a shame. I was hoping that we could . . . Well, you know.'

Gazing at the tight crotch of his jeans, I recalled taking his cock into my mouth and swallowing his sperm. My stomach somersaulting, I thought of the many times we'd slipped into the woods after school. He'd drop his trousers and I'd kneel on the ground and suck on his fresh young cock. But we were older now. I'd moved on, hadn't I? Eyeing the path that led into the woods by the bus shelter, I felt my clitoris swell expectantly. Brian had not only been a regular, but . . . I suppose I'd always fancied him. He was very good-looking, had a lovely smile and . . . Taking his hand,

I led him into the woods to what used to be our favourite spot behind the school.

'The usual?' I asked, kneeling on the ground as a cold wind whipped up.

'Why not?' he said and smiled, dropping his trousers.

'Are you still . . . you know, seeing the other lads?'

'No, I . . . I don't live here, so . . .'

'You'll have to give me your address.'

'Yes, yes, I will.'

Fully retracting Brian's foreskin, I gazed at his swollen knob, his pink sperm-slit. Although older now, his cock was still fresh, unblemished. Sucking his salty glans into my hot mouth, I closed my eyes and ran my wet tongue around its rim. I shouldn't have been doing this, I knew. But I'd been unable to help myself. The thought of young Brian's beautiful knob, his tight ball-bag, his gushing spunk . . . I was supposed to have moved on and yet I'd been fucked by the vicar and his friend and was now sucking on Brian's purple sex-globe. Was I really a slut? Or was I trying to find some comfort? Slipping his knob out of my mouth, I pulled his shaft up and licked the hairy bag of his scrotum. I was a slut, there was no denying it.

'You're as good as ever,' he said, looking down at my pink tongue lapping at his balls. Saying nothing, I knew I was good. I was the best cock-sucker in the land. I was a princess, good enough to eat, good enough to fuck. Taking Brian's glans into my mouth again, I sank my teeth gently into his young shaft. His pubes tickled my nose as I fondled his rolling balls, desperate for his sperm to jet from his sex-slit. I was in control, I reflected, kneading his beautiful balls. There'd been no blackmail, no threats . . . Brian wasn't using me, I was using him.

I'd used all the boys, although they'd not realized it. Every boy I'd wanked, every knob I'd sucked . . . The boys had thought that they were having their wicked way with me when, in reality, I was simply taking what I'd wanted. I'd always loved sucking the boys off, feeling my mouth flood with sperm, swallowing their orgasmic fluid as they'd gasped and swayed on their sagging legs.

'I'm coming,' Brian announced shakily. Slipping his knob out of my mouth, I licked the rim of his glans as his spunk jetted from his slit. Splattering my face, running over my nose, down my cheeks, his white sperm shot from his throbbing cock-head in long threads. Taking his purple plum into my mouth, I drank from his prick, his fountainhead, swallowing hard as he clutched my head and breathed heavily in his coming. I couldn't get enough cock, I realized that as I sucked and repeatedly swallowed. The salty taste, the throbbing glans, the feel of a hard shaft between my lips . . . I'd rather have had a beautiful cock fucking my pretty mouth than shafting the wet sheath of my vagina.

'You get better,' Brian murmured, the last of his spunk oozing from his sex-slit. He was right, I did get better. Better with time, age, experience. Finally slipping his sperm-glistening cock from my mouth, I licked his deflating shaft, lapping up the spilled orgasmic liquid as he looked down at me with a mixture of admiration and satisfaction reflected in his dark eyes. I should have gone into prostitution rather than 'hands-on housekeeping', as Robin had put it. With my gobbling mouth and snaking tongue, I could have earned a fortune and satisfied my craving for spunk.

'You love it, don't you?' Brian smiled as I stood up and licked my creamed lips.

'Love what?' I asked, grinning back at him.

'Cock-sucking.'

'How ever did you guess?' I giggled.

'Crystal, I have a . . . No, it doesn't matter.'

'Go on.'

'My cousin has come down from Yorkshire to stay with us. He's a virgin and it's worrying him. He's an OK guy, it's just that he . . . well, he seems to think that, because he hasn't been with a girl, he might be gay.'

'Gay? He must know whether or not he fancies other boys.'

'He . . . he knows he's not gay. It's just that, never having been with a girl . . . I was wondering whether . . .'

'I suppose I could,' I said, and smiled. 'How old is he?'

'Fairly young.'

'Fairly young? What does that mean?'

'Well . . . Do you want to meet him?'

'Yes, but since I've moved away I don't know when or where.'

'I could go and get him now.'

'Now? I'm supposed to be catching the bus and . . .'

'Some other time, then?'

I had no control over my craving for young boys, I knew as I imagined taking a virgin cock into my mouth. I'd gone to the village to grab the incriminating photographs and had ended up being fucked by the vicar and his friend, sucking the spunk out of Brian's beautiful knob and now . . . The icy wind gusting around my legs, I was feeling cold. As much as I wanted the boy's virgin cock, I wasn't prepared to hang around the woods in midwinter.

'It's too cold,' I finally said. 'If it was summer, then—'

'Come back to my place,' Brian cut in. 'My parents are out. You could go up to my room with Jeff.'

'All right,' I conceded. 'But I have to be getting home soon. Just half an hour, OK?'

'OK,' he said, grinning and leading the way along the path.

The feel of my panties rubbing against my shaved pussy lips sent quivers through my womb and I could hardly wait to meet the young male virgin. Thinking again that this was wrong, I knew that I should have gone home. I was never going to escape the vicar if I kept returning to the village in search of young boys' cocks. *Just this one*, I thought as we reached Brian's house. I'd initiate the young virgin, suck the spunk out of his purple plum, and then keep well away from the village.

Sending me up to the lad's room, Brian said that he'd wait in the lounge while I did the business. 'You know your way around,' he said, a knowing smile on his face. 'He's in the spare room.' I thought, as I climbed the stairs and tapped on the bedroom door, that an introduction would have been in order. But then, I reckoned it would be a nice surprise for the boy to find an attractive blonde at his door, offering to suck his cock. I felt my clitoris pulsate again in expectation.

'Oh,' the good-looking lad breathed as he opened the door. 'Who are you?'

'Crystal,' I replied, smiling and walking past him into the room. 'Brian thought that you might like to get to know me.'

'Get to know you?' He frowned, closing the door as I stood by the single bed.

'Slip your trousers off and lie on the bed with your feet on the floor.'

'But . . .'

'Just do it, Jeff. You're a virgin, and I'm here to change that.'

Eagerly dropping his trousers, Jeff kicked the garment aside and lay on the bed. He was young – too young, I thought as I gazed at his erect penis, his small balls rolling within his tight scrotum. There again, what the hell did his age matter? I reckoned that he wanked his fresh, youthful cock, splattering his stomach with spunk as he lay on his bed, so what the hell? Kneeling between his feet, I watched his young cock twitch as I kissed his balls. He'd come quickly, I knew as I ran my tongue over the taut skin of his scrotum. But that was probably just as well since I wanted to get home.

Running my tongue up Jeff's solid shaft, I finally pulled his foreskin back and sucked his purple knob into my hot mouth. He breathed heavily, his young body shaking uncontrollably as he lifted his head and gazed at my lips encompassing his beautiful cock. He must have thought about this sort of thing as he wanked, I mused, lowering my head until his knob touched the back of my throat. He'd have imagined his hard cock sucked into a girl's mouth as he'd brought out his fresh cream.

'That's amazing,' he breathed, brushing his fair hair away from his eyes as he gazed at my bloated mouth.

'I thought you'd like it,' I breathed, grinning and slipping his cock out of my mouth. 'Have you ever seen a girl's cunt?'

'Er . . . no, I haven't,' he admitted sheepishly.

Standing, I lifted my short skirt and pulled my wet panties down. 'There,' I smiled.

'God, you're . . . How old are you?'

'What does that matter?' I asked, realizing that my

hairless pussy lips made me look a lot younger than I was. 'You wanted to see a girl's cunt, so there it is. I want you to fuck me, Jeff,' I said, lying down next to him on the bed. 'Get on top of me and I'll slip your cock up my tight cunt.'

I didn't know why the hell I was doing this as Jeff clambered on top of me and stabbed at my sex-slit with his rigid cock. I should never have returned to the village. I should have known that my insatiable thirst for young cocks would get the better of me. *So much for moving on*, I mused, taking his fleshy shaft by its base and guiding his swollen knob into the wet sheath of my yearning pussy. As he fully impaled me, he let out a long low moan of pleasure. I, too, let out a rush of breath as my vaginal muscles tightened around his virgin cock.

'You must know what to do,' I whispered, as he withdrew and drove into me again.

'Yes, yes, I do,' he gasped, fucking me hard in his sexual frenzy.

'Is that nice?'

'Yes, yes . . .' he murmured, fucking me like a maniac.

Unfortunately, Jeff pumped out his spunk and filled my pussy in less than a minute. But I didn't mind. He'd lost his virginity and was now a man, that was all that mattered. Making his last thrusts, he finally rolled off me and lay gasping on the bed. That was that, I thought, climbing off the bed and tugging my panties back up. Kneeling on the floor, I sucked his cock clean, tasting the heady blend of his sperm and my girl-juice as he writhed and shook uncontrollably. Announcing that he was going to come again as his cock stiffened fully once more, he rocked his hips, fucking my mouth in his soaring arousal.

He was young enough to come several times, but I

wanted him to enjoy my mouth before shooting his spunk down my throat. Slurping and licking his girl-wet cock, I teased him, taking him to the verge of orgasm and expertly holding him there. His shaft glistening with saliva, sperm and girl-juice, I cleansed him, lapping up the aphrodisiacal cocktail of sex fluids. He was desperate to come again, I knew as he repeatedly tried to slip his cock-head into my wet mouth. Finally allowing him entry, I sucked on his swollen knob and licked his sperm-slit.

'Coming,' he gasped within seconds. His spunk filled my cheeks as he thrust his cock in and out of my mouth, obviously wallowing in his illicit ecstasy while I drank his young seed and drained his heaving balls. He must have thought this a dream come true as he mouth-fucked me. I knew that, from that day on, he'd be forever trying to slip his knob into girls' mouths, get his hands inside their knickers, fuck their tight cunts and drain his balls. Hopefully, now that I'd stripped him of his virginity, he knew for sure that he was heterosexual.

'No more,' he gasped as I slipped his purple globe out of my sperm-drenched mouth. 'God, that was amazing.'

'I thought you'd like to come again,' I said softly, smiling and licking my glossed lips.

'I'd like to . . . I mean . . . I'd like to see you again,' he stammered as I stood up and moved to the door.

'You mean you'd like to fuck me again?'

'No, yes . . . I . . .'

'I'm sure we'll meet again, Jeff. In fact, I'm certain we shall.'

Leaving the room, I went downstairs and said goodbye to Brian. He fired dozens of questions at me. Did Jeff do it? Did he come in your pussy? Did you suck him? I had no time to hang around and told him to ask Jeff himself what had happened. Leaving Brian's house and walking to the bus stop, I hoped I wouldn't bump into any more young lads requiring my oral services. I could have happily taken several more cocks into my mouth and swallowed copious amounts of spunk, but I had to get back to my room, back to Robin.

Finally reaching the house, I let myself in and found Robin hovering in the kitchen. He appeared to be agitated, his frustration reflected in his pained expression as he mumbled something about a young girl calling at the house. I finally managed to get some sense out of him and discovered that a friend of mine had called to see me. He couldn't remember her name but, from his description, I knew that it was Juliette. We'd always got on well at school but I'd not seen her for several months since she'd got a job in London.

'She said that she'd be back later,' Robin mumbled.

'Are you all right?' I asked as he rummaged through one of the kitchen drawers.

'Yes, yes. I'm looking for a bottle opener. There was one here yesterday but it's gone.'

'It's in the other drawer, Robin. I cleared up in here and . . .'

'Other drawer?' he breathed, moving to the next drawer. 'Ah, there it is.' He grinned triumphantly. 'This is your kitchen now. I'm surprised that you don't know where things are.'

'Yes, well . . . Have you had a busy day?'

'Busy? Busy? I've been inundated with clients.'

'Oh, that's good.'

'Is it?'

'Isn't it?' I asked.

'I suppose it is. The trouble is, they all have severe mental problems. They're all bloody mad.'

'That's why they come to see you, Robin,' I sighed. 'You're a psychiatrist, remember?'

'Oh, yes, of course. Still, that's no reason to come here harping on about their bloody nightmares. Anyway, where have you been?'

'I went out for a walk,' I replied, filling the kettle. 'Would you like some tea?'

'Yes, thanks. A walk, you say?'

'I went back to the village for . . . I met an old friend and went for a walk.'

'Ah, sex,' he chuckled.

'Sex? What do you mean?'

'You've had sex, I can tell. In the woods, more than likely.'

There really was something uncanny about Robin. His perception, insight or whatever was truly amazing. Thinking that he was like Sherlock Holmes, I slipped my coat off and looked down at my skirt and blouse. Had he seen the tell-tale signs of spunk? I couldn't see any marks, and wiped my face with the back of my hand in case sperm had dried on my chin. There were no signs of my having sex, I concluded, wondering again at his uncanny insight.

'Why do you think I've had sex in the woods?' I asked, pouring the tea.

'Because I'm a psychiatrist,' he replied. 'Psychiatrists know these things.'

'Yes, but how?'

'They just do. Now, where did I put that crate of beer?'

'I put it outside, by the back door.'

'Why on earth . . .'

'It's lager, Robin. And lager should be served chilled.'

'Ah, right. Good thinking,' he said, opening the back door.

'I thought you wanted tea?'

'No, no. I'm going to hit the booze. It's time I went on a bender.'

Hit the booze? A bender? I'd had no idea that he was a heavy drinker. Watching him grab a bottle of beer from the crate outside, I sat at the table and sipped my tea. He opened the bottle and gazed out of the window as if deep in thought. Swigging from the bottle, he spun round on his heels and grinned at me. He was a peculiar man, I thought as he made a funny face and told me that the lager tasted like a Dutch prostitute's bottom-hole.

'How do you know what a Dutch prostitute's . . .' I began.

'Because I'm a psychiatrist,' he laughed. 'Psychiatrists know these things.'

'Yes, I'm sure they do.'

'How many men?'

'What?'

'Sex. How many men did you have sex with?'

'Robin!' I gasped. 'I went for a walk with a friend.'

'Two men? Three?'

'None, for goodness' sake.'

'That girl . . . she's a lesbian.'

'Which girl?'

'The one who came here looking for you. She's a lesbian.'

He was right, Juliette did have lesbian tendencies. She'd often eyed me up, but she was in a long-term relationship with some other girl so nothing had ever come of it. We were friends, that was all. But how the hell did Robin know about her? She wasn't obviously butch or anything, so there was no way anyone could tell just by looking at her. His perception was almost frightening, and I wondered what else he knew, particularly about me. As he sat opposite me and swigged his beer, he gave me a knowing look.

'Oral,' he said mysteriously. 'You've had oral sex.'

'Robin,' I breathed, my face flushing. 'I have not . . .'

'Why lie about it? What are you trying to hide?'

'Nothing. I'm not trying to hide—'

'And you still haven't told me what it is you're running away from.'

'OK,' I sighed, finishing my tea. 'You tell me. Tell me all about myself.'

'Well, I'd say that you've had a heavy burden, a weight to bear for some time now. It's to do with that vicar, I know that. He either has something on you, knows something dreadful about you, or he . . . Yes, that's it. He knows something about you and you're afraid that he might tell.'

'Go on,' I murmured, gazing to Robin's dark eyes.

'You're running away from him. He's the main one, but you're also running from others. There are people you know, people with whom you'd rather not be involved any more. Boyfriends, I reckon. And quite a few of them. How am I doing so far?'

'Just keep talking,' I said, reckoning that he had some kind of psychic power.

'OK. An older man, probably the vicar, has a sexual hold over you. To counteract this, you like to have a sexual hold over younger men. You feel with them that you're in a position of power, using your body as a weapon . . . No, no. You use your body as a means to gain the upper hand over young men. Subconsciously, you're trying to find a balance. On the one hand, the vicar has control over you. On the other, to bring about a balance, you have this need for dominance over young men.'

'I think I know what you're getting at,' I said, a chill running up my spine. 'OK, you reckon that's what happened in the past. What about the future? Can you tell me anything about the future?'

'The future holds . . . that girl, the lesbian. She'll get what she wants.'

'Get what she wants?'

'She wants you, has done for a long time. She'll get you into bed.'

'Now that *is* daft,' I giggled. 'There's no way . . .'

'You asked me, Crystal. And I'm telling you.'

'All right, what else can you tell me?'

'I can tell you that I'm going to grab another bottle and go and sit in my consulting room. I've finished for the day, so I'm going to relax. By the way, I've left a little present by your bed.'

As Robin took another bottle and left the room, I mused on his revelation. I had no idea how he knew so much about me, but he was right on every count. If he was right about the past, then . . . then he might be right about the future and I'd end up having sex with Juliette. Was that what I wanted? I wondered. Apart from my young friend licking me during the sleepover, I'd never had a lesbian relationship. Two young girls messing about could hardly be called a proper lesbian relationship. I loved playing with the boys, wanking their hard cocks, their knobs spunking in my mouth. There was no way I wanted another girl's clitoris in my mouth.

Leaving the kitchen, I went up to my room to see what Robin's present was. Closing my door behind me, I looked at the bedside table and found myself staring at a small vibrator. After sucking Brian and Jeff, the vicar fucking my mouth, his friend shafting my bottom-hole ... I was desperate to come. But Robin couldn't have known that, could he? Perhaps he wasn't mad after all, I reflected. Reckoning that he just liked to come across as eccentric, I relaxed on my bed and examined the vibrator.

My clitoris swelling, my juices of arousal flowing. I slipped my wet panties off and lay with my legs wide apart. Robin would probably know that I'd used the vibrator and brought myself off. Was there anything he *didn't* know about me? The vicar, oral sex in the woods with young men ... He knew too much for my liking. But he hadn't mentioned the merciless thrashing I'd been forced to endure, my stinging buttocks.

Switching the vibrator on, I parted the hairless lips of my wet pussy and pressed the buzzing tip against the solid nub of my clitoris. The sensations were heavenly, and I wondered why I'd never used a vibrator before. I supposed that I'd never had the opportunity. Vibrators weren't the sort of thing that was sold in the village shop. Imagining Juliette using a vibrator on another girl, I realized that my mother must have given her my new address. End up in bed with her? No, I wasn't a lesbian.

My clitoris becoming painfully hard, pulsating wildly, I shuddered as the birth of my desperately needed orgasm stirred deep within my contracting womb. This was far better than using my fingers, and I ran the tip of the device up and down my gaping sex valley, inducing my hot juices of lust to flow from my open hole. Breathing deeply, I could feel my juices seeping between the engorged inner lips of my pussy and trickling down between my burning buttocks. The sensations were heavenly. Arching my back as my young body became rigid, I ran the buzzing tip around the base of my swollen clitoris, gasping for breath as my pleasure built.

'Yes,' I breathed, my clitoris exploding in orgasm, my vaginal juices gushing from my gaping sex hole. My eyes rolling, I tossed my head from side to side as shock waves of pure sexual bliss crashed through my young body. I pictured fresh young cocks fucking my mouth as I rode the crest of my orgasm, white sperm jetting from the sex-slits. Wanking penises, the sperm jetting, splattering my face . . . If only I'd had a cock to suck while I'd masturbated with the vibrator.

I was hooked on young boys' penises, I knew as my orgasm peaked. Their unblemished shafts, their full balls rolling within their scrotums . . . I loved bringing out their spunk, sucking and licking their purple sex-globes and bringing out the fruits of their orgasms. I'd return to the village, stupid though it was. I'd return in search of fresh young cocks and solid knobs. The vicar . . . My climax peaking again, my juices gushing from my spasming cunt and spraying my inner thighs, I tried not to think about the evil vicar.

Ripples of sexual pleasure reaching out to every nerve ending, tightening every muscle, I shook violently as the buzzing vibrator sustained my incredible climax. My solid clitoris pulsating, my vaginal muscles rhythmically contracting, I lay gasping on my bed in the grip of my multiple orgasm. Just as I was thinking that my pleasure would never end, my body began to relax as my orgasm subsided. Finally switching the vibrator off, I writhed on the bed, my hair matted with the perspiration of sexual abandon, the crack of my vulva hot and sticky with my lust juices.

It had been a long day, and an interesting one. Pleasantly tired now, I slipped out of my clothes and crawled beneath the quilt. Sleep soon engulfed me when I curled up into a ball. What tomorrow held, I had no idea. The vicar had demanded that I visit his cottage for another session of enforced sex . . . I was going to have to speak to Robin, get him to say that I'd moved out if the vicar came hunting for me. I'd also have to find a way of sneaking into the woods to meet the boys without walking through the village first. But, for now, I was going to sleep – to dream of hard young cocks and fresh sperm.

4

Robin was banging around downstairs at seven-thirty. As sleep left me, I wondered what time he normally had breakfast, and whether I should have been up before him. After all, I was supposed to be his housekeeper. Slipping into my dressing gown, I crossed the landing to the bathroom and took a shower. Dried pussy-juice, starched sperm . . . I could wash away the evidence of my debauchery, but not the weals fanning out across my crimsoned buttocks.

'Fuck me,' Robin cursed from his consulting room as I made my way downstairs, dressed in my red miniskirt and a white blouse. Ignoring him, I went into the kitchen and filled the kettle for tea. I was going to have to do some shopping, I decided, opening the fridge and gazing at the empty shelves. Making a mental note of the things I needed, I poured the tea and made some toast with what was left of the bread.

'Fuck me,' Robin cursed again as he entered the kitchen.

'I thought you didn't like swearing,' I said, looking up at him from the table.

'Normally I can't abide swearing,' he sighed, sitting opposite me. 'But I can't find the bloody telephone.'

'It's on your desk, Robin.'

'Is it? Who the hell put it there?'

'You did, I would imagine.'

'Would you believe it? I've been searching high and low for the damned thing.'

'I'm going shopping after breakfast. Is there anything in particular you want me to get?'

'Yes, a new telephone. Get one that doesn't hide from me and ring all the bloody time.'

'All telephones ring, Robin.'

'Well, they shouldn't. It's the height of rudeness. When are you going to give me my bed bath?'

'Your bed . . . I'm *not* going to give you a bed bath.'

'In that case, I shall go upstairs and take a shower. Don't forget the phone when you go out.'

'No, I won't,' I sighed as he left the room.

Finishing my tea and toast, I went into the consulting room and opened the safe. Fifty pounds would be enough, I reckoned, grabbing the money, I was about to close the safe when I noticed a pile of photographs. As Robin was in the shower, I couldn't resist taking a look and I began to flick through them. To my surprise, they were of girls' vaginal cracks. Some hairy, some shaved, some gaping wide open . . . Robin enjoyed making lewd comments, that I knew, but the photographs were wholly indecent.

Slipping them back into the safe and closing the door, I grinned as I left the room with the money. Perhaps Robin took pictures of his clients, or they might have been . . . He was a naughty man, that was for sure. Not that I could talk. Grabbing my coat from the kitchen as I heard him cursing in the bathroom, I left the house and walked to the local shops. I couldn't stop thinking about Robin's uncanny insight as I did the shopping. There was no way he could have guessed that I'd had oral sex in the woods, so how the hell *did* he know? Not buying too much on my first trip, since I didn't have a car, I lugged the bags home and decided to ask him more about my future that evening.

'The lesbian's in your room,' he announced as I stocked up the fridge.

'Oh, right,' I said, wishing he'd stop sending people up to my room.

'She wants sex,' he said, grinning. 'Rampant lesbian sex.'

'Of course she doesn't,' I laughed, closing the fridge and walking into the hall. 'Is that all you think about?'

'Yes, it is.'

Juliette was sitting on my bed, wearing a loose-fitting blouse and a very short skirt. Her long dark hair cascading over the rise of her full breasts, her make-up impeccable, she was an extremely attractive young girl. Thanking God that I'd slipped my vibrator beneath my pillow, I asked her how she was, pondering again on Robin's words. He was wrong, I knew. There was no way I was going to have sex with Juliette. She might have been a lesbian, but *I* certainly wasn't and I had no intention of becoming one.

'I've left the London job,' she said as I sat down next to her. 'It was boring, and London is a nightmare after living in the village.'

'I would have thought you'd love London,' I said. 'The people, the life . . .'

'I did at first. But it's a rat race. The bars are heaving, the buses jam-packed . . . I just didn't fit in. Anyway, you seem to have done all right for yourself. This is a lovely room.'

'It is, and the money's pretty good. Robin's OK. He's my boss, the man who let you in.'

'He called me a lesbian.'

'Er . . . yes, he . . . Don't take it personally,' I laughed. 'He calls everyone lesbians. He's not insane, exactly. Actually, I think he is.'

'There's something weird about him, certainly. Anyway, your mum said that you were a housekeeper. Do you enjoy it?'

'It's OK. Cooking, cleaning . . . It's not exactly hard work and, as I said, the money's good.'

'I do like your room,' she said, reclining on the bed as I stood up and slipped my coat off. 'You really have done well.'

'The best thing about it is that my father isn't here to nag me. That skirt's too short, what time did you get in last night . . . Nag, nag, nag. And I'm well away from . . .'

'From what?'

'Well, everything.'

Standing at the end of the bed, I gazed at Juliette's shapely thighs as she made herself comfortable. Did she want sex with me? I wondered, focusing on the triangular patch of her white panties hugging her pubic mound. I'd never have thought about lesbian sex had Robin not mentioned it. My thoughts had always concentrated on fresh young cocks, not pussies. But, sitting on the end of the bed, I couldn't drag my eyes away from the bulging material of her panties. My young friend had licked my pussy crack, but I'd never thought about touching another girl. Wishing, as my stomach somersaulted, that Robin hadn't said anything, I asked Juliette whether she'd like some coffee.

'No, I'm fine,' she said. 'So, have you got a boyfriend at the moment?'

Ray Gordon

'No, no one special. Have you . . . well, you know.'

'We split up,' she sighed, parting her thighs as she stretched her limbs and sprawled out on the bed. 'It was for the best, really. We were OK together but she started looking at other girls and that was that. Now I'm as free as a bird. I expect the vicar misses you.'

'The vicar?' I echoed. 'What do you mean?'

'You were always in the church mucking about with flowers or going to his cottage. He must miss your help.'

'Oh, yes, he does.'

Moving to the window, I couldn't stop thinking about Juliette's tight panties, the material stretched, swollen by the fleshy lips of her teenage pussy. I had to drag my mind away from lesbian sex but, after Robin's revelation, I couldn't stop wondering what it would be like to slip my finger into her tight sex hole. We talked about this and that for a while and then I sat on the end of the bed again. Her thighs wide, the narrow strip of material running between her legs did nothing to conceal her outer love-lips. I couldn't see her pubes, which I thought odd as I gazed at her most private place. Perhaps she'd shaved, I mused, my clitoris swelling, my juices of desire flowing between my sex lips.

'Why don't you come and lie next to me?' she said and smiled. 'You look tense, wound up. Come here and relax.' Joining her, I knew what she was after. But how the hell had Robin known? Juliette didn't waste any time. Her fingers wandering up my inner thigh, pressing into the soft material of my panties, she leaned over and kissed my cheek. Breathing in her perfume, I shuddered as her fingertip ran up and down my tight panties, following the opening valley of my sex groove.

'You're beautiful,' she murmured, her finger slipping

beneath the hem of my panties and stroking the top of my leg. My mind spinning, my juices flowing, I didn't move as she parted my inner lips and explored just inside my vaginal opening. I didn't want this – did I? But there was something about her touch, her sensual female touch. She knew exactly what to do, where to find my G-spot and how to massage me there. Again recalling Robin's words as Juliette slipped her finger deep into the wet heat of my vagina, I wondered whether I'd have been on the bed with the girl like this had he not said anything. We'd have probably chatted over coffee, reminisced and . . .

'Want me to lick you?' Juliette asked huskily, her long black hair tickling my face as she kissed my full lips.

'I . . . I don't know,' I replied hesitantly. Her mouth tasted of sex. 'Juliette, I . . .'

'You won't know until you try,' she whispered as she smiled, moving down my young body.

Allowing Juliette to pull my panties down and slip them over my ankles, I parted my legs and waited with bated breath as she settled between my thighs and commented on my hairless pussy. She liked it – the smooth flesh of my vulva, my bared valley of desire. She said that I looked good enough to eat. Was I a princess? Did I want this? I wondered as she kissed the fleshy hillocks of my sex cushions. I didn't know what I wanted. A tongue was a tongue, I decided as she licked the naked flesh of my mons. Male or female, a tongue was a tongue. But I could smell her perfume, feel her long hair caressing my inner thighs. There was no way I could pretend that she was anything other than a girl, a lesbian. Was *I* a lesbian?

She parted my sex lips, exposing my wet inner folds, the solid nub of my sensitive clitoris as I lay trembling on the bed. I wasn't in control now. Unlike my cock-sucking sessions where I called the shots, here I wasn't in control at all. But, unlike when I was with the vicar, I didn't feel threatened or intimidated in any way. Juliette was soft and gentle, her female caress sending my arousal sky-high. Her wet tongue lapping at my inner sex folds, tasting me there, she breathed deeply as I closed my eyes and let myself go completely. To my surprise, I'd given myself to her, offered my open pussy to another girl. Years ago, my young friend had licked me there but we'd been too young to know what we were doing. Was I too young now?

Since I'd left the village, I'd thought more about sex than ever before. I supposed it was the prospect of losing the boys, going without their hard cocks, their beautiful purple knobs and fresh sperm. I'd not expected to suck young Brian's cock in the woods. Leaving the village, I'd doubted that I'd meet any more young lads. I only had such a following because we'd all met at school. Living away from the village, in a new town, I'd thought my days of cock-sucking in the woods were over.

'You taste gorgeous,' Juliette breathed, her wet tongue teasing the sensitive tip of my solid clitoris. Staying silent, apart from my heavy breathing, I let myself drift through clouds of lesbian sex, revelling in the incredible pleasure another girl was bringing me. She was so soft, gentle – feminine. Breathing in the heady scent of her perfume, I parted my thighs as far as I could, allowing her full access to my most intimate place. Moving down, she pushed her tongue into my sex-hole, licking me there, lapping up my creamy juices of lesbian desire.

'God,' I breathed involuntarily as her tongue worked deep inside my contracting sex-sheath, sending delight-

ful ripples of sensation though my pelvis. Listening to
the slurping sounds of oral lust, I could feel her hot
breath against my splayed inner lips, her nose pressing
on the erect bulb of my clitoris. She was taking me to
heights of sexual ecstasy I'd never known before, lifting
me higher to my sexual heaven with each sweep of her
wet tongue. Shuddering uncontrollably, I was desperate
for the feel of her tongue against my expectant clitoris.
Swivelling my hips to align my sex spot with her snaking
tongue, my arousal soared as she deliberately avoided my
pleasure button.

'Please,' I gasped as her tongue delved deep into the
drenched duct of my young cunt. I heard her giggle as
she continued to tongue-fuck me and tease me, holding
me back from the explosion of orgasm. She sucked out
my creamy juices, drinking from my hot pussy as I
writhed and squirmed on my bed. I didn't think that
I could take much more as my clitoris swelled painfully.
The teats of my breasts fully erect, I ripped my blouse
open and massaged my nipples, adding to my immense
pleasure.

Was this what I wanted? I asked myself again. Was this
the beginning of a long-term lesbian relationship with
Juliette? I'd already returned to the woods, sucked the
sperm out of Brian's throbbing knob, sucked and fucked
his young friend, been subjected to the vicar's perverted
ways . . . And now a female tongue was working between
my thighs, licking, teasing, tasting. I'd hoped to escape
the vicar, but I could never escape myself, my insatiable
thirst for sex.

Finally moving up my gaping sex-crack, Juliette
sucked my clitoris into her hot mouth and snaked her
tongue around its engorged shaft. My climax immedi-

ately exploded, sending tremors of pure lust throughout
my shaking body. Never had I known an orgasm of such
power and duration. My body perspiring, my limbs
thrashing about, my breasts heaving, I screamed as
the sensations rocked my very soul. I was sure that
Robin would hear me as I cried out again in sheer lesbian
ecstasy, but I didn't care. After all, he'd said that Juliette
would get me into bed, so I doubted that he'd be
surprised to hear my cries of lesbian lust. Did he want
to mouth-fuck me?

Finally, my orgasm began to wane, leaving me gasping
for breath, my limbs twitching uncontrollably. Moving
up by my side, her face pussy-wet, cream-drenched,
Juliette smiled at me. She murmured words of lesbian
lust, but I couldn't answer. My mind floating, drifting, I
was in a state of seeming semiconsciousness. I could hear
Juliette in the distance, her words echoing around inside
my head as her pretty face came in and out of focus. She
was beautiful, young and sensual. Would she visit me
again and love me?

'Are you all right?' she asked me.

'Yes,' I gasped finally, my body calming at last.

'I won't ask whether you enjoyed it,' she giggled,
stroking the sensitive teats of my firm breasts. 'I think
I know the answer.'

'God, that was incredible,' I breathed. 'I've never
known anything like it.'

'Only a girl knows how to pleasure another girl,
Crystal. Remember that. And on that note, I must be
going.'

'Going? Already?'

'Yes, I have things to do.'

'But don't you want me to—'

'I don't think you're in a fit state to reciprocate. I'll call round this evening, if you'd like me to.'

'Yes, yes, do that.'

'OK. I'll bring a couple of bottles of wine. Red or white?'

'I don't mind. Anything.'

'Until this evening, then.'

'Until this evening.'

As Juliette left, I managed to haul my sated body up and sit with my back against the bed's headboard. I'd not been joking about the pleasure she'd brought me – I really hadn't known anything like it before. She certainly knew what to do, how to use her tongue, and I could hardly wait for her to return that evening so I could . . . Did I really want to lick and suck another girl to orgasm? Again thinking about fresh young cocks, sucking the lads to orgasm and swallowing their warm spunk, I wasn't sure that I could drink the sex-juices from a girl's hot pussy. I'd tasted my own juices, sucked my fingers clean after fingering my tight pussy – but to drink from another girl's pussy?

Parting my thighs, I looked down at the swollen lips of my hairless vulva, the girl-cream oozing from my sex-slit, running down my inner thighs. I'd never been so wet, I thought, imagining Juliette's tongue there again, licking and sucking my insatiable clitoris to another massive orgasm. Slipping two fingers into the hot duct of my vagina, I massaged my inner flesh, closing my eyes as the beautiful sensations transmitted deep into my trembling womb. Wondering about using my vibrator, I heard Robin crashing around in the kitchen and thought it best to wait until the evening.

Clambering off the bed, I adjusted my clothing and

slipped my panties back on. Realizing that I'd not done
any housework, I wondered where the vacuum cleaner
was. Knowing Robin, he didn't have one, nor any dusters
and polish. Hearing his cursing, I thought I'd best make
an effort to at least appear to be doing my job. After all,
he was paying me two hundred a week and giving me a
room for nothing. Perhaps he wanted the occasional blow
job in return?

Bounding downstairs, I found him in his consulting
room with his corduroy trousers down around his knees.
His hair was dishevelled, his bow tie crooked. He was a
mess, both physically and mentally. Staring in disbelief
as he adjusted his boxer shorts, pulling the end of his
penis out and tucking it back in, I asked him what he was
doing.

'Making myself comfortable,' he replied nonchalantly.
'My scrotal sac becomes entangled in my shorts and my
penis tries to escape through the leg hole.'

'Er . . . I don't have that problem,' I breathed.

'Perhaps you'd give me a hand? If you could just . . .'

'No, I think not,' I said, frowning as he thrust his hand
down his shorts and began groping around. 'Do you have
a vacuum cleaner?'

'I don't see how a vacuum cleaner would help,' he
sighed. 'I mean, being sucked off is one thing, but . . .'

'Robin, I didn't mean . . . I need a vacuum cleaner for
the carpets, not for your . . . your dick.'

'Ah, right. There was one somewhere. I remember
seeing one about three years ago. I know, take a look in
the cupboard beneath the stairs.'

Leaving Robin to sort his equipment out, I opened the
cupboard door and peered into the darkness beneath the
stairs. Fumbling for the light switch, I eventually found

it and turned it on. The mess in that cupboard was unbelievable. An old radio that should have been in a museum, a vacuum cleaner that should have been at the rubbish dump . . . Clearing the cupboard out was going to be a major operation, but it had to be done.

I worked for an hour or so while Robin fiddled about in his consulting room and then I decided to make some coffee. Once I'd got the house straight, sorted out cupboards and cleaned the place up, it would be easy enough to keep it that way. It was just the initial workload that seemed daunting. Placing Robin's coffee on his desk, I thought I'd better mention the vicar. I wasn't sure how to broach the subject but, seeing as Robin knew everything about me, I decided to dive in at the deep end.

'If the vicar calls, would you tell him that I've moved out?' I asked.

'He called earlier,' Robin murmured, looking up from his desk. 'He called while you were having lesbian sex. I told him that you no longer lived here.'

'But how did you know that I—'

'Have you seen my pen anywhere?'

'It's there, on the desk. Robin, how do you know so much about me, about my life?'

'Psychiatrists know everything,' he replied, tapping the side of his nose and grinning.

'*Psychics* might claim to know things they can't have any actual awareness of, but not psychiatrists. Is there anything else you can tell me about my future?'

'The future depends on the past.'

'What do you mean?'

'Whatever happened in the past moulds the future. For example, your thirst for sex stems from the abuse you endured in the past.'

'I *wasn't* abused, Robin.'

'And your thirst for sex will very soon . . . There's a room, like a torture chamber.'

'Like this room, with those handcuffs and . . .'

'They're only there to help my clients talk about the past. They look at the dildos and handcuffs and the past comes flooding back. It helps them to open up.'

'This room you claim to know about . . . Where is it?'

'I don't know. The woods are like a magnet, attracting you, pulling you.'

'The woods?'

'Not too far from here. You'll meet someone there today. A man, a young man.'

'This afternoon?'

'As I said, you're attracted to the woods, You won't be able to keep away.'

'But what about the room?'

'The torture chamber? It's very odd. You don't want to return to the room but, for some reason, you won't be able keep away. Unless you go back to the room, the consequences . . .' Robin looked grim.

'How can I put an end to it?'

'By discovering the truth.'

'What truth?'

'I don't know. But I *do* know that it will get worse before it gets better. By the way, I saw the ghost last night.'

'Really?' I asked mockingly. 'And what was he up to?'

'Hanging around outside your bedroom door. He could probably smell fresh pussy and thought he'd—'

'Yes, Robin. Fascinating though your ghost is . . .'

'Your phone's ringing.'

'Er . . . yes, right.'

Rushing upstairs, I dashed into my room just as the phone stopped ringing. It had to have been my mother. I'd left my number on the kitchen table when I'd gone back for my things. Lifting the receiver absent-mindedly, I replaced it again when I heard only the dial tone. I'd call her later, I decided. She tended to go on a bit and I wasn't in the mood for a half-hour chat. Fresh pussy? Robin must have had one of his crazy moments if he'd thought he'd seen a ghost, I mused. A ghost hanging around outside my bedroom door? Wondering what Robin wanted for lunch, I was about to go down to the kitchen when the phone rang again.

'Crystal?' a male voice asked as I answered. Hesitating, I wondered whether it was the vicar. 'It's Ian.'

'Ian?' I breathed. 'How did you get my number?'

'Your mum gave it to me.'

'I wish she'd stop . . . Anyway, how are you?'

'I'm OK. What are you up to today?'

'Why?'

'There are a few of us . . . Want to meet in the woods?'

'Er . . . what, now?'

'Yes.'

'Who's there with you?'

'Charlie, Joe, Don and me.'

'All right. Give me twenty minutes.'

Replacing the receiver, I knew that I shouldn't go to the woods and meet the boys. I was supposed to be moving on, I reminded myself as I licked my full lips. But the thought of their tight ball-bags, their hard cocks, their rounded knobs and gushing sperm . . . Robin was right, I reflected. I'd meet someone in the woods in that day. How the hell had he known? I wondered, grabbing my coat as I walked to the front door. Telling him that I was going to the shops, I left the house and walked to the village. I was a fool, I knew. Returning to the village was dangerous. The vicar might see me and . . . Was this really my destiny?

Had the vicar not introduced me to cock-sucking at such an early age . . . But was it really his fault? He'd initiated me, yes. But I was the one who'd got a name around the school as a cock-sucker. I could hardly blame the vicar for my insatiable thirst for sperm, could I? I didn't know what to think as I walked along the street. Did my craving for young cocks really matter? It wasn't harming anyone. On the contrary, I loved every minute of it – and so did the boys. But something nagged me. I was a tart, a cock-sucking whore. If that was the case, then what were the boys? I was trying to justify my actions. Whether or not it was the vicar's fault, whatever the boys were . . . I was a cock-sucking slut.

Walking to the woods from the back of the village to avoid the lane, I felt my stomach somersault. I'd been the village bike for years, and nothing had changed. One boy, a proper boyfriend, would have been different. But I craved several boys at once – sucking their cocks, wanking them and drinking their sperm . . . Was I somehow trying to find a balance, as Robin had said? On the one hand, the vicar had control over me. On the other hand, to bring about a balance, I had a need for dominance over young men. I really didn't know what to think as I approached the clearing behind the school. The boys knew that I was a tart. And they knew that I was the finest cock-sucker in the land.

There was no one there when I entered the clearing. The thought struck me that it might have been a trick, the vicar might have . . . No, I was being ridiculous. At least the weather had brightened up, I thought, slipping my coat off and tossing it over a bush. The sun reminded me of the summer months ahead. I couldn't wait for the summer to arrive. The hot weather was ideal for cock-sucking in the woods. Stripped naked, the boys' hands wandering over my breasts, between my thighs as I sucked one of them to orgasm . . .

'Hi,' Ian greeted me, grinning as he led his friends into the clearing.

'And what do you lot want?' I giggled.

'You know what we want,' he laughed. 'The same as we always want.'

'All kneel in front of me and beg me to suck your cocks,' I ordered them. I loved being in control.

'Please, Crystal,' they said, kneeling and looking up at me, their mistress. 'Please suck our cocks.'

'I don't know whether I want to,' I responded haughtily. We always played games like this. 'Have you all been good?'

'Yes,' they replied in unison.

'Take your trousers off and stand in a row. I'll inspect your cocks and, if I feel like it, I might suck one or two.'

Eagerly tugging their trousers down, they lined up before me with their young penises already fully erect. I was in my element, I knew as I kneeled on the ground and kissed the first boy's tight scrotum. Greedily inhaling his male scent, I pressed my lips hard against his balls, my head dizzy with the thought of fresh sperm. I have to admit that I couldn't help myself. I shouldn't have gone to the village, I should have kept away from the woods . . . But when four lads offered me their hard cocks, I just couldn't resist. No one would be any the

wiser, I consoled myself. My parents would never know
. . . Robin would know what I'd done. How the hell . . .

'Aren't you going to suck it?' the boy asked as I licked
the tight skin of his scrotum.

'I might,' I said, and grinned, looking up at him.
'There again, I might not. Pull your foreskin back and
show me your knob.'

'There,' he said proudly, following my instructions
and fully retracting his foreskin.

'Not bad,' I murmured, gazing longingly at the
rounded knob of his solid cock, his small sperm-slit.
'I'm only going to suck two cocks.'

'How will you decide which two?' someone asked me.

'That's a good question. Gather round me and I'll feel
each cock in turn, see which is the hardest.'

Squeezing each shaft in turn, I realized that they were
all as hard as granite. I was going to suck the spunk out of
all four knobs, and the boys knew that. But we enjoyed
playing the games. Ordering all my students to pull their
foreskins back, I gazed at their purple plums. Licking
one, tasting the salt, I moved to the next and rolled my
tongue over its velvety surface. Finally tasting the last
two, I sat back on my heels. The boys were very patient,
standing in silence as I licked my lips and made out that I
was deciding which two cocks would mouth-fuck me.

'When did you last wank?' I asked Ian.

'This morning,' he replied proudly.

'And you?' I asked, smiling as I looked up at the next
boy.

'Yesterday.'

'Charlie?'

'Yesterday.'

'Don?'

'About two hours ago.'

'That's it, then,' I said authoritatively. 'Joe and Charlie haven't come since yesterday. I'll suck their cocks.'

Taking Joe's purple knob into my hot mouth, I ran my tongue around its rim. The boy breathed deeply, his legs visibly trembling as I kneaded his balls and sucked his knob to the back of my throat. The others watched, their solid penises twitching as the queen of cock-suckers went to work. I felt that I had power, sexual prowess as I moved my head back and encompassed the boy's glans between my succulent lips. I was a princess, good enough to eat.

Joe came quickly. His cock twitching, his sex-plum throbbing as he pumped out his orgasmic cream and filled my gobbling mouth, he rocked his hips and drained his balls. I slurped and sucked and swallowed, drinking from his beautiful organ to quench my thirst for spunk. But there was no quenching my thirst. The minute his sperm-flow ceased, I slipped his spent cock out of my mouth and grabbed Charlie's rock-hard member. *Another firm cock*, I mused, sucking his salty plum into my well-spunked mouth. *More fresh spunk*.

Eagerly gobbling on the gasping lad's swollen glans as the other boys watched, I wondered whether Robin was sitting at his desk getting some kind of psychic report on my illicit sexual activities. If he really was psychic, receiving messages from the *other side*, then he'd probably know exactly what I was up to. *Perhaps he's sent the ghost along to see what I'm doing*, I giggled inwardly, taking the boy's knob halfway down my throat and sinking my teeth gently into the root of his beautiful cock. The ghost might well be in Robin's mind, but his revelations were nonetheless extremely accurate. Forgetting about ghosts, I pulled the lad's penis out of my mouth and licked his purple globe. I wanted to see his spunk jet from his slit, feel his white cream splatter my face. Was I a whore?

Taking Charlie's solid shaft in my hand and sweeping my tongue around the rim of his helmet, I wanked his cock in my desperation for his sperm. Announcing that he was coming, he pumped out his male fluid, bathing my tongue and showering my face as I milked his fleshy rod and tongued his sex-globe. The taste of his sperm was heavenly. The feel of his white liquid raining over my face, running down my cheeks, my chin . . . Yanking his foreskin right back, I almost swallowed his whole orgasming knob, sucking out his cream and gulping hard.

I could have had a dozen lads lined up ready to fuck my mouth, I could have drunk from a dozen throbbing cocks, and still I'd have been thirsty for spunk. The boys were my princes, good enough to eat, good enough to swallow. I wasn't going to stay away from the wood, I knew that as I sucked out the remnants of the lad's orgasmic liquid. I'd be there every day in the summer, licking, sucking, gobbling, swallowing. Slipping the second deflating cock out of my mouth, I looked up and grinned at the two remaining lads.

'Well,' I breathed. 'That's that, then.'

'Come on,' one said, wanking his rock-hard shaft. 'You want this in your mouth and you know it.'

'And this,' the other expectant boy urged, running his hand up and down his firm shaft.

'I've had two cocks, two loads of spunk,' I said. 'But I suppose I could have some more. Both at once, though. Both of you fuck my mouth at once.'

They could hardly wait to sink their engorged cock-heads into my wet mouth. Standing in front of me, they presented me with their purple globes, their foreskins retracted, their small slits bared. Opening my mouth wide, I sucked both their knobs inside and rolled my tongue over their velveteen surfaces. To add to their pleasure, and to mine, I slipped my hands behind the fleshy bags of their scrotums, my fingers easing between their buttocks, seeking out their bottom-holes. Sucking and mouthing on the ballooning knobs, I slipped a finger into their anuses, pushing deep into the heat of their tight rectums as they gasped and swayed on their sagging legs.

I've never fingered anyone's bottom-hole before, and was surprised by the dank heat. Did I want to lick them there, taste their tight anuses? Maybe one day I'd slip my tongue into a bottom-hole and enjoy an anal tongue-fuck. Juliette's bottom? The boys shuddered as I pushed my fingers further into their hot ducts, their cock-shafts swelling, their knobs throbbing. To my delight, they came together, pumping their fresh cream into my mouth as their anal sphincter muscles spasmed, gripping my pistoning fingers.

Their gushing spunk seemingly never-ending, I swallowed hard repeatedly, trying not to waste one drop as they shuddered and swayed above me. Bobbing my head back and forth, taking their orgasming knobs as far as I could into my spermed mouth, I pistoned their rectal ducts for all I was worth. On and on their spunk gushed, filling my cheeks and cascading down my chin as I did my best to drink from their purple fountainheads. Trying to force more fingers into their tight arses, I was disappointed as the boys moved back, their cocks slipping out of my mouth, my fingers sliding from the dank sheaths of their anal canals. They were done in their coming, I knew as they collapsed to the ground, writhing in the aftermath of their debauchery.

'Had enough spunk?' Ian asked me.

'Enough is never enough,' I replied as the boys tugged their trousers back on.

'We could always bring a few more lads along.'

'The more the better,' I said and grinned, climbing to my feet and licking my sperm-glossed lips. 'I'd better be going. I'll see you all again, I expect.'

'Tomorrow,' Ian said, his dark gaze locked to mine. 'How about ten or more of us?'

'All right,' I agreed, wondering what the hell he must have thought of me.

'Ten, maybe more.'

'I can swallow the spunk from fifty cocks,' I giggled, grabbing my coat from the bush and leaving the clearing. 'You'll never hear me say that I can't swallow any more spunk.'

Walking back through the woods, I felt disgusted with myself. A whore, a tart . . . One of the boys had once called me a dirty little cumslut. I supposed I *was* a cumslut. Sitting on a log to rest, I thought about my life, my future. Robin had said that I'd go to the room, the torture chamber, again. I honestly couldn't see that I'd return willingly to the vicar's cottage, allow him to tie me to his table and then let him sexually abuse me. It just wasn't my scene. I had to be in control, to call the shots. The boys were like slaves, doing as I asked, pleading for me to take their silky knobs into my hot mouth and suck out their sperm. The vicar was . . . The vicar was a perverted bastard.

Realizing that I needed to speak to someone to air my

worries, I decided to turn to Robin. He'd said that he'd be there if I needed to talk, and I thought the time was right. As I continued walking home, I also realized that I'd have to catch him in the right frame of mind. If he was going through one of his peculiar mental phases, I might just as well talk to myself for all the sense I'd get out of him. Finally reaching the house, I let myself in and hung my coat in the hall before venturing into the consulting room.

'Ah, the wandering lesbian returns,' Robin chuckled, looking up from his desk. 'How was your trip to the woods?'

'I haven't been to the woods,' I lied, sitting opposite him. 'I went to the shops.'

'That's a funny place to put a shop,' he frowned. 'Right in the middle of the woods is . . .'

'Robin, I need to talk to you.'

'Of course,' he said and smiled, closing a notepad. 'I was just making some notes for my thesis on the uses and abuses of toilet paper in the Western world.'

'The uses and abuses of toilet—'

'Would *you* like to talk about toilet paper?'

'No, I would *not* like to talk about toilet paper. You said that I could talk to you if I felt the need. Not about toilet paper.'

'And you feel the need now?'

'Yes, I do. What's wrong with me? I mean, I have this obsession with—'

'Young boys' dicks. Yes, I know.'

'*How* do you know? And don't say that psychiatrists know everything.'

'How do I know how I know? I have no idea how I know how I know. I just know that I know.'

'What?'

'OK, Crystal. This is your problem, as I see it. You enjoy oral sex with boys. That in itself isn't a problem. If I were a girl, then I'd love sucking dicks. However, as I'm not a girl – and never have been, I hasten to add . . .'

'Yes, yes, all right.'

'And I have no wish to be a girl . . . Doing what you do to these boys concerns you, but that's not the main problem. As I see it, you love dick-gobbling. But you're now torn between dick-gobbling and clit-licking.'

'I have *never* licked a—'

'No, but you're about to. What you must do is stand back and evaluate the situation. Lick a clit, by all means. Suck a dick, or two or three or . . .'

'Or fifty. I mean . . .'

'From the psychiatric point of view, your obsession with dick-gobbling strongly suggests penis envy.'

'You mean that I want a penis of my own?'

'Yes and no. You're leaning towards homosexualism.'

'What? But I'm a female.'

'Homosexuals want men's dicks. You want men's dicks so you're a homosexual.'

'Robin, that's ridiculous. Look, I'll come back later when you're a little more . . .'

'Does your bottom still hurt?'

'My bottom?'

'After the thrashing, does your bottom sting?'

'How do you . . .'

'I'm going to try an experiment.'

Standing, Robin moved around the desk and stood beside me. Dropping his trousers and undershorts, he presented me with his erect penis, the succulent purple plum hovering invitingly in front of my mouth, which had fallen open in shock. Had he no shame? I wondered. There again, he had nothing to be ashamed about. I'd never seen such a magnificent specimen. His long shaft was thick and solid, his glans huge. I was reminded of the first time I'd seen the vicar's cock. I'd thought it gigantic but, in comparison with Robin's, it was quite normal.

'What do you see?' Robin asked me.

'I see your cock,' I laughed.

'What do you feel?'

'I . . . I feel . . .'

'Do you feel the urge to suck it?'

'Robin . . . is this what you do to all your clients?'

'Only when necessary. Tell me what you feel, Crystal. You're gazing at my hard cock, my knob . . . Can you control the urge to suck on my knob?'

To be honest, I *was* having great difficulty in controlling the urge to move forward and suck his beautiful plum into my hungry mouth. But I had to resist and pass Robin's test – if that was what it was. Apart from that, I knew that, once I'd embarked on a sexual relationship with him, then everything would change. I'd turn from housekeeper to live-in sex partner, and I didn't want that. What *did* Robin want? I wondered, licking my full lips as I gazed at his sperm-slit.

'Aren't you thirsty?' he asked, retracting his foreskin further and exposing the rim of his helmet. 'Sperm, Crystal. You want sperm, don't you?' I tried to black out his words of enticement but, despite myself, I moved a little closer to his delicious plum. 'You want to feel the throb of a glans in your mouth, the sperm jetting, gushing, overflowing, running down your chin as you swallow.' Moving a little closer still, I hesitated again, desperately trying to fight the urge to swallow his gorgeous knob. 'Sperm, Crystal. Sperm pumping into your mouth, bathing your pink tongue, jetting to the back of your throat . . .'

Finally giving in, I sucked Robin's glans into my wet mouth and rolled my tongue over its velveteen surface. I could feel his cock-shaft twitching, his knob swelling as he breathed deeply. The salty taste of his sex-globe driving me wild, I held his mammoth organ by its base and moved my head back and forth, mouth-fucking myself in my desperation to swallow his sperm. I knew that I shouldn't have been doing this as I sucked and gobbled. I had no doubt that Robin would be pleading for oral sex at every opportunity from that day on. Or perhaps I'd be the one pleading to suck his knob and swallow his spunk?

Cupping his full balls in my palm, I wanked his solid cock-shaft and licked the rim of his ballooning helmet as he began to sway on his sagging legs. Did he want to slip his huge cock deep into the hugging sheath of my hot pussy and fuck me senseless? It was strange, I mused as I filled my hungry mouth with his beautiful cock. Robin hadn't come across as sexual in any way. He'd made his lewd comments, obviously trying to shock me, but he just didn't seem the type of man to . . . Of course, I hardly knew him. He might have had a string of sexual relationships for all I knew. And now he was mouth-fucking me. Again, I wondered whether this had been a good idea. Boss and employee were now—

'Here comes your prize,' Robin gasped, his swelling glans bloating my mouth. His sperm pulsing from his slit, flooding my snaking tongue and filling my cheeks, I repeatedly sucked and swallowed. On and on his salty spunk pumped, gushing out of his twitching cock, the white liquid overflowing and dribbling down my chin. Wondering how much sperm I'd drunk in the last couple of hours, I bobbed my head back and forth faster, taking his glans to the back of my throat and then encompassing his rim between my spunk-glistening lips.

As I sucked out Robin's spunk, I found myself wondering how many pussies he'd thrust his cock into. Had he had girlfriends? A penis the size of his would have kept any woman satisfied. He must have been with a woman, I decided as his sperm-flow dwindled. He was as mad as a hatter, but very likeable. He probably had sex with his clients, I reflected, slipping his saliva-dripping knob-head out of my salty mouth. Yes, that had to be the answer. He fucked his female clients and then charged them for his time.

'You're very good,' he praised me, tugging his trousers back up. 'You certainly know how to . . . But you're well practised, aren't you? I mean, what with sucking off all those boys in the woods and—'

'I suppose I failed,' I sighed, licking the spunk off my chin.

'Failed? On the contrary . . .'

'I mean, I failed because I succumbed and sucked your cock. I yielded to my inner desires.'

'So did I,' he laughed. 'Er . . . oh, I see what you mean,' he murmured, retaking his seat behind the desk. 'It's better to have failed and tried.'

'Don't you mean, it's better to have tried and—'

'I know what I mean, thank you. Which reminds me. When are we going to have breakfast?'

'Breakfast? That was ages ago, Robin.'

'As was my boyhood. We'll resume our chat and sexual activities later. I have a client due at any minute, so . . .'

'Resume our sexual activities later?'

'Why not?'

'Yes, well . . . I'll go up to my room. I have some serious thinking to do.'

'About?'

'About my future, Robin. I seem to be lost.'

'Ah, no direction in life. Yes, I know the feeling. Right, I'll see you later.'

Climbing the stairs, I went into my room and flopped down onto my bed. No direction in life? Robin was right, I had no idea where I was going. I seemed to be lurching from one cock-sucking incident to another. And now Juliette had barged into my life and . . . woken sleeping desires? Was I a lesbian? If anything, I was bisexual. Closing my eyes, I decided to rest for a while. Robin would want feeding later, Juliette was coming round that evening . . . I needed to rest before taking on the next bout of Robin's madness and Juliette's . . . Did I want to suck and lick her ripe clitoris to orgasm? Would the vicar come searching for me? Or would he distribute the photographs around the village since I'd defied him and not gone to his cottage? The vicar could go to hell.

5

Juliette arrived at seven, just after I'd finished washing up the dinner things. Clutching a bottle of white wine, she was wearing an incredibly short skirt and no bra beneath her loose-fitting blouse. And the grin of a Cheshire cat. Grabbing a bottle opener and two glasses from the kitchen, I led her up to my room, all too aware of Robin spying on us through the crack in his consulting room door. Lesbianism was obviously a turn-on for him. Wasn't it for all men? He'd probably wank, imagining Juliette fingering and licking my pussy as he shot his spunk over the floor. Perhaps I should have invited him in to watch?

'I do like this room,' Juliette commented again, gazing out of the window. 'It's perfect.'

'I'm looking forward to the summer,' I said, opening the wine. 'The window open, the sun shining . . .'

'Will you be allowed to sit in the garden?'

'Oh, yes. As housekeeper, I have the run of the place. Knowing Robin, I'll also be the gardener. There we are,' I said, and smiled, passing her a glass of wine. 'Cheers.'

'To us, Crystal,' she beamed, chinking her glass against mine.

'Er . . . yes, to us.'

To us? Was Juliette thinking of a permanent relationship? I wasn't even sure that I wanted sex with her, let alone . . . I felt confused, torn. Images of my wet tongue sweeping up her yawning vaginal valley, snaking around her erect clitoris as she writhed and squirmed on the bed . . . Would I become as hooked on pussy-tonguing as I had on cock-sucking? Was I really bisexual? I'd loved the feel of Juliette's wet tongue delving into my vaginal sheath, licking the sensitive nub of my clitoris and taking me to orgasm. But did I want to reciprocate? It would be selfish to take and not give, but . . .

'Excuse me,' Robin said, knocking before popping his head around the door. 'You might want to look at the back room.'

'The back room?' I echoed, wondering whether he was having one of his mental turns.

'At the end of the hall. It's a nice room with a TV and everything. Not quite as big as this one but it overlooks the garden.'

'Oh, right,' I smiled, deciding to humour him. 'I'll take a look at it later.'

As he left, Juliette frowned at me. I had no idea what Robin was going on about and wondered how to explain to Juliette that he was crazy. Her frown turning into a grin, she leaned against the windowsill and sipped her wine. I got the impression that she knew something, and wondered whether she'd spoken to Robin about the back room. Although I couldn't see why they'd talk about a spare room.

'What is it?' I finally asked, eyeing the swell of her white panties as she leaned further back.

'You tell me,' she replied. 'What have you said to Robin?'

'Said? About what?'

'I'm looking for somewhere to live,' she enlightened

me. 'I was going to ask whether there was a spare room here, but you've obviously mentioned it already.'

'I haven't said anything, Juliette. I didn't even know that you wanted a room, let alone . . .'

'Well, I do want a room and it looks as if there's one going.'

'You want to live here?' I asked, wondering whether it would work out.

'Why not? I'd have to pay rent, seeing as I wouldn't be working for Robin. After living in London, I don't want to live back at home with my parents. This place is ideal. You're here, it's on the edge on town . . . What do you reckon?'

'Well, yes, I suppose . . . You'd better speak to Robin.'

'Yes, I will,' she murmured. 'I'll speak to him later.'

I supposed that Juliette would be company, but I didn't want her in and out of my room every five minutes. Wishing I'd not allowed her to lick my pussy, I reckoned that she'd be slipping into my bed every night for lesbian sex. Had I kept our relationship as friends rather than . . . But what was done was done. Robin must have had one of his psychic flashes, I mused. He knew far too much for my liking, and I decided to go and speak to him.

'Let's take a look at the room,' Juliette said, moving to the door.

'All right,' I sighed, following her along the hall. I really wasn't sure that this was a good idea.

'Oh, it's lovely,' she beamed, wandering into the room.

'Yes, it is,' I agreed. 'TV, hi-fi, double bed . . .'

'That will come in useful,' she giggled, sitting on the bed. 'I'll take it.'

'Take it? We haven't spoken to Robin yet.'

'Let's go and see him now.'

'Juliette, I don't think . . .' I began as she left the room.

Following her downstairs, I decided that this had nothing to do with me. If Robin wanted to let a room, then that was his business. If things went wrong, I wouldn't be involved. As Juliette tapped on the consulting-room door, I hovered in the hall. The vicar calling to see me, my mother giving my phone number to people, and now Juliette wanting to move in . . . This wasn't what I'd envisaged. Leaving the door partially open as she went in, I listened outside.

'So, you want the room?' Robin asked before Juliette had said anything.

'Yes, it's lovely. How much?'

'We'll discuss that later. Normally, you'd have to undergo a vaginal examination, but . . .'

'What?' she gasped.

'As Crystal is about to examine you . . .'

'Crystal is—'

'Do you wash regularly?'

'Yes, of course I do. Look, I want a room, not a—'

'No eating in the toilet, no throwing sanitary towels down the—'

'Robin,' I interrupted him, entering the room. 'I'll explain the house rules to Juliette later.'

'Ah, yes, of course. Juliette, are you a lesbian or bisexual?'

'I'm . . .'

'Robin,' I sighed, glaring at him. 'Juliette's sexual preference has nothing to do with you. Instead of talking about vaginal examinations and lesbianism, you should be talking about the room.'

'I *am* talking about the room. OK, that's that. Crystal will have to have a front-door key cut. You can move in whenever you wish.'

'That's great,' Juliette exclaimed, beaming. 'Thanks very much.'

'You're not a smelly straphanger, are you?'

'A what?'

'Come on, Juliette,' I said, taking her arm and walking her to the door. 'I'll tell you the house rules over a glass of wine.'

'May I join you?' Robin asked hopefully.

'No, Robin. You get on with your work while we—'

'Have lesbian sex?'

'Robin!'

'Sorry.'

Back in my room, I closed the door and gazed at Juliette as she sat on the bed. Eyeing her naked thighs and the tight crotch of her panties as her short skirt rode up, I felt my stomach somersault. The inevitably pussy-licking was getting closer, I knew as she parted her thighs, feigning innocence as she tugged her skirt even further up. It was different with the boys. With them, I was in control, ordering them to drop their trousers and show me their stiff cocks. With Juliette, I wasn't sure what to do, how to . . .

'Well?' she asked, standing in front of me. 'Aren't you going to undress me?'

'Yes,' I replied sheepishly, my trembling fingers un-buttoning her blouse.

'I've been looking forward to this,' she murmured. 'You've never eaten pussy, have you?'

'No, I haven't,' I confessed, parting the silky material of her blouse and gazing longingly at the ripe teats of her firm breasts.

'I'm all yours, Crystal. Don't feel embarrassed, just do what you want.'

Leaning forward, I sucked one of her brown nipples into my wet mouth and ran my tongue around her sensitive teat. She breathed deeply, her young body trembling slightly as I sucked harder and sank my teeth gently into her areola. I could feel my own nipples growing erect, my lubricious juices of desire seeping between my love-lips as I squeezed and kneaded the firm mound of her breast. Was this what I wanted? I again wondered, her milk teat stiffening within my hot mouth. Another girl's erect nipple in my mouth, her clitoris awaiting the intimate caress of my wet tongue . . .

I'd licked and sucked my own nipples many times. I loved wanking the boys' cocks, kneeling in front of them with my breasts bared, their spunk raining over my newly developed mammary globes. Three boys wanked over my firm breasts one afternoon after school. We'd gone to the woods and I'd stripped beneath the summer sun. I'd ordered them to drop their trousers and wank over my naked breasts. Once they'd drained their tight balls, they watched me lap up their sperm from my milk teats, my tongue snaking around my elongated nipples.

But now I was sucking and licking another girl's nipple and . . . I felt confused. The feel of Juliette's sensitive teat in my mouth sent quivers running through my young womb. She'd want a permanent relationship. She'd move into the house and come to my room for lesbian sex and . . . I didn't know what I wanted as I squeezed the hard melons of her teenage breasts. This was harmless, I tried to convince myself. Experimentation, sexual discovery . . . This was harmless.

Running my fingertips over the smooth plateau of

Juliette's naked stomach, I slipped her nipple out of my mouth and kneeled on the floor. I'd never seen another girl's pussy, and this was my opportunity to learn, to discover. Tugging her skirt down, I gazed longingly at the tight material of her white panties bulging to contain her full sex-lips. My pulse racing as she stepped out of her skirt, I eased the sides of her panties down, gazing wide-eyed as the top of her hairless sex-slit came into view. Tentatively pulling the flimsy material down further, I focused on the pink wings of her inner lips protruding alluringly from her naked vulval crack. She looked so young without pubic hair. Her naked lips were beautifully symmetrical, the creases between her sex-pads and her thighs forming a perfect V. Would I now meet young girls in the woods and tongue their pink slits?

Juliette's panties slid down her long legs to her ankles and she kicked them aside to stand with her feet wide apart. Moving forward until my knees were between her feet, her gaping vaginal valley only inches from my thirsty mouth, I pushed my tongue out and tasted the inner petals of her beautiful pussy. She shuddered, parting her feet further as I sucked on her inner labia, pulling them out of her crack and breathing in the aphrodisiacal scent of her young body. She tasted heavenly, slightly salty, reminding me of the boys' knobs.

Easing her back and sitting her on the bed, I settled between her splayed thighs as she reclined. I licked the fleshy cushions of her outer lips, running my tongue over the smooth contours of the hillocks rising on either side of her valley of desire. Again breathing in her female scent, I sucked the wings of her inner lips into my wet mouth and gently bit her. She tasted beautiful – salty, tangy, bitter. Parting the fleshy pads of her love-lips with my thumbs, exposing her pinken inner folds, I ran my tongue over her most intimate flesh. Her juices of lesbian desire seeping from the pink entrance to her sex-sheath, trickling down between the firm orbs of her buttocks, she let out a long low moan of pleasure as I lapped up her creamy girl-cum.

I was fast becoming hooked on pussy-licking, I knew as my inquisitive tongue slipped into her vaginal duct and licked the sex-dripping inner walls of her tight cunt. Had my sexual preference changed? I wondered, lapping up Juliette's hot vaginal cream. Would I discard the boys now that I'd discovered the delights of lesbian licking? As sweet as Juliette's sex-juice tasted, I knew that I couldn't go without sperm. A purple knob throbbing within my wet mouth, pumping out its spunk, bathing my tongue . . . I could never suppress my craving for fresh sperm.

'You're good,' Juliette murmured, moving my hands aside and peeling the swollen lips of her teenage vagina wide apart. 'I love having my cunt licked out.' Pressing my lips hard against her glistening inner flesh, I sucked out her preorgasmic cream, drinking from the hot sheath of her vagina and swallowing her aphrodisiacal offering. She was so wet, her juices bubbling within her sex duct, flowing in torrents from her trembling body. I could feel my own juices of arousal seeping between the engorged lips of my pussy, wetting my panties, as I pushed my tongue deep into her sex-drenched cunt.

Cunt. The harsh word echoed around the wreckage of my mind, hurting me, tormenting me. It was a word tarts used, whores, slags, sluts . . . The boys had liked me talking about their stiff cocks, telling them that I loved ball-sucking, knob-tonguing, sperm-swallowing. But the

word 'cunt' somehow went against the grain. In my
ignorance, I'd thought that lesbians didn't use the word.
I'd thought they were soft and gentle, using words of
love rather than 'cunt'. *I love having my cunt licked out*.
Did her crudity excite me?

'My clitoris,' Juliette breathed, peeling the lips of her
pussy so wide apart that I thought the delicate tissue of
her inner folds would tear. 'I need to come now, Crystal.
Suck my clitoris.' Moving up, I encircled the erect
protuberance of her solid clitoris with my wet tongue,
concentrating on the sensitive tip as she gasped and
writhed on the bed. I could feel her preorgasmic juices
wetting my chin, running down my neck as she gyrated
her hips, grinding the intimate flesh of her vagina hard
against my mouth. She was almost there, I knew. Her
back arched, her stomach rising and falling, her head
thrown back . . .

'Yes,' she gasped, her naked body shaking violently as
her orgasm exploded within her pulsating clitoris. Her
juices of lust gushing from the gaping entrance to her
young vagina, her solid clitoris throbbing within my wet
mouth, Juliette squirmed and moaned as her lesbian
pleasure rocked her naked body. I'd done it, I thought,
my tongue sweeping over her solid clitoris. I'd performed cunnilingus, I'd drunk from another girl's cunt,
sucked another girl's clitoris to orgasm. I knew what she
wanted, how to sustain her pleasure, and I drove two
fingers into the drenched sheath of her spasming cunt
and massaged her inner flesh.

'Don't stop,' Juliette murmured as I finger-fucked her
wet cunt and sucked on the solid nub of her pulsating
clitoris. My face drenched with her hot orgasmic juices,
my fingers squelching the lubricious cream flooding her

tight sex-duct, I expertly sustained her lesbian-induced orgasm. I was good, I knew. Cock-sucking, sperm-guzzling, clit-licking, pussy-fingering . . . I was a princess, a goddess of sex. Even Robin had discovered my knob-sucking expertise, I reflected. Would he come up to my room the next time he felt the need to drain his balls? Would I go down to his consulting room the next time I was desperate to drink sperm?

'That was amazing,' Juliette murmured, her head lolling from side to side as I slipped my fingers out of her sex duct. 'Are you sure you've never eaten pussy before?'

'Never,' I replied softly, sitting back on my heels and gazing at the opaque juices of sex oozing from her gaping love-hole.

'When I've moved in, we'll spend some sexy nights together.'

'Yes, yes, we will.'

'I wonder whether you're as good at bum-licking as you are at cunny-eating,' she giggled, rolling over onto her stomach, her thighs spread, her hairless vaginal lips bulging below the tight brown hole of her bottom. 'Go on, show me what you can do.'

Kneeling again, I leaned forward and planted a kiss on the taut flesh of her firm buttocks. Reaching behind her back, she parted the cheeks of her bottom, opening her anal crease and fully exposing the brown eye of her anus. Recalling the vicar licking my bottom, pushing his tongue into my rectal tube and tasting me there, I wasn't sure that I really wanted to lick Juliette's anus. Easing her buttocks further apart, she opened her secret hole, asking me to show her how good I was at anilingus. Moving closer, my mouth an inch or so from her delicate brown ring, I wondered why I'd never heard the term. It made sense, I decided. Cunnilingus, anilingus . . .

'Lick me,' Juliette breathed, obviously desperate for the feel of my wet tongue caressing the sensitive flesh of her bottom-hole. Pushing my tongue out, I tentatively licked her, tasting the brown tissue of her anus. Bitter, tangy . . . Repeatedly sweeping my tongue over her anal iris, wetting her with my saliva, I quite liked the taste of her most private hole. She shuddered, squirming on the bed as she asked me to tongue-fuck her arse. Another word I disliked. Arse, cunt . . . Common words used by common sluts.

Easing my thumbs into Juliette's anus, I opened her rectal inlet and peered into the dank tube. Again, she asked me to tongue-fuck her, projecting her rounded buttocks and offering the gaping hole of her bottom to my mouth. Deciding to take the plunge, I slipped my tongue into her open hole and licked her inner flesh. Breathing in the heady scent of her anal gully, I stretched her anus open wider, pushing my tongue deeper into her rectum. I was going to become hooked on anilingus, I knew as the unfamiliar flavour of her inner rectal flesh woke my taste buds. Fellatio, cunnilingus, anilingus . . . Was there any part of a body, male or female, that I *wouldn't* lick and suck?

'You must have done this before,' Juliette breathed shakily as my tongue snaked around within her dank rectal sheath. 'God, you certainly know how to arse-lick. Have you got a candle or something to fuck me with?'

'No, I haven't,' I replied, my tongue briefly leaving the bitter tube of her rectum.

'You must have something,' she persisted. 'What

about a hairbrush handle?'

'Wait a minute,' I breathed, reaching back to the dressing table and grabbing my hairbrush.

Easing the broad plastic handle into her gaping hole, I pushed slowly, sinking the makeshift phallus deep into Juliette's bottom as she squirmed delightfully on the bed. Would the boys enjoy an anal fucking? I wondered. I had no doubt that they'd enjoy forcing a hairbrush handle up my bottom-hole. The next time I was in the woods, I'd try licking their anuses, tonguing their tight rectal ducts as I reached between their legs and wanked their fresh cocks to orgasm. They'd like that, I thought, picturing the lewd scene.

Just for fun, I decided to ease a boy's cock into another boy's bum-hole. Would they agree to such an obscene act? I wondered. I loved the notion of watching a boy fuck another boy, his cock sliding in and out of his friend's rectum. I was becoming more decadent by the day, I reflected, twisting the hairbrush handle and pistoning Juliette's tight anal sheath. Would she allow a boy to fuck her bottom while I watched? Perhaps the time had come to invite the boys back to my new home.

'It's not big enough,' Juliette complained, lifting her head and turning to face me. 'I can take more than a hairbrush handle. Haven't you got a bottle or something?'

'Yes,' I replied, reaching to the dressing table and grabbing a plastic bottle. 'Are you sure you'll be able to . . .'

'Oh, yes,' she grinned, eyeing the bottle. 'I can take anything.'

Easing the hairbrush handle out of Juliette's tight anal duct, I pressed the end of the plastic bottle against her brown ring and pushed gently. She yanked her buttocks wide apart, opening the inlet to her rectum as I pushed and twisted the bottle. I thought that she was going to split open as the delicate tissue of her anus yielded, opening to accommodate the plastic phallus. The bottle was almost two inches in diameter and about six inches long, and I didn't think that she'd be able to take the entire length into her rectal tube. Watching in amazement as I eased the shaft into her anal canal, I thought that she'd order me to stop as inch after inch sank into her trembling body.

'That's beautiful,' Juliette gasped as I completely impaled her on the phallus, leaving only the plastic cap sticking out between the firm cheeks of her bottom. 'And now my cunt,' she murmured, turning and looking at me. 'Get something bigger for my cunt.'

'Are you sure?' I asked, taking a shampoo bottle from the dressing table

'Yes, that's perfect. Force it right up my cunt and then frig my clitty.'

Parting the hairless pads of Juliette's fleshy love-lips, I pressed the end of the bottle into the pink funnel of wet flesh around the opening of her love-sheath. The bottle was suddenly sucked into her sex-duct, swallowed by her vaginal throat. I couldn't believe my eyes. The brown tissue of her anus stretched tautly around the smaller bottle, the pink wings of her inner pussy lips hugging the larger bottle, I gazed transfixed at the lewd sight as she writhed and breathed heavily in her obvious ecstasy.

'I'd never have believed that anyone could stretch so much,' I said, wondering whether she was in pain.

'This is nothing,' she replied proudly. 'I'm well practised in the art of bum-fisting. Christine taught me . . .'

'Christine?' I echoed.

'The girl I lived with. She used to grease me up and fist my arse. Have you ever tried—'

'No, I haven't,' I cut in, trying to imagine what it would be like to have a fist embedded deep within my rectum.

'We're going to get on very well,' Juliette said, parting her knees and raising her bottom. 'OK, do my clitty and bring me off.'

Reaching beneath the larger bottle, I located the solid nub of her clitoris and massaged her there. Her sex-spot was huge, and as hard as a rock. Her vaginal juices dripping onto my hand as I masturbated her, I wondered whether to ease a bottle into my own rectal canal when I was alone. I'd slipped fingers into my pussy and even tried a candle, but to force a plastic bottle into my anus . . . The notion sending delightful quivers through my contracting womb, I grabbed the end of the smaller bottle and pistoned Juliette's rectum as I massaged her swollen clitoris. She gasped, burying her face in the quilt as her naked body shook violently. I felt in control again, as I had when sucking the boys' cocks to orgasm. Was I a control freak? I wondered, managing to piston both her sex-holes with the bottles as I frigged her clitty.

'God, yes,' she breathed as her orgasm erupted and her juices of lust sprayed from her bloated vagina. Imagining taking a young girl to the woods and initiating her into the crude art of lesbian fucking, I remembered that Ian had a sister. She was still at school, but . . . *I do believe that you're old enough. It's all right, I won't tell your mother*. Was I following in the vicar's footsteps, becoming like him? Ian's sister was extremely attractive, an angelic little beauty. The thought of leading her into the woods and stripping her excited me no end.

Sustaining Juliette's massive orgasm, I pistoned her sex-holes with the plastic bottles, fervently massaging the solid protuberance of her clitoris until she slipped into what appeared to be a state of semi-consciousness. Leaving the phalluses embedded deep within her inflamed sex-ducts, I sat back on my heels and gazed at the lewd sight. Juliette was a nymphomaniac, I concluded. Her insatiable hunger for crude sex . . . But wasn't *I* a nymphomaniac? My thirst for sex was unquenchable, there was no denying it. But, whatever I was, I'd never asked the boys to fuck my sex-holes with plastic bottles.

'Take them out,' Juliette murmured. 'Take the bottles out, gently.'

'Are you all right?' I asked, easing the larger bottle out of her drenched vaginal sheath.

'God, yes. That was absolutely incredible.'

'You should see your bum,' I giggled as the bottle popped out of her rectum like a cork. 'It's gaping wide open. I'm sure it can't do you any good having a bottle—'

'Put your tongue up my arse. Christine used to do that after fisting me. With my arse wide open . . .'

'Juliette, I think you should rest,' I broke in, gazing into the dark passage of her rectum.

'Tongue my arse and then I'll rest before I use the bottles on you.'

Easing Juliette's buttocks wide apart, I drove my tongue into the cavernous entrance to her inner core. She tasted delicious, and I again realized that I was hooked on anilingus. Were there no limits to my decadence? I wondered, licking deep inside the dank tube of her arse. Come the summer months, I'd go to the woods every day and seek out the boys' swollen knobs, lure

Ian's sister there and tongue-fuck her tight bottom-hole. But the woods and the village were dangerous places. The vicar lurked there, and should he ever see me . . .

'Have you had any dealings with the vicar?' I asked Juliette, slipping my tongue out of her yawning bottom-hole.

'Dealings?' she murmured.

'Has he ever . . . Oh, I don't know.'

'I think *I* do,' she said, rolling over and lying on her back. 'I've heard one or two rumours over the years.'

'What about?'

'Involving the vicar. I never thought there was anything in it but . . . What have *you* heard?'

'I've heard nothing,' I sighed. 'But I think I might have something to do with those rumours.'

'I doubt it, Crystal. The things I've heard are . . . Hang on. What did you do when you went to the church? You were always going to the vicar's cottage and—'

'Tell me about the rumours.'

'Rumour had it that a few young girls were involved with the vicar. I don't know who they were but apparently they visited the vicar for sex. Are you saying that . . .' Juliette's voice tailed off as suspicion began to dawn.

'Yes, I am. The vicar has been abusing me for years.'

'God. I had no idea, Crystal.'

'No one had any idea. Now he's discovered where I'm living.'

'Has he been here?'

'Yes.'

'Crystal, you have to do something.'

'Don't you think I know that?' I snapped. 'I'm sorry, I didn't mean to . . .'

'That's OK. We'll trap him.'

'Trap him?'

'Set a trap and catch him, expose him.'

'No, no, you don't understand. He's got photographs of me. It's not as straightforward as you think.'

'Listen, if he's trapped, exposed . . . All we have to do is lure him into a trap and have someone witness whatever he does. I'll do it. I'll lure him into the church and—'

'Juliette, it'll never work. He has so much on me that I'll never be free.'

'This will have nothing to do with you. If he's exposed, he'll be thrown out of the church. And the village, more than likely. You won't come into it. I have a friend, a young girl. She'll act as bait.'

'It might be worth trying,' I conceded finally.

'Anything's worth trying, for God's sake. How does this sound? The vicar is caught in his church, mucking about with a naked girl. The girl . . .'

'Testifies? I doubt it.'

'I see your point. OK, so the vicar is caught by a woman he believes is the girl's mother. I spread rumours around the village and word spreads like wildfire. I'll set it up. You won't be involved, so don't worry.'

Watching as Juliette leaped off the bed and dressed, I pondered on her plan. It was worth trying, she was right. Realizing that I should have confided in someone long ago, I turned my thoughts to Robin. I had at least tried to talk to him, I reflected. It was just my luck that he was in the middle of one of his weird mental trips. Wondering what the vicar was up to, I brushed my long blonde hair and tidied myself up. He'd no doubt be fuming because I hadn't turned up at his cottage and . . .

'I'll start the ball rolling,' Juliette said, moving to the

door. 'I'll speak to the girl and set up the plan. When I've done that, I'll get my things and move in.'

'Yes, all right,' I murmured non-committally as she left the room.

Hearing the front door close, I sat on the bed and thought about Juliette moving in. If I controlled her, only had sex with her now and then, I couldn't see that there'd be a problem. I'd make it clear that we had our own rooms and should retain a certain amount of privacy and space. If I had a friend back for coffee, I wouldn't want Juliette bursting in and joining us. Feeling more confident as Robin yelled up the stairs, I left my room and went to find him.

'Ah, there you are,' he grinned as I walked into his consulting room. 'How was it for you?'

'We talked, Robin,' I said firmly. 'That was all.'

'Oral? Yes, of course. I have a client arriving at any minute and I want you to sit in on the session.'

'Sit in?'

'She's a lesbian, so I thought that you might be able to help, seeing as you're also—'

'Robin, I am *not* a lesbian.'

'As I was saying, seeing as you've just stuffed bottles up your friend's—'

'Bottles? OK, I want to know what's going on. Have you been spying on me?'

'Of course not. As it happens, I've been out. I got back five minutes ago.'

'Then how do you know what we did?'

'I'm a psychiatrist and . . . Let's not go through that again. Ah, the doorbell. OK, you sit over there in the corner.'

I really didn't think that this was a good idea as I

settled in the old leather armchair in the corner of the room. I wasn't interested in Robin's clients, especially not lesbian clients. Perhaps I felt guilty? Watching him lead an attractive young woman into the room, I smiled as he introduced me as a trainee psychiatrist. She was in her early twenties and had long auburn hair cascading over her shoulders. She didn't look like a lesbian, I mused. There again, neither did I. As she settled at the desk and placed her handbag on the floor, I wondered what her problem was. Robin could have at least told me a little about her, I reflected.

'So, Jane,' he said, smiling and opening a notebook. 'How have things been?'

'Terrible,' she sighed. 'I can't sleep, I can't eat . . . I did as you suggested and pretended to be a caterpillar, but the postman looked through the window and saw me inching across the floor. He must have thought I was mad.'

'I'm sure he didn't.' Robin smiled reassuringly. 'Lots of people pretend to be things they're not. For example, my mother used to pretend that she was married when she didn't even know who my father was.'

'I could have coped with being a horse. I like horses.'

'Try being a horse, if you feel comfortable with it.'

I was right: Robin was completely insane. A caterpillar? A horse? How the hell would that help the woman? Wondering what on earth I was doing, sitting in his consulting room and listening to his inane drivel, I thought about Juliette's plan. Whatever happened, even if the vicar was caught red-handed, he'd still have the incriminating photographs of me. Robin had told him that I'd moved out, but I doubted that he believed it. He'd be lurking, lying in wait for me, I knew. Perhaps he'd already gone running to my parents with the photographs.

'Is your ex-husband still causing problems?' Robin asked.

'Yes, he is. He had a private detective follow me.'

'Oh? What happened?'

'I cornered the man in a shop doorway and unzipped his trousers. I sucked his cock and now he's working for me.'

'That was a good move, Jane – a very good move. As you're a lesbian, it must have been extremely difficult for you.'

'I tried to think of his prick as a huge clitoris, which helped. The detective reckons that my ex-husband is obsessed with me. If he can't have me, then he'll make sure no one else can.'

'How does he intend to do that?'

'By defaming me, telling people that I'm a dirty, filthy, immoral, lesbian slut-whore.'

'But you *are*, Jane.'

'I know I am, but I don't want the world told about it. I do have some pride. How would you like the world to know that you tried to throat-fuck me?'

'Er . . . yes, well . . .'

'If your friends and neighbours knew that you tried to force your cock down my throat and . . .'

'I couldn't help myself,' Robin whispered through gritted teeth. 'Anyway, it's a family trait.'

'Fucking women's throats is a family tree?'

'*Trait*, as in . . .'

'Let's move on to your fascination with your anus.'

As Robin rambled on, I decided that *he* was the one in need of a psychiatrist. The woman was obviously mad, but Robin was far worse. Deciding to leave them to their insane conversation, I eased myself out of the armchair. I had enough problems of my own, and had no wish to listen to other people's troubles. As I neared the door, Robin looked at me and frowned. I mouthed to him, trying to say that I had work to do, but he didn't seem to understand.

'Crystal shoved bottles up her lesbian girlfriend's bottom,' he told the woman unashamedly.

'Robin!' I gasped, walking towards the desk. 'I've never done anything of the sort.'

'Yes, you have. You pushed your tongue into her anus.'

'That sounds interesting,' the woman said, looking up and grinning at me.

'It may sound interesting, but it's not true,' I retorted indignantly.

'And she sucks cocks,' Robin added.

'Ah, you lean both ways,' the woman murmured. 'My husband leaned both ways. He loved men's bottoms and women's pussies. That's why I left him.'

'Because he was gay?' I asked.

'No, because he preferred men's bottom-holes to mine. What else do you get up to with your lesbian girlfriend?'

'They both shave their pussies,' Robin announced.

'Really?' The woman beamed, winking at me. 'We'll have to become better acquainted.'

'Er . . . I have work to do,' I murmured, walking to the door.

'Don't forget to feed the caterpillar,' Robin said as I left. 'The dog food is in the oven.'

Feed the caterpillar? Dog food? Wandering through

the kitchen, I went out into the back garden for some fresh air. I had to clear my mind of lunatic trash and try to retain my sanity. The garden was nice. Laid to lawn with borders along each side, it was conveniently secluded behind a huge wall. *Ideal for sunbathing in a bikini*, I thought, imagining Robin spying out of the window at my rounded breasts, trying to glimpse my pubes sprouting from either side of my bikini bottom. Not that I had any pubes right now.

Noticing a shed at the end of the garden, I went to take a look. If I was to be gardener as well as housekeeper, which I undoubtedly was, I thought I'd check out the tools. Opening the door, I wandered inside, surprised to find a nice carpet on the floor. With lighting and a heater, the shed was more like a den. Sitting at the oak table, I gazed at what appeared to be radio equipment. Wires, a Morse-code key . . . It was like a scene from a spy film, and I imagined Robin sitting there communicating with foreign agents. Glancing at a notebook, I wondered why there were series of numbers listed in groups of five on the page. *Some kind of code?* I wondered. Deciding that Robin was into CB radio or whatever, I left the shed and walked towards the house. Noticing a long wire running from a pole by the shed to the house, I assumed it was an aerial. 'Ten-four, good buddy,' I laughed.

It was nice to have a hobby, I thought as I filled the kettle for tea. Playing about with his radio would probably take his mind off his insane clients. *I've got a hobby too*, I giggled inwardly. *Cock-sucking*. It was more of an obsession than a hobby, I knew as I heard Robin saying goodbye to his client. The front door closing, I called out to him. Walking into the kitchen, he rubbed his lined forehead. He looked tired, drawn.

'Are you all right?' I asked him.

'I was up late last night,' he replied, taking his tea from the table.

'Playing with your radio in the shed?'

'What?' he gasped, spilling tea down his velvet jacket. 'What do you know about that?'

'I went into the garden and . . .'

'Snooped around my shed.'

'I didn't snoop around, Robin. I was seeing what you had in the way of gardening tools.'

'I'm not a spy.'

'I didn't say you were.'

'I'll have to inform Moscow of this.'

'Moscow?'

'I mean . . .'

'I thought you were into CB radio.'

'Er . . . yes, yes, that's right. Roger-dodger, and all that.'

'Ten-four, good buddy.'

'What? Oh, yes. I see what you mean.'

'What's your handle?'

'Handle?'

'What name do you use?'

'Oh, er . . . Rob Insane.'

'That's appropriate.'

'Yes, I thought so. Where's Juliette?'

'She's gone to get her things.'

'Ah, right. She seems like a nice girl. You obviously get on very well with her. Intimately, even.'

'Robin, how do you know . . .'

'About the plastic bottles? She told me on her way out.'

'She didn't. As if she'd say—'

'She told me, Crystal. She said that you'd done her sex-holes with bottles. Has she got psychiatric problems?'

'No, she hasn't. And I did not *do her sex-holes with bottles*, as you so crudely put it. I'd better go and get her room ready. The bed will need making up, for starters.'

'Ready for lesbian sex? Right, I must get on. I have to feed the dog and clean out the fish tank.'

'Yes, you do that. And then you can send a Morse-code message to Moscow.'

'Don't ever mention Moscow.'

'Why not?'

'People might think I'm a spy.'

Making my way up to Juliette's room, I decided to lay down a few ground rules when she got back with her things. Privacy was of paramount importance. She had to understand that our rooms were our homes, and we'd both knock before entering as we would on anyone's front door. We'd also have to arrange bathroom times so that we didn't clash in the mornings. I still hadn't bought any locks, and I made a mental note about that as I entered Juliette's room.

Gazing out of the window at Robin's shed, I wondered whether he *was* a spy. Morse code, talk of Moscow . . . Perhaps his clients were foreign agents, the consulting room a cover for exchanging government secrets. *Why not?* I thought, pulling the quilt off the bed. Wondering where to find some clean sheets, I thought it might be an idea to do some washing. Wandering into Robin's room to strip his bed, I couldn't believe the mess. Clothes, magazines, coffee cups . . . The place was an absolute tip. Leaving the room and closing the door, I thought it best to mention it to him before tidying up. I dreaded to think what I'd find beneath his bed.

Juliette would just have to make do with the sheets that were already on her bed, I decided, straightening the quilt. They looked clean enough, and would certainly do for her first night. Besides, she'd probably creep into my room and slip into my bed. No, I wasn't going to allow that. Not on the first night, anyway. Back in my own room, I switched the radio on and yanked the sheets off my bed. Vacuuming, washing, ironing, cooking . . . I was going to have to get into a routine. I didn't mind housework as long as I was allowed to get on with it. Thinking that I should have helped my mother around the house, I realized that I'd not been in contact with her since I'd left home. Another mental note that I'd probably forget.

Stuffing the sheets into the washing machine, I grabbed the powder I'd bought and switched on. Nothing. The water taps were turned on, the power switch was on . . . This was bloody typical, I thought, wondering what to do. Robin probably hadn't used the thing in years and it had seized up. The front doorbell rang and I peered round the kitchen door as Robin went to answer it. 'Shit,' I breathed, spying the vicar standing on the step.

'I've already told you . . .' Robin began.

'Yes, I know,' the vicar said and smiled. 'I was wondering whether you could give her a message should you happen to speak to her?'

'I won't be speaking to her. She's moved to Australia.'

'If you do, tell her that the photographs are ready to post to certain people.'

'Me included?'

'You?' The vicar frowned.

'I'd love to have some photographs of Crystal naked,

doing naked things with people.'

'You know?'

'I know everything. I'm a psychiatrist.'

'She told you?'

'Better than that, she allowed me to take some lovely photographs of her. Why don't you come in and I'll see whether I can find them?'

'All right.'

This was a mistake, I knew as I hid behind the door. What the hell did Robin think he was playing at? Inviting the bloody vicar in, making out that he had photographs of me . . . Whatever his plan, I didn't like it. The vicar was no fool, and even a fool like Robin couldn't fool him. Watching as they went into the consulting room, I slipped across the hall and listened at the door.

'I can't think where I've hidden the photographs,' Robin said. 'They were really good. You know, open-pussy shots, candles up her bum . . .'

'You sound like a man after my own heart,' the vicar chuckled. 'It's a shame she's moved away.'

'Yes, it is. It was that man from the church, I suppose.'

'Man from the church?'

'He came here and spoke to Crystal. I heard him saying something about exposing someone or other and she seemed worried.'

'This man . . . What did he look like?'

'Balding, in his sixties . . . I think he said he was a bishop.'

'Oh, my God. Er . . . what else did he say?'

'He was talking about the police and . . . That was when Crystal panicked. Shortly after he left, she moved out.'

'I see.'

'Ah, I've just remembered. Crystal took the photographs with her. She said something about the police searching a cottage, and she thought it best that I didn't have any pictures of her in the house. She was a funny girl. I thought she'd stay here for a few years, not just for a few hours.'

'Yes, well . . . I think I'd better be getting back,' the vicar muttered.

'I'm sorry about the photographs. I'd forgotten that Crystal took them to Australia with her. It's a good time of year to have a bonfire, don't you agree?'

'A bonfire?'

'You know, to burn garden rubbish and anything else you might want to do away with.'

'Oh, yes. Well, it's nice to have seen you again.'

'And you, vicar. Call in any time you're passing.'

'I will, thank you.'

Lurking in the kitchen while Robin saw the evil man out, I decided to make out that I'd not overheard their conversation. Opening the back door, I slipped out into the garden and messed about with the dustbin. I was aware of Robin watching me through the window, and wondered whether he was going to say anything. After a few minutes, he disappeared. Closing the back door, I went into the hall to find him in his consulting room. He just looked up and smiled. He wasn't even going to mention that the vicar had called, let alone tell me what had happened. I liked Robin, I reflected as I climbed the stairs to my room. Strange, eccentric, completely and utterly mad . . . But I liked him very much.

6

Three days had passed since Juliette had moved in. I hadn't seen much of her, which had surprised me, and Robin seemed to be keeping a low profile. Nothing from the vicar, no phone calls . . . But I'd had the chance to get the house in order, and even to get the washing machine repaired. Housekeeping really was a doddle, particularly as Robin had told me not to bother with his bedroom. The bedroom from hell. I was relaxing on my own bed when the doorbell rang, and I thought it best to let Robin answer it in case the vicar had returned. Peering over the banister, I was surprised to see Juliette leading a young lad up the stairs. *Perhaps she fancies a bit of cock?* I mused.

'Someone to see you,' she said.

'*Me*?' I'd never seen the lad before, but he looked tasty. 'Oh, right,' I murmured, wondering who the boy was, and what he wanted. 'Er . . . come into my room.'

'Thanks,' he replied, smiling and displaying a lovely row of white teeth.

'Have fun,' Juliette giggled as I showed my visitor into my room and closed the door. Did she know him?

'Aren't you going to introduce yourself?' I asked as he stood awkwardly by the bed.

'Oh, sorry. I'm Steve.'

'And?'

'And? Oh, I see. A mutual friend sent me to see you. He reckons that . . .'

'Sit down and tell me who this mutual friend is.'

'Duncan, Duncan Williams. He said that . . .'

'I haven't seen Duncan since I left school. He doesn't know that I'm living here.'

'He must do. Anyway, he said that you . . . well, that you take money.'

'Take money? What are you talking about?'

'For sex.'

'Oh, he did, did he? Well, you can tell Duncan bloody Williams that I've never taken money in return for sex and I never will. Hang on. I thought Duncan had gone to live in America. Where did you see him?'

'In the village. He said that you're known as Cumslut Crystal.'

'Cumslut . . . And you've come here to pay me for sex?'

'Well, yes. Duncan said that—'

'I don't care what Duncan said. I am *not* a prostitute.'

'There's been a mistake, then,' he sighed.

'How the hell does he know where I'm living?'

'He didn't say. All he said was that you're an ace cock-sucker and you'd do a blow job for twenty pounds.'

'An ace . . . What a bloody cheek. You just wait until I get my hands on him.'

'I'd better go. I'm sorry . . .'

'No, no. You don't have to go yet.'

Scrutinizing Steve as he sat on the bed, I thought again that he wasn't a bad-looking lad. A couple of years my junior, his fair hair flopping over his smooth forehead, he was wearing tight blue jeans and a T-shirt. I'd never seen him in the village, and I felt a bit suspicious. Duncan

Williams hadn't been one of the lads I used to meet in the woods, and he'd definitely moved to America with his parents. Even if he *had* returned to England, he knew nothing about my reputation, and he certainly didn't know where I lived.

'Is Duncan living in the village with his parents?' I asked.

'Yes, he is. I saw him yesterday – that was when he told me about you.'

'I suppose he's still got that shocking head of red hair,' I laughed.

'Er . . . yes, red hair.'

'How tall is he now? He was over six feet when we were at school.'

'Huge,' Steve said and smiled. 'He towers over me.'

Duncan Williams had black hair and was a five-foot short-arse. This was some kind of trick, I knew. *The vicar?* I wondered. Had he sent the boy to . . . Yes, that was it. He was trying to find out whether I still lived in Robin's house. He'd sent the lad along to check up on me. Offering the young snoop a cup of coffee, I went down to the kitchen and grabbed a length of washing line from the cupboard beneath the sink. Steve was going to wish he'd never agreed to play a part in the vicar's evil plan. And he was going to regret coming to see me.

'The kettle's on,' I said, returning to my room and locking the door. 'Steve, I've been thinking about your proposal.'

'Oh?'

'I *am* rather short of cash at the moment, so . . . Did you say twenty pounds?'

'Yes.'

'OK, slip your clothes off and lie back on the bed.'

'Really?' He beamed, yanking his T-shirt over his head. 'That's great. I thought that Duncan was . . . What's the washing line for?'

'To tie you down,' I replied, eyeing his erect penis as he stood up and slipped his jeans off. 'I want to make sure you get your money's worth.'

'So it is true? You are a—'

'Yes, but I had to make sure that you were genuine. I've already had trouble with the cops.'

'Oh, right. God, I've never met a prostitute before.'

'You have now. And you're going to do far more than just *meet* one, believe me.'

As Steve lay on his back, I pulled his hands behind his head and bound his wrists to the bedposts. Spreading his legs and securing his ankles, I stood over his naked body, admiring his tight ball-bag, the unblemished shaft of his young cock. There was something about young boys, I mused, eyeing his sperm eggs that were clearly defined through the taut flesh of his scrotum. Fresh, hard, able to come more than once . . . Steve had a beautiful young body, but there was something about him that worried me. He was bait of some kind, that was for sure.

Deciding to start by shaving him, I grabbed my razor and shaving foam from the dressing table and sat on the bed beside him. He lifted his head and frowned as I squirted the foam over his balls and around the base of his erect cock, but then he lay back and closed his eyes. He was obviously looking forward to my intimate attention, even if it did mean losing his pubic curls. He'd be thinking about my hot, wet mouth engulfing the globe of his solid penis, my tongue licking his sperm-slit. I'd allow him his pleasure – *my* pleasure – when I was ready.

Working the razor over the fleshy sac of his scrotum, I

pulled his cock down and shaved his pubic mound. The razor left pale, smooth flesh in its wake, stripping years from his genitalia. I finished the job and admired my handiwork.

'You look like a little boy,' I said softly and grinned, wiping the foam away from his baby-smooth flesh. 'Good enough to eat.'

'God,' he breathed, lifting his head and staring at his bald genitalia. 'It'll take ages to grow back.'

'We won't let it grow back. I'll shave you whenever you come and see me. So, what did the vicar say?'

'He said . . . er . . . the vicar?'

'When he sent you here. You've come to check whether I'm still living here, haven't you?'

'No, no . . .' he stammered, fear mirrored in his blue eyes. 'Who is this vicar?'

'You've made a fatal mistake, Steve. Several mistakes, in fact. Duncan Williams is in America. He has black hair and is short and stocky. Are you going to tell me about the vicar?'

'I don't know any vicar.'

'What are his plans?'

'I don't know anything about—'

'Where's that leather belt?' I muttered, moving across to the wardrobe. 'It'll make an ideal whip.'

'A whip?' he breathed, tugging against his bonds.

'Ah, here it is.' I grinned nastily, taking the belt from the wardrobe and standing by the bed. 'I shaved your balls because I want to see your flesh redden when I whip you. Shall I start with your cock?'

'No, please . . .'

'What's the matter? I thought you wanted sex?'

'Yes, but I don't want to be whipped.'

'You want a blow job?'

'Yes, yes, I do.'

'And you'll get a blow job. After I've whipped your pretty cock. I'm somewhat of an expert when it comes to playing with cocks. I love pushing things into little knob-slits. I very often use a pen. I push the end of the pen into the knob-slit and then slide it all the way down the middle of the shaft until—'

'No! Please, let me go. I won't tell the vicar that you live here. I'll say that—'

'Yes, you will. You'll tell him that I'm here and he'll probably pay you for your trouble. Was that the deal?'

'No, no. He's not paying me.'

'I think I'll taste your knob,' I said, leaning over and pulling his foreskin back. 'I love tasting knobs. When did you last have a good wank?'

'I don't know. Yesterday, I think.'

'You think? It can't have been very good. Would you like to fuck my wet mouth?'

'Yes, yes, I would. But I don't want to be whipped.'

Taking Steve's salty plum into my mouth, I sucked gently, running my tongue around the rim of his ballooning helmet. His breathing deepening, his solid cock-shaft twitching, I wondered whether or not to whip him. It would be interesting to whip his cock. I'd watch him squirm as his genital flesh reddened. Was I wicked? No. He was as bad as the vicar, I concluded. I doubted that he knew of the years of abuse I'd had to endure at the vicar's hands – and cock. Whether he knew it or not, he was helping the evil man, aiding and abetting him. And he had to pay for his crime.

Slipping his cock out of my mouth, I licked his hairless balls. Nibbling his tight sperm-bag, I decided that I really would whip his cock. He had to be punished, after all. Leaving the bed, I slipped my well-juiced panties off and stuffed them into his mouth. I didn't want Robin or Juliette to hear his cries of protest as I thrashed his pretty cock.

'And now for your punishment,' I said, taking the leather belt in my hand. 'I once whipped a boy's cock so hard that he shot his spunk all over his stomach. That was after he'd pissed over it. I wonder whether you'll piss or spunk first?'

Raising the belt above my head, I brought it down across the flaccid shaft of Steve's cock with a loud crack. His naked body convulsing, his eyes wide, he moaned through his nose as I raised the belt again. Lashing the reddening shaft of his penis, I imagined that the boy was the vicar, fantasizing that I was punishing the so-called man of God for his wicked sins. Again and again I lashed the boy's cock, chuckling as he squirmed and pulled futilely against his bonds. He didn't piss himself, which I found most disappointing. I'd have loved to watch his golden liquid spurting from his knob-end, raining over his stomach. But his cock didn't even stiffen, let alone pump sperm over his stomach.

Dropping the belt on the floor at last, I sat beside Steve and gazed at the crimsoned flesh of his young cock. I felt wicked in the extreme, thoughts of torturing the boy even more viciously looming in my mind. Squeezing his balls, I watched him grimace. I squeezed a little harder, delighting in his plight as he again struggled to break free. Taking his foreskin between my finger and thumb, I pulled it up, stretching his young cock as he tried to spit my panties out of his mouth. Moving to the dressing table, I grabbed an elastic band and returned to my victim. Slipping the band around the neck of his scrotum, I watched his balls ballooning through his stretched sac.

'I might decide to keep you here,' I said, flicking his purple knob with my fingernail. 'You've annoyed me, Steve. The last boy who annoyed me . . . I forced him to suck other boys' cocks and swallow their spunk. I had him on his knees, tied to a tree in the woods. The boys fucked his pretty mouth and spunked down his throat. I know a few lads who would just love to fuck *your* mouth and spunk down *your* throat. Of course, we might be able to do a deal.' Taking his wallet from his jeans, I pulled out fifty pounds. 'This will come in handy,' I told him, grinning evilly. 'Oh, and what's this? A girl's phone number. Annie, eh? Is she your girlfriend?'

Lifting the phone, I punched in the number while Steve watched me with wide eyes. Reckoning that she was his girlfriend, I decided to cause some trouble. A woman answered and I asked for Annie. I heard the woman calling the girl, then what sounded like someone bounding down a flight of stairs.

'Hello,' a young female voice finally said.

'Annie, this is Selina,' I said softly. 'I thought I'd better tell you that Steve—'

'Is he all right?' she broke in.

'Oh, yes, he's fine. I thought I'd better tell you that he's been seeing another girl.'

'What?' she gasped. 'Who *are* you?'

'I'm a friend. I don't like the idea of people cheating on each other so I thought I'd give you a call. You see, I've just seen Steve in the woods behind the village school. I was out walking and . . . well, he didn't see me, but I saw him.'

'What was he doing?'

'To put it bluntly, he was fucking a young girl's mouth.'

'The bastard!' Annie hissed.

'Yes, he *is* a bastard. He's also been seeing the vicar. Did you know that Steve's bisexual?'

'Bi . . . I don't believe it. Whatever Steve is, he's not . . . Wait a minute. How do you know my number?'

'Steve was fucking me up until last week. He's told me all about you. Just to prove that I'm telling the truth, there's a mole on the base of his cock.'

'Anyone could have a mole . . .'

'If you want real proof, ask him to show you his cock when you see him. The girl he was with in the woods shaved his pubes off. I hid behind a bush and watched the whole thing.'

Replacing the receiver, I turned and grinned at Steve. He looked completely devastated, but it was his fault. He'd come to me for sex and had offered to pay me for a blow job. He'd been eager enough to strip naked and have me suck the spunk out of his knob. If he'd lost his loving girlfriend in the process, then he only had himself to blame. Flicking his glans with my fingernail again, I decided that the time had come to take him to orgasm.

'I'm going to suck out your spunk,' I giggled, licking the smooth surface of his glans. 'Seeing as you no longer have a girlfriend to suck you off, I'll give you a little treat.' Almost swallowing his knob completely, I sank my teeth gently into the root of his stiffening cock. As my lips pressed against the hairless sac of his ballooning testicles, I decided to leave the elastic band in place. I'd bring out his spunk, swallow the cream of his orgasm – and then whip his spent cock again with the leather belt.

I was enjoying myself. A young lad tied to my bed, his naked body mine to do with as I wished . . . What more could a girl want? What more could a cumslut want? Thinking about Juliette, her creamy-wet pussy, her erect clitoris pulsating in orgasm beneath my sweeping tongue, I again wondered whether I preferred boys or girls. For some reason, I wasn't sure that I wanted to be bisexual. It was as if I was torn between pussies and dicks, drawn to both but . . . *Why not have my cake and eat it?* I thought, stroking the taut skin of Steve's ball-sac.

'Crystal,' Juliette called, tapping on the door.

'Er . . . what is it?' I asked.

'May I come in?'

'I'm still with my . . . my friend. I'll see you later.'

'Are you being naughty?'

'I'll see you later, Juliette,' I repeated loudly, wishing she'd go away.

'I only want to come in for a minute.'

'Juliette,' I breathed in exasperation, opening the door. 'I have a visitor and—'

'Bloody hell,' she gasped, walking past me into the room. 'What the—'

'He's . . . he's a friend,' I stammered.

'What the hell have you done to his cock? An elastic band around . . .'

'He likes being tortured,' I lied.

'Tortured? Where on earth did you meet him?'

'We've known each other for a year or so.'

'Really? Mind if I join you? I'm not into cocks, but . . .'

'Juliette, I . . . Oh, all right,' I conceded, thinking that it might be fun. 'Why not?'

'Mind if I finger his bottom?' she giggled. 'I love fingering tight bottoms.'

'Go ahead.'

Watching the girl settle beside my prisoner, I couldn't help but feel sorry for Steve. His eyes widened as Juliette forced his buttocks apart and drove a finger deep into his rectum. His cock twitched expectantly. He was lucky to have two girls attending his sexual needs, I reflected, imagining his girlfriend gazing in horror at his shaved balls. But he was going to have some explaining to do if he wanted to hang on to Annie. There again, it was probably too late to hang on to her.

Juliette sucked Steve's swollen knob into her pretty mouth as she fingered his arse, pistoning his tight rectum as he writhed on the bed. She was a dirty bitch, I mused. She'd made out that she wasn't really into cocks, and yet she seemed to be enjoying herself immensely. She certainly had a thing about bums, I thought, watching her force another finger into Steve's rectal duct. I doubted that she would try to force her fist into his anal canal, but I thought she might like *me* to fist *her* tight bottom.

I should never have opened the door to Juliette, I reflected, realizing, as she bobbed her head up and down, repeatedly taking the boy's knob to the back of her throat, that my room was fast becoming a sex den. I should have kept Steve to myself rather than . . . Was I jealous? Had I really wanted to keep *Juliette* to myself? Confused, I moved behind her and yanked her skirt up, pulling her tight panties down to her thighs and exposing the beautiful orbs of her firm buttocks.

Holding her arse-globes wide apart, I was amazed to see the end of a candle protruding from the tight hole of her anus. She must have enjoyed the sensations as she walked and moved around. She really was a dirty little cow, I thought, taking the end of the waxen phallus and sliding it partially out of her hot duct. Ramming the candle back into her bowels, I grinned as her buttocks tensed. I could hear her slurping, sucking on Steve's solid cock as she fingered his bum-hole and I pistoned her anal canal with the candle. She was no more pure lesbian than I was, I knew as Steve shuddered in his climax and I heard Juliette gulping down his fresh spunk.

'You *are* a dirty little slut,' I giggled as she drank from the boy's throbbing knob. 'Walking around with a candle rammed up your bum and drinking spunk . . . You're a dirty little slut,' I repeated. My crude words obviously aroused her and she moaned loudly through her nose, her hips rocking, her bottom thrusting back to meet the lunges of the wax phallus as I arse-fucked her with it. Slapping her naked buttocks with the palm of my hand, I noticed the leather belt lying on the floor. Would Juliette enjoy a naked-buttock thrashing? I wondered, leaving the candle embedded deep within her rectum and grabbing the strap.

Standing by the bed, I raised the leather belt above my head and brought it down as hard as I could across the firm globes of her young bottom. Her shapely body jolting, she didn't leap off the bed and protest as I thought she might have. I reckoned that Juliette liked having her bottom thrashed as I brought the belt down again, lashing the pale flesh of her tensed buttocks. What Steve would think, I had no idea. He'd go home without his pubes, his balls drained . . . He'd think we were nothing but a couple of sluts. We *were* a couple of sluts.

Eyeing the hairless lips of Juliette's vagina bulging between her young thighs as I continued to thrash her firm buttocks, I noticed her creamy pussy-milk trickling from her lickable sex-crack. What *did* I want? I wondered? Male or female? Or both? Finally discarding the leather belt, I gazed at the glowing flesh of Juliette's pert bottom. She was still busily gobbling on Steve's knob, sucking out the remnants of his sperm. Pushing my face between her thighs, I lapped up her creamy sex-fluid, sweeping my tongue up and down her hot valley of desire as she trembled and moaned through her nose.

'Let's take the gag out of his mouth and sit on his face,' Juliette trilled eagerly, slipping the boy's cock out of her mouth.

'No, not yet,' I replied softly, sure that Steve would yell at me for whipping his cock.

'Come on, Crystal,' she persisted. 'I want to piss in his mouth.'

'Piss in his . . .' I began, wondering whether I'd heard her correctly.

'I love it. Aren't you into water sports?' she giggled, clambering off the bed and slipping her wet panties off.

'No,' I said, somewhat shocked by her revelation.

'That's a shame,' she breathed, straddling Steve with her knees either side of his hips. 'Come on, boy, stiffen up and fuck me,' she laughed.

Watching as Juliette rocked her hips, massaging Steve's cock with her vaginal flesh, I noticed the candle sticking out of her tight bottom-hole. Were there no bounds to her sexual exploits? I wondered. Although I'd always been heavily into cock-sucking, Juliette seemed to be into anything and everything. Was I missing out? As she lifted her young body, I watched her grab Steve's erect cock and slip his swollen knob between the pink petals of her inner lips. Lowering herself, she threw her head back and let out a sigh of pleasure as his penile shaft entered the tight sheath of her young pussy. Feeling redundant, I sat on the edge of the bed and grabbed the end of the candle.

'I'll give you a hand,' I said, pistoning her rectum with the candle as she bounced up and down on Steve's solid cock.

'Mmm, that's nice,' she sighed. 'This reminds me of the double fucking I had a few weeks ago.'

'Two men?' I asked.

'Two men, two cocks, two holes . . . Sheer heaven.'

Juliette had duped me, I reflected. Making out that she was all lesbian . . . Had she been after Robin's cock? I wondered. I'd not seen much of either of them for three days. Perhaps they'd been shagging in the consulting room? Was I jealous? I'd preferred things before Juliette had moved in. Just Robin and me, our insane conversations, eating meals together . . . And sucking his cock. I wasn't in control, that was the problem. Robin was the boss, but I'd run the house, cooked and cleaned. With Juliette there . . . I just didn't like the way things were turning out.

Listening to the squelching of Juliette's vaginal juices as she fucked herself on Steve's beautiful cock, I repeatedly drove the candle deep into her tight arse. She was close to her orgasm, I knew as she murmured incoherent words of lust. Steve's moans of pleasure resounding around the room, I imagined the spunk issuing from his orgasming knob, filling Juliette's vaginal cavern. When the blend of his spunk and Juliette's girl-cum oozed from the bloated shaft of her pussy and ran down over his hairless balls, I'd lap it up, swallow the blended products of their orgasms.

Resting my head on Steve's leg, I had a close-up view

of the crude coupling, his cunny-wet cock driving in and out of Juliette's dripping cunt, her outer lips repeatedly squashing his swollen ball-bag. Slipping the candle out of the tight canal of her bum-hole passage, I drove two fingers past her anal sphincter muscles, massaging deep inside her rectal sheath and adding to her pleasure. My own juices of arousal oozing between the engorged cushions of my outer labia, my clitoris painfully hard, I was desperate for the feel of Juliette's wet tongue snaking between my thighs.

Steve's sperm finally gushed from Juliette's pussy and streamed over his balls. I moved in and lapped up the highly aphrodisiacal blend of spunk and girl-cum. Juliette leaned forward to allow me better access, and I licked Steve's cock-shaft and slurped at Juliette's fleshy labia as she gasped and shuddered in the grip of her own orgasm. The sight of Steve's glistening penis sliding in and out of her cunny drove me wild with desire. Licking and mouthing at their sex-dripping genitals as I finger-fucked Juliette's spasming anal canal, I swallowed the heady cocktail of their love-juices.

My fingers slipping out of Juliette's arse as she rolled off Steve's tethered body and lay beside him on the bed, I moved in and sucked his spent cock into my hot mouth. Sucking his wet knob, licking Juliette's girl-cum from his shaft, his scrotum, I cleansed him, hoping that he'd soon restiffen so I could impale myself on his fleshy rod and flood my thirsty cunt with his male cream. Juliette fell asleep as I worked my tongue over Steve's cock and his smooth scrotum. She was probably exhausted after her pussy-fucking, her anal fingering, but I knew that she'd soon recover and demand another cock-induced orgasm.

As Steve's young cock stiffened within my wet mouth,

I clambered on top of him with the gaping entrance to my hungry pussy hovering over his knob. At last it was my turn to fuck him, and I guided him deep into my vaginal sheath, lowering my trembling body until the hairless outer lips of my pussy pressed against his ballooning scrotum. I could feel the bulbous head of his cock against my creamy-wet cervix, his solid shaft swelling within the hugging sheath of my hot cunt. Bouncing up and down, the juices of my drenched pussy squelching, I knew that I'd have to release Steve before long. The vicar would be desperate for news of my whereabouts, but I didn't reckon that Steve would tell him. I doubted that he'd enjoyed having his cock and balls whipped, but he was bound to return to Robin's house now that he knew there were two nymphomaniacs living there.

'Are you there, Crystal?' Robin called, tapping on the door.

Shit. 'Er . . . I'm sleeping,' I lied, sitting on Steve's balls with his solid cock embedded deep within my hot pussy.

'You're awake,' Robin persisted.

'I am now, but I was sleeping. What do you want?'

'You're having sex, aren't you? I can smell sex in the air.'

'No, Robin. I am *not* having sex.'

'Yes, you *are*. OK, I'll come back later. When you've finished your three-way orgy.'

Thinking that Robin must have been spying on me, I gyrated my hips, stirring my hot pussy cream with Steve's beautiful cock-shaft. Robin was a damned nuisance, I reflected. With his uncanny insight he knew exactly what I was doing, and it unnerved me. Wondering whether he could read my mind, I thought about the sea, the waves crashing over rocks, as I bobbed up and down and fucked Steve. Robin would become confused as images of the sea loomed in his mind. No, of course he couldn't read my mind. But he must have had *some* method of spying on me. If Robin knew what other people were doing, then he might be able to enlighten me about where the vicar kept the incriminating photographs. More than that, he might be able to give me the names of other girls the evil man had been using and abusing.

As Steve's solid cock throbbed deep within my spasming vagina in yet another climax, I could feel his creamy spunk bathing my cervix. My pulsating clitoris massaged by his sex-wet shaft as I bounced up and down, I reached my own massive orgasm, my juices of lust spewing from the bloated cavern of my hot cunt as I shook violently. I couldn't get enough sex, I knew as I watched Steve's eyes rolling, his tethered body trembling beneath me as his balls drained yet again. Slowing my bouncing as my orgasm began to fade, my long blonde hair cascading down over my flushed face, I couldn't believe the incredible intensity of my climax.

Clambering off Steve's naked body, I swayed on my trembling legs as my sperm-flooded sex-sheath drained, the creamy cocktail of blended male and female cum streaming down my inner thighs. Juliette finally opened her eyes and smiled at me before she got up off the bed. We were both well and truly fucked in our orgasm-induced exhaustion. Our pussies brimming with spunk, our young bodies sated, we'd had enough of Steve for the time being.

'You'd better go,' I said, releasing his wrists and ankles.

'You can come back whenever you want,' Juliette giggled as he pulled my panties out of his mouth and climbed to his feet.

'And don't say anything to you-know-who,' I said as he grabbed his clothes.

'Do you think I'd ruin my chances of coming to see you again?' Steve riposted, and grinned.

'I don't know. Maybe you would.'

'No chance.'

'You'd *better* come back,' Juliette said, sitting back down on the bed, opening her smooth young thighs wide and peeling the hairless lips of her cunt wide apart. 'If you want more of this, of course.'

'Seeing as I've lost my girlfriend, you can count on me.'

'What will you say to—' I began.

'You're not here. You moved out, and no one knows where to.'

'Great.'

As Steve finished dressing and left the room, I wasn't sure whether I could trust him. The prospect of two nymphomaniacal girls to fuck would probably dissuade him from telling the vicar where I was, though, I mused. The orgy over, I watched Juliette slip her candle back deep into her rectal duct before pulling her panties up her long legs. The front door closing, signalling Steve's departure, I thought I'd better go and see what Robin was up to. And ask him about the whereabouts of the photographs, if his psychic powers would reach that far.

'I'll see you later,' Juliette said, leaving the room.

'OK,' I murmured pensively, wondering whether to try out a candle up my own bottom-hole.

'Let me know when your friend comes round again.'

'Yes, yes, I will.'

Making my way downstairs, I found Robin lurking in his consulting room. Sitting in his chair, he was fiddling with something beneath his desk. Wondering whether I should have knocked before entering since he seemed oblivious to me, happily playing with his erect cock, I was about to let out a little cough when something started buzzing. Peering over the flat surface of the desk, I watched as he pressed the tip of a vibrator against his swollen knob.

'Ah, er . . .' he gasped, looking up. 'I was just—'

'Bringing yourself off?' I giggled.

'No, no. I was checking my penile response,' he replied sheepishly, tossing the vibrator into the drawer and zipping up his trousers. 'It's in the rules, you see.'

'Yes, I'm sure it is,' I laughed.

'The garden's looking nice now that you've dug out the weeds.'

'Weeds? I haven't—'

'Ah, that reminds me. I found your bikini behind the shed. You shouldn't leave it there. It'll get filthy.'

'Right, I'll remember that,' I said and smiled, realizing that he'd lost his marbles again.

'Talking of sheds, I see a small outbuilding. Very small, rather like a brick coal bunker. It's behind a cottage and—'

'And I know exactly what you're talking about,' I cut in. 'I'll see you later.'

'Where are you going?'

'To see a coal bunker about some photographs.'

Grabbing my coat, I left the house and walked to the village. Robin must have known that I was going to ask about the photographs. How his psychic powers worked,

I didn't know. And I didn't care. All I wanted was to get my hands on the evidence and then tell the evil vicar to go and fuck himself. Juliette had said nothing more about her plan, and I presumed that her young girlfriend hadn't wanted to get involved. I was the only one who could deal with the man of Satan.

Reaching the woods behind the school, I followed the path to the rear of the vicar's cottage and peered over the garden wall. Determined not to make the same mistake as I had on my previous visit when I'd ended up in his sex chamber, I slipped into the garden and hid behind a bush. I could see the coal bunker. Robin was right – so far. Stealing across the lawn, my stomach churning, I realized that I might be about to put an end to years of threats and sexual abuse. My heart racing as I opened the lid of the coal bunker, I peered down into the black hole and noticed a shoebox. Recalling the vicar's words as I grabbed the evidence, I felt a little despondent. *Boxes full of photographs. Boxes – plural*, I thought.

Noticing the garden shed, I wondered whether there were more boxes stashed there. But it was too risky to hang about, so I dashed across the lawn with my spoils and made my escape into the woods. When I was a good distance away from the cottage, I sat on a log and opened the box. It contained dozens of photographs of my naked body: my open pussy, my bare buttocks and crudely exposed bottom-hole, sperm running down my chin and over the mounds of my petite breasts. I could hardly believe my eyes as I gazed at my tongue licking a huge swollen purple cock-head, sperm jetting from its slit and splattering my face. The vicar had been careful to keep not only his face out of frame but the rest of his body too – and no one who saw the photos would be likely to be able to identify him by his prick. But I knew that it was his cock fucking my pretty mouth.

If I'd got all the photographs, and the vicar believed Steve and thought that I'd moved away, I was in the clear. He wouldn't come to Robin's place looking for me, he'd have no evidence of my early sexual encounters . . . All I could do was pray that I'd finally put an end to the nightmare. Walking through the woods clutching the shoebox, I had a feeling that this wasn't the end of the matter. I don't know what it was, why I felt like that, but *something* was niggling me. Perhaps Robin's psychic powers had rubbed off on me? Whatever it was, I felt uneasy.

As I walked along the lane, wondering what to do with the photographs. I felt that I should hang on to them. Posterity? A reminder of old times? The photographs depicted a very real part of my young life, nightmarish though that part had been. There again, my sexual exploits in the woods with the young lads from school . . . Lifting the lid off the box and pulling out some photographs as I walked, I gazed at several shots of me in the woods, a young lad's cock fucking my mouth, his spunk running down my chin. I'd been so young, I reflected, wondering where the vicar could have been hiding to take such a close-up photograph.

'Where are you off to?' a male voice called from behind.

'Oh, Mr Carter,' I breathed, turning and facing my old English teacher. 'Er . . . how are you?'

'I'm very well, Crystal. How are you faring in the big wide world?'

'I'm a housekeeper,' I replied, rather too proudly. 'I

mean . . . it's a live-in job. Just temporary until I get something better.'

'I should think so, too. You're a bright young lady. Don't go wasting your life, will you?'

'No, no, of course not.'

'I'm on my way home so I'll walk with you,' he said, smiling and placing his arm around my shoulder. 'I've been into the village to post a letter.'

'Do you live this way?' I asked.

'I moved a few months back. The village was too confining, so I bought Grange Cottage. Do you know of it?'

'Yes, I do. I've heard about it, although I've never been there. It's about four hundred years old, isn't it?'

'Almost. Would you like to come and take a look round?'

'I'd love to.'

'I'm still in a bit of a mess, but I know where the kettle is if you'd like some tea.'

'That would be nice.'

As we walked, I held the shoebox tightly, wondering what on earth Mr Carter would think if he saw the photographs. I'd always got on all right with him, but he'd kept himself to himself at school. He must have been about forty. Word had it that he'd never been married and was a bit of a loner. I was surprised that he'd asked me back to his cottage as no one had ever really got to know him. As far as I knew, he didn't have any friends and had never joined the other teachers for their regular Friday-evening drink in the pub.

'Here we are,' he said, leading me down a narrow track to the cottage. I'd not seen the place before. As a kid, I'd played in the woods and gone exploring, but had never come across the beautiful old cottage. Reckoning that Carter must be fairly well off financially as I followed him through the hall into the lounge, I settled on the leather chesterfield and looked around at the antique furniture. A couple of cardboard boxes were on the floor; he still had a lot to do, but it was a lovely room.

'What's in the box?' Carter asked, sitting in an armchair opposite me.

'Just some odds and ends,' I lied. 'I've left home and had to pick up a few personal things.'

'Ah, the live-in housekeeping job. It's not in the village, then?'

'No, no. It's . . . it's not far. Do you live alone?'

'Yes, I'm afraid so. Crystal, what's in the box?'

'I've told you,' I said, frowning at him. 'A few personal things from home.'

'Are you going to show me?'

'There's . . . there's nothing to see,' I laughed, realizing that he knew what was in the box. Was he in with the vicar? 'Well, I'd better be going.'

'Not until you've shown me what's in the box.'

'Mr Carter . . . it's just a few things, like I said. My birth certificate, passport and—'

'Then you won't mind showing me.'

I stood up and was about to leave the room when Carter leaped to his feet and grabbed my arm. Snatching the box from me, he moved to the centre of the room and looked inside. I'd never felt so humiliated as when he flicked through the photographs, flashing me an accusing look every now and then. I'd failed again in my plan to be free of the evil vicar, I was sure as I watched my erstwhile English teacher scrutinizing the photographs of my naked body.

'Where did you get these?' he asked.

'The vicar,' I confessed, wondering whether he'd ring the man and tell him what I'd done. 'How did you know what was in the box?'

'I didn't. I've been watching the vicar for some time now.'

'Watching him?'

'A girl came to see me. Jenny Carlton – you probably know her.'

'Yes, I do.'

'The vicar had been . . . well, I think you can guess. Anyway, I've seen this shoebox several times before. The vicar takes it to the church, carries it home again . . . I had a pretty good idea what it contained. I must admit, though, that I thought I'd find photographs of Jenny, not of you.'

'I think there may be more boxes,' I said, thankful that he wasn't in with the vicar.

'I'm sure there are. I only wish I'd known of your involvement.'

'What are you going to do?'

'Leave these with me,' Carter said, placing the box on the coffee table.

'But . . .'

'It's all right. They'll be safe enough. I'm working on a plan which I hope will . . . I won't say anything yet. Where do you live? I'll need to get in touch with you.'

Giving Carter my phone number, I felt that I could trust him. After all, he'd been my English teacher, Jenny had confided in him . . . and he was well respected in the village. There again, so was the evil vicar. Offering me a cup of tea, he went into the kitchen and filled the kettle. He was all right, I was sure. Leaving me in the lounge like he had, he must have realized that I could have grabbed the box and run. He *was* to be trusted, I was sure as I joined him in the kitchen.

'Are there other girls?' I asked.

'I'm not sure. I have an idea that there might be several from the school. I'm having to play this very carefully, Crystal. Obviously, I'll bring the police in when I've gathered enough evidence. If I go to them now . . . I need to be sure that he won't wriggle off the hook.'

'He's slimy, I know that.'

'When I saw you in the lane with that shoebox, I put two and two together. Where was it?'

'In the coal bunker at the back of his cottage.'

'What made you look there?'

'I . . . It was a hunch. I'll have to speak to Jenny, see what she's been through.'

'No, no: I'd rather you kept this to yourself until I've gathered enough evidence to nail the vicar. There's your tea. Do you take sugar?'

'No, thanks.'

Sipping my tea, I gazed out of the kitchen window, wondering about Jenny. I *would* speak to her, I decided. I'd not really known her that well at school but, now that we had the perverted vicar in common, I thought I'd have a chat with her. I could see Mr Carter's point about secrecy, inasmuch as he wanted to get as much evidence as possible together, but just talking to Jenny wouldn't do any harm, surely. Thinking about the box of photographs, I wasn't too happy about leaving them with him. He was bound to look through them again and gaze at my mouth sucking the spunk out of a purple knob, my gaping pussy, sperm running over my hairless love-lips . . . I'd feel highly embarrassed the next time I saw him.

'When you ring, leave a message and it'll be passed on to me,' I said, wishing I'd not given him my number.

'Passed on? Don't you have a phone where you are?'

'Not yet. I've only just moved in. When I said that I was a live-in housekeeper . . . well, I now live out. In fact, I've left the job. I wasn't going to mention it but . . . It's a long story.'

'Oh, I see. Where are you living now?'

'In Barnhampton.'

'Give me the address and I'll—'

'Better still, give me *your* phone number and I'll ring you when I get a phone installed.'

Carter seemed rather agitated as he wrote his number down. Deciding not to trust anyone after all, I thought it best to take the box of photographs with me when I left. He'd seemed pretty angry when he'd grabbed my arm, and I knew that I've have a job getting hold of the box. Gazing down the garden again, I told him that I'd seen someone lurking in the bushes. As I'd thought he would, he went to investigate, giving me a chance to grab the box and hide it in the bushes beside the track that led to and from the cottage. Thinking quickly, I left the front door open and returned to the kitchen before he got back.

'I couldn't see anyone,' Carter said, closing the back door.

'I thought you'd gone round to the front,' I said, frowning. 'I heard the door open.'

'What?' he breathed, walking into the hall. 'What the hell's going on?' he asked, closing the front door and joining me in the kitchen.

'I don't know. Perhaps the front door wasn't closed properly and it blew open. Well, I'd better be going.'

'Ring me, OK?' he said, smiling as he followed me into the hall.

'I will, the minute I get a phone. It should only be a day or two. Thanks for the tea.'

'You're more than welcome.'

Leaving the cottage, I walked round a bend in the narrow track and grabbed the shoebox. Reckoning that Carter would come after me once he realized that the evidence had gone, I ran down the lane and slipped the box into the bushes growing beneath the spreading branches of a huge oak tree. My plan couldn't have turned out better. Carter would believe that the photographs had been stolen, the vicar now had no evidence – and I was perfectly innocent. Quickening my pace, I wondered why Carter hadn't come after me. Perhaps he'd gone back into the garden to look for the intruder. Whatever happened, I thought that it would be best to move out of Robin's house. *Perhaps I should get my own flat somewhere?* I mused, reaching the front door. I'd give it some thought while I was preparing the evening meal.

7

After having an early night, I woke at seven, walked down the lane and retrieved the box of photographs from beneath the bushes. I'd been lying in bed thinking about Mr Carter, and had decided to determine whether or not I could trust him. Unfortunately, Robin had been going through one of his mental episodes so I'd not been able to ask him about the man. Carter might have been genuine, I reflected. Jenny might have confided in him and poured out her story, and maybe he really was trying to nail the vicar. But I had to be sure. Ringing him from a call box, I wanted to see what his reaction was to the missing photographs.

'Did you take the box of photographs with you?' he asked me the minute I'd said hello.

'*You* took them,' I replied. 'They were in your lounge.'

'They've gone,' he snapped. 'Someone must have come in through the front door and taken them.'

'You mean to say that someone has all those incriminating—'

'They must have known about them,' he broke in agitatedly. 'Who had you told?'

'No one. This is great. I *knew* I should have taken them with me.'

'It's not my fault, Crystal. Look, don't worry. I'll get them back.'

'You'd better,' I sighed.

'Give me your address and I'll come round.'

'I'm out today.'

'This evening, then.'

'I'm . . . I'm going to London. I won't be back for a couple of days. Do you think someone's going to black-mail me? Ask for money and . . .'

'Maybe. I really don't know what to think. I'm *sure* the front door was closed. I just don't understand . . . It must have been someone who knew about the photos.'

'The vicar?'

'No, no. Well, it might be. Someone must have fol-lowed you.'

'This is a bloody mess,' I said, still unsure whether or not to trust him. 'I'll ring you tomorrow.'

'It's a shame I can't see you today. If you could come round . . .'

'I'm on my way to the station. I'll ring tomorrow.'

'All right,' he conceded. 'Until tomorrow, then.'

Replacing the receiver, I left the phone box and walked down the lane towards Carter's cottage. Hiding the photographs beneath the bushes again, I slipped into the field and approached the cottage from the rear. I wasn't sure what I had in mind as I crept into the back garden. Listen at the window? Watch him? It did occur to me that if Carter went out I could search his place. Search for what, though? Slipping behind the shed as I noticed him in the kitchen, I thought that I was wasting my time. It was a cold and wet winter day. What on earth was I doing hiding in someone's garden?

I was about to go home when I heard Carter's phone ringing. Making my way towards the cottage, I hid by the back door and listened. The top kitchen window was partially open so I could just make out what he was saying. He mentioned something about things going wrong and he was going to have to take the day off work to sort it out. Was he talking about me? Again, I thought that I was wasting my time. Then an idea struck me. I went round to the front of the cottage and rang the bell. This was stupid, I knew, but I had to find out what was going on.

'Oh, Crystal,' Carter said, opening the door. 'I thought—'

'I'm on my way to the station,' I breathed. 'I'm really worried about those photographs.'

'So am I. Come in and I'll put the kettle on.'

'Thanks.'

'I can't believe that someone walked into my lounge and took the box,' he said, leading me into the kitchen. 'It doesn't make sense. Firstly, they must have known what they were after. Secondly, I'm sure the front door was shut so how the hell did they—'

'Has the vicar ever been here?'

'No, he hasn't. Why do you ask?'

'I just wondered. As there's now been a robbery, I think we should go to the police.'

'The police? Er . . . no, I don't think that's a good idea, Crystal.'

'Someone's been into your cottage and stolen some-thing,' I persisted. 'You should at least tell the police about it.'

'We don't know that someone . . . What I mean is . . .'

'What you mean is, you still have the photographs,' I ventured.

'What? Of course I haven't got them. Why would I tell you that they'd been stolen if I still had them?'

'Perhaps you want them for yourself. Perhaps you enjoy looking through them.'

'That's ridiculous.'

'Is it?'

'Of course it is. Don't get me wrong, I'm a normal man. Of course photographs of naked women turn me on. But to keep the evidence would be . . . well, it would be crazy.'

'I suppose so,' I sighed, wondering how to catch him out. Perhaps he *was* genuine? 'Luckily, I still have the other box.'

'Other box? You mean, you have *more* photographs?'

'Yes. I took them from the vicar's cottage yesterday. There are several photographs of another girl.'

'Where are they?'

'Well hidden, so you needn't worry.'

'Who's the girl?'

'I don't know. The point is, you can see the vicar's face in one of them.'

'Right, let me have them and I'll go straight to the police.'

'Let you have them?' I laughed. 'After what happened to the others?'

'Crystal . . .'

'Look, I have to go or I'll miss my train.'

'Go? Crystal, I don't think you realize how serious this is.'

'Oh, but I do. That's why I'm going to London.'

'What do you mean?'

'I'm meeting someone, someone who's going to deal with this once and for all.'

'I wish you'd told me before. We should work together, Crystal. Who is this person?'

'A private detective.'

'And you're going to give him the photographs?'

'Yes. I was talking to him on the phone and he reckons that the vicar isn't working alone. Right, I'd better get going. I have to pick the photographs up and catch the train.'

'Ring me, OK?'

'Yes, I will.'

As I left the cottage, I wondered whether he'd follow me. If he was involved, and believed that I was taking photographs to London, he might get someone to snatch them from me. My mind flooding with images of a man grabbing me and pulling me into the bushes, I kept turning my head as I walked along the lane.

Not wanting to be seen entering Robin's place, I decided to turn off into a side street and make my way around the back of the house. Hammering on the back door and getting no response, I wondered where Robin had got to as I managed to climb in through a window. He wasn't in his consulting room, and Juliette was out. At least I had some time alone to think. Making a cup of coffee, I sat on my bed and tried to relax.

My life had never been particularly enjoyable. I hadn't liked school, my father and mother had been strict, the vicar had used and abused me . . . Sipping my coffee, I came to a decision. Having to hide, keep my address from people, having to lie – it was all down to the vicar. One man had dominated my life. One man had ruined my life. And the time had come to put a stop to it. Stealing the photographs, making up stories, living on a knife's edge – I'd had enough. The time had come to put a stop to the vicar's continual threats, his perverted ways. Lifting the phone, I rang my mother to ask her when the next church meeting was. With the vicar out of the way for a few hours, I'd have time to search every inch of his cottage.

'Mr Carter has just been to see me,' she said. 'I rang you earlier but you were out.'

'What did he want?' I asked. 'I haven't seen him since I left school.'

'He wanted your address.'

'Did you give it to him?'

'Yes, I did. And your phone number. He seemed to think that you'd moved. He said that he'd spoken to you.'

'He's mixing me up with someone else.'

'That's what I thought. He said that you'd been to his cottage and—'

'I don't even know where he lives.'

'Oh, well, no doubt he'll tell you what he wants when he rings you. So, how are you? I would have thought you'd have been to see us.'

'What with settling in and everything, I haven't had time. I'll see you soon, I promise.'

'You make sure you do.'

'OK, I'd better go.'

'All right. Take care, Crystal.'

'I will. And I'll come over very soon.'

Replacing the receiver, I knew now that Carter was in with the vicar. Asking my mother for my address and phone number . . . Wondering when he'd ring, I finished my coffee and paced the floor. Should I answer the phone? Should I move out of Robin's place and find somewhere else? Wondering where Robin and Juliette had got to, I passed the time by getting on with some housework. When my phone rang, I was in the kitchen. My hands trembling, my heart racing, I dashed upstairs and grabbed the receiver.

'Hello,' I said, disguising my voice.

'Crystal?' Carter asked.

'I think you must have the wrong number.'

'This is the number I was given. Has Crystal moved out?'

'The young girl who lived here moved out, yes.'

'Do you know where to?'

'No, I'm sorry. I live here now and . . .'

As he hung up, I wondered whether I'd fooled him. I doubted that he'd ring again, but he might come to the house. Robin had already told the vicar that I'd moved out, but Carter might decide to check for himself. I thought about disguising myself as an old lady and answering the door, but realized that it would be stupid to carry on like that. For one thing, I'd have no idea when he was going to come round, if at all. Hearing the noise of the front door slamming shut, followed by Robin's curses, I went downstairs to see him.

'Bloody people,' he complained as I reached the bottom of the stairs.

'Are you all right?' I asked.

'Yes, I am now. Your car is outside.'

'My car? I haven't got a car.'

'You'll need these,' he said, thrusting his hand into his jacket pocket and passing me two keys. 'It's insured, so you can drive it right away.'

'What? You've bought me a car?'

'You're always going out in the cold, so I thought it might be a useful present.'

'A present? That's great,' I said, beaming.

'The bloody salesman had the audacity to suggest that I couldn't afford it. He noticed that I was looking at a small car and when I went to look at this one . . .'

'What car is it?'

'Bloody wanker. To suggest that I couldn't afford a Jag. Huh.'

'A Jaguar?'

'I was going to buy you a little Ford runabout, but I bought the Jag to show the bastard up. Fancy suggesting that I . . .'

'Robin, you bought me a *Jag* as a present?'

'That *is* all right, isn't it?'

'All *right*? It's *amazing*! Thank you.'

'You're welcome. The bloody insurance cost an arm and a leg. Still, you're worth it. Why don't you go for a drive?'

'I will,' I cried, opening the front door. 'I'll see you later.'

'Don't go and crash it, will you?'

'No, I won't.'

Leaving the house, I forgot all about the vicar and Carter as I climbed into the new Jag. Robin must have been crazy, I thought, starting the engine. He hardly knew me and he'd bought me a new car. Moving off, I drove around the side streets until I got used to the automatic gearbox. Leather seats, CD player . . . I couldn't believe it. Driving to the village, I half hoped that the evil vicar would see me. Again thinking that Robin must have been crazy, I wondered whether he'd had one of his mental turns and would later regret spending the money.

On the way to the village, I picked up the box of photographs. They were safe, at last. Driving into the village, I noticed Juliette talking to the vicar outside the church. Keeping my head down, I drove past them and parked in the lay-by outside the local shop. 'What's she up to?' I murmured, watching them in the rear-view mirror. My mind running wild, I imagined that Juliette was a member of the evil vicar's gang of perverts. She headed my way as the vicar went into the church, and I slid down in the seat as she approached. Stopping outside the shop, she rummaged through her handbag.

'Hi,' I said brightly, grinning as I opened the window.

'Crystal . . . What are you . . . Whose car is that?'

'Get in,' I said, checking the mirror for the vicar. 'Get in and I'll tell you.'

'Blimey, it's new,' Juliette gasped, sitting beside me.

'Brand new,' I trilled, driving off. 'It was a present.'

'*What?*'

'From a friend.'

'It must be a very good friend.'

'Don't worry about the car. What were you saying to the vicar?'

'Ah, yes. My plan is in motion. Where have you been? I wanted to talk to you.'

'Busy. OK, what's been going on?'

'Well, I spoke to the young girl I know and she's up for it. I was asking the vicar whether he'd mind if a friend of mine took a look around his church and made notes for her school project. One thought of a schoolgirl in his church and he was dead keen on the idea. Where *did* you get this car from? It must have cost a small fortune.'

'When's this girl going to the church?'

'This afternoon. I've also arranged for a woman I know to act as her mother. She'll go into the church and, hopefully, catch the vicar with his trousers down and his cock up the girl's arse.'

'Charming.'

'Where are we going?'

'Just for a drive. I want to get used to the car. So, what's going to happen when this woman catches him in the act?'

'I have to work out the details but, basically, she's going to threaten him. I'll happen to walk in and witness the proceedings. I'll do my horrified act and . . . well, we'll see what happens. At the very least, I reckon that the vicar will leave the village.'

'What, sell his cottage?'

'The church owns it.'

'Ah, right.'

I reckoned that Juliette's plan was full of holes, but she had the basics worked out quite well. A distraught mother catching the vicar fucking her little girl's bottom-hole, Juliette arriving just in time to witness the ugly scene . . . If nothing went wrong, it just might work. The vicar would hardly hang around if the police were mentioned. There again, he . . . But there was no point in speculating. Besides, it would be better to have tried and failed. I imagined the vicar's face, his expression when a woman burst into the church and saw his cock up a young girl's bottom. What the hell would he say? What *could* he say?

Parking outside Robin's house, I invited Juliette into my room for a chat about her plan. She went on about the car as we passed Robin in the hall. He said that I'd already told him about my new car, winking at me as he disappeared into his consulting room. Juliette sat on the bed as I closed my door and took my coat off. The plan was going to have to be well organized, the timing perfect.

'How will the woman know when to go into the church?' I asked her.

'I'll give her the signal. I'll be watching through the side window and I'll whistle at the appropriate time.'

'What if the vicar sees her enter the church, whips his cock out and moves away from the girl?'

'No, no. She's going to slip into the church and creep down the aisle. The girl will be by the altar, the vicar with his back to the doors.'

'He might decide that it's too risky and take her into his office or—'

'The girl knows what to do. She's going to stand by the altar and slip her panties off. If the vicar suggests going into the office or moving somewhere else, she'll bend over the altar and pull her skirt up. One look at her hairless cunny lips ballooning between her thighs, and he'll be up her as quick as lightning.'

'What if . . . I'm not trying to criticize your plan, I just want to make sure that everything's covered. For example, he might lock the doors.'

'Good point. OK, so the girl makes sure that he doesn't. If he does, then she leaves.'

'Or she could allow him to do her, and then scream out. The woman finally gets in and . . .'

'And sees nothing. She'll have to make sure that he doesn't lock the doors. I reckon that he'll be too excited to think about anything other than his cock. Anyway, he wouldn't lock the doors. The girl walks to the altar and then gives him the come-on. I don't reckon he'd walk back to the doors.'

'OK, Juliette. I think you've got it all worked out.'

'I'm sure I have. And the beauty of it is that you won't even be in the village, let alone the church. It will have nothing to do with you.'

'I like the sound of that. So, the woman threatens to go to the police – and then what?'

'Well, he'll probably talk to her, try to wriggle out of it. Of course, I'll have walked in by then. I do my shock-horror act, and the vicar's stumped. There's the poor girl – who'll be in floods of tears – two witnesses . . .'

'Yes, I like it. The more I hear, the more I like it. What if he's not there?'

'He will be. He's expecting the girl at three o'clock.'

I couldn't see that anything would go wrong. Juliette had planned it well, perhaps too well. If the priest became suspicious . . . I had to try to think positively. After all, this was the first time that the end of the evil man's reign had even remotely been a possibility. Perhaps things were changing for the better? I reflected as Juliette went down to the kitchen to make some coffee. Not only was the vicar's reign of abuse about to end, but I had a brand new Jag. I even had the box of photographs.

Wondering whether to park somewhere close to the church that afternoon, I thought about wearing some sort of disguise. No one except Robin and Juliette knew about my car . . . My thinking was becoming muddled. The danger, excitement, anticipation . . . Realizing that I had to try and relax, I looked at Juliette's naked thighs as she brought two cups of coffee into my room. Perhaps an hour of lesbian sex would relax me but I wasn't sure. Sperm was rather like a calming drug, I reflected. Now that I had a car, I could suck young boys' fresh cocks into my mouth in comfort. The woods were ideal in the summer, but in midwinter . . .

'I'll ring you from the village once it's over,' Juliette said. 'Once the vicar has been caught red-cocked, I'll let you know.'

'Yes, all right,' I murmured pensively, distracted by images of a young cock fucking my wet mouth.

'All you have to do is stay here and wait. You won't go into the village, will you?'

'No, no. I'll sit here by the phone.'

'Right. I'm going to my room to get ready. What are you going to do now?'

'I'll go for a drive. Don't worry, I'm not going anywhere near the village. I think I'll go up to Cranmead Hill and take a walk.'

'OK, I'll talk to you later.'

Leaving my coffee on the bedside table, I grabbed my car keys and left the house. I felt a great sense of freedom driving my new car. It was like slipping into another word, a world where there were no problems, a world far removed from the stark reality of the vicar. Recalling the evil man's accomplice, the young man in the sex chamber, I wondered what he'd do once the game was over. Perhaps he was married. It would be interesting to find out where he lived, I mused, putting my foot down once I was on the open road.

Cranmead Hill held fond memories for me. Parking the car, I recalled the picnics I'd enjoyed there with my parents, running through the bracken with my father laughing as he chased me. But that was long ago. My father became more strict as I grew, my mother seemed to grow sadder and I . . . I became involved with the vicar. Taking the box of photographs from the back seat, I looked through them. The vicar's knob pumping sperm over my face, the white liquid hanging in a long strand from the tip of my pink tongue . . . I needed a cock to suck. A purple knob throbbing in orgasm, pumping spunk into my thirsty mouth . . . I had to find myself a young lad.

Cranmead Boys' School was just over the hill, and I
wondered whether to go searching for fresh cock there.
Locking my car, I walked to the brow of the hill and
gazed at the old Victorian building. There was a rugby
match going on, the sports master blowing his whistle,
shouting at the boys as they raced after the ball in their
shorts. Deciding to have some fun, I followed a narrow
path to the edge of the playing field and crouched behind
a bush.

'Go on, Davis!' the master yelled as the ball came my
way. Another boy dived onto the ground and grabbed the
ball as Davis approached. The game moved on, the boys
racing to the far end of the field, leaving Davis looking
somewhat bewildered. Getting his breath back, he began
to walk away. Desperate for the feel of his young cock in
my mouth, the taste of his spunk bathing my tongue, I
couldn't allow him to leave. The master was right down
the far end of the field, supervising what appeared to be a
fight and giving me the opportunity to borrow one of the
lads.

'Davis,' I called softly. Turning, he gazed at the
bushes. 'Davis, come over here.'

'What?' he murmured, frowning as he walked around
the bushes and stared open-mouthed at me. 'God . . .
who are you?'

'I'm an attractive teenage girl,' I giggled.

'I can see that. What are you doing here? If you're
caught . . .'

'No one ever catches me. Why don't you pull your
shorts down?' I grinned, kneeling in front of him. 'Show
me your lovely cock.'

'But . . .'

'We haven't got much time. Pull your shorts down and

I'll suck your cock, lick your purple knob and swallow your spunk.'

Without hesitation, Davis tugged his shorts down, exposing the flaccid shaft of his beautiful penis snaking over his small balls. I immediately moved in, fully retracting his foreskin and sucking his purple plum into my wet mouth. He looked down at me, gazing at the fleshy shaft of his cock stiffening as I ran my tongue over the salty globe of his young cock. He was stunned, obviously unable to believe what was happening as he stroked my long blonde hair. Fondling his tight balls, I took his knob to the back of my throat, my full lips encompassing the root of his penis, which had become engorged and rock-hard with incredible speed.

Bobbing my head back and forth, I breathed heavily through my nose as Davis began to tremble and gasp. His dark pubic curls tickling my nose as he mouth-fucked me, I doubted that he'd ever had a girl suck his cock and swallow his sperm. Breathing in his male scent, I imagined him wanking. He probably looked through dirty mags at pictures of girls' juice-streaming cunts. He probably jerked off in his bed at night, his sperm flooding across his stomach as he imagined fucking a pretty girl's wet mouth. His fantasy was about to become reality.

Tonguing Davis's swollen glans, my succulent lips rolling along the unblemished rod of his young cock, I was desperate for his spunk. I'd known since I was very young that the boys' school was there. My father would walk with me along the narrow path and point out the Victorian building. It was a posh school, he'd said. A school especially for the rich lads. In my tender years, I'd not understood why parents paid huge amounts of

money to send their children to school. My father had
wanted me to go to a posh school. He'd said that I'd
become a refined young lady if I went to a decent school.
In reality, I'd become a dirty little slut.

'I'm coming,' the boy gasped, clutching my head and
rocking his hips. His sperm flooding my mouth as I
snaked my tongue over his throbbing sex-globe, I swallowed the fresh fruits of his young balls, gobbling and
slurping at his twitching cock-head as he let out long low
moans of male pleasure. Would he tell his friends? I
wondered, my mouth overflowing, his orgasmic liquid
dribbling down my chin. They wouldn't believe his
fantastic tale, I was sure as I sucked the cream out of
his knob, drinking from his male fountainhead. They'd
call him a liar, probably rough him up for trying to make
out that he was a man at last.

'Davis!' the sports master yelled at the top of his voice
as the boys' shouts grew louder. 'What the hell are you
doing there, boy?'

'Coming, sir,' the lad replied as I sucked the last drops
of his spunk from his beautiful cock. 'I have to go,' he
said, looking down at my spermed lips as I moved my
head back and slipped his sex-globe out of my spunk-
flooded mouth.

'I enjoyed that,' I whispered huskily.

'So did I,' he murmured, tugging his shorts up.
'Where are you from?'

'Heaven,' I smiled. 'Why don't you send one of your
friends along to see me?'

'Yes, OK,' he said as the sports master yelled again.
'Don't go away.'

'Oh, I won't.'

Licking my salty lips, I peered over the top of the bush

and watched young Davis running at top speed across the field. He talked excitedly to one lad, and then another, and I wondered whether I'd get to suck the entire team to orgasm. One fresh cock after another filling my thirsty mouth with sperm . . . Sheer sexual bliss. Noticing one of the lads nearing the bushes, repeatedly turning his head and keeping his eye on the master, I felt my clitoris stir, my juices of lust seeping between the hairless lips of my young pussy. Should I allow him to fuck my hot cunt or my wet mouth? I pondered as he hovered by the bushes. Calling him, I yanked his shorts down as soon as he rounded the bush and stood in front of me.

'God,' he breathed, obviously stunned to discover that Davis hadn't been lying. Licking his tight scrotum as his penis stood to attention, his purple globe rubbing against my forehead, I opened my mouth wide and sucked his ball-sac into my hot mouth. He looked down at me, total disbelief evident in his expression as I took his foreskin between my finger and thumb and wanked him. I could feel his sperm eggs as I snaked my tongue over his full sac, sucking gently as I increased my wanking rhythm. His foreskin rolling back and forth over the plum of his young organ, his spunk-slit appearing and disappearing, I wanked him faster and sucked harder on his heaving balls. Again, I realized that we had very little time. He had to get back to the rugby match before the sports master missed him and began yelling. But I just *had* to suck the creamy sperm from his knob-eye, so I slipped his balls out of my mouth and pulled his cock shaft down.

Engulfing the lad's swollen knob in my wet mouth, I tongued his slit and sucked hard on his silky-smooth sex-globe. He let out a rush of breath, his knees bending as I worked my tongue expertly around the rim of his solid glans. He tasted heavenly, salty, tangy . . . Wondering how many boys were in the rugby team, I decided to bring him off quickly. I wanted every boy in the team to cock-fuck my pretty mouth and sperm over my snaking tongue. I'd set my goal, and was determined to win. Before the game was over, I'd have swallowed spunk from every boy's glans. Wondering why I'd not been to the playing field before, I kneaded the boy's full balls as he shuddered violently. I'd obviously been missing out on a constant supply of young cock.

The lad's creamy sperm jetted to the back of my throat, filling my cheeks, and he let out stifled whimpers of sexual satisfaction as I drank from his twitching cock. This was doing me good, I reflected, moving my head back and forth to meet his penile thrusts, mouth-fucking myself with his beautiful sex organ. Juliette's plan, the vicar, Carter . . . My mind was calming, relaxing as I sucked out the young lad's spunk and drained his tight balls. I had no idea when the rugby match would end, but I felt I could quite easily spend an hour or more sucking off each boy in turn. This was far better than sitting in my room waiting for news of the vicar's downfall.

'Blimey,' my young pupil breathed as I slipped his deflating cock out of my mouth and looked up at him. 'That was—'

'You'd better go,' I whispered, wiping sperm from my mouth with the back of my hand.

'Yes, I suppose I had.'

'Did you like fucking my mouth?'

'Like it? It was fantastic. Do you want me to send someone else to see you? Do you want another boy to . . . to fuck your mouth?'

'Oh, yes,' I breathed, grinning as he tugged his shorts

up. 'I want all the boys to fuck my pretty mouth and spunk over my tongue. Have you ever been sucked off before?'

'No, no – never.'

'Ever seen a girl's cunt before?'

'No . . . well, only in pictures.'

'The next time I'm here, I'll let you push your sweet cock into my hot and very wet cunt and fuck me senseless.'

'When? When will you be here again?'

'Soon. OK, when does the match end?'

'We've only just started.'

'Good. OK, send me another boy. I need another hard cock pumping fresh sperm down my throat.'

Dashing across the field, he bounded up to a blond lad and waved his hands about excitedly. They were enjoying my intimate attention as much as I was, I mused as the blond looked towards the bushes and frowned. If the sports master realized what was going on . . . I could always suck the spunk out of *his* purple knob, I thought in my rising wickedness. Watching the blond lad walk towards the bushes while his mates raced down to the far end of the field, I got on all fours and tugged my panties down. My skirt up over my back, my knees apart, my naked buttocks projected, I decided to have the boy fuck my pussy. I'd suck and lick his cock clean after he'd fucked me and filled my tight sex-sheath with his cream. Once I'd stripped him of his virginity, felt his throbbing knob sperming deep inside my hot cunt, I'd take him into my spunk-thirsty mouth and . . .

'Bloody hell,' he gasped as he rounded the bush. 'Rogers *wasn't* lying.'

'Of course he wasn't,' I giggled, turning my head and gazing at him. 'What did he say to you?'

'He said that there was a pretty girl in the bushes who had sucked his dick.'

'He was telling the truth. And when you go back onto the field, you can tell your friends that there was a pretty girl in the bushes and you fucked her tight cunt. Now, kneel behind me and fuck me hard,' I breathed, reaching behind my back and yanking the hairless lips of my vagina wide apart. 'Hurry up before you're missed. Fuck me really hard.'

'Who are you?' he asked, kneeling behind me and yanking his shorts down.

'A girl in desperate need of a good cunt-fucking,' I replied in my crudity.

As he stabbed between the wet lips of my cunt with his swollen knob, trying to find my cuntal opening, I listened to the shouts coming from the field as one of the teams scored. Suddenly, it was the blond who scored, his bulbous knob driving deep into the wet sheath of my aching vaginal duct, his young balls pressing against my naked mons, his pubes caressing the sensitive flesh within my gaping valley of desire. Wasting no time, he partially withdrew and then rammed deep into me again, his rock-hard cock-shaft gliding in and out of my spasming pussy, the juices of my desire squelching, pouring in torrents down my inner thighs.

'Rogers was right. You're a dirty girl,' he breathed, repeatedly ramming his ballooning knob deep into the contracting duct of my tightening pussy. My young body rocking with the illicit fucking, I listened to the lad's lower stomach slapping against my rounded buttocks. His small balls swinging, I reached beneath my stomach and grabbed his full sac, kneading his sperm eggs as he neared his orgasm. My clitoris solid with expectation, I swivelled my hips, pressing my swollen pleasure spot hard against his cunny-wet shaft as he fucked me hard and fast in his sexual frenzy.

His spunk soon flowed into my cunt, jetting from his knob, bathing my cervix as he fucked me like a dog. Holding my hips, he repeatedly yanked my bottom hard against his firm lower belly, his knob battering my spunked cervix as his gasps of gratification filled my ears. My own orgasm erupting within the solid nub of my clitoris, I felt the cocktail blend of my juices and his sperm spraying from my bloated sex hole and splattering the naked flesh of my inner thighs. I thought that the boy's balls would never empty as he continued to fuck me, pumping his male sex-liquid deep into the tight sheath of my teenage cunt as his virginity fell away. My clitoris pulsating, sending shock waves of crude sex deep into my quivering womb, I pressed my face against the cold grass as the boy took his pleasure. Again and again he drove his swollen glans deep into the spasming duct of my cunt, fucking me, spunking me.

'Where the hell's Johnson got to?' the sports master yelled. Little did he know that young Johnson was scoring his own goal and finding manhood behind the bushes with a whore-slut. His balls finally drained, Johnson slipped his drenched cock out of my sperm-bubbling pussy and yanked his shorts up. Rolling onto my back, I lay with my limbs spread wide, the gaping valley of my shaved pussy bared before the lad's wide eyes. The blond boy stared at my blatantly displayed inner flesh as the master yelled out his name again. It was as if Johnson was stunned, his gaze transfixed on the sperm-oozing open hole of my cunt. His face flushed, his mouth hanging open, he stammered something as the master again called out.

'You'd better go,' I whispered.

'Yes, yes, I will.'

'Have you not seen a girl's cunt before?'

'Er . . . no.'

'I'll meet you here again some time. You can lick my cunt, tongue-fuck my wet cunt and bring me off.'

'God, yes.'

'*Johnson*! Where the hell *are* you, boy?'

'And I might allow you to push your cock into my mouth and spunk down my throat.'

Grinning as the lad leaped to his feet and ran off, I wondered whether he'd send another fresh young cock to fuck me. The taste of sperm lingering on my tongue, male cream oozing from the inflamed sheath of my teenage cunt, I slipped my panties off and massaged the solid nubble of my clitoris as I awaited the next lucky lad's arrival. Come the summer months, the boys would be playing cricket, I mused, my clitoris responding to my fingertip caress. I should have moved several miles away from the village, I ruminated, imagining living far away from the evil vicar but close to a posh boys' school. Perhaps I should have got a job at a boys' school. My ripening clitoris sending delightful ripples of sex through my trembling womb, I stilled my massaging fingertip when I heard voices nearing the bushes.

'Welcome to heaven,' I grinned as two boys rounded the bush and stared in disbelief at the yawning valley of my vagina, the sperm dribbling from the open hole of my sex duct. 'So, who's going to fuck me first?'

'I will,' the bigger of the two lads said, grinning wolfishly and eagerly ripping his shorts down.

Settling between my spread thighs, he grabbed the shaft of his huge cock and drove his purple globe deep into my sex-dripping cunt. I was in my heaven, I thought happily as the boy's friend stared at the crude fucking. My sperm-saturated body rocking with the vaginal pistoning, I tossed my head back and listened to the squishing sounds of sex as the bigger lad fucked me senseless. My clitoris exploding in orgasm again, I tossed my head from side to side, my eyes rolling, my young body shaking violently as he quickly reached his climax and filled me with spunk.

He was good, I mused, my clitoris throbbing, pulsating wildly as he continued to shaft my teenage pussy with his young organ. He'd come too quickly for my liking, but he was still solid, his beautiful shaft driving in and out of my sperm-drenched cunt as his friend awaited his turn. I thought that, with the stamina of youth, the boy was going to come again as he repeatedly cock-fucked me, battering my young cervix with his wet knob. Sadly, his penis deflated and he slid his member out of my inflamed vagina with a loud sucking sound.

No sooner had the boy moved aside than his friend was between my legs, driving his granite-hard penis deep into the sperm-brimming sheath of my burning cunt. Again, I rocked with the vaginal fucking, my breasts bouncing, my stomach rising and falling as his bulbous knob pummelled my spunk-drenched cervix. Resting his weight on his arms, the new boy increased his fucking rhythm, shafting my young body as hard as he could with his beautiful penis, stretching open the tight sheath of my fiery cunt. I could feel his sperm gushing into me as he gasped and shuddered, the male cream cascading from my gaping sex-hole and coursing down between the naked globes of my firm buttocks. His swinging balls slapping my wet arse-cheeks, his knob battering my sperm-flooded cervix, he finally collapsed on top of me, breathing heavily in the aftermath of his illicit fucking.

His friend ran off as the smaller lad slipped his spent cock out of my cream-filled vagina and kneeled between my trembling thighs. He wasn't at all bad-looking, I thought. His dark hair flopping over his suntanned face, his muscles rippling, he was also a good fuck. Rolling onto his back, he lay there and rested. He was in no fit state to play any more rugby, I knew as I gazed at his sex-juiced cock snaking over his hairy balls. Wondering how many more fresh cocks I'd enjoy before the match was over, I stared in horror as the sports master appeared as if from nowhere.

'Watkins!' he yelled, his eyes darting between the lad's juiced cock and my sperm-oozing sex-hole. 'What the bloody hell do you think you're—'

'Oh, er . . .' the boy stammered, leaping to his feet and hauling his shorts back up.

'Go to my study and wait there. Never have I—'

'Yes . . . yes, sir,' the lad jabbered before running off.

'And as for you . . . Who are you?'

'A girl from heaven,' I giggled, parting my thighs wider. 'I've been giving the boys a little sex education.'

'Sex . . . How old are you?' he asked, eyeing the hairless lips of my vulva.

'Old enough to get myself fucked.'

'This is private property,' he growled. 'You shouldn't . . .'

'*This* isn't private property,' I said huskily, parting the fleshy lips of my spunked pussy. 'It's all yours, if you want it.'

'I . . . Look . . . You can't just turn up here and—'

'Fuck me,' I breathed, fingering my burning sex duct. 'Fuck my tight little cunt and spunk up me.'

He was every bit as male as his pupils, I thought as he glanced at the playing field and then slipped his shorts down. Kneeling between my parted thighs, he grabbed his huge cock by the root and rammed his solid knob into me. My stomach rising, my vaginal canal bloating, I gasped as he completely impaled me on his beautiful weapon. That was obviously the end of the rugby-team cock-sucking, I mused as the sports master began his fucking motions. But I'd be back. Come the summer months . . .

'Christ,' the man gasped, his knob hammering my cervix. 'You're a tight bitch.' I could hear the boys shouting as their master's swinging balls battered the firm cheeks of my bottom. Jeering, laughing and joking, the lads obviously knew what was going on behind the bushes. But it was only fair that their master too should enjoy the wet sheath of my little pussy, I reflected. It was only fair that the filthy slut behind the bushes should offer her dirty little cunt to everyone.

My inflamed vagina flooding with sperm, I watched the man's face grimacing as he fucked me and drained his balls. He'd obviously been in desperate need of a young girl's pussy, I reflected as his solid shaft glided in and out of my tightening cuntal sheath. Wondering whether he'd like to bend me over a desk and cane the firm globes of my pert bottom, I thought about entering the school one day. I could go to the headmaster's study and show him my little pink pussy. The headmaster would love me to suck him off, I was sure. All men were the same, I reflected. They all wanted me: my naked body, my tight cunt and firm tits. And I had power over all men, I knew as the sports master grunted and gasped, making his last thrusts while a roar rose from the playing field.

'I don't want to see you here again,' the man breathed, withdrawing his cock as the boys approached.

'Don't you?' I asked impishly, licking my full lips. 'I would have thought that you'd want to see me here every day!'

'Well . . . not when there's a match on,' he said, pulling his shorts up.

'What's the score, sir?' someone called.

'It's a shame you didn't last a little longer,' I sighed. 'I was just beginning to enjoy your lovely cock.'

'Right, you lot!' the sports master bellowed, leaping to his feet. Looking down at me, he smiled. 'I've changed my mind. I'll see you again.'

'Yes, you will.'

'OK, you lazy, unfit layabouts. Let's get this match going!'

Slipping my panties back on, concealing the sperm-oozing crack of my fiery pink cunt, I made my way back to my car and started the engine. I was freezing cold, my buttocks icy, my wet pussy chilled. The heater on full, I listened to the radio for a while, basking in the warmth as I ran my tongue around my salty mouth. I'd enjoyed my trip to Cranmead School. Wondering how the match was going, I was sure that the sports master wouldn't admonish the boys. After all, he was as bad as they were. Perhaps he was better? With a never-ending supply of hard cocks and fresh sperm, the school playing field was going to become one of my regular haunts. And it was far away from the vicar and his evil ways.

Checking the time, I wondered whether I should drive

into the village. Only one hour to go, I thought as sperm filled my wet panties. I'd told Juliette that I'd wait in my room by the phone, but intrigue was getting the better of me. No one except Robin and Juliette knew my car, so . . . One mistake, and I could ruin the plan. Perhaps I should return to the playing field and play with some more cocks? Glancing at the box of photographs on the back seat, I wasn't sure what to do.

8

I'd parked my new Jag outside the shop just down the lane from the church and had been twiddling my thumbs for almost an hour. Nothing had happened. No vicar, no Juliette . . . I was beginning to wish that I'd stayed at the playing field and enjoyed gobbling some more cocks. I could still taste sperm, feel the male cream oozing from my inflamed vagina and filling my wet panties. I was becoming obsessed with cocks and sperm. *Becoming*? I had to stop thinking about sex all the time.

I'd decided to wait another five minutes before going home when I saw the vicar enter the church. 'Where the hell's the girl?' I murmured, looking up and down the road. To my relief, a young girl emerged from behind the church and slipped in through the main doors. *So far, so good*, I thought, imagining her lifting her short skirt and displaying her tight panties to the vicar. Noticing a middle-aged woman hovering outside the door, I wondered where Juliette had got to. Then I glimpsed her creeping around the side of the church. This was going to work, I was sure.

My smile turning to a frown as a man headed for the church gates, I felt my stomach sink. 'Oh, no,' I breathed, realizing that it was Carter. Leaping out of my car, I called out to him.

'Crystal? I thought you'd gone to London,' he said, crossing the road.

'A change of plan,' I smiled, moving away from my car. 'Where are you off to?'

'The church. I thought I might have a snoop round if the vicar's not there.'

'I've just seen him,' I said, keeping one eye on the middle-aged woman. 'He went into the church a couple of minutes ago.'

'I think I'll go in anyway. I might be able to get him talking and learn something.'

'No, I wouldn't. He . . . he might become suspicious.'

'Perhaps you're right. So, what are you up to?'

'Now that my London trip has been postponed . . .'

'You're still going, then?'

'Oh, yes. I'm meeting the man tomorrow.'

'Are you on the phone yet?'

'No, not yet.'

'It's a bit awkward, not being able to contact you. If there's a development . . . Look, give me your address and then I'll at least be able to see you.'

'I . . . I think I'll be moving again,' I stammered shakily. 'I'm not sure what's happening with the flat yet. The man who owns it is in Australia and . . . well, it's a long story. My mother said that you'd called.'

'Er . . . yes, that's right. I wondered whether you'd got a phone. She gave me what must have been your old number.'

'She's becoming forgetful,' I laughed, wondering what was happening in the church. 'She knows that I'm not living there any more.'

'Oh, right. Crystal, would you mind if I asked you something personal?'

'No, of course not.'

'You have . . . I should say, you *had* a bit of a name for yourself at school.'

'Did I?'

'You were pretty friendly with some of the boys.'

'I always got on well with the boys. Far better than with the girls, for some reason.'

'No, I mean . . . Apparently, you were quite, er, *intimate* with some of them.'

'Intimate?' I murmured. 'I had the odd kiss, I suppose. But I was young.'

'Are you still . . . What I'm trying to say is . . .'

'What have you heard about me?'

'Just one or two things about you meeting boys in the woods. I overheard a couple of boys talking.'

'When was this?'

'When you were at the school. I was going to say something to you at the time but . . . Well, I wasn't sure what to say.'

'So what are you trying to say now?'

'I live alone, as you know. I really don't know how to put this. Look, we can't talk here. Would you like to come to my place for a coffee?'

'Now?'

'Yes. If you're not doing anything?'

'Well, I . . . I suppose so. Is it important? What you want to ask me, I mean.'

'It is to me. After seeing the photographs of you . . . Walk to my cottage with me.'

I'd locked my car and it was parked safely, so I didn't mind leaving it there for a while. I knew what Carter was after, and decided to play along with him up to a point. I'd tease him, make out that I had no idea what he was talking about. I might even learn something, I reflected as we walked to his cottage. If he *was* in with the vicar, he might let something slip. He probably thought that, as I was well known for cock-sucking in the woods, I might allow him to cock-fuck my mouth. The notion began to excite me as we reached his cottage. My old English teacher fucking my mouth, pumping sperm over my tongue . . .

'I've heard quite a few things about you, Crystal,' he said, walking into the kitchen and filling the kettle.

'Nothing too bad, I hope.'

'The things you did with the boys . . . Is it true?'

'What things?'

'You had sex in the woods with the boys, didn't you?'

'We played about,' I said softly, feigning embarrassment as he poured the coffee. 'We were young – learning, discovering.'

'And now that you're older?'

'I don't see the boys any more.'

'No, I mean . . . Shall we sit in the lounge?'

'All right.'

Following Carter through the hall, I felt my stomach somersault. I was enjoying the game, and decided to tease him as I sat on the sofa. Passing me my coffee, he sat opposite me and gazed at my young breasts straining my blouse as I slipped my coat off. He wanted to fuck my mouth, I knew as I parted my thighs, deliberately displaying my sperm-soaked panties. Again wondering whether he was in with the vicar, I wondered what was happening back at the church. Had the middle-aged woman burst in and caught the evil man with his cock up the girl's bottom yet? I should have stayed at home and waited for Juliette's phone call, but the prospect of sucking my old English teacher's cock and drinking his spunk had excited me.

Parting my thighs further as I reclined on the sofa, I imagined his lonely penis stiffening, his sperm-laden balls heaving within their hairy sac. He might not have had sex in years. Living alone, he probably resorted to wanking every day, shooting his spunk over his stomach as he thought about the schoolgirls' tight knickers and petite tits. Were all men the same? I wondered, recalling him sitting at the front of the class, his eyes darting beneath the desks in the hope of glimpsing a pair of tight panties. As he adjusted the crotch of his trousers, I knew that he was eager to slip his knob into my mouth. Little did he know that I was equally keen to have him mouth-fuck me. Perhaps he'd become a regular mouth-fuck, I mused as he focused on the wet crotch of my tight panties.

'Now that you're older, do you still enjoy it?' Carter asked.

'Enjoy what?' I asked, feeling sorry for him.

'I heard that you had oral sex with the boys.'

'Who told you that?'

'I overheard things at school, Crystal. Do you have a boyfriend?'

'No, not at the moment.'

'I was wondering whether you'd like to come and visit me now and then.'

'Yes, of course. I like your cottage. The garden will be lovely in the summer.'

'Yes, yes, it will. Crystal, what I'm trying to say is . . . Would you have sex with me?'

'Sex with you?' I gasped.

'I get pretty lonely here.'

'I know, but . . .'

'I've always liked you, Crystal. When you were at school, I often thought . . . Now that you're older . . .'

'Old enough to be loved properly?'

'Well, yes. I heard that you had oral sex with the boys.'

'So you reckon that, because I used to suck the boys' cocks, I'll suck yours?'

'I suppose you think that I'm a dirty old man?'

'No, not at all. It's just that I wasn't expecting you to ask me for sex.'

'What did the vicar make you do?'

'Terrible things,' I sighed, lowering my head. 'I'd rather not talk about that evil man.'

'No, of course not. So it's true about you and the boys?'

'Yes, it is. I'll show you what I did to the boys,' I said softly and smiled. 'Come and stand in front of me.'

Unbuckling Carter's belt as he stood with his crotch level with my face, I yanked his zip down and watched his trousers fall around his ankles. Tugging his shorts down, I gazed longingly at his erect penis. It was huge, the broad shaft standing to attention before my wide eyes, his purple knob glistening, inviting my wet mouth. Running my fingertip up his veined rod, I circled his swollen plum, grinning as I imagined him spunking in my mouth. Finally leaning forward, I kissed his glans, his shaft twitching as he looked down and gasped.

Allowing Carter his pleasure, I engulfed his salty knob in my hot mouth, my full lips closing around his fleshy shaft, my wet tongue snaking over his sperm-slit. He shuddered, breathing heavily in his ecstasy as I sucked and gobbled. Trying to remember how many cocks I'd already sucked that day, I wondered whether I'd ever meet a man whom I wouldn't allow to mouth-fuck me. It seemed that every man I met ended up with his cock fucking my mouth, his spunk jetting down my throat. Taking Carter's beautiful glans deeper into my mouth, I cupped his heavy balls in my hand, kneading his sperm-spheres and sinking my teeth gently into the fleshy shaft of his massive penis. Did it matter how many cocks I'd sucked? The more the better.

'You're good,' Carter breathed as I moved my head back, his salivated knob slipping out of my mouth. 'Very good.'

'You used to look beneath my desk, didn't you?' I asked, grinning at him. 'You wanted to see my tight knickers, didn't you?'

'Yes, I did,' he confessed as I licked his sperm-slit.

'You used to picture my hairless cunny, didn't you?'

'Yes. I always liked you, Crystal. You were my favourite.'

'You liked the idea of my little pink cunt, you mean?'

'Yes, yes. I used to look at your thighs when you were sitting at your desk. Every day, I hoped to catch a glimpse of your knickers. I imagined your little cunny, my tongue licking your crack.'

'You should have asked me to show you my little crack. We could have gone into the stockroom. I'd have shown you, and allowed you to lick me. All you had to do was ask.'

'I wish I'd known that.'

'I would have pulled my knickers down and let you lick the cream out of my little slit.'

'God, I think I'm coming already.'

Taking Carter's saliva-wet knob between my lips again, I tongued his sperm-slit, desperate for his spunk to gush as I imagined him licking my hairless pussy in the stockroom. I should have been more adventurous when I was at school, I reflected. There again, I was rather young to be sucking the boys off, let alone swallowing my English teacher's sperm. The vicar was another matter, of course. As I sucked and mouthed on this latest trembling man's cock, I decided to call on him again and allow him to spunk down my throat, just as he was going to do any minute now. I might even charge him for the pleasure next time, I mused as he gasped. His glans swelling, his penile shaft twitching, I knew that he was about to shoot his spunk and drain his balls.

Carter's sperm flooding my mouth, I swallowed hard, drinking from his throbbing glans as he let out grunts of pure sexual pleasure. I'd never known a man come so much. His spunk filling my cheeks, streaming down my chin, he clutched my head and mouth-fucked me for all he was worth. On and on his sperm flowed, pouring from him in torrents, jetting down my throat as I did my best to swallow the creamy fruits of his orgasm. Perhaps he didn't wank after all, I reflected. He might not have drained his huge balls in years.

'Suck really hard,' Carter ordered me, stilling his throbbing knob between my spermed lips. Sucking as hard as I could, I listened to his moans of sexual ecstasy resounding around the room as his spunk gushed again and filled my cheeks. In my wickedness, I wondered how many cocks I could suck to orgasm in one day. Two rugby teams would be a good start, I mused, wondering again how many players made up a team. One thing that fascinated me about cocks was their diversity. Long, short, thin, fat, circumcised . . . God only knew how many cocks I'd sucked during my sweet short life. And

God only knew how many more I'd gobble before my life was over.

'That was amazing,' Carter breathed as I slipped his spent penis out of my spermed mouth. 'I do wish we'd got to know each other a little better when you were still at school.'

'Really?' I grinned, licking my spunk-glossed lips as he pulled his trousers up and buckled his belt. 'You'd have pushed your cock into my mouth and spermed down my throat?'

'That's what the boys were doing to you, so why not?'

'Why not, indeed? So, after all this time, you finally got what you wanted. You got your cock into my mouth.'

'Yes, I did,' he said and grinned. 'And it was every bit as good as I'd imagined it would be.'

'Mr Carter, I need to know something.'

'Please, call me Barry.'

'OK, Barry. Are you in with the vicar?'

'In with him?' he echoed, frowning darkly. 'How do you mean?'

'Are you involved?'

'God, no. Involved in sexually abusing young girls? Never.'

'You'd have quite happily fucked my mouth in the stockroom, wouldn't you?'

'Well, yes, but . . . That's different.'

'Is it?'

'Of course it is. I would never have forced you or taken pornographic photographs of your naked body. Talking of which, who the hell stole them?'

'I don't know,' I sighed, wondering whether to trust him. 'OK, I took them,' I confessed.

'*You*?'

'I took them because I didn't know whether or not I could trust you. Also, the phone number you rang . . . It *was* mine. I answered and made out that Crystal didn't live there.'

'I wish . . . I wish you'd told me before,' Carter complained. 'There I was thinking that someone had walked into my cottage and . . . I suppose I can understand why you didn't trust me. Did you leave the front door open?'

'Yes. I hid the box beneath a bush and left the door open so that you'd think someone had come in. OK, what did Jenny tell you about the vicar?'

'She came to me and said that the vicar had been abusing her.'

'Why did she approach *you*?'

'I was her teacher. I suppose she looked up to me. This man you're meeting in London . . .'

'I'll tell you tomorrow, after I've talked to him,' I said, still not completely sure that I could trust Carter. 'Well, I'd better be going.'

'Oh, er . . . I'll ring you, shall I?'

'All right. When I get back from London tomorrow, I'll call in and see you.'

'That would be nice, Crystal.'

Seeing me to the door, his face beaming, Carter waved goodbye. I reckoned that I must have made his day by allowing him to mouth-fuck me. But could I trust him? He now knew where I lived, he had my phone number . . . If he *was* in with the vicar, I'd probably soon find out. Making my way back to the village, I noticed that all was quiet outside the church. *The explosion must be over*, I mused as I climbed into my car, wondering what had happened. I was tempted to go into the church and look for the vicar, but thought better of it.

Arriving home, I slipped my coat off and went up to Juliette's room. There was no sign of her, or of Robin. Back in my room, I grabbed the phone and punched in the dialback number. No one had called. I couldn't stand waiting, pacing the floor waiting for the phone to ring or the front door to open. I took a shower, prepared the vegetables for the evening meal, and then sat on my bed, staring at the phone. Juliette finally rang at six o'clock.

'Where are you?' I asked irritably.

'In the pub,' she replied. 'We're celebrating the vicar's downfall.'

'Why the hell didn't you ring me earlier?'

'I couldn't find your number. I've only just found it scribbled on a piece of paper in my—'

'Don't worry about that. What happened at the church?'

'God, it's a long story. Come down to the pub and I'll tell you about it. We're in the Duck's Arse.'

'The Duck's Arse? Don't you mean the Duck's Egg?'

'That's the one.'

'OK, I'll see you soon. Get me a vodka and lime.'

'Will do.'

Replacing the receiver, I wondered who Juliette was with. I grabbed my coat and left the house. Perhaps Robin was with her, I thought, walking down the street to the local pub. At least I hadn't wasted the afternoon sitting in my room waiting for her to call. In fact, I'd had a most interesting afternoon, not only at the playing field but at Barry's cottage too. Walking into the dimly lit pub, I noticed Juliette sitting at a table and made my way over to her.

'There's your drink,' she said, looking up and smiling at me as I sat opposite her.

'Thanks. I thought you were with someone?'

'I was with the woman who played the role of the distraught mother. Unfortunately, she had to go.'

'OK, so what happened? I want to know everything, every detail.'

'My young friend went into the church and did her bit. She ended up over the altar with the vicar's cock up her pussy.'

'Not up her bum?'

'No. Anyway, the *mother* walked into the church and had a fit. The vicar was caught red-handed. I made my entrance just in time to see the vicar pulling his cassock down.'

'And?'

'The mother said that she was going to the police. I agreed with her, the girl was sobbing . . . The vicar came out with all sorts of lies and excuses but quickly realized that he wasn't going to get away with it.'

'Is he leaving the village?'

'The woman took the girl outside, saying that she was going to calm her down, leaving me with the vicar. I told him that the woman wouldn't hesitate to go to the police, and that I'd have to come forward as a witness since I'd seen the sordid episode. He didn't know what to do or say, apart from panic. Anyway, I said that I'd talk to the woman once she'd made sure that her daughter was all right and she'd composed herself. He offered to give her money if she didn't go to the police, so I said that, at the very least, she'd want to see him leave the church and the village.'

'What did he say to that?'

'He said that he wouldn't be able to get a job and he had nowhere to go. I said that I knew the woman well and she was a terrible gossip. I made it clear that word would get round the village within a few hours. The upshot of it is that he's leaving tomorrow morning.'

'That's great,' I said and beamed, knocking back my vodka. 'It seems too good to be true. What if he doesn't leave?'

'I don't know. Obviously, the girl wouldn't want to cry rape – then she'd have to go to court. The woman would have to say that she wasn't the girl's mother, but she did witness the—'

'The police would realize that the vicar had been set up,' I interrupted her.

'Exactly. All we can hope for is that the vicar won't risk hanging around. He believes that word is going to get round so, police involvement or not, he knows he can't stay in the village.'

I still wasn't convinced that the vicar was really going to leave the village. He might dismiss the gossip, telling anyone who questioned him that he had no idea what they were talking about. Would he take that risk? I really didn't know what to think as I went to the bar and bought two more vodkas. Would the vicar realize that he'd been set up? And, if so, would he believe that I'd been involved? There were too many ifs and buts, I knew as I went back to the table and passed Juliette her drink.

'Don't worry,' she said, smiling as she noticed my pained expression. 'He'll leave tomorrow, you'll see.'

'I hope so,' I sighed. 'If he doesn't, then *I* will.'

'It won't come to that. By the way, have you seen Robin recently?'

'No, I haven't. God knows what he gets up to. I've prepared the evening meal so I hope he turns up. What are you going to do about work? Are you looking for a job?'

'I have enough money to get by on for a few weeks. But I'll have to do something eventually. The thing is, a normal job takes up so much time so for little money. There must be something I can do that pays really well and doesn't take up all my time.'

'There is,' I giggled.

'No, Crystal, I'm *not* going to do that. It's all right for you. You're Robin's housekeeper, which basically means that you cook the meals and piss about.'

'There's more to it than that, Juliette. There's the shopping and . . .'

'You're never in the house,' she laughed. 'You're always out somewhere or other.'

'Yes, but . . . Anyway. Robin seems happy. Talking of meals, I'd better get back before Robin does. He'll probably come in starving and complain if there's nothing to eat.'

'Oh, I was hoping you'd stay here with me. We could spend the evening together, drinking vodka and relaxing.'

'I'd like to, Juliette. The thing is . . .'

'I'll bet Robin won't be back for ages. Just say that you didn't know what time he'd be in so you thought it best not to cook. Say that you went out looking for him.'

'I'm not his keeper.'

'Maybe not, but there's no point cooking his dinner if he's not there. I'll get you another drink.'

As she went to the bar, I decided to stay. She was right, Robin might not be back until late – at at all. Perhaps he had a secret woman somewhere, I mused. No, not Robin. The vodka already going to my head, I began to feel a little more relaxed as I looked around the pub. There were only a handful of people at the bar, and I wondered whether it would get more busy during the evening. I might even meet an attractive man, I reflected. There again, any man with a solid cock and huge balls brimming with sperm was attractive to me.

Noticing Juliette talking to the barman, I wondered whether she knew him. They were both laughing as if they'd known each other for years. Knowing her, she'd never seen him before and had decided to lure him into her bed. So much for her lesbianism, I reflected. Glancing at the door as it swung open, I gasped. Dressed in jeans and a jumper, the vicar walked up to the bar. Noticing Juliette, he kept well away from her, but if he discovered that she was with me . . .

Mouthing to her as she turned and faced me, I nodded in the direction of the vicar. Fortunately, she saw him and realized what I was trying to tell her. My heart racing, my hands trembling, I went to the bar, grabbed my drink from Juliette and went back to my seat. I should have left the pub, but I knew that the evil man would join me once he saw me and I wanted to hear what he had to say. Within a couple of minutes, he'd looked around the bar and noticed me. I'd never felt so nervous, but I didn't know why. After all, he could hardly do anything to me in the pub.

'Mind if I join you?' the priest asked, placing his pint on the table.

'If you have to,' I replied coldly.

'I might be going away,' he said, licking his lips as he gazed at my pretty mouth.

'That would be a dream come true for me,' I replied, forcing a smile.

'It'll only be for a week or two, just until I resolve a little problem that's cropped up.'

'Oh, what's that?'

'Just a minor glitch. In fact, you might know something about it.'

'I doubt it,' I breathed, fear welling from the pit of my stomach. He couldn't have known about my involvement, could he?

'Do you know a girl called Alison?'

'No, I don't. Why?'

'Her mother, perhaps? Her name's Mary.'

'I have no idea who you're talking about.'

'Haven't you? I had a slight problem in the church earlier today. That girl at the bar was involved,' he said, glancing at Juliette. 'Do you know her?'

'I've never seen her before. Look, I really don't know what you're talking about. What was this problem you had?'

'I believe that I was set up.'

'Set up? You're not making any sense.'

'A young girl came to the church to see me. Her name was Alison and she wanted to look around the church and make notes for some school project or other.'

'So?'

'I don't think there's any need for me to tell you what happened because I believe that you already know the story.'

'What story? Look, I have to be going. You're not making any sense at all.'

'Don't leave, Crystal – not yet. This girl, Alison, came into the church and pulled her knickers down.'

'What?'

'She then leaned over the altar, pulled her short skirt up over her back and invited me to fuck her arse.'

'Now you've completely lost me,' I laughed.

'Then her mother came into the church.'

'I suppose you're going to tell me that her mother did the same?'

'On the contrary. Her mother came in and . . . Well, as I said, it was a set-up.'

'And you believe that this had something to do with me?'

'I thought you'd moved away?' he said accusingly, staring hard into my eyes. 'But I know for a fact that you're still living at that psychiatrist's house.'

'No, I'm not.'

'I think it's time you started being honest with me, Crystal. You *do* know that girl at the bar. She was at your school.'

'Was she?' I said, frowning as I gazed at Juliette. 'I don't recognize her.'

'I spoke to that psychiatrist you're living with. He said that you'd gone to Australia, and that he had photographs of you. It was pretty obvious that he was lying, especially when he started going on about a balding man from the church asking questions. *He* needs a psychiatrist, if you ask me.'

'Yes, he does have his strange ways. Still, I don't live there any more so it doesn't bother me.'

'You stole a box of photographs from me, Crystal. And, please, don't deny it. I have several more boxes packed with photographs so it's no real loss to me.'

'There you go again,' I snapped, wondering whether he'd been talking to Barry Carter. '*I* stole a box of photographs? What the hell are you going on about now?'

'There's no point in continuing this conversation if you're going to deny everything.'

'There's no point at all.'

'Bear this in mind, Crystal. I have photographs of you in the woods and—'

'And I've been talking to Jenny.'

'Jenny?' he frowned. 'Jenny who?'

'The other girl you've been abusing.'

'I don't know any Jenny.'

'As you said, there's no point in continuing this conversation if you're going to deny everything.'

'I *do* deny it. I don't know anyone called Jenny. Wait there and I'll get you another drink. Vodka, isn't it?'

'And lime.'

I was beginning to have serious doubts about Carter. He'd specifically said that Jenny had confided in him. Perhaps the vicar was playing games and . . . I really didn't know what to think or who to trust. I even began to doubt Juliette as the priest stood next to her at the bar and said something to her. She glanced at me and then frowned at the vicar. He certainly didn't seem too bothered about the incident in the church. Going away for a week or two? Reckoning that he was as unsure about the situation as I was, I decided to raise the stakes.

'I *do* remember that girl at the bar,' I said as he placed the drinks on the table and sat down. 'Juliette something or other. Her father was a policeman.'

'A policeman?' he echoed, frowning at me. 'Are you sure?'

'Yes, in London. I think that's where she lives now. I don't know what she's doing here. Visiting, I suppose. Did you say that she was involved in the church? With what happened earlier, I mean.'

'Yes, yes, she was,' he murmured pensively. 'I thought her father worked—'

'You want to keep on the right side of her. Her dad's pretty high up in the police. Why are you going away? Is it because you got caught abusing yet another young girl?'

'I told you, it was a set-up. By the way, the young man who was in my sex den . . . he can't wait to meet you again. He rather enjoyed your visit.'

'That was my first and my last visit. Your evil reign is over, you do realize that?'

'Far from it, Crystal. As I said, I'm going away for a week or two. But I'll be back.'

'Excuse me,' Juliette said, smiling and standing by the table. 'It's Crystal, isn't it?'

'That's right,' I replied.

'I'm Juliette.'

'I thought I recognized you. This is the local vicar.'

'Yes, we met earlier. Mind if I sit down?'

'I can see the whole picture now,' the vicar said, grinning malevolently. 'You two are in this together. You set me up and—'

'The woman has spoken to the authorities, if you get my meaning?' Juliette murmured, flashing him an accusing look.

'I doubt it,' he said, finishing his drink and standing up. 'I can see the plan now. Do you really believe that that girl will stand up in court and . . . I'll leave you to discuss the set-up.'

As the priest left the pub, I felt sure that the plan had failed. He'd put two and two together and come up with the truth. He knew damned well that the woman wouldn't go to the police. It was a shame that he'd come into the pub when Juliette and I were there. But what would he now? Would he go away for a week or two?

Feeling despondent, I sipped my vodka and thought again about moving far away from the area.

'Don't worry,' Juliette said and smiled reassuringly.

'Don't worry? Juliette, he's sussed us. He knows that we set him up.'

'Does he? He can't be sure, Crystal.'

'When nothing happens after a week or so, he'll be sure.'

'I was talking to the barman.'

'Yes, I saw you chatting him up.'

'I wasn't chatting him up. Mind you, he's not bad-looking.'

'So, what did you say to him?'

'I pointed out the vicar. I started the rumour.'

'Oh?'

'I said that the vicar had been caught in the church screwing a young girl.'

'God. What did the barman say?'

'He was stunned. I'm not sure whether he believed me or not. But, when he hears more rumours . . . That's our mission, Crystal. We have to spread the word.'

'Right,' I said softly – and smiled.

'If the barman tells, say, three people and they each tell three people . . . Nine, twenty-seven, eighty-one . . . That's how rumours spread like wildfire, especially in a village.'

'The barman will probably tell more than three people,' I said, feeling more confident.

'I'm sure he will. And the source of the rumour will quickly be lost. Once someone tells someone who already knows . . . No one will know who started the rumour.'

'Except for the vicar.'

'That won't matter. With a malicious rumour like that

flying around the village, he'll have to leave. Of course, we could always throw a few more lies into the pot. By the time we've finished, the man will have to run.'

Juliette was right: the vicar would have no choice other than to flee the village. Deciding to enjoy the evening, I knocked back my vodka and bought two more. The barman *was* good-looking, I mused as he placed the drinks on the counter. In his early twenties with black hair and dark, deep-set eyes, he'd make a fine bed-partner. Thinking about hauling his cock out and sucking his purple knob, I returned to our table and sat down. Juliette was definitely up for an evening of heavy drinking. Downing her vodka, she giggled as she undid the top two buttons of her blouse.

'She's rather tasty,' she said, nodding towards the door as a teenage girl walked in with a young man.

'You are awful,' I laughed, gazing at the half-moons of Juliette's pert breasts where they showed through the gap in her unbuttoned blouse. 'Put your tits away, for God's sake.'

'Shan't,' she retorted impishly. 'Don't you like my tits?'

'Yes, very much, but I don't think you should get them out in here.'

Watching her stagger to the bar in a state of near-undress, I cringed as a middle-aged man stared at her. We were going to get thrown out at this rate, I was sure as her giggles resounded around the pub. Juliette was good company, I reflected. She was fun, and I wished that I was free of problems so that I too could enjoy life to the full. I'd had fun with the boys at the playing field and had enjoyed teasing and sucking my old English teacher, but

I'd still had the constant nag of the vicar and his threats at the back of my mind. Hopefully, that would change before long.

'Guess what?' Juliette said excitedly as she returned with the drinks. 'We're going to get free drinks all evening.'

'Why? What have you done?' I asked, frowning at her.

'*Me*? I haven't done anything.'

'Come on, tell me.'

'Well, I *did* tell the barman that we'd both suck his cock if he gave us free drinks.'

'Juliette! God, I thought you were a lesbian.'

'I am. To be honest, since breaking up with . . . well, let's just say that I'm playing the field. The female and male fields.'

'I played in the field earlier,' I whispered.

'Oh?'

'The playing field by that posh school. There was a rugby match on and . . . I hid in the bushes and helped the team members.'

'Helped their members? Yes, I'll bet you did. God, you say that *I'm* awful.'

'We'll have to go there together sometime. So, where are we meeting the barman?'

'We're staying on here, after the pub closes.'

'What about Robin?' I sighed. 'I'm supposed to be cooking his dinner.'

'Fuck Robin,' Juliette laughed, standing up and making her way to the loo.

Now there was a thought. Perhaps I could appease Robin by allowing him to slip his massive cock into my little pussy, I mused. I had a feeling that he was going to be angry. He had said that I could come and go as I wished, as long as the house was clean and the meals were on time. Noticing the barman winking and grinning at me, I gave him a slight smile. I was looking forward to taking his purple glans into my mouth and sucking out his sperm, but I wished that Juliette had asked me before arranging a mouth-fucking.

The pub grew busier, the sounds of laughter, glasses chinking and music playing becoming louder. What with the cheerful atmosphere and the free drinks, I decided to become a regular customer. Perhaps the vicar was a regular, I reflected, watching Juliette stagger out of the toilet. There was no way she was going to last the evening, I knew as she teetered towards our table and almost fell over as she sat down. Her eyes rolling, her words slurred, I suggested that she should get some fresh air before having another drink.

'I'll be all right,' she mumbled, grinning as the barman asked whether he could join us.

'Of course,' I said, smiling and eyeing his tight trousers as he sat down.

'I have a break,' he said. 'The guvnor's taken over for ten minutes. Sorry, I'm Julian.'

'Crystal,' I said, shaking his hand. 'You've already met Juliette.'

'Yes, I have. So, you're staying on later?'

'Apparently. But I don't know about her.'

'I'll be all right,' Juliette insisted loudly. 'Perfectly capable of a mouth-fucking.'

'Shush,' I whispered, looking around the pub. 'Julian will throw us out if you carry on like that.'

'I've got a candle up my arse,' she giggled.

'Juliette!'

'A candle?' Julian echoed, his deep-set eyes frowning.

'She walks round with a candle . . . Take no notice of her. She's pissed.'

'Is it true?'

'Of course it's true,' Juliette laughed. 'A long, thick, wax—'

'Juliette, shut up,' I hissed. 'For God's sake, I can't take you anywhere.'

'I can hardly wait until we close,' Julian said, gazing at Juliette's breasts as they almost tumbled out of her blouse.

'She's bloody dangerous in public,' I murmured, reaching across the table and buttoning her blouse.

'She seems like fun.'

'I'll give her fun if she throws up.'

'The guvnor will chuck her out if she does that. I'd better get back. See you later.'

'Yes, OK. Though I might be on my own.'

'Yes, I understand.'

Grabbing Juliette's arm, I took her outside and propped her up against the wall. She seemed to sober up after a couple of minutes, but I suggested that she went home to sleep it off. She wouldn't hear of it, insisting that she wanted a good mouth-fucking after the pub had closed. After ten minutes or so, she seemed to be fine and I was about to take her back into the pub when a familiar voice called out.

'Oh, Robin,' I said, smiling as he approached.

'What are you two up to?'

'Oh, we were just getting some fresh air. Er . . . your dinner . . .'

'You got my note?'

'Note?'

'I left a note saying that I wouldn't be in for dinner.'

'Oh, yes, I did. Are you coming into the pub?'

'I never drink alcohol,' he said, opening the door. 'So I'll just have a large Scotch.'

'Right,' I said and frowned, leading Juliette to our table.

'Two vodkas?' Robin asked.

'One, I think.'

'Two,' Juliette chipped in.

'Two it is.'

At least I didn't have to worry about Robin's dinner, I thought, sitting opposite Juliette. Hoping that the vicar wouldn't return and catch us sitting with Robin, I wondered how long it would take for the rumour to spread through the village. It was pretty easy to spread rumours about someone, I mused. In this case the rumour was true. But if someone were to spread malicious lies about another person . . . I recalled a man who'd lived in the village some years previously. His wife left him and he began slagging her off to people in the village. Telling everyone that she was a prostitute and had stolen his money and ruined his life, he initially gained some sympathy. As time passed, though, people realized that he was lying and the whole thing backfired on him. But that wouldn't happen with our rumour. After all, what we were spreading about the vicar was the truth.

'There we are,' Robin said, placing the drinks on the table. 'What I like about this pub is the open log fire.'

'There isn't one,' I said, looking around the pub.

'A real fire gives out a lot of heat and the burning wood smells nice. So, how are you both?'

'Fine,' Juliette replied. 'When the pub closes later, we're going to—'

'We're going to go home,' I cut in. 'Where have you been, Robin? Anywhere nice?'

'The police station,' he replied as Juliette went up to the bar.

'The police . . . What for?'

'They arrested me earlier.'

'Why?'

'The Jag . . . I didn't pay for it.'

'What?'

'I took it for a test drive and forgot to go back to the showroom and pay for it.'

'Bloody hell. You mean to say that I've been driving around in a stolen car?'

'Sort of. It's all right now, though. I've explained my mistake to the police and paid for the car. I was overcome with excitement and just forgot to pay for the thing. Still, not to worry. I saw the ghost earlier.'

'Ghost?'

'In the house. He was pacing the hall outside your room. Looking for fresh pussy, more than likely.'

'Fresh . . . You are terrible, Robin.'

'I know. Terribleness runs in the family. Did you enjoy the rugby match?'

'What . . . How do you know about that?'

'I have my ways. What was the score?'

'Robin, I wish you'd tell me how you know these things.'

'I just sort of know. I don't know how I know that I know, I just—'

'Don't start that again.'

'Sorry. So, you're staying on after the pub closes?'

'We . . . we were going to stay on for late drinks but I'm not so sure now.'

'Late sex, you mean?'

'OK, that's it. How the hell do you know my every move, my every plan?'

'I know that I know but I don't know how I know that I know.'

'It's hopeless trying to talk to you, Robin.'

'That's exactly what my great-great brother used to say. Well, I'd better be going home.'

'What about your Scotch?'

'I don't drink alcohol.'

'Then why did you buy it?'

'I move in mysterious ways. See you later.'

As Robin left, I breathed a sigh of relief. Mysterious ways? He was right there. Watching Juliette chatting to the barman, I realized that the evening wasn't going to be particularly enjoyable. Finishing my drink, I was about to leave when the door opened. To my horror, the young man who'd abused me in the vicar's sex den walked into the pub and looked around. Noticing me, he came over to my table and asked whether I'd like a drink. He obviously wanted to talk to me about something, so I asked for another vodka and lime. The vicar must have told him that I was there, I reflected, wondering what he wanted. With so many undesirable types wandering into the pub, I was rapidly going off the place.

'So,' he said brightly and smiled, sitting down next to me. 'How are you?'

'None the better for seeing you,' I replied.

'Don't be like that. I was talking to the vicar earlier.'

'That doesn't surprise me. Birds of a feather and all that.'

'He told me about the problem he'd had in the church. I want that girl's address.'

'What girl?'

'Alison, the girl who was the bait for your trap.'

'I don't know who or what you're talking about.'

'OK, Crystal, if that's the way you want it. I'll be waiting in your room for you.'

'In my room?'

'We'll have a proper chat when you get home.'

'Are you threatening me?'

'Yes, I am. I don't like the idea of teenage girls fucking me about, or my friends. The vicar is . . . I don't like what you're doing to him.'

'And I've never liked what he's done to me.'

'I'll be waiting for you, Crystal,' he said again, downing his drink. 'I may have to deal with the psychiatrist if he gets in my way.'

'You just dare to—'

'I'll see you later.'

Watching him bang his glass down on the table and leave the pub, I felt my heart racing, my hands trembling. 'Shit,' I breathed, wondering what the hell to do. Looking at Juliette as she slumped over the bar, I realized that she was too drunk to be of any help. Perhaps I should ring Robin and warn him, I thought, wondering whether there was a phone in the pub. Or should I dash home before the young thug got there? No, I'd be too late. If he hurt Robin . . .

'Shit.'

9

Realizing that I had no choice, I finally walked home. I felt guilty, worried about Robin, fearful . . . What did the vicar's accomplice plan to do? Kidnap me? Tentatively opening the front door, I slipped into the hall and crept up to the consulting-room door. I'd expected to find Robin gagged and tied to his chair, but he was sitting at his desk, going through some papers. Perhaps the young man was waiting in my room, I mused, climbing the stairs. Terrifying thoughts filled my head as I stood on the landing. He might be behind the door waiting to pounce. He'd grab me, put sticky tape over my mouth, bind my wrists . . .

'He was just trying to frighten me,' I murmured, entering my room and finding nothing. Breathing a sigh of relief, I took my coat off and sat on the bed. Why had the vicar sent the man to the pub to threaten me? Some last-ditch attempt, perhaps? I didn't know what to think, but I was sure that the vicar was more than a little anxious about his predicament. Pubs were ideal environments for gossip to spread, and I wondered how many people the barman had told about the incident in the church. If he'd told six people and they'd each told six . . .

Hearing the front door close and someone coming up the stairs, I leaped to my feet. Had Robin let the young man in? My hands trembling, I knew that I couldn't go on like this. Living my life having to watch my back, not daring to answer the phone . . . Someone was outside my door, lurking, waiting. My heart banging hard against my chest, I heard a tap on the door, watched the handle turning.

'Who is it?' I asked shakily.

'Who do you think it is?' Juliette asked, grinning as she walked into the room. 'Father Christmas?'

'God,' I sighed. 'I do wish you wouldn't creep around like that.'

'Robin's gone to bed, that's why I crept up the stairs. Where did you get to? I went back to our table and you'd gone.'

'I was feeling tired. Apart from that, you were getting totally wrecked on vodka, and you were chatting to the barman so I didn't see any point in staying.'

'You're all uptight, Crystal,' she said and smiled, unbuttoning my blouse. 'Let's get into bed and I'll relax you.'

Slipping my blouse off my shoulders, Juliette unhooked my bra and peeled the silk cups away from the rounded mounds of my firm breasts. My nipples immediately responding as she ran her fingertips over the sensitive protrusions, I let out a rush of breath. I did need to relax, but I wasn't sure that I wanted lesbian sex. Her hands ran over my hips and she tugged my skirt down, kneading my fleshy pussy-lips through the tight material of my panties. My arousal soaring, I thought that this might indeed be the best way to relax. Juliette's intimate attention, her massaging, fingering, tonguing . . . yes, this *was* the best way to forget about my problems.

Slipping my wet panties down to my ankles, Juliette
kneeled on the floor and licked the full length of my sex
crack. Lapping up the creamy blend of sperm and girl-
juice as I stood over her and shuddered in my lesbian
ecstasy, she dug her fingernails into my rounded buttocks, pressing her face hard against my vulval flesh as
her tongue snaked into my vaginal sheath. Thoughts of
the young man's threats slipping away, I closed my eyes
as my pleasure built and my juices of lesbian desire
flowed from my tightening quim.

'Get into the bed,' Juliette whispered, rising to her feet
and standing in front of me. Slipping beneath the quilt, I
watched her undress, slowly revealing the violin curves
of her naked body. She was beautiful. The hairless crack
of her vagina seeming to smile at me, her erect nipples
pointing alluringly to the ceiling, her naked body invited
my hot mouth, my wet tongue. Reaching beneath my
pillow, I grabbed my vibrator and placed it beside me
beneath the quilt. Climbing into the bed, Juliette gazed
at the pink cylindrical device, her sparkling eyes lighting
up. She ordered me to lie on my back with my legs
parted.

Settling between my thighs, she parted the fleshy swell
of my vaginal lips and presented the tip of the buzzing
phallus to my clitoris. 'This will relax you,' she whispered, watching my sex button emerge from its hiding
place as she pulled my outer labia further apart. 'There,
that's nice, isn't it?' she asked as I began to tremble.

'Yes, I like that,' I replied dreamily, the sensations
permeating my contracting womb

Vibrating my erect sex bud, watching my girl-juice
ooze from my hot, yawning valley, Juliette forced my legs
wider apart. Biting my inner thighs, sinking her teeth

into the sensitive flesh of my naked mons, she seemed to be overwhelmed by a rampant desire to use my naked body roughly. For some reason, I recalled the thrashing I'd endured in the vicar's sex den. Would Juliette enjoy a naked-buttock thrashing? Images of hanging her naked body from chains and whipping her firm buttocks filled my mind as I cried out and shook uncontrollably in my sexual ecstasy. I could feel my swollen cunt-lips swelling, my slippery juices decanting as my clitoris pulsated in the beginning of an orgasm.

'God,' I breathed as my pleasure exploded, my clitoris pulsating wildly, my juices of lust spewing from the gaping entrance to my hot cunt. Her fingers delving into my spasming sex sheath, massaging the wet inner flesh of my pussy, Juliette ran the tip of the vibrator around my throbbing clitoris, sustaining my mind-blowing climax as I writhed and squirmed on the bed. My naked body shaking violently, my breathing fast and shallow, I dug my fingernails into the mattress as my orgasm peaked, sending electrifying shock waves through my trembling pelvis. I thought that my pleasure would never end as the liquid sound of my squelching juices mingled with the noise of the buzzing vibrator. Again and again my orgasm peaked, my young body convulsing, my eyes rolling as I endured one of the most intense orgasms I'd ever experienced.

Finally discarding the vibrator as my incredible climax began to recede, Juliette rolled me over onto my stomach and spread my trembling legs still further apart. Half dazed, I didn't know what she was doing as she leaped off the bed. Settling back down between my spread thighs, she rubbed cooling cream between my buttocks, paying particular attention to the brown ring of my anus. I felt my juices flowing as her fingertip teased my sensitive brown tissue, waking sleeping nerve endings there. My cunt aching for her pistoning fingers, I knew that she was going to finger-fuck my anal canal. *A double pistoning*? I mused in my dreamlike state.

I felt something hard pressing against my anus, my brown tissue yielding as she pushed what I thought was her candle into my bottom-hole. As she eased the waxen phallus deep into the tight duct of my dank rectum, I imagined the intimate tissue of my brown ring stretching, dilated by the thick shaft of the candle. My cunt-milk pouring from my gaping sex-hole, I knew that Juliette intended to spend half the night playing with me, teasing and pleasuring my teenage body. As the candle glided deeper into my very core, stirring my bowels, I buried my face in the pillow.

'What does it feel like?' Juliette asked, twisting the shaft.

'It's amazing,' I gasped. 'God, it's heavenly.'

'There's more to come,' she giggled, pushing still deeper into my spasming bum-hole.

'No, no more!' I cried, the end of the candle now embedded within the hot depths of my very core. 'Please, I can't take any more.'

Ignoring my protests, Juliette pushed and twisted the candle, massaging the hot flesh deep within my arse as I gasped and shuddered in my new-found lesbian ecstasy. Five, six, seven inches embedded in my rectal duct? I wasn't sure how long the candle was, but I knew that I couldn't take another inch. Leaving the bed, Juliette fiddled with something on the dressing table, giggling as she returned and positioned herself again between my splayed thighs. I could feel her slender fingers peeling

my swollen pussy-lips open, exposing the pinken entrance to my aching vagina. She was examining me there,
I knew as her long hair tickled the backs of my legs, the
sensitive flesh of my naked buttocks.

Driving her fingers deep into my cunt-hole, stretching
my inner flesh, Juliette massaged me there. Forcing more
fingers into my bloated vagina, stretching my pink
sheath wide open, she sank her teeth into the firm orbs
of my naked buttocks. I shuddered, whimpering into my
pillow as my naked body shook uncontrollably. Her
fingers leaving my wet sheath, she pressed something
hard and cold against the pink funnel of flesh surrounding the portal of my pussy. She'd taken something from
the dressing table, something to use as a phallus to fuck
me with. Twisting and pushing whatever it was, she
eased the huge shaft deep into my contracting cunt. The
cold object slipped easily into my accommodating pussy
until I could feel the end pressing hard against my cervix.
My fleshy outer lips stretched around the massive phallus, my clitoris forced from beneath its pink bonnet, my
bloated anal canal aching, I knew that I had reached the
bottom of the pit of debauched lesbian sex.

'Do you like it?' Juliette asked me as she massaged the
sensitive nubble of my erect clitoris. 'You want me to
make you come, don't you?'

'God, yes,' I breathed.

'Your bum's stretched wide open by the candle, your
cunt's bloated by the shampoo bottle . . . I'll vibrate your
beautiful clit and make you come.'

The vibrator pressed hard against my solid pleasure
nodule, sending soothing sensations deep into my quivering pelvis, and I gasped and squirmed as Juliette
expertly stiffened my throbbing clitoris with the buzzing

device. I was going to come and come until my cunt
burned and my clitoris could take no more. Juliette was
going to give me no mercy, I knew as the birth of my
second orgasm stirred deep within my hot womb. She
was going to bring me one multiple orgasm after another
until I passed out from sheer sexual pleasure.

'God, I'm coming,' I cried as my clitoris pulsated in
orgasm. I could feel my small sex-protrusion exploding,
throbbing, pumping, swelling beautifully. Working the
candle in and out of my tight anal orifice, Juliette
continued to vibrate my aching clitoris, taking me from
one mind-blowing sexual peak to another. Thrusting the
candle between my twitching anal orbs, moving the tip of
the vibrator around the base of my pulsating clitoris, she
giggled as I cried out again in my coming. My entire
body shuddering violently as my climax rode on and on,
I tossed my head from side to side, gasping, perspiring in
my sexual bliss. 'No more,' I panted as my orgasm
peaked yet again. 'No, no . . . Please . . .'

My cunt-lips painfully swollen, my clitoris pumping
in orgasm, I shuddered as she turned the vibrator up to
full power, increasing my incredible pleasure. Imagining
a young cock in my mouth, sperm jetting from the
throbbing knob, I gyrated my hips, sandwiching the
buzzing vibrator between my solid clitoris and the mattress. Juliette moved her attention to the candle emerging
from between my tensed buttocks, grabbing the end and
pistoning the tight sheath of my arse as I let out whimpers of lesbian sex and murmured incoherent words of
girl-lust.

All thoughts of the vicar and his evil accomplice faded
as I revelled in my exquisite pleasure. My mind blown
away on clouds of orgasm, I had no worries, no pro-

blems. If only I could have been free of problems all the time, I reflected. I'd have been able to enjoy my young life. But at least now the vicar might be planning to flee the village. If he'd got wind of the gossip, he might have decided that it was time to move on. All I could do was hope and pray.

Finally coming down from my amazing orgasm as Juliette switched the vibrator off, I lay quivering on my bed. I couldn't have taken any more, I knew as she slipped the candle out of my inflamed rectal sheath. Withdrawing the shampoo bottle from my drenched vagina, she kissed my naked buttocks, licking the sensitive brown tissue surrounding my sore anal eye. Moving away, I sat up and laid her down on the bed. I wanted the feel of her tongue inside my wet pussy, caressing my inner flesh. I knelt astride her head and lowered my open pussy over her pretty face, settling my sticky vaginal lips over her mouth.

Coughing and spluttering as my juices poured from my cunt and filled her mouth, Juliette pushed her tongue deep into my sex duct, lapping up my cream as I trembled violently. I could feel her tongue exploring me, delving deep inside my sex-sheath to seek out the source of my girl-cum. The sensations were mind-blowing, taking my lust for sexual fulfillment to amazing heights. Swivelling my hips, I aligned my erect clitoris with her open mouth, gasping as she swept her tongue over my small protrusion, sending electrifying shudders of pleasure through my quivering body.

'Don't stop,' I ordered Juliette as her tongue circled my aching clitoris, swelling my budlette until it was near to bursting point. 'Yes,' I gasped as my climax erupted in a powerful explosion of sheer lesbian lust. Rocking my naked body, sliding my drenched girl-slit back and forth over her hot mouth, I pumped out my slippery juices of lust, lubricating our illicit union as she trembled beneath me. Spluttering through the wet cunt-flesh between my thighs, she drank from my teenage body. Rubbing my orgasming clitoris over her mouth, bringing out shock waves of pure sexual ecstasy, I hung my head briefly and breathed heavily in my lesbian loving.

Another wave of immense pleasure sweeping through my sex-drenched body, I tossed my head back, my long blonde hair cascading down my back as my cunt again pumped out its orgasmic cream. Grinding my inner vulval flesh hard against Juliette's cum-flooded face, I sustained my orgasm, gasping and squirming on top of my lesbian lover as she did her best to drink from my juice-brimming cunt. Finally stilling my sated body, I relaxed in the aftermath of my climax, allowing her to drain my sex duct until I rolled to one side and lay exhausted on the bed. I needed to sleep, but Juliette sat up and rolled me onto my stomach again. I heard her moving about in the room, but had no idea what she was doing until the leather belt cracked loudly across the sensitive orbs of my naked buttocks.

'No,' I whimpered as the savage strap flailed my stinging bum-flesh. Unrelenting, Juliette continued with the merciless thrashing, her giggles echoing around the room as my buttocks burned like fire. Burying my face in the pillow, I wondered whether Robin was listening to the sounds of illicit lesbian sex as he lay in his bed. Perhaps he was wanking, shooting his spunk over his pillow as he pictured my naked body, imagined Juliette's tongue fucking my hot wet cunt.

'That's too hard,' I complained as Juliette brought the

leather belt down with such force that my teenage body convulsed wildly. Swishing the strap through the air again, she was obviously taking great delight in watching as the leather cut across my taut buttocks. Driven by lesbian lust, she continued to thrash my young buttocks, giving me at least fifteen good lashes before she had to rest her aching arm. Lifting and turning my head, I gazed at the burning orbs of my arse as she rested her whip arm. Glowing crimson, the sight of my burning flesh excited me, and I hoped that she'd allow me to give *her* a thrashing before the night was over.

Settling between my naked thighs, Juliette smeared more cream into my anal crease, wiping the cooling lubricant around the snugly puckered pinky-brown entrance to my bowels. I knew that I was in for another anal pistoning as she held my stinging buttocks wide open and slipped the end of the candle into my dusky hole, past my defeated sphincter muscles, driving it deep into my hot body. She slid the candle in and out of my beautiful bottom-hole, fucking me there with the waxen phallus as I gasped and writhed in my sexual ecstasy. The obscene image sent a wonderful shudder up my spine and a delightful throb through my clitoris. My brown anal tissue stretched tautly around the thrusting candle, my fiery buttocks held wide apart . . . I couldn't deny that I'd found my domain. I was in my sexual heaven.

'You have a beautiful bum,' Juliette murmured, easing the candle out of my inflamed rectal duct. 'I think it's time I gave you a good arse-fisting.'

'No, Juliette,' I murmured dreamily.

'Why not? Just relax and allow yourself the pleasures you deserve.'

'I don't want your fist up my—'

'Be still,' she said, stretching the globes of my burning bottom wide apart.

I could feel Juliette's creamed fingers entering me, slipping past my brown ring, delving deep into my yielding rectal tube. My dusky pink hole opening, widening as she forced more fingers into my fiery bottom-hole, I was sure that I'd split open. Never had I known such incredible sensations of debased sex. Her knuckles slipping past my dark portal, driving deep into my most private sheath, she pushed and twisted her hand, trying to sink what felt like half her arm into the very core of my young body.

Lifting my stomach clear of the bed, raising my weal-lined buttocks, I allowed Juliette better access to my inner core as she continued to force her hand into my rectal channel. She was opening me slowly, stretching my anal duct open as she eased her hand into my trembling body. My eyes squeezed shut, my face grimacing, I held my breath as she finally accomplished her mission, her fist buried deep within my inner core, the stretched ring of my anus hugging her wrist.

'I've done it,' she breathed proudly, flexing her fingers, sending exquisite sensations deep into my pelvis. 'How does that feel?'

'God,' I gasped, my naked body shaking. 'It's . . . it's incredible.'

'Just relax and allow me to massage inside you. Relax completely and I'll fist your pussy too.'

'No,' I murmured. 'I'll tear open.'

'Of course you won't. The secret is to relax your muscles, Crystal.'

'I'll try. But stop if I say so.'

'Of course.'

Her fingers parting the fleshy cushions of my outer labia and delving into my wet cunt, Juliette straightened the fingers of the hand already in my rectum to lessen the restriction of my vaginal canal. I could hear my juices squishing, bubbling as she pushed and twisted her other hand. My pelvic cavity felt completely bloated, my insides inflating as she eased her hand into my vaginal cavern. Suddenly, her entire fist was sucked into my ravenous cunt, sending shudders through my teenage body as I gasped.

Twisting both her fists, massaging the thin membrane dividing my sex canals, Juliette leaned forward and bit each of my burning buttocks in turn. Shuddering uncontrollably in my new-found ecstasy, I tried to relax, breathing deeply and allowing the crude sensations to ripple throughout my young body. I felt as if I was drifting through a sexual heaven, floating through warm waters of pure sexual rapture. Raising my hips and parting my knees, my naked body on all fours, I rocked back and forth, double-fisting my sex sheaths. Juliette matched my rocking, pumping my squelching ducts, sending electrifying tingles of sex through my very soul.

'I'm going to come,' I announced dreamily as my clitoris was massaged by her cunny-wet wrist. I could feel my pleasure spot inflating, pulsating as my orgasm welled from the depth of my pelvis. Suddenly, the eruption came, my clitoris pulsing fiercely, my vaginal juices squirting from the bloated cavity of my teenage cunt. Again and again waves of sex crashed through my trembling body, touching every nerve ending as I panted and gasped for life-giving breath.

My long blonde hair matted with the perspiration of crude sex, my flushed face burning, I rocked back and forth faster. What had I become? I wondered as my orgasm rolled on. Another girl's fists fucking my private ducts, my pussy shaved and hairless, the intimate flesh-depths of my body awash with spunk from my trip to the playing field . . . This had to be the bottom of the pit of depravity, I was sure as my vaginal muscles tightened around Juliette's fist. I'd been mouth-fucked, cunny-fucked, double-fisted . . . I could fall no further, I was sure. had the Devil taken my soul in exchange for this incredible new sexual pleasure that I was experiencing?

'Slow down,' I gasped, my orgasm beginning to fade. Stilling my rocking body, I felt my pelvic muscles spasm as Juliette twisted her fists more slowly. Gently, she massaged the inner flesh of my inflamed sex-caverns, sending ripples of intense pleasure through my young womb. Withdrawing first from my bloated vagina, she eased her other fist out of my cavernous rectum, leaving my sex holes gaping. Lying on the bed, my thighs twitching, I waited for my sated body to calm down. Never had I known such crude sex, such incredible ecstasy. If I'd had a solid young knob spunking into my mouth as Juliette had fist-fucked me . . .

'Feeling more relaxed now?' Juliette asked me, stroking the sensitive flesh within my anal crease.

'God, yes,' I murmured. 'Totally relaxed.'

'How about a little whipping?' she giggled. 'Just to bring some warmth to your buttocks.'

'No, I . . . I don't want the belt again.'

'Come on, Crystal. I know what's best for you.'

'Just gently, then,' I conceded, tucking my arms beneath my body and closing my eyes, 'Just a gentle spanking with the belt.'

My hands clasped beneath the hot flesh of my vulva, I

smiled as the belt trailed over my smooth buttocks. The first lash tensing my already red arse-globes, I moaned softly through my nose. The leather meeting my burning flesh, gently increasing the stinging sensation, I felt the hot, creamy juices of my abused cunt decanting over my clasped hands. Drifting in my sexual ecstasy as Juliette continued the gentle whipping, I slipped a finger between the pouting lips of my pussy and caressed my expectant clitoris.

As Juliette increased the intensity of the whipping, lashing my burning buttocks harder, I massaged the solid nub of my clitoris faster. The continual abuse of my teenage body was exhausting me, but I was desperate for another orgasm, desperate for more crude sex. The belt cracking repeatedly across my tensed buttocks, the pain permeating my bottom-cheeks, I began to tremble as my clitoris swelled beneath my vibrating fingertip. Picturing a young cock fucking my wet mouth, fresh spunk jetting from its knob-slit, I shuddered as my orgasm exploded within the pulsating nodule of my solid clitty.

'God,' I breathed, the sensations driving me wild. Realizing that I'd brought myself off, Juliette frenziedly thrashed my naked buttocks with the belt, repeatedly bringing the leather strap down as hard as she could. My buttocks on fire, my cunt-milk spewing from the inflamed opening of my sex-sheath, my clitoris pulsating, I didn't think that I'd survive my massive climax. My mind blown, my head dizzy, I convulsed wildly on the bed, drowning in my own lust as the gruelling thrashing continued and my orgasm peaked.

My teenage cunt had become the very centre of my being, my naked body bringing me nothing but immense sexual pleasure. Lesbian sex, cock-sucking and spunk-swallowing, double-fisting, naked-buttock thrashing, clit-licking . . . I was into anything and everything. Delighting in the thrashing, I again imagined a cock fucking my pretty mouth as my latest orgasm shook me to the very core. This was sex – real sex, crude sex – and I was loving every minute of it. Sadly, just as my crimsoned buttocks became numb and I was looking forward to at least another twenty lashes, Juliette complained about her arm aching.

'I can't go on,' she sighed, tossing the belt onto the floor.

'I was really beginning to enjoy it,' I said shakily, my clitoris retreating beneath its pinken hood again.

'I've thrashed a few girls in my time, but I've never known anyone like you,' she giggled, lying next to me and pulling the quilt up.

'How many girls?' I asked, snuggling next to her warm body.

'I don't know. Ten, maybe more. God, I'm knackered.'

'Me, too. We need to sleep.'

I woke in the morning to find that Juliette was already up. Hoping that she'd gone to make some tea, I hauled my aching body out of bed and stretched my limbs. Wondering what the day would bring, I looked out of the window. It was snowing thick and fast, the huge flakes falling swiftly to the ground, which was already virgin white. Not a good day for cock-sucking in the woods. Waiting ten minutes or so for Juliette to return, I thought that she must have gone to her room so I took a shower and got dressed.

As I was about to go downstairs to make Robin's breakfast, I noticed a piece of paper tucked under the telephone. *I'll be back*, I read. Wondering where Juliette had gone, and why she'd bothered to leave me a note, I jossed the paper into the kitchen bin.

I cooked Robin bacon and eggs for breakfast. He seemed to be relatively normal, talking about his clients and the day ahead. I decided to have a good go at the housework. What with the snow, the best place to be was at home. I'd clean the bathroom properly, have a go at getting the kitchen straight and do the washing, which had piled up again.

'Juliette went out early,' Robin commented as he ate his breakfast at the kitchen table.

'I didn't realize that she'd gone out,' I said, washing the frying pan. 'It must have been important for her to go out in this weather. It's like Siberia out there.'

'Siberia?' he echoed. 'What do you know about Siberia?'

'Not a lot, apart from the fact that it's freezing cold and snows all the time.'

'They've been developing over-the-horizon radar.'

'Who have?'

'No one. Have you fed the cat?'

'Yes, Robin,' I sighed.

'Good. Well, I have to spend an hour in the shed.'

'Won't you get cold out there?'

'I'll switch the heater on before I send the message.'

'What message?'

'To my contact . . . I mean . . .'

'You are a spy, aren't you?' I asked him accusingly.

'Of course not. I'm simply going to send a message to an old friend to tell him that it's snowing here.'

'What's the weather like where he is?'

'Worse than this, I would imagine. At this time of year, Moscow . . . I mean, Scotland . . .'

'Have you finished?' I asked, taking his plate.

'Yes, thank you. That was very nice, Crystal.'

'You go and send your Morse-code message and I'll start the housework.'

Watching Robin wander down the garden to the shed, I realized again how fond I was of him. He was totally mad, but extremely likeable. Wearing his corduroy trousers, velvet jacket and bow tie, sending Morse-code messages from the shed . . . An incredibly strange man, but extremely likeable. Finishing the washing-up, I wondered again how Robin knew things. What was his strange power? If I could catch him when he was in normal mode, I might be able to discuss it properly with him. Until then, I'd just have to accept it.

Jumping as the doorbell rang, I walked into the hall and peered through the stained glass. I could see a figure, but couldn't make out who it was. Perhaps one of Robin's clients had turned up early, or Juliette might have forgotten her key. There again, it might have been the vicar or his evil accomplice. Wondering whether to go and get Robin, I thought that it could easily be the postman or someone who'd come to read the electricity meter. I had to stop being paranoid. If I was going to live my life in fear of the doorbell and the telephone ringing, then life wouldn't be worth living. Taking a deep breath, I opened the door.

'Oh,' I breathed, gazing at more than half a dozen boys.

'Hi, Crystal,' Ian said and grinned. 'We thought we'd come and keep you company.'

'Well, I'm pretty busy right now,' I said, imagining six young cocks, six loads of fresh sperm. Making a quick headcount, I realized that there were eight boys. 'All right, come in for a while,' I conceded.

Leading the boys up to my room, I locked the door and gazed at them as they lined up by the bed. *Keep me company*? I mused. They wanted to push their hard cocks into my hot holes. Eight rock-hard cocks, eight swollen knobs, sixteen full balls . . . Robin was busy in the shed, Juliette had gone out . . . The housework would have to wait, I decided, eyeing the tight crotches of the boys' jeans. Not knowing how long Robin would be in the shed, I wasn't sure how much time I had. The sooner we got started, the better, I mused.

Ordering the boys to strip, I knew that I was a whore-slut. I just couldn't resist hard young cocks and fresh spunk. Was there something wrong with me? I reflected, hurriedly slipping my T-shirt over my head and un-hooking my bra. One girl, eight boys. The notion excited me, wetted the groove of my vulva as I slipped my skirt down and kicked it aside. My young body would soon be awash with sperm, my holes overflowing, my pussy and belly full. God, how I loved the youthful shafts of boys' penises. No, there was nothing wrong with me.

Tugging my panties down, I lay on my bed with my limbs spread and waited until the boys were all naked. I could feel my stomach somersaulting as they gathered round the bed, four boys either side of me, scrutinizing my teenage mounds and crevices. Their wide eyes trans-fixed on the elongated teats of my breasts, my hairless pussy slit, my eyes darting between their solid cocks, their full balls . . . I was surrounded by what I most loved in life, eight solid penises, eight purple knobs, eight pairs of tight balls. I was in for yet another session of crude sex, I knew as Ian ordered me to get on the floor.

Leaving the bed, I followed his instructions, positioning my naked body on all fours. Hoping that I'd be allowed the pleasure of a simultaneous mouth-fucking and pussy-shafting, I wondered whether they were going to queue up behind me and take me in turn. One young lad crawling beneath my naked body and stabbing upwards between the fleshy pads of my vaginal lips with his bulbous knob, I realized what the gang had in mind.

As the lad beneath me slid the entire length of his solid cock deep into my accommodating vaginal sheath, another kneeled behind me. My inner labia stretching as the lad beneath me fully impaled me, I felt my solid clitoris emerge from beneath its fleshy hood. My full outer lips hugging the root of the boy's fresh young cock, I shuddered as the lad behind me parted my anal hole with his thumbs.

Feeling a wet tongue lubricating my anus, I looked down at the boy beneath me and grinned. His cock was motionless within the hugging sheath of my sex-drenched pussy, his solid knob pressing hard against my ripe cervix. He was obviously waiting for the second penis to enter my rectum before he began his shafting movements, his fucking motions. I could feel the ballooning globe of the other boy's knob pressing hard against the delicate brown tissue surrounding my dilated anus. Suddenly, his glans was sucked past my anal sphincter muscles. Driving his knob into my rectal canal, his swollen plum opening me as it journeyed along my tight channel to the cavern of my bowels, he let out a huge gasp of pleasure.

Lifting my head as the double impalement inflated my

pelvic cavity, I gazed longingly at another swollen sex plum hovering in front of my wide eyes. *Three cocks entering my orifices*, I mused happily, licking my succulent lips. Opening my mouth wide, I sucked the beautiful cock-head inside, running my wet tongue over its silky-smooth surface, exploring the small sperm-slit. Snaking my wet tongue around its rim, I savoured the salty taste, my womb contracting delightfully as my arousal went through the roof.

I really was in my sexual heaven, I mused as the beautiful cocks between my splayed thighs withdrew partially and then thrust deep back into my inflamed lust-ducts. Taking the twitching knob bloating my mouth to the back of my throat, I sank my teeth gently into the broad root of the solid organ, delighting in the three-way illicit union as gasps echoed around the room. Breathing in the scent of the boy's pubic curls, I gobbled and sucked on his magnificent member as he clutched my head and rocked his hips.

Listening to the squelching juices of my vagina as the boys fucked my tight sex-sheaths, I licked and sucked the third lad's knob, gobbling and mouthing fervently in my desperation for his fresh spunk to gush and bathe my snaking tongue. To my delight, another boy settled next to the lad fucking my hot mouth and offered me his swollen glans. Moving my head back, the first cock slipping out of my wet mouth, I watched the two boys press their purple cock-heads together. Taking them into my mouth, I sucked and tongued both salty knobs. Four cocks embedded deep within my teenage body, four knobs about to pump out their fresh spunk and fill my every orifice . . . This was, indeed, sexual heaven.

Rocking back and forth as the four granite-hard cocks

fucked me, I again thought what a whore-slag I was. I
lived, breathed, slept, ate and drank crude sex. But that
was how I'd been brought up, wasn't it? The vicar
regularly fucking my mouth and spunking down my
throat, abusing me, spanking me, arse-fucking me . . .
I knew no different. But I was eighteen now. I should
have learned by now. *Learned what*? I wondered. *How to
behave as society expects me to behave*? Most people would
have called me a dirty little slut if they'd discovered that I
masturbated regularly, frigged my clitty to orgasm and
fingered my tight cunny-hole. What the hell would they
call me if they discovered that I had four cocks simultaneously fucking my spunk-thirsty orifices?

'Right up her sweet arse,' the lad behind me cried as
his organ swelled within my anal sheath, his spunk
gushing from his throbbing knob, lubricating the illicit
union. The boy beneath me gasping as he reached his
shuddering climax, pumping his creamy spunk deep into
my contracting cunt, I moaned through my nose as the
two knobs bloating my mouth swelled and throbbed and
flooded my tongue with sperm. Drinking from the orgasming cock-heads, swallowing hard, I listened to the
gasping and squelching sounds of debased sex, delighting in my crude and wanton act of debauchery as my own
orgasm erupted within the solid nubble of my pulsating
clitoris.

Dizzy with sex, my eyes rolling, spunk gushing from
my mouth and running in rivers down my chin, I realized
that there were another four boys waiting to use my
teenage body. Another four cocks, rivers of sperm . . . By
the time they'd finished with me, the first four would
have recovered, their cocks stiff and eager to give me
another quadruple fucking. The first cocks making their

last thrusts, the first four boys' balls drained, I shuddered my last orgasmic shudder as the spent knobs left my well-spermed mouth. I needed to rest, I knew as the deflating shafts withdrew from my inflamed rectum, my burning vaginal duct. Rolling onto the floor, I lay on my back, trembling uncontrollably in the aftermath of the illicit, wonderful abuse of my young body.

Two boys lifted my feet off the floor, pulling them high in the air above my head, and I felt the succulent lips of my inflamed vagina open wide as they parted my feet. The others gazed at my sperm-oozing sex-holes, the humiliatingly exposed sexual centre of my naked body. I opened my mouth as a boy kneeled on the floor and lowered his balls onto my flushed face. Sucking his scrotal sac into my mouth, I gobbled on his balls as a solid penis drove deep into the hot sheath of my wet cunt.

My trembling body rocking with the vaginal fucking, I sucked and mouthed on the heaving balls filling my mouth as my erect nipples were licked and nibbled. The electrifying sensations driving me crazy, I jumped as at least three fingers forced their way deep into my sperm-brimming rectal duct. My vaginal cavern repeatedly inflated by the pistoning cock, my inner anal flesh massaged by the intruding fingers, I sucked on the balls bloating my mouth as teeth sank into my areolae. Every inch of my body tingling with sex, my womb spasming, my clitoris painfully swollen, I knew that I was nearing another mind-blowing orgasm.

How many orgasms I could achieve in one session of crude sex, I had no idea. When I was young, too young, I'd masturbated one morning in my bed. After five massive climaxes, I'd rested for half an hour before massaging my inflamed clitoris again. My sex juices had flowed freely between the hairless lips of my young pussy, soaking the mattress as I'd frigged myself off. Managing another three orgasms, I was completely exhausted, waiting another half an hour before resuming the abuse of my rubicund clitoris. It had been Saturday, no school, my parents having a lie-in . . . What else was there to do apart from finger the tight sheath of my little pussy and masturbate until I almost passed out? I'd used a candle, fucking myself with the waxen shaft until my tiny cunt was sore and inflamed. I rubbed my clitoris relentlessly, managing to achieve a dozen orgasms before my aching hand fell limp by my side.

It was that particular morning that the vicar had called. I'd washed and dressed and was looking forward to the weekend when my mother had sent him up to my room. He'd made me bend over a chair with my skirt up over my back and my knickers around my thighs. He'd forced his huge cock deep into my sore cunt, remarking on how wet I was as he'd grabbed my hips and fucked me in his wickedness. His hairy balls had slapped between my thighs, his lower belly smacking the orbs of my young bottom. I remember my mother calling up the stairs to say that she'd made the vicar a cup of tea. He'd called back to say that he was coming, which he was. His spunk had gushed into my burning cunt, filling me, his sperm overflowing and running in rivers of milk down my inner thighs.

Finally slipping his cunny-wet penis out of my tight vagina, the priest had made me kneel in front of him and lick his deflating cock. His penis snaking over my fresh face, his sperm oozing from his slit, running down my cheeks, he'd ordered me to suck the remnants of his cream out of his dripping knob. I'd complied, sucking and gobbling, swallowing his orgasmic liquid as my mother had again called up the stairs. The vicar had taken my hand and led me down to the kitchen where my mother was waiting with the tea. My face dripping with spunk, he'd not allowed me to wash, delighting in my plight as my mother had asked me what the white stuff was running down my cheeks, my chin. I looked sheepish, and she accused me of taking her face cream without asking. The cleric had grinned at me, lifting his cassock and displaying his wet cock each time my mother turned away.

'Now suck my knob,' the boy with his balls in my mouth ordered me, breaking my reverie. He sounded like the vicar. *It's all right, I won't tell your mother.* His balls slipping out of my mouth, he leaned over, gripping his solid cock by the root as he planted his prick-plum in my mouth and instructed me to use my tongue. My stomach rising and falling with the vaginal pistoning, my milk teats painfully bitten, I sucked and licked the fresh knob inside my hot mouth.

Recalling the netball team, the young lads sneaking behind the bush and spunking down my throat, I found myself wondering how old boys were when they started wanking. When did they first produce sperm? I was becoming obsessed with teenage boys, I knew as my mouth flooded with sperm, the boy above me gasping as he forced his throbbing knob to the back of my throat. My burning vagina filling with the other boy's orgasmic flow, my nipples painfully bitten, pulled and twisted, I reached another mind-blowing climax.

I'd planned to spend the morning catching up with my housework, and yet my naked body was lying on the floor at the disposal of eight young lads and their rampant cocks. More sperm flooding my orifices, my clitoris pulsating in yet another orgasm . . . There were two boys left, I calculated, swallowing the spunk filling my cheeks. My vaginal throat gulping down the other lad's gushing sperm, my naked body shaking violently as my climax rocked my very soul, I recalled my erstwhile English teacher's throbbing knob spunking in my hot mouth. Where would it all end? I wondered, sucking the last of the spunk from the boy's sperm-slit. My naked body collapsing on the floor as my feet were released and the cock inside my cream-bubbling pussy withdrew, I knew that there'd be no end to my life of sex and debauchery.

My naked body was hauled up off the floor, four boys holding my arms and feet as if they were going to give me the bumps. My legs wide apart, the spermed crack of my pussy gaping, I watched a lad stand between my thighs, the purple head of his solid cock aligned with the open entrance to my drenched cunt. Suddenly, he entered me, his ballooning glans driving along my sex-shaft and pressing against my spunk-bathed cervix. The boys rocked me back and forth, my naked body swaying, the lad's penis thrusting in and out of my sex-bubbling pussy.

Sperm soon gushed, once more filling the hot cavern of my cunt, running down between my naked buttocks as the boy drained his balls. My body rocking back and forth, all the boy had to do was stand there with his cock in my cunt, his spunk filling me as he gasped and his mates chuckled. I was like a rag doll, swaying, rocking, my cunt fucked and spunked by the throbbing cock. The taste of sperm lingering on my tongue, male cream oozing from the inflamed eye of my bottom-hole, I shuddered as the spent penis left the sheath of my cunt with a loud sucking sound.

'One to go,' someone chortled. Another fresh knob stabbing between the dripping lips of my abused cunt, the huge knob gliding along my sex sheath, pressing against my sperm-drowned cervix, I knew that I couldn't take much more. My body rocking again, the squelching sound of my vaginal cream-and-spunk cocktail filling my ears, I was sure that I could hear sperm dripping onto the carpet. My room had become a sex den, I reflected as the boy's balls battered the spunk-dripping orbs of my firm buttocks. Fingering, sucking, fucking, spunking, orgasms . . . My home was nothing more than a den of iniquity.

'Rock her faster,' the gasping lad ordered his friends. Swinging back and forth, I gasped too as his sex-shaft repeatedly rammed into my aching cunt, his knob pummelling the ring of my inflamed cervix. Reaching beneath my naked body, he clutched my buttocks in his hands, his fingernails biting into my sensitive flesh as he rammed his cock-head into me with a vengeance. Again and again his glans battered my cervix, his swinging balls slapping my crimsoned bottom as he fucked me.

His spunk flooding the cavern of my convulsing pussy, the boy fucked me still harder. I listened again to the squelching sounds of illicit sex as the boys rocked me back and forth, repeatedly impaling me on the lad's solid organ. They chanted as they swung me. In, out, in, out, in, out . . . Used and abused, gang-banged . . . I was a slut-whore, a goddess of sex, the best cock-sucker in the land. I'd found my domain.

Tossing my naked body onto the bed as the lad slipped his deflating cock out of my fiery cunt, the boys laughed and joked as they got dressed. Quivering uncontrollably, gasping for breath, sperm oozing from my burning sex-holes, I lay on my back with my eyes closed. I'd been well and truly fucked and spunked, used and abused. And I'd loved every minute of it. Would there be another rugby match that afternoon? I wondered as I heard the door open and the boys file out of the room. More tight balls to fondle, cocks to suck, more sperm to swallow . . . I was a goddess of decadence.

IO

Although I was exhausted, I had a shower and managed to make Robin some lunch before going shopping and stocking up with food. There was still no sign of Juliette, and I assumed that she'd gone job-hunting. Either that or cock-hunting. By mid-afternoon, I was feeling really good. Relaxed, happy . . . Wondering whether to go out for the evening, I decided to go to the pub and check up on the local gossip. Word of the vicar's wrongdoing should have spread through the village, I reflected. If it hadn't, then I'd fan the flames and make sure that the rumour got a real hold.

Wearing a very short skirt, I didn't bother to slip my panties on. It was best to be prepared for sex, I thought wickedly as I made my way down the road. Prepared for crude sex, pussy-fucking, cock-sucking. Wondering whether I'd meet a young man in the pub, I imagined flashing my naked pussy. I'd sit at a table with my thighs slightly parted, the hairless crack of my vagina displayed. A pang of excitement coursing through my stomach, I hoped I'd meet Juliette. Perhaps we could stay until closing time and then share the barman's purple knob, drink his spunk before going home – make up for disappointing him the previous evening.

I arrived at the pub at seven and bought a vodka and lime. Not bought, exactly. The good-looking barman didn't charge me. After meeting Juliette, he obviously had something else in mind by way of payment, rather than cash. That suited me, I thought, sitting at a table by the window and imagining his stiff cock driving in and out of my hot mouth. Why use cash when I could use my mouth or my pussy to get what I wanted? Had the barman known that I was naked beneath my short skirt . . . He'd have come in his trousers. What a waste of fresh spunk.

Sipping my drink, I couldn't think where Juliette had got to. She must have got up pretty early to go somewhere. She'd not mentioned a job interview or any other appointment, and I began to wonder whether the vicar had kidnapped her. Why bother to leave me a note? Kidnapped? My mind was running wild. She was probably with some man or other, wanking his cock, bringing out his spunk. No doubt she'd turn up at some stage, I mused, gazing out of the window at the dark sky and wishing that summer would hurry up.

Noticing a young man standing at the far end of the bar, I swivelled on my chair, turning to face him and parting my thighs a little. Sitting at the bar, gazing at the rows of optics, he didn't notice me. He appeared to be deep in thought, oblivious to his surroundings, and I wondered whether he had marital problems. I began fantasizing as I waited for him to notice me. He'd rowed with his wife and was drowning his sorrows. He'd see me, gaze longingly at my naked vulval lips. I'd ask him to join me, reach beneath the table and haul his cock out. I'd wank him, his spunk flowing over my hand . . .

Turning, he smiled at me and then lowered his eyes. A thrill ran through my stomach as he focused on the crack of my pussy. He must have thought me a filthy little slut, a tart, a whore. I felt wicked, parting my thighs further and displaying the shaved flesh of my vulva. Would my fantasy become reality? I wondered, licking my succulent lips provocatively as he stared at my pussy, my cunt. I wanted him, needed to feel his sperm running over my hand as I rolled his foreskin back and forth over the purple plum of his solid cock.

'Good evening, Crystal,' Barry Carter said, making me jump.

'Oh, I . . . I didn't see you come in,' I said softly and smiled.

'All alone, then?'

'Yes, just having a quiet drink.'

'I'll get myself a pint and join you. Are you all right?' he asked, nodding at my glass.

'Yes, yes, I'm fine.'

My fantasy would never see the light of day, I knew as the young man turned and faced the bar again. Perhaps I'd wank Barry's solid cock beneath the table, bring out his spunk, feel the white liquid running in rivers over my hand as he gasped and doubled up with pleasure. The young man sipped his drink, not looking at me again as he returned to his thoughts of loneliness. Was I lonely? Where the hell was Juliette? What the hell did Barry want? Another blow job?

I had to find out more about Jenny, what she'd told Barry. I didn't like being in a position where I didn't know whether or not I could trust him. Hoping that this would be an opportunity to discover the truth, I decided to start by mentioning Jenny. The vicar had seemed pretty genuine when he'd denied all knowledge of the girl, leading me to believe that Barry was lying. He'd said that he'd put two and two together when he'd seen me in the lane with the shoebox. Did he know that the box contained photographs because the vicar had shown him? Or had he already got hold of some evidence? As he joined me, I asked him whether he'd heard any more from Jenny.

'Nothing,' he said, sipping his beer. 'But that's not surprising because she's waiting to hear from me. Now that you've come on the scene, things have changed.'

'Changed? How do you mean?'

'You've taken a box of photographs, Crystal. The vicar must be aware that they're missing so I'm going to have to be careful. I don't want him discovering that I'm onto him.'

'You talked about having enough evidence. Apart from photographs, what evidence is there? Is Jenny going to talk about her ordeal? Is she going to open her mouth and shop the vicar?'

'No, she doesn't want to have to go through that. And I can't blame her. What I'm hoping to do is to take some photographs of young girls going into the church, or into the vicar's cottage.'

'Are there other girls involved?'

'I'm not sure.'

'So, what evidence have you got?'

'I . . . I'd rather not talk about it in here.'

I still wasn't sure whether or not I could trust Barry. He was being evasive, to put it mildly. What evidence did he actually have? None, I concluded. I needed to talk to Jenny, but I had no idea where she was. I hadn't seen her in ages. She might have moved away for all I knew. All I could rely on to be rid of the vicar was the rumour that Juliette had started. How many people had the barman told? Barry obviously hadn't heard the gossip, and I began to wonder whether Juliette was right about rumours spreading like wildfire.

'Have you heard the gossip?' I asked, watching for his reaction.

'Gossip? There's so much gossip in the village that it's difficult to keep up with it. I did hear that Mrs Baker from the post office is pregnant yet again.'

'God, she's already got five kids.'

'Her husband . . . Yes, well.'

'So, you've not heard the rumour about the vicar?'

'The vicar? OK, what's the story?'

'I overheard someone in a shop this morning. I didn't hear it all, but it seems that the vicar was caught with his trousers down in the church.'

'Good God,' he laughed. 'His trousers down in the church? I can't say that I've heard that one. What was he doing, bringing himself off?'

'All I heard was that he was with a young girl and he was caught in a compromising position.'

'That might explain it,' he murmured pensively.

'Explain what?'

'Who caught him with the girl?'

'The girl's mother, apparently.'

'I saw him walking to the station with a suitcase earlier.'

'You mean he might have gone away?'

'If a horrendous rumour like that gets around the village . . . What choice would he have?'

'Particularly if it's true and he really *was* abusing some girl or other.'

'Crystal, I think this might be our chance.'

'To do what?'

'To search his cottage. If he has gone away, then I

doubt that he'll have left incriminating photographs behind. But we might discover something else, some other sort of evidence.'

'We don't know for sure that he has moved away. He might just have gone to visit someone.'

'Possibly. He only had one suitcase, so I reckon that he'll be back. Whether to collect the rest of his things or . . . We should search his place tonight, Crystal.'

'When did you see him going to the station? How long has he been gone?'

'About two hours ago. If we go to his place now and . . . Damn. My mother's coming over later. We'll have to leave it.'

'That's a shame. I'm sure that he has a stash of photographs of me – and of other girls, more than likely. If he only had one suitcase, he might not have taken the photographs.'

'A chance like this, and my mother's coming over. Unless . . . No, no.'

'Unless what?'

'I was just wondering . . . You could go to his cottage and take a look round.'

'No, no . . .' I said shakily. 'I'm not going anywhere near that place.'

'He keeps a front-door key beneath a flowerpot by the step. I know that because I've seen him use the key. You could—'

'What if he comes back and finds me there?'

'Flick the latch on the front door. If you hear him outside, trying to open the door, make your escape through the back garden.'

'No, it's too risky. I've been there once and . . . I won't go into that.'

'I understand. Crystal, I have an idea.'

'Go on.'

'You go to his place and search . . .'

'No, Barry. I told you, I don't want to go there, let alone search—'

'Listen to me for a moment. After you've searched his cottage, come round to my place on your way home. If you don't turn up within, say, an hour, I'll come and find you. I'll break in, if I have to.'

'All right,' I conceded, finishing my drink.

'Good. It's quite a walk into the village. I'll drop you off and then go back to my place and wait for my mother. Call in on your way back, OK?'

'I don't like this, Barry.'

'Neither do I. But this is the chance we've been waiting for. When you told me about the rumour . . . It all fits. I reckon that he's moving away.'

'One suitcase,' I murmured. 'If he left two hours ago . . .'

'The sooner you search his cottage, the better.'

'OK, let's go.'

Barry dropped me off a few yards from the vicar's cottage and then drove home. Standing in the cold lane, I gazed at the place, looking up at the front-room window. The sexual torture chamber. The cottage was in darkness, but the vicar could return at any minute. I was wasting time, I knew as I looked up and down the lane. My thoughts muddled, I wondered whether the vicar had heard the rumour and was in the process of moving out. Perhaps he'd already taken his belongings and Barry had seen him with the last suitcase. I didn't know what to think. The vicar had said something about going away for a week or two, so I reckoned – eventually – that it was safe enough to search his cottage.

Finding the key beneath the pot, I let myself in and flicked the latch as Barry had suggested. Unable to see a thing in the dark, I felt along the wall and switched the hall light on. If the vicar came back, he might believe that he'd left the light on, I mused as I climbed the stairs. By the time he'd fiddled with the lock and managed to get in, I'd have raced downstairs, slipped through the back door and got away. Reaching the top of the stairs, I realized that I should have taken someone with me. Safety in numbers? But I had no idea where Juliette was, and Robin . . . Trying to calm my mind, I decided to search the sex den first.

Slipping into the room, I switched the light on and looked around me. Nothing had changed, which I thought was odd. If the vicar was going to do a runner, surely he'd have dismantled the torture chamber, done away with the evidence of his perverted ways. Perhaps he intended to come back, I thought anxiously. If the cottage belonged to the church, then the furniture . . . The vicar didn't have a car and might have been moving his personal belongings out in stages. Clothes, papers, bits and pieces . . . He probably didn't have a great deal to take with him. Two or three trips might do it.

Searching a cupboard, I was amazed by the host of horrendous-looking devices I discovered. Speculums, metal clamps, huge dildos . . . This was evidence enough, and I couldn't understand why he'd not cleared the sex chamber before moving anything else out of the cottage. Opening a drawer, I found several large candles, handcuffs, shaving equipment . . . Noticing a bundle of photographs, I stood beneath the light and flicked through them.

'Good God,' I breathed, gazing at a photograph of a young girl's naked body tied to the table in the torture chamber. Her hairless vaginal lips held wide apart with clamps and thin chains, a huge candle emerging between the rounded cheeks of her buttocks . . . Gazing at the girl's face, I frowned. It was Lorraine, a girl from my class at school. I'd not seen her for a year or so and had assumed that she'd moved away. How many victims had the vicar lured to his sex den? I wondered, looking through the photographs. Finding another one of Lorraine with thin chains and weights attached to her elongated nipples, I realized that it must have been taken fairly recently. She was about my age, and by the look of . . .

'Great,' I beamed, discovering several photographs of the vicar's cock fucking my pretty mouth, his sperm flowing down my chin. Placing the bundle of photographs on the table, I rummaged through the drawer again. More speculums, vibrators, weird-looking metal contraptions with screws and levers . . . This was evidence enough that the vicar was far from a man of God. A man of Satan, more like. If the villagers knew that he had a sexual torture chamber in his cottage, they'd lock up their daughters.

'Hello,' the vicar said softly, grinning sinisterly as he stood in the doorway. He was dressed in some sort of leather bondage gear. Frozen to the spot, I could say nothing as I gazed at the shaft of his erect penis emerging through a hole in the leather pouch over his crotch. 'Now this really *is* a stroke of luck.'

'You . . . you bastard,' I finally breathed shakily.

'Your friend Juliette has been dealt with,' he said. 'And now . . .'

'What have you done to her?'

'Suffice it to say that she won't be bothering anyone again. Least of all me. And now I have to deal with *you*, Crystal. You've been fun over the years as a plaything, but now I have no further need of you.'

'People know that I'm here,' I hissed. 'Unless I'm back within an hour, they'll come looking for me.'

'Of course they will,' he laughed. 'By the way, the psychiatrist is in on this. He supplies me with fresh meat. Fresh female meat, I mean.'

'I don't believe you,' I gasped, sure that Robin would never abuse young girls.

'Whether you believe me or not doesn't really bother me. Didn't you ask him about his previous house-keepers? They disappeared, Crystal. One by one, the young girls he employed vanished into thin air.'

'Robin would never—'

'I see you've found the photographs of Lorraine. Now, she didn't work for Robin, as a matter of fact. She came to the church and . . . well, that's another story. Would you take your coat off, please?'

'No,' I gasped, fear welling from the pit of my stomach as the priest grabbed a leather whip and moved towards me.

'We can do this one of two ways, Crystal. Either you remove your clothes, or *I* remove them. The choice is yours.'

'I'm leaving,' I retorted. 'And if you think you can stop me . . .'

'Leaving already?' the vicar's accomplice asked, grinning as he blocked the doorway.

Raising the leather whip over his head, the vicar flashed me a triumphant grin. I stared at his penis, the veined shaft rising above his heaving balls, the taut purple crown I'd sucked to orgasm hundreds of times in the past. This couldn't be happening, I thought, wondering whether Barry had set me up. I should never have trusted the man. I should never have trusted anyone. I'd flicked the latch on the front door, so the vicar and his partner in sexual crime must have been expecting me. They'd been hiding in the cottage already, lurking, waiting to pounce.

The young man hurriedly removed his clothes and stood with his huge cock pointing to the ceiling. He'd shaved his balls, his mons. His genitalia smooth and soft, his crotch looked like that of a young boy. Wondering what they'd done with Lorraine and Juliette, I knew that I was in real danger. My only hope was that Barry hadn't set me up and would come looking for me. There was no hope, I was sure. Of course Barry had arranged this. How else would the vicar know that I was planning to search his cottage?

'We're waiting,' the vicar said.

'Where's Juliette?' I asked.

'Somewhere far away,' he chuckled. 'Now, are you going to take your clothes off or shall I—'

'Let me do it,' the young man cut in. 'I'l rip her skirt to shreds, tear her panties off . . . What was that?' he asked as a dull thud sounded downstairs.

'Nothing,' the vicar said. 'This old place is always full of creaks and thuds at night. Now then, Crystal. Clothes off, please.'

'All right,' I conceded, hoping that the noise had meant that someone had come to rescue me.

Taking my coat off, I wondered whether Robin had followed me. He seemed to know all about me, my every move, and might have picked up some psychic message or other telling him that I was in danger. Sure that I'd heard a creak downstairs as I unbuttoned my blouse and slipped the garment off my shoulders, I thought that Barry might not have set me up. He might have come to make sure that I was all right. I was trying to cling to a glimmer of hope that didn't exist. Only Barry had known that I was going to the vicar's cottage, I'd told no one else. The chances of the cleric seeing me arrive, turning the lights out and hiding . . . Barry had told him that I'd be there, that was for sure.

Stepping out of my skirt as it fell around my ankles, I slipped my shoes off and stood naked in front of my captors. They laughed, asking me why I wasn't wearing any panties. The young man called me a slut, suggesting that I never wore panties so that my cunt was always ready for cocks. I supposed that he was right – my cunt *had* been ready to receive a hard cock. Someone was moving about downstairs, I was sure as I heard another creak. It had to be Robin. He was my only hope now.

'I'd better go and check downstairs,' the vicar said, leaving the room. 'Get her onto the table.'

'You heard the man,' the Devil's assistant chortled. 'Get on the table, on your back.'

'You won't get away with this,' I said, climbing onto the table and lying on my back under the light. 'When Juliette realized that—'

'Didn't you get my note?' he asked. 'I left a note under your telephone saying that I'd be back.'

'*Your* note?' I breathed.

'I said that I'd be back, and I was. I took Juliette.'

'You couldn't have.'

'Couldn't I?'

As he bound my wrists and ankles, my stomach churned. So he *had* been up to my room the previous evening. I'd thought that Juliette had left the note and . . . Why hadn't he waited for me to get back from the pub? Perhaps Robin had disturbed him, I reflected. If the vicar's accomplice had been into the house, then he might have taken Juliette, it was true. Perhaps she'd got up in the night to go to the loo and he'd leaped out of the shadows and grabbed her. My mind aching, I watched the young man finish his job of bondage and stand back to admire his handiwork. My legs wide apart, my hairless vulval lips gaping, I knew that I was in for a horrendous time.

'I thought it might have been Robin but there was no one there,' the vicar said as he walked into the room. 'Just the old beams creaking in the night.'

'You're expecting Robin?' I asked, lifting my head off the table.

'Of course,' he laughed. 'As I said, he supplies me with fresh meat. He should be here before long.'

'You're a pervert and a liar,' I spat as he ran his fingertips up and down the yawning crack of my vagina.

'Crystal, I have no need to lie to you any more. You won't be leaving here, so it doesn't matter whether or not you know the truth. Robin has been working with us for a long time. He employs you girls as housekeepers and . . . well, they end up here.'

'Who else is in on this?'

'Several people. You know nothing, Crystal. You and your bloody meddling, poking your nose in where it's not wanted . . . You obviously thought that you were the only girl. I've lost count of the girls who have been to this room.'

'What about Barry Carter? Is he in on this?'

'Ah, the English teacher. Yes, of course he's working with us. He needs young girls as much as we do. He's supplied several young beauties from the school. It's so easy, Crystal. He's an English teacher, a man in a position of trust. I'm a vicar, a man of God. It's so easy.'

'Let's get on with it,' the young man said, taking a bamboo cane from the corner of the room.

'A word before we get started,' the vicar murmured, leaving the room.

Wondering what was going on as they whispered outside the door, I thought what a fool I'd been. Robin wasn't psychic. He, and probably others, had been following me, spying on me. His radio equipment in the shed was probably for keeping in touch with the other perverts. Carter had conned me, I reflected. How the hell did he know that there was a key beneath the flowerpot? Telling me that his mother was visiting him and . . . I'd been such a fool. Juliette was missing, I'd not seen Jenny around the village for some time . . . It wouldn't have surprised me if the young lads had been involved with the vicar. Perhaps half the village were in on it, the men fucking the young girls, using and abusing them until they were no longer needed and . . . And what?

Again thinking what a fool I'd been, I wondered why the girls hadn't been missed. There again, a lot of the girls from school had left the village, moved away to find work in London or wherever. Or had they? How many housekeepers had Robin employed? I couldn't believe that he was working with the vicar. He was strange, to say the least, but . . . Recalling his consulting room, the dildos and handcuffs, I felt my stomach churn again. He had several spare rooms in his house. How many girls had lived there before disappearing from the face of the Earth?

'We'll start with a pussy-thrashing,' the young man announced, grinning evilly as he followed the vicar into the room. Tapping my hairless vulval lips with the thin bamboo cane, he turned to the vicar. 'An *internal* thrashing, I think,' he said.

'Of course,' the vicar chuckled, taking something from a drawer. 'Just to get her warmed up.'

'She's a nice specimen. One of the best we've had for quite some time.'

'It's a great shame that she had to interfere,' the vicar sighed, passing something to his accomplice. 'However, she *did* interfere and now she has to be silenced.'

Fixing two metal clamps to the fleshy cushions of my outer labia, the young man ran two chains from the clamps over my hips and down either side of the table. I knew what he was doing as he fixed heavy weights to the clamps. I'd seen the photographs of Lorraine, her tortured pussy lips. My vaginal lips stretched wide apart, exposing the sensitive inner flesh of my sex valley, I couldn't imagine what it would be like to be caned there. The funnel of pink flesh surrounding my vaginal entrance, my clitoris . . . The pain would be excruciating.

'It's no good,' the young man said, lowering the top section of the table so that my head fell back. 'I've got to fuck her mouth before I do anything else.'

'She enjoys having her mouth fucked,' the vicar laughed as I stared upside down at the young man's solid penis.

'I know I've said it before, but you did a brilliant job on this table. With her head at this angle, I'll be able to push my cock straight down her throat.'

He was right: my head back, my mouth open wide, he slipped his purple knob into my mouth and drove it right down my throat. My nose pressed against his hairy scrotum, my lips stretched tautly around the broad shaft of his huge organ, I breathed heavily through my nose as his knob seemed to travel all the way down my throat to my stomach. I'd never taken a cock down my throat, and was surprised that it was possible to swallow the entire organ without choking. Withdrawing until his swollen knob settled between my full lips, the vicar's accomplice drove into me again, his glans gliding down my throat until the base of his cock met my lips. I could feel his glans deep within my throat, his balls pressed hard against my nose as I stared between his legs at the far wall. This was sexual degradation beyond belief.

Sliding his solid shaft in and out of my mouth, his bulbous knob repeatedly gliding down my throat, he pinched and pulled on the sensitive teats of my nipples. Had I not been fearful for my safety, I'd have enjoyed the deep-throat fucking, the painful abuse of my sensitive nipples. My tethered body jolting as the vicar thrust what felt like a huge candle deep into the tight shaft of my wet cunt, I wondered what horrendous abuse the evil pair had planned for me. I couldn't see what the vicar was doing, but I could hear the repeated click of a camera shutter. More incriminating evidence, I thought. Evidence? If they were going to do away with me, it didn't matter what evidence they had.

'While you're busy fucking her throat, I'll do her arse,' the vicar said, lowering the bottom end of the table. My feet almost on the floor, my naked buttocks over the edge of the table, I wondered how many other girls had been in this very position. The table was an ingenious contraption, the work of perverted minds, and I recalled Robin's examination couch. How many girls had he tied to his couch and sexually abused before delivering them to the vicar? Still finding it hard to believe that he was in with the evil pair, I remembered the internal examination I'd endured. He was probably evaluating me, scrutinizing my naked body to determine whether or not I was worth sending to the vicar to use for crude sex.

My sore nipples painfully stretched, I felt something encircling the base of my breasts. It was rope, tightening around my mammary spheres, my tits ballooning as the pressure increased. Tightening the rope further, the vicar chuckled in his wickedness, remarking on the dark discs of my areolae, my inflating nipples. The camera shutter clicked again as the young man continued to throat-fuck me. Did they sell the photographs to perverts? I felt the vicar's fingers between my firm buttocks, painfully parting my bum-cheeks, exposing the sensitive ring of my anus. Tensing my buttocks in readiness to defend my bottom-hole, I felt his bulbous knob pressing hard against the eye of my tightly closed anal portal.

'Hot and tight,' the vicar gasped, his ballooning knob slipping past my defeated sphincter muscles and journeying along my rectal tube to my bowels. The bloating sensation within my pelvis was incredible. My cunt stretched to capacity by a massive candle, the vicar's huge cock embedded deep within my arse, the young man's knob repeatedly gliding down my throat . . . Never had I known such degradation. My teenage body rocking with the double fucking, I prayed for my freedom, prayed for someone to come to my rescue. But there was no one to come to my aid. Robin had betrayed me, Carter had . . .

'Ah, yes,' the young man breathed, his spunk gushing from his throbbing knob, pumping down my throat and into my stomach without my having to swallow. The vicar releasing his sperm, lubricating the inflamed sheath of my rectum with his orgasmic cream, I wondered whether to make an effort to save myself from my inevitable fate. I could offer to supply the evil men with fresh meat, as the vicar had put it. They were obviously aware that I knew young girls, and might spare me if I offered to become a supplier. A purveyor of teenage cunt? How far would I go to save my own skin?

The young man finally withdrawing his spent cock from my throat, his sperm dribbling from his knob-slit and running up my nose, I raised my head and gazed at my tortured breasts as he moved away. The ropes tightly bound around the base of my mammary globes, my tits looking like two purple balloons, I wondered what had become of my teenage body. I'd offered my cunt, my mouth, my arse, to dozens of cocks. I'd swallowed gallons of spunk, allowed men to use and abuse me, fuck me, finger me, spunk me . . . What the hell had I done with my young life?

My father had always been away on business, my mother had been too strict, the vicar had entrapped me at an early age . . . Could I blame others for my wanton behaviour? Had my mother not been so trusting in the vicar, had the vicar been a man of morals, had the young boys at school not been saturated with testosterone and better able to control their cocks . . . Hormones weren't to blame for my debauchery. And neither were other people. It was my life, my body, and the things I'd done that had been my undoing. There again, had the vicar not introduced me to crude sex . . . Someone else would have. At some stage in my young life, someone would have taught me the delights of orgasm, cock-sucking, sperm-swallowing, arse-fucking. Why were so many girls normal? I wondered. They grew up into fine young ladies, never masturbated, retained their virginity until an age society deemed decent . . . Or did they? Was I deluding myself?

The vicar's cock finally slipping out of my spunked arse like a cork out of a bottle, I recalled an incident I'd long since pushed to the back of my subconscious. I was young, naive, innocent. Wasn't that always my excuse for my sexually wanton behaviour? Perhaps it *had* been my fault that a very good friend of my father's had toyed with the fleshy lips of my little pussy.

My parents had gone into town, leaving me to do my homework. It was a beautiful summer day and I was sitting in the garden in my bikini when the man called. He joined me on the patio, saying that he'd help me with my homework. He looked at me, stared at the cleavage between my small breasts, my nipples clearly defined by my flimsy bikini top. Taking no interest in my work, he said that he liked teenage girls and wanted to look at my naked body. I wasn't shocked, I even half expected him to make a move. I suppose that I was used to men gazing at me, their lecherous looks. I was used to the vicar pushing his purple knob into my mouth or the sheath of my tight pussy.

The man was in his thirties and had something to do with my father's work. He also wanted to have something to do with his daughter. When he reached out and pulled my bikini top down, exposing the firm mounds of my teenage breasts, I moved away and told him that I had to get on with my work. He just laughed and said that I'd better do as he asked, otherwise he'd tell my parents about me. I didn't know what he meant. Tell my parents about what? He left me guessing, stroking my long blonde hair as I sat on the patio beneath the hot sun. He said that he liked my body, and he wanted me to stand up and show him my pussy.

I was confused. He was a family friend, a man who'd often visited us, stayed for dinner. He'd watched me grow, develop, and must have decided that I was old enough. Old enough to be loved properly? I could trust no one to keep their hands off my young body, even family friends. Hadn't the vicar been a trusted family friend?

'If your parents knew . . .' the family friend began, massaging his solid penis through his trousers. 'I don't know what they'd think about you.'

'What?' I asked, frowning at him. 'If my parents knew what?'

'If they knew that you came to the front door naked. If they knew that you'd asked me to fuck you . . .'

'Lies,' I breathed.

'Let's not complicate matters, Crystal. I don't want to get you into trouble so just do as I ask. Come and stand here and show me your little pink cunt.'

I stood in front of him, innocent in my guilt as he pulled the front of my bikini down and gazed longingly at the tightly closed slit of my pussy. He talked about masturbation, asked me whether I fingered my pussy and frigged my clitoris to orgasm. He said that my mother would be horrified if she discovered that I masturbated. Taking my pencil from the table, he pushed it between the fleshy swell of my cunny lips, driving the thin wooden shaft deep into my vaginal canal.

His hands were trembling, his trousers bulging, and I knew that he wanted to fuck me. Every man I met wanted to fuck me. Had other men fucked my mother?

Yanking the pencil out of my pussy, he made me bend over with my feet wide apart, the rounded cheeks of my naked bottom displayed to his wide-eyed stare. Following his instructions, I reached behind my back and eased a finger into my bottom-hole, pushing it deep into the heat of my tight rectum. Stroking my firm buttocks, he said that he knew about my activities. I thought he meant the vicar, but discovered later that he knew nothing about me. He was hoping that I'd have a few secrets, as many teenage girls do. Most young girls masturbate, and he knew that, played on that. He made out that he knew things about me, dreadful secrets that would shock my mother.

'Bend over the table,' he ordered me. Slipping my hot finger out of my bottom-hole, I leaned over the patio table, standing with my feet apart, my naked buttocks projected. I heard his zip sliding down, movements behind me, and then felt the bulb of his solid penis inside my anal gully. My tight brown ring was dry, in need of lubrication. Slipping his knob between my vaginal lips, he creamed his glans and then moved up to my anus again.

'Yes,' he breathed, his purple crown slipping past my anal sphincter muscles, driving deep into the core of my young body. 'You like that, don't you?' he asked, grabbing my hips and fucking my bottom. I said nothing, clinging to the table and allowing him to arse-fuck me, wondering what secrets he knew about me. 'Can you feel my cock up your arse?' he breathed, his swinging balls slapping the wet lips of my teenage cunt. 'I'm going to spunk up your arse, Crystal. I'm going to fill your sweet arse with my spunk.'

Ramming his cock-head deep into my bowels, his belly slapping my tensed buttocks, he let out a low moan as his sperm gushed and filled my inflamed rectal tube. Listening to the squelching sounds of sperm as he arse-fucked me, I gazed at my homework lying on the table. Suffragettes, women's rights. What rights did *I* have? Wherever I was, wherever I went, men were after my teenage body. Even sitting in the garden doing my homework, I was used and abused.

The family friend finally slipped his spent cock out of my bottom-hole, leaving me with sperm oozing from the inflamed eye of my anus. I slipped my bikini back on and carried on with my homework as he left. He'd had what he'd wanted: he'd fucked and spunked my teenage arse and drained his balls. Some family friend *he* was.

'Come in, come in,' the vicar exclaimed jovially as someone entered the room, bringing me back to the stark reality of my predicament. 'I'm pleased that you could make it.'

'I wouldn't miss this for anything,' Robin chuckled, eyeing the curves and crevices of my naked body.

'You've betrayed me,' I hissed, my already crumbling faith in humanity shattering as I stared hard at Robin. 'I thought you were—'

'He's not only betrayed you,' the vicar said and grinned triumphantly. 'He's about to fuck every hole in your body.'

A tear rolled down my cheek as Robin ran his finger-tips over the painfully clamped lips of my vagina. I'd been bad, sucking cocks, drinking spunk, allowing young lads to mouth-fuck me and . . . I'd hoped that things would change as I grew. When I'd met Robin, I'd thought I'd found not only a friend and confidant in the eccentric man but a . . . Foolishly, I think I'd fallen in love with him. His eccentricity, his dress sense, his garden shed with its radio equipment . . . Never having a proper father figure, let alone a friend and a lover . . . I'd thought that Robin . . . I didn't know what I'd thought.

One thing was for sure. Never would I escape the perverted desires of men, of all ages. The boys had used me to satisfy their craving for crude sex, older men had fucked my mouth and my cunt and my arse without giving a thought for my feelings. There was no such thing as love, I concluded. Parental or otherwise, love didn't exist. I'd stupidly believed that Robin and I would become . . . I didn't know what I'd stupidly believed.

'Got any more girl-meat lined up?' the vicar asked the treacherous psychiatrist.

'You bet,' Robin chuckled. 'Now that this little slut's room is vacant, I'm planning on getting some students in. Are you up for a bit of Mediterranean pussy?'

'I'm up for any breed of pussy, as long as it's young and fresh,' the vicar laughed.

Girl-meat? Was that all I was to Robin? A lump of female flesh to be used, fucked, spunked . . . How long had he been working with the vicar? I wondered. Where was Juliette? As they talked about my naked body, discussed my tight cunt and my firm tits as if I wasn't in the room, I couldn't understand why Robin had bought me a new Jag. He must have owned the car already, I reflected. Making out that he'd bought it for me, there must have been some method behind his madness, some plan or other. Was he really mad? Perhaps it was an act, although I couldn't see the point in pretending to be insane.

'Who the hell's that?' the vicar whispered as the front doorbell rang. 'I'm not expecting anyone.'

'Shit,' the young man breathed. 'You'd better slip your cassock on and go and answer it. Whoever it is will see the light on, they'll know that you're in.'

'This is all we need,' the vicar complained as the bell rang again and someone knocked loudly on the door. 'What the hell are we going to do with her?'

'I doubt that we've anything to worry about,' the young man said, releasing the vaginal lip clamps. 'It's probably nothing important.'

'No, but we can't be too careful. Get her out of here. Hide her in the garden until I've dealt with this.'

Releasing the ropes, the young man hauled me off the table and ordered me to put my coat on. Praying that I'd have a chance to make my escape as he frogmarched me downstairs, I couldn't understand why they were panicking. It could have been a neighbour at the door, so why drag me out into the garden? Perhaps the vicar was afraid of the police, I mused as Robin opened the back door. The rumours, the police . . . Stepping out into the garden as they hovered in the kitchen, turning their backs to me for a split second, I ran like hell across the lawn and made my escape into the woods. It was dark, but I knew my way around and I raced along the narrow path, heading for a small clearing surrounded by bushes. I could hear someone coming after me in the dark, twigs cracking, heavy breathing.

Behind the bushes, I crouched in the clearing, the icy-cold air wafting around my ankles as I held my breath and pulled my coat collar up. I tried not to shiver, tried to be still as someone neared the clearing. I could hear Robin calling me, saying that he'd conned the vicar and would help me to get home. Home? I reflected. I could hardly go to Robin's house. Barry Carter was in on the act, so I couldn't go there. I had nowhere to go, no one I could trust . . .

'Where are you, Crystal?' Robin called again. 'I'm on your side, for God's sake. I came to rescue you.' He was lying, I knew. His talk about supplying fresh meat . . . He was in with the vicar, there was no doubt in my mind. My only hope of escape was to head for my mother's cottage. No, they'd be watching, spying, ready to pounce from the shadows. With only a coat to keep me warm, I knew that I couldn't stay in the clearing all night. My only hope was . . . There was no hope.

II

I waited in the woods for an hour or so, the cold penetrating my flesh, my body shivering uncontrollably. All had gone quiet, and I hoped that they'd called off the search as I emerged from my hiding place and headed along the narrow path to the lane. With nowhere to go, I decided to make my way to Robin's house. If I could get into the shed and switch the heater on, I'd at least keep warm and hopefully be safe enough until the morning came. What I'd do then, I wasn't sure. Possibly head for my mother's cottage, slip in through the back garden unnoticed?

Walking along the lane, I realized that I'd lost all track of time. I had no idea how long I'd been in the vicar's sex dungeon, but the time was the least of my worries. Becoming colder by the minute, I started to trot along the lane to try and warm up. I longed for the summer, the warm evenings, meeting the boys in the woods. Where would I be once the winter had gone? Abroad? Bronzed Mediterranean men, the sun, the sea . . . Or in the vicar's sex dungeon?

Hearing a car approaching from behind, I dived into the bushes, praying, as the headlights closed in on me, that it wasn't Robin coming after me. I was pretty vulnerable, walking along the lane alone at night, but I had no other choice. Not recognizing the car as it passed, I ran the rest of the way to the house and slipped around the side of the building into the back garden.

As I'd expected, the shed was padlocked. There were no lights on in the house, and I reckoned that Robin was still at the vicar's cottage, probably making plans to recapture me. Shivering uncontrollably, I knew that I had to get warm before much longer. The shed was my only hope. I was trying to force the padlock off the door with a piece of wood when I happened to look up and notice that Juliette's light was on. Reckoning that Robin was back, probably clearing out her room to make way for his next victim, I gazed up at the window, wondering what to do. He'd be clearing *my* things out before long. I must have been mad to trust him. And to think that fallen in love with him was . . .

'Juliette,' I breathed as she appeared at the window and drew the curtains. She was fully clothed – no chains or handcuffs, either. What the hell was she doing there? I wondered, grabbing a handful of small stones and tossing them at her window. As she looked out, I waved frantically, doing my best to attract her attention without shouting. Shortly after she'd drawn the curtains again, the kitchen light came on. Where the hell was Robin? Shivering in the dark, I saw Juliette at the sink, filling the kettle. I didn't know what was going on as I walked up to the back door and tapped on the glass. The young man had said that he'd taken her, so why . . .

'What on earth are you doing out there?' she asked, opening the door.

'Where's Robin?' I whispered, slipping into the kitchen.

'Out. Why?'

'I'll go up to your room. If he comes back, you haven't seen me, OK?'

'OK, but . . .'

'I could do with a cup of coffee.'

'I'll bring one up in a minute. Crystal, what the hell's going on?'

'I'll tell you later. You haven't seen me, Juliette. Do you understand?'

'Yes, of course.'

Dashing upstairs, I dived into Juliette's room and huddled up against the radiator. The perverts had been lying about Juliette – but why? The young man had been into my room and left the note beneath my phone, I knew that much. Had Juliette managed to escape, she'd hardly be making coffee in Robin's kitchen. My mind confused, I couldn't work out what was going on. Beginning to warm up, I sat on the bed as Juliette came in with two coffees and locked the door behind her. She looked all right, clean and tidy. It was pretty obvious that she'd not been to the vicar's sex den. My coat fell open and she shook her head, frowning as she stared at my naked breasts.

'Where the hell have you been?' she asked, standing in front of me. 'More to the point, where are your clothes?'

'It's a long story,' I sighed, sipping my coffee. 'Basically, the vicar, some other man and Robin captured me and sexually abused me.'

'Robin?' she said, staring at me in disbelief. 'He captured you and abused you?'

'Yes, our beloved Robin.'

'That's ridiculous,' she giggled. 'When was this?'

'This evening. He's at the vicar's cottage now. There were three of them. Oh, and Barry Carter is in their gang.'

'Carter, the English teacher?'

'The very same.'

'Ah, that'll be Robin,' she said as the front door closed.

'Don't . . .' I began, my eyes wide with fear.

'I'll go down and talk to him. It's all right, I won't say that you're here.'

As Juliette left the room, I listened at the door. I could hear her bounding down the stairs, saying something to Robin in the hallway. Easing the door open, I crept to the top of the stairs as she followed Robin into the kitchen and offered him a cup of coffee. He asked her about me, whether or not she'd seen me come home. Juliette lied, changing the subject to make out that she knew nothing.

'Are you sure she's not in her room?' Robin asked.

'Positive,' she replied. 'Do you need to speak to her or something?'

'Yes, urgently. There's been a right cock-up and I'm afraid for her safety.'

'What are you talking about?'

'Crystal was . . . This business with the vicar. I went to his cottage to rescue Crystal. I'd already spoken to the vicar and gained his confidence. It wasn't easy, but I managed to convince him that I was . . . well, like him.'

'A pervert?'

'Yes. He'd already been here, looking for Crystal. I chatted to him, talking about dirty photographs and young girls. We met a couple of times and I managed to get in with him. He hadn't said anything to me, but I had a feeling that Crystal was going to his cottage this evening.'

'And did she?'

'Yes, she did. I decided to go along to make sure that she wasn't in any danger. I got there and chatted to the vicar, made out that I'd got a young girl lined up for him. He told me that Crystal was upstairs in the sex den and he invited me to join him and his friend. It was terrible. Crystal was naked, tied to a table in the vicar's sex den. Playing the part, I made out that I was joining in with the debauchery until . . . Luckily, Crystal escaped.'

'Where to?'

'That's just it. I have no idea where she is. She was only wearing her coat and, if she stays out in this cold for much longer . . . I dread to think.'

Was Robin telling the truth? I wondered. His story did sound feasible. But I couldn't understand why he'd not told me that he'd become friendly with the vicar to the point where the man trusted him. I was still feeling cold and tired, but I dared not go to sleep until I was certain that Robin was genuine. For all I knew, he had the vicar waiting outside in a car, ready to whisk me back to the torture chamber. I wasn't even sure that I could trust Juliette. She'd left the house early, been gone all day . . .

'What I don't understand—' Juliette began.

'There are several things I don't understand,' Robin said. 'Firstly, if there's life on other planets, then why don't they make contact with us?'

'*What*? Robin, what the *hell* are you on about?'

'Thirdly, what on earth was Crystal doing at the vicar's place? She must have been mad to go there alone.'

'I've not seen her since I left the house this morning, so I wouldn't know. How come you know so much about the vicar?'

'When he decided that he could trust me, he told me a few things about his clandestine activities.'

'Oh, I get it. You get in with him on this abuse racket, you knew that Crystal was going to his cottage . . .'

'What are you trying to say?'

'What Crystal would say if she was here.'

'You don't trust me?'

'Crystal has told me everything about the perverted vicar. She confided in me, and yet she said nothing about going to his place.'

'How could she have told you? You've been out all day.'

'Then how did you know? Unless the vicar told you, there's no way you could have known. Think about it, Robin. Do you expect her to trust you?'

'I see what you mean,' he sighed. 'And after this evening . . . I don't suppose she'll ever set foot in this house again. I blame the bloody Martians.'

'Where are you going?' Juliette asked as I heard the back door open.

'To sulk in my shed. And to switch my radio on and communicate with any passing spaceships.'

'You're mad, Robin.'

'I will be if the Martians don't answer my call.'

I was in two minds as to whether to go downstairs and confront Robin or not. He seemed genuine, but didn't everyone? Returning to Juliette's room, I sat on her bed, wondering who had been at the vicar's front door. Perhaps Carter had called to join in with the debauchery. Feeling more confused than ever, I thought about leaving, getting away. All I had to do was grab a few things and drive off in the Jag.

'He's gone out to the shed,' Juliette said as she walked into the room and locked the door. 'He said that he went to the vicar's cottage to make sure that you were all right.'

'Yes, I heard you talking. Should I trust him?'

'God only knows,' she sighed, gazing out of the window. 'He *might* be telling the truth.'

'He might be lying. I'm thinking of going away, Juliette.'

'Away? Where to?'

'Anywhere. Wales, Scotland . . . Anywhere that's far away from this place.'

'What does he do in that shed? I can see him fiddling with a radio or something.'

'I don't know what he gets up to. I think he might be a Russian spy.'

'Don't be daft,' she giggled. 'Robin, a Russian spy?'

'Why not? This psychiatrist thing might be a cover. He doesn't have many clients. Perhaps the few clients he has are contacts.'

'You've been watching too much television.'

'I never watch TV. Think about it. He has radio equipment in the shed, a few strange people call, he pretends to be mad, he has loads of money . . .'

'Spies usually have access to government papers or whatever. Living here in the sticks, what information could Robin get that would be useful to anyone?'

'He might be some sort of middleman, passing information on to Moscow.'

'You're talking nonsense, Crystal. Anyway, you shouldn't be thinking about Robin. You should make some plans, decide what you're going to do.'

'All I can do is get away from here.'

'Look, I'll go and talk to Robin. If I can find out the truth . . . I'll talk to him, OK?'

'OK. But you must promise not to tell him that I'm here.'

'I promise.'

Finishing my coffee, I slipped my coat off and climbed into Juliette's bed. Exhausted, tired, cold, I desperately needed to sleep. Thoughts swirled around my racked mind: the vicar, Carter, Robin, Lorraine, Juliette . . . I had to get far away from the area. I'd escape during the night. Grab my car keys and a few things from my room and drive off into the dark of the night. My head aching with a million thoughts, I finally fell asleep.

Waking at seven to find myself alone in bed, I wondered where Juliette had got to. Slipping out of bed, I crept onto the landing, listening for signs of life. Finally donning Juliette's dressing gown and venturing downstairs, I discovered that I was alone in the house. This was my chance to leave, I knew as I raced upstairs to the bathroom. Taking a shower, washing away the dried sperm and girl-juice from my inflamed vaginal crack, I went to my room and dressed. Not wanting to take too much with me, I stuffed a suitcase with clothes and a few bits and pieces and grabbed my car keys. My phone rang as I left my room and went downstairs. It might have been my mother, I reflected. Or the vicar.

Surprised to find my car outside the house, I wondered why Robin hadn't at least taken the keys back. I shouldn't have been bothering about Robin, I knew as I drove off. The chains had gone – I was free. Slowing up as I approached Carter's cottage, I stopped outside. Robin had betrayed me, and the vicar, Carter . . . Why? I wondered. Was their thirst for crude sex so insatiable that they'd go to any lengths to get their hands on young girls? Pulling into Carter's drive, I knew that I was making a mistake. But I had to talk to him, discover . . . I didn't know what I was doing as I rang his doorbell. Walking into a pervert's lair, more than likely.

'Crystal,' he said warmly, beaming and opening the door. 'Come in, come in.'

'I can't stay,' I said, following him into the hall.

'What happened last night? I went to the vicar's cottage and—'

'Before we go any further,' I cut in as he closed the door, 'the police know that I'm here.'

'The police? I'm not with you.'

'I told them that I was coming here, so don't get any ideas.'

'Crystal, you're not making any sense. What do you mean, *don't get any ideas*?'

'I think you know what I mean. Anyway, I'm leaving. You'll never see me in the village again.'

'Where are you going?'

'I'm hardly likely to tell *you* that, am I? Besides, I don't know yet.'

'I have to say that I'll miss you. We were just getting to know each other. Would you like some coffee?'

'Yes, please.'

'Why tell the police that you're here?'

'Because I know that you're working with the perverted vicar. He told me everything, Barry, so don't deny it.'

'I emphatically deny it,' he returned, filling the kettle.

'You supply him with young schoolgirls, don't you?'

'*What*? Young schoolgirls? I don't know what he's been saying, but he's lying, I can tell you that. I supply him with young schoolgirls? Good God. I'm the one who's been trying to nail the man, if you remember. By the way, I have some more evidence.'

'Oh?'

'Do you remember Lorraine Dickson?'

'Yes,' I murmured pensively, recalling the photographs of her in the vicar's sex den.

'She rang me last night. She's been talking to Jenny and—'

'She rang last night? Did she say where she was?'

'No, but if you want to see her, she'll be here in an hour or so.'

This was a trick, I was sure. What did he know about Lorraine and the vicar? I'd known nothing about it, having discovered the photographs only the previous evening. The only way Carter could have known about Lorraine was if the vicar had told him. And he'd only mentioned her calling to see him as a ploy to keep me there. Hopefully, he wouldn't try anything if he believed that the police knew where I was. Following him as he took the coffees into the lounge, I sat on the sofa and decided that I'd wait for Lorraine to arrive – if she arrived at all. I wouldn't let Barry out of my sight, determined. I'd not allow him an opportunity to make a phone call to the vicar and tell the evil man that I was at his place.

'You've got it all wrong, Crystal,' he said, sitting back in the armchair.

'Have I?'

'Yes, you have. I realize that the vicar might have lied to you, told you dreadful things about me. I also realize that you can't be sure whether you should trust me or not. I can't prove anything to you, Crystal. However, if you wait for Lorraine to arrive, I'm sure she'll put your mind at rest.'

'We'll see,' I murmured. 'Did your mother turn up last night?'

'No, she rang to say that she couldn't make it. Which

was just as well, what with all this going on. I've discovered that the vicar is working with a young man named Bridlington. I know where he lives, so he's on my hit list.'

'Where does he live?'

'Leicester. He obviously travels down to see the vicar and—'

'How did you discover his address?'

'It was something Jenny said. She overheard the vicar talking to Bridlington and Leicester was mentioned. Bridlington isn't a common name so it wasn't too difficult to find his address. I know you don't trust me, Crystal, and I can understand why. I'll be honest with you. I'm not as squeaky-clean in all this as I make out.'

'What do you mean by that?' I asked fearfully.

'When Jenny first came to me and told me about the vicar, I have to admit that I was turned on. What I did was wrong, I know. I said that I'd help her in return for sex. I'm a normal man, Crystal. A young attractive girl like Jenny talking about sex, the vicar shaving her pussy, coming in her mouth . . . I'm afraid I succumbed to my male desires.'

'Did she agree to your proposal?'

'Yes, she did. The same thing happened with Lorraine. She visits me regularly for sex. I know that you must think I'm evil to take advantage of young girls, but they were being subjected to crude sex anyway. They were handcuffed and whipped, used for debased sex . . . I did nothing like that, I hasten to add.'

'You're no better than the vicar, are you?'

'No, I suppose not,' he sighed. 'When I saw the photographs of you . . . You're young and attractive.

Seeing those pictures of your naked body, your beautiful breasts, your hairless pussy . . .'

'I reckon that you want to nail the vicar, get him out of the way, so that you can have the girls to yourself.'

'No, Crystal. It's not like that at all. I really thought you'd understand. Men look at young girls and . . . I suppose you can't see the attraction.'

'I know exactly what you mean. The thing is—'

'Look, we have an hour or so before Lorraine arrives. Shall we . . .'

'You want sex with me? How many girls do you want, Barry?'

'I'm sorry. It's just that . . .'

'OK, take all your clothes off.'

'All of them?'

'The choice is yours. All or nothing.'

Watching as he unbuttoned his shirt, it occurred to me that the vicar might be calling. Barry had probably realized that if I thought that Lorraine was due, I'd hang around. I didn't know what to think as he slipped his shirt off and tugged his trousers down. Perhaps he was planning to strip me naked. Once the vicar arrived . . . Eyeing Barry's erect penis catapulting to attention as he pulled his shorts down, my stomach somersaulted. He really was well endowed, his massive shaft rising above his heaving balls, his foreskin fully retracted, exposing the swollen plum of his magnificent penis.

Walking towards me, he stood with his purple knob only inches from my sperm-thirsty mouth. I was a fool to succumb to my insatiable craving for hard cocks. I should have driven past the cottage, found freedom several hundred miles away from the village of perverts. But wasn't I a pervert too? I mused, opening my mouth and licking my full lips. I wanted to suck the sperm out of Barry's knob as much as he wanted to mouth-fuck me.

'Ah, that's good,' he breathed as I engulfed the salty globe of his solid cock in my wet mouth. It *was* good, I mused, running the tip of my tongue around the rim of his helmet and savouring the aphrodisiacal taste of his beautiful glans. As I sucked and mouthed on his cock-head, I realized again that I was taking a huge risk. I'd been driving along the lane to freedom, planning to leave the village behind me for ever. Why the hell had I pulled into Barry's drive? Was it my craving for his cock that had driven me to risk my chance of freedom? Or had curiosity got the better of me?

I supposed that I hadn't wanted to leave the village without discovering the truth. Why I'd thought that Barry would reveal all to me, I had no idea. After the things the vicar had said about him, I should have kept well away from the man. Kneading Barry's heavy balls, his gasps of pleasure filling my ears, I wondered whether Lorraine was into lesbian sex. Would she allow me to push my wet tongue into the tight sheath of her young pussy? Would she allow me to suck and lick her ripe clitoris to orgasm? A terrible thought struck me as I sucked on Barry's knob. Did I really *want* my freedom? Leaving the village, I'd also be leaving the boys, Juliette, Barry . . . Even the vicar's sexual torture chamber attracted me.

'Here it comes,' Barry breathed, clutching my head as he rocked his hips and mouth-fucked me. His sperm gushing, bathing my tongue, filling my cheeks, I doubted that I'd find as much sex anywhere else as I already had in the village. How long would it take me to establish intimate relationships with both men and women in a new town? I'd have to trawl the bars looking for potential sex partners, which could be dangerous. Wanking Barry's solid cock-shaft, bringing out the seed of his balls, I repeatedly swallowed his spunk as I pondered on the prospect of setting up in a new town.

A new home, a new job, new friends . . . The notion didn't appeal to me at all. I'd probably end up working in a shop or a pub and living in a seedy bedsit with next to no money. There'd be no way I could run the Jag. Sucking out the last drops of Barry's orgasmic fluid, I moved my head back and tongued his sperm-slit. Licking around the rim of his engorged knob, lapping up the spilled spunk, I finally released his deflating penis and looked up at him.

'Was that OK?' I asked, knowing that it had been more than OK.

'God, yes,' he breathed, swaying on his sagging legs. 'I know you think badly of me, but I just can't help myself when it comes to teenage girls.'

'The only reason that I think badly of you is because you haven't licked my bottom yet,' I giggled teasingly.

'You'd like that?' he asked, his eyes wide with expectation.

'Like it? I'd *love* to feel your wet tongue licking my bottom-hole.'

'In that case . . .'

'In that case, you'd better do it,' I breathed, grinning.

Kneeling on the floor, I laid my head on the sofa cushion and pulled my short skirt up over my back. Barry settled behind me, almost ripping my panties down in his eagerness to get to the dusky ring of my anus. Yanking my naked buttocks wide apart, he wasted no time, his wet tongue repeatedly sweeping up my anal gully, teasing the sensitive opening of my rectal inlet. Shuddering, I breathed heavily as he pushed the tip of his tongue into my secret hole, waking the sleeping nerve endings there, sending tantalizing ripples of decadent sex through my trembling body.

'You really like this sort of thing, don't you?' Barry asked, lapping at my anal hole.

'I can't get enough,' I replied.

'Lorraine and Jenny . . . You beat the others hands down. Wait there a minute. I want to go and get something.'

'OK, but be quick.'

As he dashed out of the room, I could feel his saliva running down my anal crease, trickling into the yawning crevice of my vagina. Perhaps he was going to get a candle, I mused, imagining a huge waxen shaft driving deep into the dank heat of my bowels. Whatever it was, I was sure that I'd love every minute of it. 'Shit,' I breathed, realizing that he might be ringing the vicar. Again, my hunger for debased sex had got the better of me. I could hear Barry moving about upstairs. Was he on the phone? Again, I had a chance to get out, to leave the village and find freedom, but . . .

'You'll love this,' Barry said, holding something behind his back as he walked into the room. 'OK, relax your muscles.' I could feel him pressing something hard against the delicate tissue surrounding my bottom-hole. Was it a candle? I wondered as my anus yielded, allowing a cold shaft to glide along my rectal duct. The cooling phallus stretching me wide open, I imagined that it must have been at least two inches in diameter. As the shaft drove deeper into the very core of my teenage body, I also reckoned that it was at least eight inches long.

'God,' I breathed as the thing started buzzing, sending electrifying vibrations deep into my trembling pelvis. Was this what Barry did to the other girls? I wondered as he sank the pulsating shaft deeper into my contracting anal canal. Perhaps he had a sex den upstairs, I reflected fearfully. He might have lured girls from the school to his cottage, taken them to his den and . . . Having only just moved into the cottage, I doubted that he'd had a chance to set up a dungeon of sexual torture. But he might have handcuffs and whips, I reflected hopefully. Could I really leave behind the village of decadence? Would I even survive without regular debased sex?

Feeling Barry's bulbous knob slipping between the pouting lips of my hairless pussy, I gasped as he drove the entire length of his beautiful organ deep into my contracting cunt. God, he was big. My vaginal canal already narrowed by the huge vibrator embedded deep within my arse, I thought I'd split open as Barry's cock-shaft expanded, his huge knob pressing hard against the creamy ring of my cervix.

'I used to look up your skirt when you were at school,' he breathed, withdrawing his swollen penis part-way and driving back into my wet cunt again. 'Many times I saw the triangular patch of your tight knickers.'

'You wanted to tongue-fuck my little cunt, didn't you?' I said, building his fantasy.

'God, yes. I used to imagine that I was underneath your desk, licking your sweet pussy-crack.'

'I'll let you into a little secret, Barry. I used to masturbate in the toilets at school, and I imagined that I was wanking your huge cock – your spunk raining over my face, splattering my hair.'

'You really thought that?'

'I used to imagine that your spunk was splashing over my small titties, running over my stomach to my little pussy-crack.'

'God, I'm coming,' he breathed, my words of arousal obviously driving him crazy.

His sperm filling the spasming sheath of my cunt as he pistoned my tight arse with the buzzing vibrator, he continued with his fantasy. My own orgasm erupting within the pulsating head of my clitoris, his words of illicit schoolgirl-fucking sending my libido through the roof, I imagined my tongue sweeping up and down a young girlie's hairless vaginal slit. I was into anything and everything, I knew as I imagined fingering a young pussy, inducing cunny-milk to flow over my hand.

Waves of pure sexual ecstasy rolled on and on through my abused body, my muscles twitching, my limbs convulsing wildly. Imagining another man's cock filling my thirsty mouth with spunk, knew that I'd become so decadent, so perverted in my ways that I could never enjoy a proper relationship with just one partner. Had Robin and I got something together, I'd still have been looking for illicit sex with other men, and probably with women too. There was so much I'd yet to experience, I reflected. My tongue lapping up spunk from a girl's pussy as two men fucked the tight holes between my legs, three purple knobs pumping spunk into my mouth, two cocks forced deep into the sheath of my arse . . . There was so much I had to look forward to.

My orgasm receding as Barry pumped the last of his creamy spunk deep into my inflamed vaginal sheath and slowed his anal ramming, I shuddered in the wake of my incredibly debased pleasure. My rectum stretched by the buzzing vibrator, my cunt spewing out its blend of sperm and girl-juice as Barry withdrew his spent cock . . . I was left gasping for life-giving breath, shaking violently. Switching the vibrator off, Barry slowly withdrew the shaft, allowing my anal duct to close. The eye of my anus was burning, tingling in the aftermath of the abuse.

'Lick my bum,' I gasped, desperate for the cooling sensation of Barry's saliva. He complied willingly, wetting my inflamed dusky tissue with his lapping tongue, cooling me there as I recovered from my session of debauched sex. The time was running on, and I wondered, as Barry swept his wet tongue over the dark ring of my bum for the last time, whether I should make my escape. Sitting on the floor, he smiled as I hauled my quivering body up and relaxed on the sofa. Had he phoned the vicar?

'I must be going,' I breathed shakily, raising my naked buttocks and tugging my panties up my thighs. 'I have things to do.'

'Already? But I thought you wanted to see Lorraine?'

'I do, but I don't want to see the vicar.'

'The vicar? What do you mean? Oh, you think he's coming here to—'

'Did you phone him when you went upstairs?'

'No, of course I didn't,' he laughed. 'Crystal, you can't go through life not trusting anyone.'

'If I had, then I wouldn't be in this situation.'

'No, but . . . OK, it's up to you. If you want to go now, that's fine. But do remember this. You can't run for ever.'

'I realize that. But I want to make a fresh start, begin again. If I stay here, the vicar and his perverts will hound me.'

'Give me a little more time and, hopefully, I'll be in a position to put a stop to it.'

' "Hopefully" being the operative word,' I sighed despondently. 'If you send the vicar and his friend packing . . . There may be others, Barry. There could be several other men in the village who have copies of the photographs and they'll start on me.'

'I don't think so. I really can't believe that the vicar is running a huge sex ring. He has this Bridlington man with him, but I don't think there are any more. And before you say it, I know that I can't be certain. But on a small village like this, there's surely no way the vicar could run a ring of perverts.'

'I'm inclined to agree,' I said, glancing at the mantel-piece clock.

'And, to be honest, I really can't see that he'd use the photographs against you. Can you imagine it? He shows your parents photographs of you cock-sucking or whatever. They're going to ask him where he got the pictures.'

'He reckons that he'll make out that he found them in the church.'

'No, no. It would be too risky. He'd have to send them anonymously and, if he did, so what? OK, your mother wouldn't think very highly of you, and your father . . . your father would probably go to the police and ask them to look into it, to find the pervert who forced you to suck his cock. The vicar wouldn't take that risk, believe me.'

The more I listened to Barry, the more I realized that he was right. The vicar could do nothing with the photographs, other than gaze at them while he wanked his cock and shot his spunk over the floor. He might spread a few pictures around the village, but someone would probably call the police in and they'd have to investigate the matter. As Barry dressed, I wondered whether to go back to Robin's house and talk to him. I'd liked living there, working for him and . . . I liked Robin.

'Ah, that'll be Lorraine,' Barry said and smiled, heading for the door. Taking a deep breath, I waited in fear and trepidation. If it was the vicar, I'd curse myself. If it was the vicar, he'd probably curse *me*. My mind spinning as Barry opened the door, I could hear him murmuring. The door closed and there was movement in the hall, the muffled sound of Barry's voice. My heart racing, my breathing unsteady, I twisted my long blonde hair around my fingers. As I waited for the visitor to reveal their identity, I was reminded of an incident in my early teens when my mother had said that someone was making a surprise visit on my birthday. I'd thought it was the vicar with a special present for me. My heart had raced, my hands had trembled as I'd waited for the doorbell to ring. I'd been in a state of near-panic for almost two hours, only to find that the mysterious visitor was my aunt.

'Hi,' Lorraine said cheerfully as she breezed into the room.

'Thank God,' I breathed, my shoulders slumping as if a huge weight had been lifted off me. 'Er . . . I haven't seen you for ages. How are you?'

'All right, considering,' she replied, smiling and dumping her coat on the armchair before sitting down next to me. 'Barry's told me about you and the vicar.'

'I'll leave you to have a chat,' Barry said, peering around the door.

As Lorraine related her story, I gazed at her firm breasts billowing the front of her blouse. She was an extremely attractive girl. Long auburn hair framing her fresh face, sparkling brown eyes, succulent lips . . . I imagined Barry's purple knob between her lips, his sperm pumping into her wet mouth, dribbling down her chin and splattering the teats of her naked breasts. Having seen the photographs of her naked body, I knew that the lips of her vagina had been shaved. Hairless, firm, smooth . . . I couldn't help but imagine my tongue there, running up and down the wet slit of her pussy, lapping up her girl-cream.

'So, that's how it all started with the vicar,' Lorraine sighed. 'Were you listening?'

'Er . . . yes, I was.'

'I need to find somewhere to live,' she said. 'I've been staying with a friend, but I need my own place.'

'Robin has a spare room,' I blurted out.

'Robin?'

'He's . . . he's my landlord, and my boss. I don't know whether he'll agree to it. In fact, I don't even know whether I'll be staying on there.'

'Shall we go and see him?' she asked, hope mirrored in her brown eyes. 'It would be fantastic, Crystal. You and me in the same house . . .'

'There are complications,' I sighed, focusing on the naked thighs revealed by her short skirt.

'Complications? If he has a spare room to let, what's the problem? I can pay the rent, if that's what you're worrying about. I work for an estate agent in Barnhampton.'

'That's where the house is.'

'Even better,' she trilled. 'I could walk to work and—'

'Lorraine, it's not that easy.'

'Why? I'm desperate for somewhere to live, Crystal. I want to get out of the village, away from the vicar.'

'I know the feeling. OK, let's go and talk to Robin,' I finally conceded. 'My car's outside.'

'That Jag?'

'Yes, that Jag.'

As we said goodbye to Barry and climbed into my car, I gave up trying to work things out. Was Robin involved? Was Barry genuine? What was the vicar up to? My thoughts were hurting my mind, and I decided to talk to Robin, get everything out in the open at long last. Lorraine went on about my car as we neared the house. Was it really mine? I wondered. Or had Robin just lent it to me? I'd not seen the documents, so I assumed that the car was on loan to me. Parking outside the house, I felt my heart miss a beat. Leading Lorraine up the path and opening the front door, I imagined being greeted by Robin, the vicar, the young man . . .

'Ah, the wanderer returns,' Robin smiled as he emerged from his consulting room. 'Where on earth have you been?'

'This is Lorraine,' I said, turning and facing the girl.

'Lorraine, I'm very pleased to meet you.'

'Crystal said that you have a spare—'

'Wait in my room,' I interrupted the girl. 'Up the stairs, first on the left.'

'So, where have you been?' Robin again asked, leading me into his consulting room as Lorraine climbed the stairs.

'After the incident in the sex dungeon, where the hell do you *think* I've been?' I hissed, sitting opposite Robin at the desk.

'We need to clear things up,' he said, resting his elbows on the desk and clasping his hands.

'Clear things up?' I retorted angrily. 'You need to tell me the truth, for a change. OK, how long have you been supplying fresh meat to the vicar?'

'The only fresh meat I supply is to the cat.'

'The cat's bloody well dead, Robin.'

'Oh, my God. When . . . How . . .'

'Cut the insanity act and start talking. Are you in with the vicar or not?'

'No.'

'Have you ever sent girls to him?'

'No.'

'This is getting us nowhere. You're lying, I know it.'

'Lorraine's a pretty little thing. I hope she'll be visiting us regularly.'

'She wants to move in.'

'Excellent. There's nothing I like more than having pretty little girlies moving into my house.'

'She's not fresh meat, Robin.'

'Oh, that's a shame. When did she go off?'

'Go off? Now, you listen to me.'

'I'm listening.'

'I want to stay on here as your housekeeper. But, if I'm to do that, you have to be honest with me. What's that radio equipment for?'

'In the shed? Oh, that's just a hobby.'

'Are you really insane or is it an act?'

'We're all insane, to a greater or lesser extent. You're keeping your guest waiting.'

'I know. So it's OK if Lorraine moves into the spare room?'

'There's nothing I'd like more than . . .'

'Robin, she's not moving in to gratify your sexual needs.'

'Isn't she? Oh well, life's full of disappointments. I'll have to go through the Housekeeper Employment—'

'*I*'m your housekeeper. Lorraine works for an estate agent.'

'The Estate Agent Employment Act, then?'

'No, Robin. I'd better go and talk to her,' I said, standing and walking to the door. 'And we'll talk again later.'

'I like a bit of oral,' he chuckled.

Lorraine was sitting on my bed, her face beaming as she looked around the room. I knew how desperate she was to get out of the village, and I must admit that I felt sorry for her. But my pity was outweighed by my insatiable thirst for sex. She was so attractive, young and curvaceous. The thought of her teenage pussy devoid of pubic hair sent quivers through my womb. My lust-juices seeping between the wings of my inner lips, my clitoris swelling, I knew that I had to have her.

'OK, the rules,' I began, standing in front of her.

'Rules?' she echoed, her brown eyes reflecting puzzlement. 'What rules?'

'*My* rules, Lorraine. Take your clothes off and I'll examine you.'

'Examine me? What for?'

'I'm Robin's right-hand man – woman. Before anyone moves into his house, they have to be examined.'

'I don't understand. Why—'

'I don't make the rules, Lorraine,' I replied, desperate to feast my eyes on her naked body. Locking the door, I smiled at her. 'Clothes off, if you want to move in.'

Standing, she unbuttoned her blouse and slipped it over her shoulders. Her bra straining to contain her full breasts, she reached behind her back and unhooked the garment. Peeling the cups away from the beautiful mounds of her teenage breasts, she looked down at the stiffening teats of her nipples. I was wicked, but I couldn't help myself. She was sensual, fresh, alluring, and there was no way she was going to escape my intimate attentions. My thoughts should have been on Robin and his involvement, if any, with the vicar. But the thought of a hot, wet, tight, hairless pussy . . . Watching with bated breath as Lorraine tugged her skirt down her long legs, I gazed at the swell of her tight panties, the damp patch on the crotch of the red material.

'Keep going,' I instructed her as she stepped out of her skirt, her wide eyes staring at me. Placing her thumbs between the elastic of her panties and her shapely hips, she pulled the garment down slowly. The top of her vaginal slit came into view, and then her full love-lips, her inner lips emerging alluringly from the crack of her naked vulva. My heart racing, my stomach somersaulting, I grinned as her panties fell around her ankles.

'Rule one,' I said, licking my lips provocatively. 'You'll attend my needs as and when I tell you to.'

'I know what you mean,' she smiled, running her hands over the swell of her young breasts. 'I'll have no problem complying with rule one.'

'Rule two. All girls living in this house will shave regularly. Rule three—'

'May I have a word?' Robin called, tapping on the door.

'I won't be a minute,' I replied, wondering what the problem was. Had the vicar turned up? 'Wait there,' I said, stroking Lorraine's auburn hair.

Leaving my room, I went downstairs and found Robin hovering by his desk. He looked pained, anguished, as he fiddled with his bow tie. I instinctively knew that something was very wrong. I'd not heard the front doorbell or the phone ringing, so I doubted that he'd received bad news. Looking at the desk as he pointed to a sheet of paper, I picked it up. 'I'll be round in an hour to collect the sluts,' I read aloud. It wasn't signed, but I knew that it was from the vicar. Again, my hands trembled, my heart raced. I couldn't take any more of this. The vicar had either got word that Lorraine was with me or he'd been watching the house.

'Go to your room and stay there,' Robin said, taking his coat from the hat stand.

'Where are you going?' I asked.

'Stay in your room and keep the door locked. And don't answer your phone.'

'Robin . . .'

'We only have an hour. I'll be as quick as I can.'

As he left the house, I wandered upstairs and mooched on the landing. It was all very well telling me to stay in my room, but wouldn't it have been better to flee the house? Had Robin done a runner, deciding to keep out of the way until the vicar had completed his dirty deed? Where was Juliette? Was she in hiding? Perhaps she was waiting until I'd been kidnapped before returning. Perhaps she had designs on my room – and my job. *One hour*, I reflected fearfully, wondering what to do. Should I stay or should I go?

12

I'd decided to lock myself in my room and toy with Lorraine while I waited for Robin to return. I needed something to take my mind off the vicar, his threat to come and get me, and what better way was there than abusing Lorraine's teenage body? She was lying on the bed, her violin curves displayed, her thighs parted. Eyeing the pouting cushions of her hairless outer labia, I wondered whether to spank her vulval flesh. Her inner lips protruding from the hairless valley of her teenage cunt, I was gripped by an overwhelming urge to torture her sexually. Was I normal? Imagining tying her down to the bed, I was about to get my leather belt from the dressing table when she propped herself up on her elbows and asked me what I required of her.

'Require of you?' I echoed.

'What do you wish me to do, madam?'

'Spread your legs wide and peel your pussy lips apart,' I said, delighting in the game.

Resting her head on the pillow, Lorraine opened her legs and took the fleshy pads of her vaginal lips between her fingers and thumbs. Parting her sex-hillock, exposing the intricate folds glistening within her valley of desire, the ripening nodule of her pink clitoris, she looked at me questioningly. I ordered her to finger her pussy to lick and suck the elongated teats of her nipples, and she complied without hesitation. She was an obedient slave, only speaking when spoken to, doing exactly as I asked when I asked. To test her obedience, I ordered her to lie on her stomach with her legs wide apart. Following my instructions to the letter, she pulled her rounded buttocks wide open and exposed the tight dark ring of her anus to my wide-eyed gaze.

'You've been trained,' I remarked as she followed my next order and drove a finger deep into her bottom-hole. 'Who trained you?'

'The vicar,' she replied, pushing and twisting her finger, obviously revelling in the lewd sensations.

'Tell me about it. What did he do?'

'I've spent many hours in his cottage, naked except for a dog collar around my neck. He enjoyed leading me round the cottage on a chain, treating me like a dog.'

'Worse than a dog, I would imagine. OK, let's see how good a job he's done. Pull your finger out of your bum and stand up.'

Lorraine immediately leaped to her feet, standing in front of me with the erect teats of her rounded breasts pointing to the ceiling. Having not seen the girl for a long time, I hardly knew her and was surprised by her obedience. To test her further, I told her to kneel behind me and lift my skirt up. Parting my feet wide as she took her position and raised the back of my skirt, I ordered her to pull my panties down and part my buttocks. Without hesitation, she slipped my panties down, opening my anal gully and exposing the sensitive eye of my anus.

'Have you ever licked a girl's bottom?' I asked her.

'No,' she replied.

'Have you had lesbian sex?'

'No, I haven't.'

'Then it's high time you learned how to pleasure another girl. I want you to lick my bottom-hole, lick me there and push your tongue inside me.'

Feeling Lorraine's hot breath within my bottom crease, I closed my eyes, my young body shuddering as she licked the dusky tissue surrounding my rectal inlet. Wetting me there, teasing the sensitive nerve endings, she opened my crease wider and slipped her tongue into my hot rectum. She was an excellent slave, and I was looking forward to having her move in. It was control, I reflected as she caressed the walls of my anal canal with the tip of her wet tongue. I'd always been in control with the boys, and now I had complete and utter control over Lorraine.

'You'll call me mistress,' I breathed, amazing sensations of debased sex rippling through my contracting womb. 'Do you understand?'

'Yes, mistress,' she replied, lapping at my bottom-hole.

'And you'll remain faithful to me. Unless I decide that you should pleasure a friend of mine, that is.'

'Of course, mistress.'

'Your duties, apart from attending my most intimate needs, will include cooking the evening meal. Now, you may finger my bottom. Push as many fingers as you can into my bottom.'

'Yes, mistress.'

Slipping a finger into the tight sheath of my rectum, Lorraine eased a second finger into my yielding hole. Parting my feet further, I bent over and touched my toes, allowing her better access to my rectal canal as she drove a third finger into the core of my young body. I rather liked the thought that she'd never had lesbian sex. I'd teach her, instruct her in the fine art of clit-licking, pussy-tonguing, nipple-biting. Managing to ease four fingers past my defeated anal ring, she massaged my inner flesh, kneading the pliable tube of my hot rectum as I looked up at her between my parted thighs. This was lesson one, I mused. A lesson in lesbian anal fisting.

My sex duct was in need of lubrication, and I instructed Lorraine to slip her fingers out of my bottom-hole and take the jar of cooling cream from the dressing table. Standing upright as she walked across the room, I had a wicked idea. Sending her down to Robin's consulting room to take a speculum from the desk drawer, I made sure that the door was locked straight after she returned with the device. My mind bubbling with debauched thoughts, I grabbed the lengths of washing line I'd used for bondage and told her to lie on the floor with her head against the wardrobe. Running two lengths of washing line from the wooden knobs adorning the top of the wardrobe, I lifted her feet high in the air and bound each ankle. Her legs wide, her feet high above her head, resting against the wardrobe, I settled on the floor and scrutinized her gaping vaginal valley.

Starting from the small of her back, I ran my tongue along her bottom crease, the different tastes driving me wild as my tongue swept over her anal eye, the gaping entrance of her creamed pussy, the solid bud of her clitoris. Again, I licked her open valleys, moving from the beginning of her anal cleft to the fusion of her inner lips just below her hairless mons. I slipped my tongue into her anus, and then licked just inside the entrance to her vagina, my mind dizzy with sex as I savoured her varying flavours.

Taking the speculum, I slipped the cold steel paddles

between the swollen lips of her vagina and drove the device deep into her young pussy. Imagining myself as a gynaecologist, I squeezed the levers, watching in awe as her sex tube opened, revealing the creamy walls of her vaginal throat. Opening her further, I peered deep into her teenage cunt, spying the doughnut-like ring of her cervix as she gasped frantically. Having unrestricted access to both her sex-holes, I pulled the creamed speculum out of her vagina and eased the paddles past her anal ring. Lorraine whimpered, her naked body trembling as the steel paddles slipped deep into her rectal canal. But she didn't protest.

'I want to look inside your bottom,' I said huskily, squeezing the levers, her anal tract dilating.

'Yes, mistress,' she breathed, her arms either side of her hips, her slender fingers yanking the rounded cheeks of her buttocks wide apart.

'Has anyone ever used a speculum to look inside your bum?'

'No, mistress.'

'Not even the vicar?' I asked in surprise. 'Well, there's a first time for everything. OK, relax and I'll open you up.'

Squeezing the levers again, I peered into the dank tube of Lorraine's gaping rectum, imagining the vicar's cock sliding deep into the very core of her young body, his throbbing knob spunking her bowels. Leaving the speculum in place, I grabbed the shampoo bottle from the dressing table and positioned the end between the swollen pads of her outer lips. She gasped, her tethered body quivering uncontrollably as I eased the huge bottle deep into the wet sheath of her beautiful cunt.

'Is that nice?' I asked her, the end of the bottle pressing against her ripe cervix.

'God, yes,' she murmured. 'It's amazing.'

'I think we're going to get on very well together,' I breathed, smiling and massaging the sensitive bud of her solid clitoris with my fingertip. 'I may have to thrash you now and then,' I added.

'Yes, mistress,' she replied.

'I have a leather belt that I may have to use on your naked bottom. Just to keep you under control, you understand. In fact, I'll try it now.'

Releasing the levers and slipping the speculum out of the inflamed duct of her rectum, I took the belt from the dressing table. Her legs wide, high in the air, the rounded cheeks of her firm buttocks were perfectly positioned for a gruelling strapping. Eyeing the shampoo bottle emerging between the swollen lips of her vagina, I thought, as I kneeled on the floor, what a beautiful photograph it would make. There again, no. I'd had enough trouble with photographs.

Raising the belt above my head, I brought it down across the tensed orbs of Lorraine's bottom, grinning as her naked body jolted. Again, I lashed her bottom-cheeks with the leather strap, watching thin weals fanning out across her twitching flesh. The shampoo bottle shooting out of her cunt like a bullet as I continued to lash her reddening buttocks, I giggled wickedly. This was my domain, I reflected. Control, power, domination over my teenage sex-slave. Lash after lash cracking loudly across her crimsoned buttocks, her juices of desire spraying from her gaping cunt-hole, I thrashed her relentlessly. Her naked body shaking violently, her sex-juices pooling on the carpet, I finally discarded the leather belt and lay on the floor.

Lapping at Lorraine's open vaginal entrance, sucking

out her pussy cream, I drank from her beautiful body. It was time for her orgasm, I decided, peeling the inflamed lips of her vulva wide apart and exposing the reddening tip of her pleasure spot. Locking my full lips to her vaginal flesh, I sucked her swollen clitoris out of its fleshy hood, running my tongue over the sensitive tip of the sex protrusion as her gasps of lesbian pleasure filled my ears. My own clitoris solid in arousal, my juices of desire flowing into my panties, I lost myself in my lesbian licking.

Nearing her orgasm, Lorraine shuddered fiercely, her cunt-milk gushing from her open hole, splattering my chin as I licked and mouthed her ballooning clitoris. I could feel her pleasure button pulsating beneath my sweeping tongue as her tethered body tensed and convulsed wildly. Her fingers clutching strands of my long blonde hair, she gyrated her hips, grinding her cuntal flesh hard against my pussy-wet face as she let out a scream and finally reached the pinnacle of her lesbian-induced pleasure.

'Yes,' she cried, her clitoris exploding in orgasm in my wet mouth. Spluttering on the copious flow of vaginal juice issuing from her burning cunt, desperate for air as Lorraine forced her sex flesh harder into my mouth, I thought I'd suffocate. The orgasmic shock waves rocking her young body, she shook uncontrollably as her climax subsided, only to peak and grip her in lesbian lust again. Driving two fingers deep into her inflamed anal sheath, I knew that she could barely stand the incredible pleasure she was deriving from her abused body.

My mouth full of cunt flesh, I gasped for breath as I finally moved back, massaging the nub of Lorraine's pulsating clitoris with my fingertip to bring out the last ripples of her climax. Crying out her pleasure as her orgasm peaked yet again, she tossed her head from side to side, completely lost in her sexual delirium. Vibrating her pulsating clitoris with my fingertip, I finger-fucked her tight arse-duct, her naked body rocking with the beautiful abuse. Arse-pistoning, clit-massaging, I attended her young body until my arms began to ache. I thought she'd never come down from her sexual heaven as she cried out again in the grip of her ecstasy. Continuing the anal pistoning, the clit-massaging, I watched her creamy cum-juice issuing from her sex-sheath, running down and lubricating my finger as I repeatedly rammed into her inflamed bottom-hole.

At last, the waves of pure lust receded, leaving her trembling, her smooth stomach rising and falling, her firm breasts heaving. Releasing her trembling body, I laid her on her stomach with the glowing cheeks of her buttocks perfectly positioned for another thrashing. Splaying her thighs, my fingers toying with her pinken girl-crack, I smiled as I kissed the rubicund flesh of her taut buttocks. Licking her sensitive orbs, wetting her with my saliva, I pulled her buttocks apart, exposing her abused anal hole to my hungry gaze. Before the thrashing, I decided to tongue-fuck her bottom, calming her before administering the gruelling punishment.

Licking around Lorraine's sensitive dusky tissue, I tasted the bitter-sweet flavour of her tightly closed bottom-hole, delighting in my wanton debauchery as she squirmed and writhed on the floor. My sex-slave would become used to my wicked ways, my dominating depravity, I reflected, slipping my tongue into the deliciously tasty sheath of her anal canal. A daily arse-tonguing, a daily clit-sucking and naked-buttock thrashing . . . She'd also have to endure a breast-lashing, I thought in my ever-rising wickedness.

As I began spanking Lorraine's fiery buttocks with the palm of my hand, each slap becoming progressively harder, she tensed her buttocks again. Grabbing the leather belt, I thrashed my slave, giving her no mercy as she writhed and cried out with the beautiful sensations of combined pain and pleasure. The cracking belt jolting her naked body, she slipped her hand beneath her stomach and caressed the nodule of her clitoris, stiffening her sex-nubbin in readiness for another massive orgasm. I whipped her crimson buttocks harder until her orgasm erupted and she cried out, screaming in her Sapphic coming.

Driven by an uncontrollable yearning for sadistic lesbian lust, I brought the belt down again, flogging the girl's taut flesh, delighting in my wickedness as deep red weals fanned out across her crimson posterior. Lifting her head off the floor and squeezing her eyes shut, biting her lip as lash after lash landed squarely across her stinging bottom-globes, Lorraine could do nothing to halt the merciless flagellation of her naked buttocks. Her fingers still massaging her swollen clitoris, she screamed again as the stinging pain permeated her scarlet bottom-cheeks, transmitting deep into her trembling pelvis as she reached her climax.

Continuing with the gruelling thrashing, wondering at my new-found obsession, I ignored Lorraine's pleas for mercy. She tried to roll over, tried to escape the leather whip as she frigged the pleasure from her clitoris, but I pinned her down with my free hand and thrashed her for all I was worth. I wondered when Robin would return as the leather strap hit home again, biting into her anal orbs, and I knew that I had no control over my lesbian lust.

Wicked in the extreme, I couldn't help myself as I thrashed Lorraine again and again until she finally managed to roll over and lie on her back.

'Please, no more,' she whimpered, driving me to abuse her even more. Ripping my cunt-soaked panties off, I placed my knees either side of her head and lowered the gaping entrance to my cunt over her gasping mouth. Gazing at her rounded breasts, I could feel her tongue snaking, working its way inside me as I grabbed the belt and raised it above my head. Bringing the leather strap down across the mounds of her tits, catching the brown protrusions of her erect milk teats, I chuckled wickedly as her naked body jolted violently. There was no escape for Lorraine now, I knew as I ground my cuntal flesh hard into her mouth and repeatedly lashed the firm hillocks of her breasts.

Finally tossing the belt aside, I leaned over her quivering body, burying my face between her slender thighs, pushing my tongue into the spasming sheath of her hot cunt as she tongued the duct of my juice-brimming cunt. Aligning the solid nubble of my clitoris with her open mouth, I moaned through my nose as her tongue snaked around my sex protrusion. I came quickly, my orgasm erupting within my pulsating clitoris, my creamy juices of lust gushing from my open cunt, flooding my slave's face as I sucked her orgasm out of her swollen clitoris.

Writhing in lesbian lust, our naked bodies entwined in our sexual passion, I let out a rush of golden liquid, flooding her face, filling her mouth as she coughed and spluttered beneath me. Fighting to push me away as the flow continued, Lorraine cried out, protesting at my crude act, pleading for me to stop. Dizzy in my sexual delirium, I couldn't halt the flow. Driven on by my own decadence, I listened to the splashing sound, delighting in my crudity until I'd drained my bladder. She finally managed to push me off, her face drenched with my golden rain as she sat up and wiped her mouth on the back of her hand.

'I don't want that,' Lorraine hissed, glaring at me as I stood up and adjusted my miniskirt.

'You'll do as you're told,' I retorted, gazing at the wet patch on the carpet. 'If you want to live here, then . . .'

'Crystal, I'll be your slave, but I won't—'

'I give the orders, Lorraine,' I interrupted her sternly. 'What was that?' I whispered, hearing movements downstairs.

'If you think I'm going to allow you to—'

'Shut up, Lorraine. There's someone downstairs.'

Moving to the door, I turned the handle, listening intently as I peered onto the landing. Again, I heard a movement. Sure that someone was in Robin's consulting room, I edged my way onto the landing and leaned over the banister. Lorraine's whimpers sounded from my room, making it difficult to hear what was going on downstairs, so I closed my door and locked her in. Praying that it wasn't the vicar as I tentatively crept down the stairs, I hovered outside the consulting room. I heard a drawer open and close, papers shuffling . . .

'Where the fuck is it?' Robin cursed.

'God, you scared me,' I complained, walking up to his desk. 'I thought the bloody vicar had got in.'

'Where the fuck is it?' he breathed again, rummaging through more papers.

'What are you looking for?' I asked.

'The electricity bill.'

'What? How you can worry about that at a time like this, I honestly don't know.'

'A time like what?' he said, looking up and frowning at me. 'God, you're naked.'

'Robin, I'm fully clothed.'

'Well, you *should* be naked. All teenage girls should be naked at all times. May I suck your tits?'

'No. The vicar, Robin. He's due here at any time.'

'No, he's not.'

'The note, you showed me the note. This vicar is coming here to . . . Where have you been?'

'I went out.'

'For God's sake,' I spat. 'I know that you bloody went out. What are we going to do about the vicar?'

'Nothing.'

'Oh, I give up,' I sighed, walking to the door.

'So did he.'

'What? What do you mean by that?'

'What's that dripping all over my desk?' he asked, looking up at the ceiling. 'Oh, there seems to be a leak.'

'It's piss,' I replied. 'I pissed all over the floor in my room.'

'Oh, that's OK then. I once pissed all over the kitchen table. By the way, I have some news about the vicar.'

'At last,' I breathed, perching my buttocks on the edge of the desk. 'Well, go on.'

'He's moved away.'

'Really? Are you sure? I mean . . .'

'I have all the photographs in that box over there. You might want to burn them in the garden later.'

'So, what happened?'

'I went to see him. I had to rough him up a bit, of course.'

'Robin, I didn't think you had it in you,' I laughed.

'We've all got it in us.'

'I wish I had it in me. Your cock, I'm talking about.'

'That could be arranged.'

'So, tell me what happened. You went to his cottage?'

'Yes, I did. He was there with another man, a younger man. I said that the police had raided my house and I'd heard that they were planning a raid on his place. The fool not only believed me but asked me to look after the box of photographs.'

'Good God. Where were they hidden?'

'In the attic. With no photographs, he has nothing on you. Or the other girls.'

'That's great, Robin,' I beamed, leaping off the desk and flinging my arms around his neck. 'I can't believe that it's over. Why did you have to rough him up?'

'I didn't. I lied because I thought it would sound good, kind of manly.'

'You are silly,' I said and smiled, kissing his cheek. 'I owe you a lot. I owe you a hell of a lot.'

'We'll sort out something by way of payment later. So, this girl who's moving in.'

'Lorraine? She's upstairs, in my room.'

'How many more girls will you be moving in? We'll end up with a harem at this rate.'

'None, I hope. Talking of girls living here, have you seen Juliette? She's always disappearing.'

'She's job-hunting. Let's not talk about her, Crystal. I'd like to talk about us, the situation here. Sit down for a minute.'

Sitting in the old armchair, I wondered whether he felt the way I did. The situation? Perhaps he didn't like the idea of having a house full of teenage girls. There again, knowing Robin, he'd like nothing better. Sure now that he wasn't involved with the evil vicar, I smiled as he sat behind his desk and rested his chin on his hands. Was I in love? I wondered, gazing at his hair cascading over his lined forehead. He was insane, had no dress sense whatsoever, lived with a dead cat that didn't exist, was probably a Russian spy . . . What did I see in him? Turning, he smiled at me.

'Well,' he said.

'Well?' I echoed. 'Well, what?'

'You'll live with me as my wife.'

'Your wife? You mean . . .'

'As man and wife. If you want to, that is.'

'I'd love to, Robin,' I trilled. 'We'll have a church wedding.'

'I meant *as* man and wife, not—'

'It's marriage or nothing.'

'Marriage it is, then. God only knows what my mother will say when she discovers that I'm marrying a teenage girl.'

'Oh, I didn't realize that your mother was around. I'll have to meet her.'

'You'll have a job.'

'Why's that?'

'She lives with the cat.'

'Robin, you've lost me again.'

'In heaven.'

'Ah, right. Look, I'd better go and see Lorraine,' I said as a loud thud sounded on the ceiling. 'I've locked her in my room and . . .'

'I hope she's not pissing on the floor,' he laughed.

'I doubt it. We need some time together, Robin. There are things to talk about, plans to make.'

'Such as?'

'The marital bedroom for starters. It's a bloody pig-sty.'

'It *is* rather untidy, but . . .'

'God only knows when you last made the bed.'

'I hoovered the sheets the other day.'

'Hoovered the . . . We'll talk later,' I said as Lorraine started calling out. 'I've locked her in and if she needs the loo . . . You don't want more golden rain showering your desk, do you?'

'Preferably not. There again, I'm rather partial to a drop of . . . We'll discuss that later, too.'

'Yes, I think we'd better.'

Finding Lorraine sitting on the bed, her auburn hair matted with my girl-juice and urine, I was disappointed in her. I'd believed that she was going to make an ideal slave. With Robin and me getting married, she could have added to our sex life, joined us in the marital bed and . . . My mind riddled with perverted thoughts, I grabbed the leather belt from the floor and held it above my head.

'Do you want to stay on in my house as my sex-slave?' I asked her.

'*Your* house?' she said, her dark eyes flashing. 'I thought this was Robin's house?'

'Robin and I are getting married,' I told her proudly.

'Oh. So that means . . . Congratulations. Yes, I'd love to stay on as your sex-slave.'

'Good. That's settled, then. Thinking about it, I suppose I'd better test you before making the final decision.'

'Test me?'

'Robin!' I called from my doorway. 'Would you come up here, please?'

bouncing in the palm of my hand as she quickened her wanking motion. 'You'll drink it all up like a good little girl.' She nodded, moving her head back and forth, repeatedly taking Robin's glans deep into her mouth. She'd join us in our bed, I decided. I'd order her to lick my clitoris to orgasm as Robin shafted the tight duct of my bottom and filled my bowels with his spunk. I'd watch Robin's huge penis driving in and out of her sweet cunt as I licked and sucked on her clitoris. We were all going to get on very well together, I was sure.

'Yes,' Robin breathed, signalling that his spunk was about to pump into the girl's mouth. I could hear her swallowing, gulping down his orgasmic fluid as she wanked the solid shaft of his magnificent cock and I kneaded his huge balls. Robin was a lucky man, I reflected. Two girls to attend his sexual needs . . . Again wondering where Juliette had got to, I imagined her joining in, sucking Robin's cock to orgasm as Lorraine licked her cunny and I tongue-fucked the tight hole of her anus. Three girls to pleasure him? He *was* a lucky man.

'You're hired,' I laughed as Robin pulled away, his penis-head leaving the girl's spunk-flooded mouth.

'She certainly is,' Robin breathed, his body trembling in the aftermath of his throat-sperming.

'I was good enough, then?' Lorraine asked, her sperm-glossed lips furling into a smile at she gazed up at Robin.

'More than good enough,' he replied. 'And now I have to go and find the electricity bill.'

Lorraine frowned at me as he left the room. She was obviously wondering what Robin was talking about, but his weirdness was something that she was going to have to get used to. I'd explain about the dead cat later, and the shed and . . . How could I explain about the shed? I had no idea what he got up to with his radio equipment. Deciding not to tell Lorraine that Robin was a Russian spy, I felt the juices of my vagina streaming down my inner thighs. I needed sex, crude sex.

As Lorraine was naked and the house was very warm, I decided to strip off. Tugging my skirt down my long legs, I slipped my blouse off and ordered my sex-slave to gather up my clothes as I threw them on the floor. Obediently complying, she folded them neatly, placing them in a pile on the end of the bed. This was going to work out very well, I knew. Marriage, a lovely house, a new Jag, Robin . . . Robin was still an unknown quantity, but I loved him.

'Oh,' Juliette gasped as she barged into my room. 'Er . . . Lorraine, isn't it?'

'That's right,' Lorraine said and smiled. 'I remember you from school.'

'So, what's going on?' Juliette asked. 'I've been out job-hunting and I come home to find two naked beauties waiting for me.'

'It's a long story,' I replied. 'Er . . . Lorraine, would you remove Juliette's clothes, please? We're going to have a party, Juliette,' I said. 'A celebration.'

'What are we celebrating?' Juliette asked as the slave girl kneeled on the floor and yanked Juliette's skirt down to her ankles.

'The end of the perverted vicar,' I announced smugly.

'The end? You mean . . . it's over at last?'

'Yes, it is. We'll send Robin out to stock up on booze and we'll have a bloody good party. A naked party.'

'Sounds good to me,' Juliette said and grinned as the slave girl tugged her wet panties down and gazed longingly at her pinken cunt-crack.

Bounding downstairs, I told Robin about the party and asked him to nip out to get the booze. He gazed at my naked body, obviously eager to get the party started. Donning his coat, he grabbed some money from the safe, told me that he loved me and then left the house. Love? What the hell was love? I wondered. Sitting on the edge of the desk, I pondered on the future. Marriage, happiness . . . I'd never envisaged myself being married. At least monogamy wasn't part of the set-up, I reflected, recalling Robin pumping sperm down Lorraine's throat. What sort of marriage was I embarking on where my husband would be fucking teenage girls and I'd be licking their clitorises to orgasm? A marriage that would last for ever, I decided. If Robin and I loved each other, then what difference would it make whether he spunked up my cunt or another girl's tight arse?

There's a moral here, I thought, looking around the untidy consulting room that reflected Robin's mind perfectly. Freedom, individualism, was the key to any successful relationship. Tie someone down, chain them, restrict them, rule them – and you have all the ingredients of ruination. Love can turn to hate in the blink of an eye. Love kills, hate kills. I was heavily into knob-sucking, spunk-swallowing, clit-licking . . . But Robin knew what I was like, and he wouldn't try to change me. I knew what *he* was like. Mad, verging on insane, crazy, unreliable, forgetful, the dress sense of a tramp, a Russian spy . . . Robin was Robin and it would be a crime to try to change him.

Giving Lorraine and Juliette some time to get to know each other, I waited in the consulting room for Robin to get back with the supplies. To my utter amazement, when I answered the front doorbell, expecting to find him on the step clutching several carrier bags full of bottles and cans, I found myself facing Ian and six of his young friends.

'You're naked,' Ian breathed, gazing at the opaque liquid dribbling from my shaved pussy slit.

'How observant of you,' I replied, smiling. 'You'd better come in. You're just in time for the party.'

'Party? That's great. Got any cannabis?'

'No, Ian. We only have sex, booze and rock and roll. I want you all to strip off. We're having a naked party, so go through to the lounge and strip off.'

'You bet,' he said, grinning and leading his gang into the lounge.

Robin returned and lugged a cardboard box full of cans and bottles into the kitchen before kissing my full lips. It was a shame that he didn't have a mother, I mused, taking the glasses from the cupboard. He was going to have to meet my parents at some stage. What my father would say when he discovered that I was marrying an older man . . . I didn't care what my father might say. I was happy, and that was all that mattered.

'There are some young lads in the lounge,' I said as laughter resounded around the house.

'Yes, I saw them,' Robin chortled. 'I suppose, since every one's naked, I'd better strip off too.'

'Yes, you had. It's going to be a good party, Robin. We're going to have a good life together.'

'I know that,' he said, taking me in his arms. 'Don't ask me how I know. I just know that I know that . . .'

'And I know, too. OK, clothes off and we'll get the party going.'

'Crystal, I'm not really mad.'

'I know that.'

'But I *am* a Russian spy.'

'If you say so, Robin.'

'You don't mind that?'

'Why should I? If you're happy playing about with your radio in the shed, then that's fine by me.'

'Right, Well, I'd better feed the cat and then get ready for the party.'

'I fed the cat earlier, so you go and get ready and I'll offer the boys a drink. Oh, tell the girls to come down, will you?'

'Right, will do.'

Watching Robin leave the room, I smiled as I heard him bounding up the stairs. Feed the cat? A Russian spy? Eccentricity must be a marvellous attribute, I reflected. Living in a world of your own, no worries, no problems . . . Perhaps I was eccentric too, I thought, pouring myself a glass of vodka and orange. My sexual exploits were hardly normal and I was marrying a man old enough to be my father . . . As Robin had said, we're all mad to a greater or lesser degree.

I'd come a long way, I mused, sipping my drink as the girls went into the lounge and laughter again resounded throughout the house. From that fateful day when I'd delivered the birthday cake to the vicar's cottage, to living in a huge Victorian house with my future husband . . . How many cocks had I wanked? How many knobs had I sucked to orgasm? How much spunk had I swallowed? I'd come a hell of a long way since visiting the vicar in my tutu. When I was younger than I should have been to see an erect penis, let alone hold one in my small hand, a young lad taught me how to wank him . . .